GIRL ON THE EDGE

A Novel

CD REISS

Flip City Media

GIRL ON THE EDGE

Part One

Chapter One

GREYSEN

SEPTEMBER, 2006

The sky in Iraq was the bluest blue I'd ever seen. It had a flat depth, as if thin layers of glass, each a slightly different shade, were stacked together. Sometimes I'd dream about that sky. Either I'd be floating in it, blue everywhere, above and below, at each side and pressure point, squeezing the breath out of me, or I'd be falling from it, from blue into blue, no Earth barreling into greater and greater detail. Just a single direction in the never-ending cerulean sky.

Caden and I had been separated by an ocean and a war for ten months. We'd married while I was on leave and spoke when our schedules matched and the wind blew the wi-fi signal in the right direction. I thought I hadn't known him long enough to miss him, but I did.

Painfully. Tenderly. Thoroughly. Our separation stretched the bond between us to a thin, translucent strand, but did not break it.

Caden's eyes had the color and layered depth of the Iraqi sky.

When I missed him, I looked up. When I wrapped his T-shirt around my neck, my dreams of the blue sky lost their nightmarish edge, and the bond became a little less taut.

Jenn and I flew to New York in our uniforms. She remained on active duty and had a job waiting at the VA Hospital in Newark. I had a husband and no job.

"You want to put on some makeup or something?" she asked.

"Why? You afraid they're all looking at me?"

The crew had moved us to first class. I craned my neck to see a jowly businessman sleeping with his mouth open. A mid-level rap star with cornrows and a name I couldn't recall was reading a book to his daughter, and two middle-aged women chatted in the row across. No one was giving my lashes the side-eye.

"Hell, no. But maybe you want to look nice for your husband?" She rooted around a quilted pink bag and found a black stick. "Here. Lip gloss.Doll it up just a little. You're a civilian now."

She handed me a compact with a mirror. I flipped it open and looked at myself in circular sections.

I was a civilian now.

I had no idea how to be that.

AS THE ONLY girl in a military family, enlisting wasn't encouraged. It wasn't unexpected either. It made them proud. And disappointed. And worried. A mixed bag of emotions that probably had nothing to do with either parent and everything with how I felt every time I wondered what they thought.

I would have stayed in the army my entire life, but Caden happened, and he saw the army as his duty to the country. A debt to pay, not a way of life.

At the gate, a little girl of about six ran up and gave Jenn and me flowers. "Thank you for your service," she said.

This wasn't uncommon. I'd learned people were in awe of my career choice and the risks it involved.

I kneeled and took the flowers. "Thank you for the flowers. And thank you for appreciating us. That means a lot."

Suddenly shy, she curtsied and ran away to her mother, who waved at me. I gave her a thumbs-up.

"Is it wrong to wish she was a single, six foot-tall black man with a nice bank account?" Jenn asked quietly, sniffing the flowers.

"Her mother might be a little surprised."

Jenn chuckled and pointed at the sign above. "Baggage claim, this way."

We didn't get two steps before I saw Caden waiting for me. He had flowers tied with stars and stripes printed on the ribbon, a grey suit, and a smile that told me he saw me the way I saw him—with a certain amount of surprise at the easy familiarity, and another bit of gratitude at the fulfilled expectations. It was as if we were seeing each other for the first time, and coming back to something very familiar.

I dropped my bag and ran into his arms. We clung to each other, connected in a kiss that held nothing back. Cocooned, shielded by love and commitment, the airport terminal fell behind the wall of our attention to the kiss.

He jerked me away with a sucking sound and a drawn breath, but kept his nose astride mine. "Welcome to New York, Major."

That was when I heard the applause.

"Are we making a spectacle of ourselves?" I let my body relax away from his.

"I fucking love you so much, I don't even care."

I looked at the people surrounding us. I was in camo and he had a flag ribbon on the flowers. We were indeed making a spectacle of ourselves.

Jenn dropped my bag at my feet. "That was so sweet I almost clapped."

Caden took it before I could. "Thank you for not."

The crowd dispersed, and we headed out of baggage claim without further incident.

"WHAT DO you want to see first?" Caden asked after we dropped Jenn off at her parents' brownstone in Fort Greene. His wrist was draped over the steering wheel of his Mercedes. The band of his expensive watch caught glints of the sun. The seats were soft black leather. There was no dust or sand on the carpets, and none of the upholstery was torn.

"The inside of my eyelids."

"Come on, Major. Push on." He squeezed my knee and kissed me at the red light. "You'll sleep when you're dead."

I put my hand over his, and he stroked my thumb. "Were your eyes always this blue?"

"Probably."

They looked bluer against the New York sky, which was fluffed with late summer clouds. I sat back and looked out the window. Maybe tomorrow I'd see the color I'd fall through.

"What are my choices?" I asked.

"The house, your new office, or any restaurant in the city."

That was more choices than I was used to, and none involved getting sand in the crack of my ass or telling a man it was okay to kill people.

"Can we eat in?"

"Yep."

The seams in the bridge's surface went *puh-puh-puh* under the tires and the web of cables holding it up blurred in my peripheral vision. Manhattan stretched ahead of me like a dense construction of grey bricks. I didn't know where people fit into such compactness.

"Okay," I finally said. "The house."

CADEN PUT the car in a garage a block away. Apparently, he'd bought the spot years ago. It required a mortgage and operating fees. Where I grew up, you parked in a lot someone else owned, your own driveway, or on the street.

This was my new normal.

On the walk along Columbus Avenue, I felt as if I were wearing a camo clown suit. Caden put his arm around me and kissed my temple as we waited at the light. The crowd crossed before the light changed to green, but I followed my husband.

"We're on 87th between Columbus and Amsterdam," he said. "Avenues run north-south, streets run east-west."

"Got it." We turned onto a narrow, tree-lined street. "This is a nice block."

"It is."

The houses were stone and connected to each other on the sides. Some were slightly set back from the street to accommodate a stoop and a few steps down to a garden apartment.

He stopped by one such house and held his hand out while the other took my duffel off his shoulder. "Here we are."

I looked up. Garden apartment. Three stories. An attic with stone carvings around the leaded windows. "Is it all yours?"

He threw the duffel up the steps. It made it halfway. "It's all ours."

He picked me up in his arms before carrying me up the stoop. I squeaked in surprise. We laughed as he tried to unlock the door without dropping me, and when he managed to do it, I cheered.

He retrieved my bag and dropped it in the foyer. We were at the base of a flight of stairs. Everything was polished dark wood carved at the corners. A beveled mirror was set into a frame with three brass hooks under it. I took off my cap and let my hair fall.

I was fully overwhelmed. He took my cap and put it on a hook before taking my face in his hands and kissing me.

"I have your back," he whispered. "Okay?" I nodded, and he kissed me again. "Say it for me."

"You have my back."

"And your front."

I smiled into his kiss. "You have my front."

"I can take you to the bedroom if you insist or on the stairs right now."

"Will you give me a minute to shower?"

"You have rank."

"That's an order then."

He got his hips under me and his hands under my ass, hitching me up until I could get my legs around his waist. He carried me to our room. I didn't see anything but his face on the way up. I only knew there were wood floors and windows. Two flights. A tower with me on top.

HE SAT me on a bench in the bathroom and turned the water on in the white claw-foot tub. He kneeled in front of me to unlace my boots. I couldn't stop looking at him in his fancy suit, kneeling on the bathroom floor to service me.

"I hate that they make us wear this shit on the way home," he said. "It's total PR."

"Yeah, well, the military is nothing without its symbols, and that's what I am."

"Were." He pulled off the boot. "Now you are Dr. Greysen Frazier, MD, with a psychiatric practice in Manhattan." He peeled off my socks. "And my wife. Stand up."

Still on his knees, he undid my buckle and fly and pulled my pants down, letting his palms spread out over the skin of my thighs. I stepped out of them and he tossed the pants aside.

"Ah, I missed this." He lifted my shirt and kissed the silver scar over my heart. He kissed my belly and the triangle below. I put my fingers in his hair, and he reached up under my clothes until he found my hardened nipples.

"Caden," I groaned. "Bath."

With a gentle suck on my belly, he stood. I started unbuttoning from the top and he unbuttoned from the bottom. We met in the middle and got all my clothes off until I wasn't wearing anything but the dog tags that hung between my breasts.

He laid them in his palm and looked at them, letting one clink against the other.

"Take them off," I said.

He closed his fist around them and pulled them over my head. The chain slid against my long, straight hair, and I was free.

Caden coiled the chain on the vanity. I shut off the water and tested it.

Scalding hot.

No one in the world knew me the way he did.

HE'D TAKEN his jacket off, rolled up his sleeves, and bathed me, touching every part of my body. His hands knew exactly how to tease me. They were accurate and subtle, driving my desire forward without letting me come.

He tossed the towel away and threw me on the bed, soaking wet.

He didn't even undress to fuck me. Not right away. He just spread my legs and fucked me as if we hadn't seen each other in four months.

The sheets were white.

The furniture was honey, and the lamps were Tiffany.

Day turned into evening, but the street didn't quiet.

That was all I noticed between orgasms.

In the darkness, we curled under the covers. He stroked my arm with his thumb, appreciating every inch of skin.

"I haven't shown you the house," he said. "I'm sorry."

"Are you going to show me all your childhood secret hiding places?"

"The speakeasy in the basement? Yes."

He'd told me about the Prohibition-era space the first owners had dug out of the basement. How it had false walls, a mosaic tile floor, a mahogany bar, and secret places to hide customers and almost a century later, small children.

"It's a really nice house," I said. "Is this a good neighborhood, as neighborhoods go in New York?"

"This block is unattainable."

"What's that mean?"

"This house is priceless. I could name a number and get it."

"Your dad was smart to buy it when he did."

"He wanted to be near enough to the hospital, but not that close. He had a space for a practice in the garden apartment, which is soon to be..." He waited for me to finish.

"My practice."

"Bingo."

"I'm nervous."

"I know."

"What if I—"

He put his finger on my lips before I could utter my litany of doubts. "You're going to do fine. And if it takes longer than you think it should, we can survive on a heart surgeon's salary for a while."

Of course we could. There was nothing to be nervous about. He had my back and my front.

"Can I see the office?"

"Yes."

WE WIGGLED into pajamas and went down the back stairs, which led to a short, carpeted hall with an old wooden door at each end.

"The door at the back leads to a shared kind of alley thing out the front, so patients won't bump into each other on the way in and out," Caden said as he turned the skeleton key that stuck out of the office's keyhole. It clacked deeply before the door swung open. He flicked on the lights.

The office defied every expectation.

I expected cold fluorescents and a dropped ceiling.

What I got was a pristine white ceiling and warm lamps.

I expected an empty space.

What I got was a 1950s era desk and chairs, tufted couch, end tables, a clock where I could see it but the patient couldn't, and a deep blue carpet to muffle the distracting scrape of chairs and footsteps. Behind the desk, a horizontal filing cabinet had framed pictures leaning on the top. Family. Friends. Caden and me on the rooftop of the hotel in Amman, with the sunset behind us. I picked up our wedding photo. My parents had set up the backyard in flowers and tables, doing the best they could when they heard we were getting hitched on two-day leave. Caden and me outside the combat hospital in Balad, dressed in dull green and smiles.

"I read up on what you'd need. They said family pictures humanized you to patients."

"That's right."

He opened the door on the far end of the room. The waiting room was bathed in the same warm lamplight. It was small. Two chairs and a love seat. A coffee table. A Wasily Kandinski print. Everything matched the interior office.

"I had speakers put in." He pointed up. Small wood-grain boxes hung in the corners where the ceiling met the walls. "I hear music soothes the savage breast."

Caden, a psychiatrist's husband, had hang-ups about mental illness that had revealed themselves after I accepted his proposal.

"I won't be working with savages," I said with a raised eyebrow. I was going to have to patiently whittle away this particular neurosis.

"They won't all have breasts either." He put his arm around me. "So you like it?"

"I love it. Madly, deeply. I love it." I put my arms around his shoulders, and his snaked around my waist. "Thank you so much."

"There's so much we're going to do together." He kissed my neck. "We're going to build an entire life out of a war."

"That would be a miracle."

"First of many. You and me. We're a miracle." He pulled back so he could see my face. "You know what I see when I look at you?"

"Your wife?"

"The worst decisions I've ever made, I made for a reason. You. You rose out of the destruction. Our life together will be built into the best from what survived the worst."

"That's very poetic."

He smiled. "I've been thinking about what to say for days. I wanted to explain how magnificent we're going to be."

"Magnificent?"

"I don't think I quite nailed it." He took me back into the hall and to an unremarkable door under the stairs. "Basement."

He opened the door, and flicked on the light. Wooden stairs led to a dirt floor in a four-by-five room. Caden reached around me and put his hands on a vase sitting on a set-in shelf. He yanked it, and the wall slid to the side, revealing a mosaic floral floor and dark wood bar stacked high with cardboard boxes.

"Chez Columbus," he said, smiling. "1925-1933."

Amazing. An actual speakeasy with a stairway to the hidden alley on the side of the house, hidden rooms, and lastly, behind the laundry room, a big wall safe. He opened it, then pushed away the wall behind it to yet another room with cylindrical holes in the concrete.

"The bottle room," he said. "This was where I hid when... you know."

"When you were scared."

"When I should have been stopping him from beating her."

"I'm going to get you out of the habit of blaming yourself."

"Good luck." He held out his hand, moving the subject away from the abuse of his mother as he always did. "Come on. It's cold in here."

The steps to the bedroom seemed like an eternal climb, but we wound up racing to the top. It didn't matter who won. We both landed on the bed.

We held each other tight, and I felt safe starting a new life with him.

THAT NIGHT, with the *whoosh* of cars outside and a police siren whining far away, he woke with a grunt and a command. "Stop!"

I reached for my revolver, but it was locked away in a strange closet, in the strange bedroom, in a city that was a sea of stone.

But he was there, the street light blue on his cheek, and all was well as long as he was next to me.

"Caden? Are you okay?"

"Yeah." He rolled over to face me. "Sorry."

"What was it?"

"Dream. Nothing."

PTSD was as real as the war itself, and I had to know if he was reliving it in his sleep. "Caden. Can you tell me?"

"Pieces of me were breaking off."

"Were you in Iraq? In the dream?"

"No." His denial was barely a whisper.

I took it for a normal nightmare and joined him in sleep.

Chapter Two

CADEN

Greysen was back, and like good news when nothing's going right or a seat by the radiator after a day in the snow, she brought relief to pain I forgot I was feeling.

As soon as she agreed to marry me, while I was still deployed, I started getting the house ready. I met with an architect and contractor on a short leave, and again on the way back from our wedding in California. I was barely off the plane before I started furnishing the house. I had an attending position waiting at Mt. Sinai, but she had nothing and I needed to give her everything.

The house had been unoccupied since I left. Dad's office was a wreck. I'd had it ripped down to the studs. Had the shitty memories scraped out of the plaster and sanded off the wood. When I resigned my commission and returned, it was all details and new furniture.

That was when the dreams started.

Or more accurately, the dream. They were all the same dream, the way a woman was the same woman from all angles, naked or dressed. Same person, only time and situations changed.

I was somewhere in the house. The windows were painted over. I was in tremendous dream pain. Meaning I was terrified to the point of pain, but I couldn't physically feel my body being torn in two.

Obviously. It was just a dream. I never felt pain in my dreams.

The dreams weren't long. They came in the middle of the night, and I woke enraged, because I wasn't just coming apart. Something was taking me apart. It had to be stopped.

But when I woke to Greysen's voice, I wasn't pissed off at the dream thing. I was fine, and I went back to sleep. It hadn't come back in two nights.

"It's nice to not have to rush through surgery," I said, swinging my racquet at the tiny blue ball. It popped off the front wall, made it past the receiving line, and took off for the back wall.

Danny thought he was in an action movie, again, and tried to climb the wall to get it, managing to just get it back into play. I slammed it to the other side of the court while he was recovering.

"How about not getting shot at? Is that an improvement?" Danny said as I helped him up. He was a buddy from my residency at NYU Medical. Pediatric surgery, but he floated into general pediatrics when he didn't have the intestinal fortitude to cut into children.

"No one was shooting at me." I snapped up the ball and got ready for my serve. "It was easy."

"I still think it was stupid," he said. "But you lived, so whatever. They were your years to waste."

"Wouldn't have met Greysen."

I served. He was better set up this time and won the point.

"Yes! One more and drinks are on you, Private."

"Captain."

"You're nothing out here, buddy. What's Greysen? A major? That higher than captain?"

"Yes, but we're nothing here."

"Your woman still ranks you."

"Trash talk won't win you the point." I bounced the ball, setting up a serve that wouldn't overpower him, which he'd be ready for, but one to surprise him.

"That's right. I forgot you were unshakable."

I served. He was off guard, recovering enough to return but not win. Two points later, I had the game.

THE CLUB'S lounge wasn't crowded on weekdays. Out the floor-to-ceiling windows, the rooftops of Manhattan were laid out like a fallen dresser with drawers pulled out randomly. Water towers, HVAC units, greenhouses, and patios dotted the rooftops, and through the slit of Second Avenue, I saw the southern tip of the island.

Danny placed our drinks on the table by the window and threw himself into the chair. Guy couldn't sit straight to save his life. I hadn't noticed that until I got back from my second deployment. Sloppiness had always bothered me, but slouching never had. All kinds of new things bugged me now, but more things seemed petty and unimportant. Status symbols. Expensive things. A woman everyone else wanted. None of that was interesting anymore.

"Sit up straight, would you?" I said. "You look like a rag doll."

"I'm entitled to sit like this today."

I tipped the Perrier bottle into the glass. The ice clicked. When it settled, I took a sip. "You blow one too many noses?"

"I had to refer a kid, thirteen... he was *thirteen*. Had to refer his parents to an oncologist they'll go broke paying. And it was hopeless. There was no... ah, never mind."

"Sorry, that's... well, it's part of the job. But sorry."

"Asshole." He crossed ankle over knee and drank his beer. He was a redhead and, in the ultimate irritating cliché, had a temper to match.

"I am an asshole."

"That some kind of opening for another war story?"

It hadn't been an opening any more than Dan's snide comments were actual insults. My friend was making a request. He'd lost his brother on 9/11 and listening to me tell a war story made him feel as if he'd deployed with me.

"I had this guy on the table," I said. "We were low on morphine, so no one got it until we put them under, so he was screaming his head off. And rightfully so. His humerus was shattered."

"Very funny."

We clicked glasses, and I continued. "His arm was hanging on his body by half a bone. Rotator cuff was torn up. Skin had third-degree burns. I could put him back together well enough to get him to Baghdad, but it would have taken five hours. So meanwhile, you know what he's screaming?"

"Get the fuck on with the story?"

"'I'm a guitarist.'" I paused with my drink at my lips long enough to mutter, "He played fucking guitar." I put the glass down. "Meanwhile, they tell me there's another guy who's about to lose his leg. They clamped off the femoral artery, but it's going stiff real fast and he's going to need a graft."

"Who's triaging these people?"

"Someone who loves rock. But what do you do? You can save the arm or the leg. You can't save both. One gets a quick amputation. The other gets screws and pins. Which is it?"

"Do I get vitals?"

"Answer."

"Was either in shock?"

"This isn't a drill, Dan."

"Hang on—"

"There's no time."

"Jesus."

"Which?"

"All right, all right, asshole. What did you do?"

I finished my drink. "Decided it's easier to hold down a job with two legs and one arm than the other way around."

"You got something against music?"

"It was a calculation. Life over limb."

"You are one sick fuck." He put his elbows on his knees and shook his head in disappointment, but his smile told me he admired me. "How does your wife even deal with your shit?"

My wife had lived it with me, that was how.

"She didn't believe me. She came to Balad Base before the second Fallujah offensive to make sure we weren't fucked in the head. She wouldn't believe I could turn it on and off. She was like a pit bull, man."

She cared. More than her big brown eyes or the silken hair she kept twisted in a bun, I remembered her caring about my psychological well-being. I was no one to her, but she didn't want me to suffer. That first session, when I laughed at her, I also started to fall in love with her.

She hadn't believed that either. How could a man so detached feel love? How could I be brokenhearted one minute and perform surgery the next without opening myself to a crippling emotional breakdown?

Eventually, she learned I could do both. More than nimble hands and the will to finish med school, at-will detachment was my most valuable skill.

"I maintain going was stupid," Danny said. "Noble, but stupid."

"Like I said, I met Greysen."

"The internet works fine, thanks." He picked up his glass. "That's where I met Shari."

"When do I get to meet Shari? Or do I have to go on the internet to do it?"

"Soon. You want another?"

"Sure."

He went to the bar. The sky turned orange with the sunset.

You didn't meet women like Greysen on the internet. She'd spent her adult life in the army, and if she hadn't met me, she'd still be wearing boots and brown. She'd be fucking some other lifer.

She'd be living her life the way she always thought she would.

I'd rescued her from all that.

She'd be just fine.

Deployment after deployment. A slave to pay grade and rank. Stable.

Greysen wanted her boundaries pushed. She wasn't happy unless she was doing more, going faster, expanding in all directions. The military limited her ability to find how far she could go.

I hadn't considered that maybe the limits were the point.

When Dan came toward the table with the drinks, I resolved yet again to make sure Greysen was happy.

Chapter Three

GREYSEN

I didn't just have to get used to New York or civilian life. I didn't just have to acclimate to finding work instead of having it given to me. I had to get used to being married.

Caden and I had met in a war zone. I'd been prepared to live in that zone my whole life. My family prized duty and loyalty to near fetish.

He had gotten a direct commission as a doctor in late 2001 out of a sense of duty he wasn't explicitly raised with. He held it in his heart next to his need to be a part of a solution. He entered the army with his privilege, his money, his medical pedigree, and a cockiness usually only found in fighter pilots and bomb specialists.

We were from different countries in the same America. When I'd arrived on base, he was just another good-looking soldier who wanted to get in my pants. Another one denying he was stressed. Too boastful, too proud, too full of himself to take no for an answer.

He broke down my professionalism by being honorable, dutiful, brilliant, and just enough of an asshole to remind me he was fully a man, and just vulnerable enough to remind me he was fully human.

He also smelled nice and had a casual way of touching me that made me want to purr.

My CO had issued me a pass just long enough to fly home and get married. We did it at my parents' house in San Diego. He had no one in New York. The night before we tied the knot, I had a vivid dream. In it, I was marrying the wrong man. On top of a tall building, guests filled the chairs. Mom congratulated me. Dad flew in on an F-14. My brother Colin wore camo and boots he wouldn't be caught dead in outside a dream.

And I was marrying the wrong man. No one would listen. They thought I was crazy. I woke up in a terror, convinced I was making the mistake of my life.

Then I saw Caden sleeping next to me, and the terror fell away. I wasn't marrying the wrong man. I was marrying Caden, and he was *right*. I was never as sure about anything in my life as I was about him.

In New York, the last place on earth I thought I'd find myself, those first months of our relationship seemed like a dream. I remembered the blood, the explosions, the prayers uttered to a God I'd forgotten a hundred times, but the hours of gentle relief with him became more of a home base to balance against the violence I'd seen. That knowledge that no, I wasn't making bad decisions because he was with me, became my anchor.

Before we were married, and after he inadvertently rescued me from an assignment that would have ended my career, we both got approved for R&R.

We couldn't acknowledge each other on the streets of Amman, but in the American hotel, we could be a couple. We became intimate with the hotel tea shop and the details of our separate rooms. On the rooftop patio, he traced the red scar down my right wrist. His lips were parted a little, as if ready to kiss at any moment, and his face was lit by the sun's reflection.

"Your eyes match the sky," I said to him. His face was framed in the blue Iraqi ceiling.

"They're actually holes in my head," he said. "You're seeing right through."

Caden ran his fingers over the top of my hand, connecting the knuckles like a man taking territory one hill at a time. We were so deep inside each other, there was no such thing as a public place.

I hadn't gone to Iraq to fall in love. I was there to do the impossible—talk to soldiers about how they felt in a situation where feelings could kill. It was exhausting.

Caden energized me.

He traced the scars I'd gotten when I broke my wrist. "Does anyone think you tried to kill yourself?"

"Everyone. My mother still thinks I'm trying to hide a suicide attempt."

"Why?"

"I was a goth teen. Eyeliner out to here. The world was *so boring*, like, *so* uninteresting." I rolled my eyes dramatically.

"Can't imagine it." His fingers kept tracing the scar.

"I did want to... well, I almost gave up after I broke it. I lost flexibility, and it was permanent. I wanted to be a medic." The admission embarrassed me, because I'd failed.

"That doesn't surprise me at all." He lifted my face by the chin. "You're an adventurous spirit."

"So are you." I nudged him.

"No, really. You're pretty angry at your limitations."

"Angry?"

"Frustrated. Don't worry, we're going to get rid of either the anger or the limits."

"When?"

"Don't rush. We have a lifetime."

———

JENN SHOWED up in leggings and a gray army hoodie, exactly on time. Five in the morning like a good soldier. I was early, stretching on the summit of a huge boulder in Central Park. She joined me.

"Ronin's coming," she said. "That all right?"

Ronin and I had dated, if that was what you called sporadic sex in the first year of enlistment, then a long separation, then a few rolls in the hay when I was a resident at Walter Reed and he was working in Intelligence.

"What's he doing in New York?"

We took off down the boulder, stopped at a small rock embedded in the grass, and dropped for push-ups.

"Who knows?" Ten then back up the rock.

"Really?"

"Left Aberdeen Proving Grounds." Top of the rock. Squat thrusts.

After everything that happened at Abu Ghraib, they'd sent him to Aberdeen. Jesus Christmas on a ladder, the army was fucked.

"They sent him here? Why?"

"He's out of uniform now."

Our breathing became unavailable for talking as we worked out. Ronin showed up midway through, in designer jeans and a sport jacket. He may have gone spook, but he was a handsome one. Dirty-blond hair, dark blue eyes in a face that had been chiseled and pristine when we met, but was wearing its ruggedness well.

"You doing it in that jacket?" I said between finishing push-ups and running back up the boulder.

"In a minute." He took out a cigarette and lit it.

Jenn gave him the finger. He waved.

I didn't think I could do another. The push-ups were murder on my wrist and my lungs burned.

"One more!" I cried, heading back down the boulder.

"I can't!" Jenn put her hands on her knees.

"You can!"

I was telling myself more than her. I pushed myself. Push-ups. Run. Squat thrusts. Run.

I fell to my knees on the grass and rolled onto my back.

Ronin slow-clapped with the cigarette dangling from his lips. "Nice work, Major One More."

Instead of telling him to go to hell, which would have taken a spare breath I didn't have, I held up my middle finger.

"Two from me!" Jenn held up both of her birds.

Ronin laughed and put his cigarette out under his shoe. "You're just jealous I don't have to work as hard as you." He picked up his cigarette butt and flicked it toward the garbage pail. It was too far to reach and too small a target, but it landed.

"What are you doing here, Ronin?" I asked.

Jenn put in her two cents. "Did Intelligence kick you out for lack thereof?"

He held his hands over his heart. "I'm wounded."

"No, really." I sat up. "I'm asking nice."

He shrugged. "Got an offer in the private sector."

Jenn and I both asked "Where?" at the same time.

"I can't say, and you both owe me a beer."

"Can't say?" I asked. "You were doing medical research."

"I still do. But, you know, it's still military shit. La-di-da." He broke a piece of grass and tossed it my way. "How's civilian life, Major? You adjusting?"

"Yeah. It's fine."

"She sucks at it," Jenn interjected.

"What's that supposed to mean?" I asked.

"You're still trying to impress the brass with one more lap."

"Shut up." I threw blades of grass at her, but she was right. I wasn't at home outside military life. Not yet.

"And the practice?" he asked. "How's it going?"

"She needs clients."

"Can I talk?" I kicked her gently.

"You're too slow."

"I could use some more clients."

"Said so."

We smiled at each other.

"Jenn here sent me a couple of guys from her art therapy group, and thank you."

"You're welcome."

"But that's only a couple."

"Most of my vets are from Jersey anyway," she added.

"Manhattan's tough," I agreed. "I specialized in battle trauma. They don't grow military here. They grow, I don't know, hedge fund managers and musicians."

"Yeah, here's the thing. How far are you going to push to do this?" Ronin asked, then continued before I could ask him what the fuck that was supposed to mean. "You're far outside your comfort zone here."

"I don't have a comfort zone."

"I'm asking if you're committed, Major One More."

"You know I am, Lieutenant Pain in the Ass."

"Good." He slapped his knees and stood as if we'd just ended a meeting. "I'll send you some people. See you around." He stepped away then turned back. "And Jenn?"

"What?"

He flipped her the bird and she laughed.

When he was out of earshot, she sighed. "Such a good-looking man with an ice-cold rock for a heart."

"Oh, not really. He had a heart once." I got my feet under me. "He never calls your rank."

"No, I guess not." I helped her up. "I never noticed."

"I think he likes you."

"I bet I can get to Columbus Station first."

"Hell, no."

And we were off for one more run.

Chapter Four

CADEN

OCTOBER, 2006

Greysen had been home three weeks the first time it happened. I was standing over a man with an empty chest. The pump kept his blood moving and the measured hiss of the ventilator told me he was breathing. We'd extracted a leg vein to replace the clogged artery.

I'd done this procedure at least a hundred times, and twice in an army hospital. I knew the rhythms of beeps and hisses. It was nothing. Vitals were good. Oxygen was good.

I held my hand out for the grafted vein. The nurse handed me the tray with the slice of flesh, and the whisper of the ventilator changed.

"What?" I said.

Everyone looked up. Pairs of dots of eyes over pale blue rectangles covering their mouths. Something was there with us, in the room, and it wanted me. If I'd been in a cave with a hungry lion, I'd be just as sure, except the lion didn't growl. It breathed in a throaty rattle with the shushing of the ventilator.

"What, what, Doctor?" Amy Sullivan, the assisting surgeon, asked.

I wasn't in a cave. There was no hungry lion. It was fine. The numbers were good. The ventilator was just...

"Can someone check the ventilator?"

"Ventilator checks out," the tech's voice came from behind me.

"You can tell that in two seconds? Can I have a swab, please?" I prepped for the graft. "Does it sound normal to you?" I said quietly to Amy.

"Yeah. Are you all right?"

I was sweating. My heart was racing. My adrenal glands were firing on all cylinders. This didn't happen to me. I always put the right feelings in the right boxes and slid the deadbolt closed until I needed them. I didn't make up stories, and I didn't hear voices in the equipment.

But the feeling of being besieged was as familiar as it was real, and I knew how to handle it.

This was war, and I could do my job in the middle of it.

"I'm fine. Let's put this guy's heart back in."

THE FEELING FOLLOWED me that night to our first anniversary dinner. When I saw her outside the restaurant, I kissed her and held her hand while we waited for our table. I decided not to ruin the evening. When I took her hand over the table and she tucked her foot between mine, I decided she didn't need to know at all. What was I supposed to say? "I was sure there was something but there wasn't?" Or, "Can you please diagnose me before bed?"

Being married to a psychiatrist had upsides. She prescribed sleeping pills when I needed them. In Fallujah, when I was in the field hospital OR for eight days without rest, she'd managed vitamins and enough amphetamine to keep me sharp enough to not kill anyone. When we were deployed together, I never worried about her getting killed. But nothing kept me sane at home like loving her. She avoided her comfort zone, never got bored or was boring. She was serious but not dull. She was a bulwark against my worst impulses, and my God, my God I loved her more than I thought I could love anything.

Her opinion meant everything to me. She'd never think I was weak, yet I was terrified she would.

Truth incoming.

I didn't want her to tell me it was nothing, even though I hoped it was.

I didn't want her to have some easy cure, but I didn't want to continue like this.

I didn't want to become a patient in my own marriage.

I wanted it to go away by itself. Prove it was a bad day and that I could handle it at the same time.

But it didn't. The second night with no relief from the feeling something was there, as Greysen breathed softly next to me, I lay awake in the silent dark, trying to isolate the problem. If I could build a wall around this feeling, hem it in, maybe I could identify it and throw it away. Pick the shrapnel out of my own guts to *plink plink* in the tray, shard by shard, observe them without the crust of shit and blood.

I must have been seconds from sleep. The shadows got deeper, outlines shifting with the passage of the moon in the window, taking on new, more threatening shapes.

Threatening, and yet... not.

My shrapnel had a shape, and it was compassion. A silent empathy and gentleness just this side of sweet. The Thing watching me, wanting me, the violent pressure on my mind I'd just gotten a shape around had a personality, and it was *kind*.

My body jolted with a cortisol flood, waking Greysen. She sat up on one arm. Her long straight hair covered her face in a veil. "Caden?"

"It's okay," I said. "Just a dream."

Why the fuck did I say that?

"Can you tell me—?"

"No."

Twisting to her side, she lay down facing me, hands tucked under her pillow. She stayed silent for a few seconds. "You should write it down."

"Go to sleep." I stroked her hair away from her face.

When I'd met her, she kept her hair just long enough to keep in a ponytail, but short enough to care for easily. Now that we were civilians, she was letting it grow.

I loved her so much, I wanted to marry her every single day for the rest of my life.

Then a realization hit me like Reveille in the morning.

The Thing? The pressure? The entity that had its own personality that was all gentle kindness?

The Thing loved her too.

Maybe my mental weakness came from being tired, or hiding things from Greysen. Maybe I was jealous of a figment of my imagination. Maybe I wanted to show it who was in charge here.

For all those reasons, and some more complex instinct, I ran my hand down her back. She wore satin nightgowns, a civilian pleasure she reserved for herself and me. She sighed when my palm landed on her ass.

"Doctor?" One eye opened under the web of hair that covered her face. "Do you know what time it is?"

"It's time for you to get on your hands and knees."

"Excuse me?"

I got up on my knees and grabbed her hips on either side, lifting them over the mattress. She flopped onto her hands, half twisted.

I bent my body over hers, reaching around her waist and talking softly in her ear. "If 'excuse me' means no, then say no."

She swiped her hand around her head to get the hair off her face, looking back at me with an unfiltered gaze. "It doesn't mean no, but..."

"Then you're excused."

I grabbed her breast harder than I normally would. She was mine. I would not be undercut, and I would not compete. I pulled her nightgown up and yanked down her underwear. Our eyes met over her shoulder.

"I can't lean on the wrist for long," she said.

"I'm aware." Normally, I'd gently slide in, but not this time. Something more primal called, and I shoved hard inside her.

Yeah.

Just like I thought.

The Thing was horrified.

"Let's get pressure off that wrist." I took her by the biceps and pulled her arms behind her, holding them together with one hand. "Better?"

"Yes." Her head dropped forward.

"This is going to be different," I said.

"No shit."

I hesitated. My desire to show the Thing my dominance couldn't be satisfied at her expense. I loosened my grip on her arms just a little.

"Don't..." She stopped, took a deep breath, and turned her head as much as she could. "Don't stop. I'll let you know." Her hips pushed into me.

Gently, I gathered her hair with my free hand and wrapped it around my fist, then I yanked her head back as I entered her with full force.

She screamed through her teeth. "God! Caden!"

"Say no," I growled.

"Yes."

I fucked her so rough, I didn't expect her to come so hard and so quickly. I kept fucking her, holding her arms behind her, pulling her hair as if it were a bridle. I unleashed deep inside her, bruising her arms with my grasp.

Right there, a whirlwind spun around us as I pounded her, whipping me into a confusion of desire and need, surrender and dominance. Even as I thrust forward physically, mentally I was spun by the force of it. Flipped like a coin, revolving in the air, landing, settling on the mattress.

The whirlwind fell away, and there was only Greysen under me.

The kind, sweet Thing shrank back into the shadows, weeping.

Take that, you fuck.

Chapter Five

GREYSEN

In the weeks after he took me from behind in the middle of the night, we went back to normal. The episode seemed like a pleasurable blip in a pleasurable routine.

We were meeting at the Mt. Sinai fundraiser. It was a cutting day. When he arrived at the fundraiser, he'd smell of rubbing alcohol and cologne if he'd put some on, fresh coffee grounds and cut grass if he hadn't. He'd touch my shoulder. He'd run his finger along the edge of my strapless gown. At home, we'd barely make it in the door before he'd strip me naked and take me. Yes, it was predictable. Some things were worth predicting.

I crawled into the back of the car where my younger brother, Colin, waited. He was an engineer who'd been inspired to go to college after I'd found a way to go to med school, and he'd moved to New York for a job just as I was settling in. The education had done nothing to tamp his roguish ways.

"You look nice," he said when I slid in next to him. He flicked one of my dangling earrings.

"You do too." I straightened his black bow tie as the limo coasted toward the museum.

He shooed my hand away. "Thanks for the plus one."

"Try to keep off the ladies."

"What's the fun in that when I have to watch your husband with his hands all over you?"

"Stop it."

"You two are so in love it makes me sick."

THE EVENT TOOK place in a ballroom lined with Regency-era portraits and heavy drapery. I plucked a champagne flute from a server's silver tray and Colin did the same.

"This is lovely." He scanned the room like a cheetah selecting the weakest in the herd.

"Behave."

"Oh, your friend Jenn is here. I like her," he purred.

I elbowed him as Jenn saw us and headed over. She was awkward in heels and her fat black glasses always slid down her nose, but her smile was a beacon of light against her brown skin. We greeted each other, and she swapped her empty flute for a full one.

"Easy there, tiger," Colin said.

Jenn took no shit, and she was a terrible flirt. "I'm grown, but thank you."

"He's on the make," I offered.

"Good luck with that." She tipped her glass to him, and he responded with a clink. "Ronin's here," she said to me.

"Where is he?" I craned my neck. "He sent me some referrals. I owe him a drink."

I saw him before the last word was out of my mouth, but he already had a drink in his hand. He wedged his way through the crowd toward us.

"What are you doing here?" I asked as he kissed my cheek.

"Business."

"Obviously," Jenn said. "No one's here for the food."

"Thank you for the referrals," I said. "I owe you a drink."

"Open bar doesn't count."

We were talking about something unimportant when Ronin put his arm around my shoulders and pulled me to him, but we were laughing.

"Blah blah," Colin complained. "Caden's here."

He crossed the room to my husband, whose eyes were on me. Caden wore a deep navy suit and a gold tie. His cufflinks sparkled, and his hair was combed off his face. The fact that he hadn't shaved contrasted the crispness of the suit against the animal body inside it.

We went quiet. He wasn't looking at me. He was looking at Ronin.

Ronin removed his arm from my shoulders.

Colin interrupted the gaze by shaking my husband's hand and making some sort of wisecrack he must have found hilarious.

Caden, not as much. He'd turned his attention back to me.

"Girl. He looks like he wants to eat you alive," Jenn said into her glass.

I turned to Ronin so I could blame him, but he was gone. Caden maneuvered to us.

"My dad never looked at my mom like that," Jenn continued.

Before I could offer a snappy answer, Caden found us and kissed Jenn on the cheek. He kissed my cheek in the same platonic way, then looked behind him, but no one was there.

"Where's Colin?" I asked.

"Bar."

When I turned to scan the bar for my brother, I leaned into Caden a little. We had a pattern. A rhythm to our interactions. The shape of the space between us, laid out over the time together, was as predictable as the phases of the moon, and his touch always came when expected.

But when we looked at Colin as he tried to charm a young lady in a gold dress, Caden didn't lean in when I did. He didn't put his hand on my back. When Bob Abramson found me and said he wanted me to meet someone, my husband didn't take my hand. When Wilhelmina, the head cardiac nurse, her hair braided into long, neat rows, gave me a kiss and asked how I was handling my husband's hours, Caden didn't come close to me and brush his thumb between my shoulder blades. When we all sat down for a presentation about the hospital's goals, he kept his hands folded in his lap.

When he released his hands and placed them on his knees, I put my left hand over his right. He patted it, smiled at me, and slipped it away before looking behind him again.

I thought he was in a bad mood.

What else could it be?

Chapter Six

CADEN

The war had been building for over a month. The ventilators were left to do their job, but the squeak of gurney wheels on linoleum, the tip-tap of computer keys, the murmurs of the hospital staff all held a thread of the Thing I thought I'd banished. I could have a conversation with Greysen, but only if I concentrated on not hearing the Thing in the boiling pasta water or the radio news. Every day, it got a little stronger. Every day I was a little more tense, a little more afraid, a little more uncomfortable. The Thing got harder to box away and cart off. Harder to hide behind a wall. Impossible to ignore. I was pressed in on all sides by a Thing I couldn't even define.

And what had become more and more clear was that it wanted my wife.

I could put on a suit and knot a tie. I could put jeweled links into a starched cuff. I could shower, shave, comb my hair, but it was all a lie. It was all a costume, a mask. Under it, I was no more than a knot of bodily needs and overwhelming sexual urges. My mind was a set of neurons firing commands to my glands, and the glands sent emotions through my bloodstream.

She was mine.

Not his.

The Thing was male, and its strength was its persistence.

The neurons said I had to have her in my line of sight, but I'd bring the Thing right to her.

The only way to keep it away from her was to keep my distance.

But the animal said no. The animal I was knew that wouldn't work because she was mine.

Navigating between all these urges was exhausting. But as I entered the fundraiser, I took a breath. The exhaustion was under my suit. Behind my smile and polite words. No one could see.

She was with her brother and Jenn. Her hair was piled on top of her head and her earrings dropped down the length of her neck. She wore nude lipstick, and under the satin bodice of her gown, her nipples were hard. She was the picture of grace and charm, with a smile that transformed everyone around her and eyes that comforted people into talking.

The Thing saw her. In the bouncing acoustics of the room, it whispered its longing.

"Hello." Colin shook my hand.

I hadn't even seen him coming toward me. Just her. Only her.

"Nice to see you." I angled myself so I could see her over his shoulder.

"I'm hitting the bar, can I get you something?"

"I'm good, thanks." I patted his shoulder and headed for her, crossing half a ballroom without acknowledging another soul.

The Thing got more vocal, hiding in the voices of the guests and the strings of the musicians' instruments.

I could smell her from farther away than normal. Apples. No matter which perfume she wore, she smelled of the first bite of an apple, breaking taut skin with teeth, juice dripping down my chin. She was the satin skin and the crisp meat of the fruit. She was the hard seed and the tenacious stem.

I found her.

Ronin.

Laughing.

Arm around her shoulders.

He'd touched her. He'd had her. He'd licked the apples off her skin and touched her body. He wanted her again. Of course he did. She was beautiful and sexy. Any man would want her. I was filled with an unreasonable fury. A foul grimace in my soul. A call to action lubricated by rage.

I headed for them, bumping into a woman from pediatrics. I excused myself, and when I turned back, Ronin was gone.

In the seven steps to my wife, I came to some sort of sense.

Ronin was not a threat.

On the flip side, I was losing my fucking mind.

Kissing Jenn first was a delay tactic. I needed a moment to reduce my pulse rate. It didn't work. When I kissed Greysen's cheek and she slipped her hand in mine, the animal threatened to burst out of his suit.

I always desired her. Every minute. But this?

I wanted to drag her out by her hair, respecting the norms of privacy only because I wouldn't be able to finish in the middle of the ballroom. I wanted to squeeze her flesh, mark her in bruises, leave streaks of semen on her. Make the Thing scream in horror and curl up in a ball far away.

I couldn't live like this anymore.

But I was in a public place.

The suit was who I needed to be.

The suit was armor against the horrifying sight of the animal.

I didn't look at her. Didn't touch her. I focused on the distance between us and the eyes of a hundred people. I listened to Bob Abramson talk about money and bullshit, concentrating hard enough to make a decent show of being civilized.

In the dark, during the fundraising video, she leaned into me, taking my hand. "What's going on?"

"Nothing."

"Caden." My name was more than a statement. It was a comment on how well she knew the animal, and how well she loved it.

If eyes could listen, hers did, gazing at me in the darkness. I couldn't lie to her for much longer.

The entire invite list was watching the video. The bar was empty. The hallway lights were dimmed. The kitchen staff moved constantly and quietly to set up the buffet.

I laced my fingers in hers. She had a gold band we'd gotten out of expediency. No big sparkling rock. No sign I'd ever courted her properly before marrying her.

My father always said a man didn't skip steps if he wanted to do something once.

I slid my cheek to hers and whispered in her ear, "I want to destroy you."

Her hand tightened in mine so tightly I could feel our bones. Her glands must have fired, because the apples and the perfume melded and became something so uniquely *her* my balls ached—but not for simple release. For something more. An agreement of ownership.

Waiting wasn't an option.

Pulling her by the hand, I headed for the hallway.

"Caden," she said when we were away from the event, "slow down."

I didn't. I couldn't. I pulled her down the carpeted steps to the lower level, stepping over a velvet rope at the bottom. The lights were out in the hall. Three doors led to three empty event rooms.

"What's with you lately?" she asked.

"Are you saying no?"

"I'm asking a question."

I backed into one of the rooms and pulled her in. It was dark but for light coming from under the doorways on each side. The Thing cowered in the shadows, emitting fear like a pheromone. Good. I walked in deeper, eyes adjusting quickly enough to avoid the tables and stacks of chairs on wheeled dollies.

"So am I." I faced her. "Are you saying no?"

"What are you hoping I'll say yes to?"

"I'm going to pull that dress up until I can get to these hard nipples." I pinched them through the dress and she groaned. "Then I'll bend you over one of these tables and fuck you so hard walking's going to hurt. Are you saying no?"

"I'm not. But I want to know what's going on with you."

"Pull your dress up before I shred it."

Scaring her wasn't my plan, but there was fear in the air. I had no choice but to breathe it in.

The fear didn't come from her. As she pulled her dress over her waist to show me her thong and the lace edges of her stockings, she bit her lower lip. The fear I detected was in the shadows.

I stepped behind her.

The Thing was going to watch me.

I pushed my hand up between the fabric and her skin, taking that taunting nipple. I twisted it. Pulled. She leaned into it.

"Does it hurt?" I abused her nipple again.

"Yes."

"I should stop?"

"No."

I pushed her into a table, bending her sharply. When she tried to get up on her hands, I shoved her down by the base of her neck. Her earring fell over her jaw and clicked against the table.

I forgot about the Thing. Forgot about how much it wanted her. There was only Greysen and me in a dark room with our suddenly elastic boundaries.

I claimed her inside and out, and the whirlwind stopped.

Chapter Seven

I ached when I woke. From the bottom up: My feet from the shoes. My trapezius muscle from the bite.

I bent over the bathroom vanity and ran my fingers over the bite bruise. It wasn't too bad. The skin was a shade redder. It looked like a mild hickey. My eyes were ringed in black. I hadn't bothered to take off my makeup. We'd had sex twice again at home, if you could call it sex. More like he took my body and made it his own, giving orgasms and taking them as if they were a marital right. I'd collapsed into unconsciousness.

I wiped the bluish-gray mascara stains from my face.

My body wasn't a marital right, of course. My body was my own, and I could refuse him at any time. Caden knew that. He must have, because even after we got home, he checked on me.

Twice, the mask of determination snapped off, leaving a man who looked disconcerted.

Twice, he asked me if I wanted to slow down or stop.

Once, I said I was fine. Once, I begged him not to stop.

Both times, his brutality returned like a Halloween mask on an elastic string.

I should have made him stop, but I couldn't.

Why?

Was I threatened? Did I believe he'd hurt me worse if I did? Would he?

No.

"No," I said into the mirror. "He wouldn't."

How did I know? Was it the orgasms he gave me? He'd acted as if my pleasure gave him power. Every orgasm drove him to greater intensity, and each increase in passion drove me deeper into a sexual fugue.

I trusted him. One, he was a doctor, and a great one. It didn't get any safer than that. Two, he wanted me to want what he did. The checking in told me that much. He wanted consent. Needed it as much as I did, but I didn't think... no, I was sure he hadn't planned the last two rough encounters, so he couldn't have asked ahead of time. He was getting the idea to hurt me in the moment.

The pain.

Next time, I should stop him when it hurt. When he bit me. When it was uncomfortable.

I should, but I wouldn't. Morning Greysen, with her mascara running down her face and a bite mark on her neck, knew it wasn't okay to cause your partner pain or discomfort during sex. Dr. Greysen Frazier knew it was okay as long as it was coupled with consent and clear boundaries.

She knew it had a name.

I tossed the mascara-streaked wipe into the trash and went downstairs before I could say the name to myself.

CADEN WAS AT THE STOVE, making breakfast. My favorite.

"Pancakes!" I fist pumped quietly. "Pow."

I kissed him and he looked down at me, mask gone. Just my husband. He moved the spatula to the other hand and squeezed my shoulders while he flipped the cakes.

"I have nothing today," he said. "What about you?"

"Session in the morning and that's it. I was going to go work out. Maybe. I don't know. It's still kind of weird, all this time to myself."

He laced his fingers in mine, nudging the disks around pensively. "You said a big rock didn't go with army green. What you wore last night would have been stunning with a ring."

Pulling his arm off my shoulder, I put my left hand next to his. "We match. That works for me."

He shut off the stove and jerked the pan until the cakes slid. "Do you miss the service?"

He deserved my honesty, but there was more to the question than a simple lament for a job I didn't have anymore. He was the reason I'd left five weeks before instead of forty years from now.

But I couldn't lie to him or myself. "Sometimes."

He shifted the pan back and forth on the burner so the pancakes would skate around.

He picked up the plate and looked right at me for the first time that morning. His gaze landed on the bite mark. Reflexively, I covered it. He put the plate down and moved my hand away.

"Broken blood vessels," he said. "You have some abrading to the skin."

"It's fine."

"Does it hurt?"

"Only when you touch it, so don't." I picked up the plate. "I'm starving."

I kissed him and went to the table. He'd set it with silverware and glasses, and as I draped the cloth napkin on my lap, I took a second to acknowledge that he didn't usually set up an elaborate breakfast. He cooked for me as often as I cooked for him, but this was a step beyond.

As if he was trying to get back into my good graces.

For the pain. For the roughness. For the use of my body.

There's a name for this.

We made love that afternoon.

And by "made love," I mean we fucked passionately and considerately. We used our mouths for pleasure. He eased into me with grace, touched me where I liked to be touched, made sure I came long and hard before he did.

The bite mark was gone the next day, and though I didn't forget about the self-doubt it had revealed, I didn't think about it much because I didn't want to.

Two weeks passed.

I picked up two more clients from Ronin, which pretty much filled my schedule. I seemed to have a gift for counseling and medicating PTSD. Go figure. My military life was of use, and as that became apparent, I missed it less and less.

One night, as I was coming out of the bathroom, I caught Caden looking into an empty corner. I say "caught" because when he heard me, he jumped as if he was doing something wrong, then he passed me to go into the bathroom without saying a word or touching me.

He usually found some way to touch me.

The last lack of affection had ended at the fundraiser where he'd fucked me on a banquet hall table. Brutal sex after days of growing emotional distance. And boom, fixed the next morning as if nothing had happened.

Was he having an affair?

I felt every pulse of blood through my veins, hot with sparking electricity at the thought of his body touching another woman's.

I breathed through it, telling myself nice things about trust and the basic goodness inside my husband. It worked to clear the room of the noise, but the hum of possibility remained in the corners, cowed but not killed.

I DIDN'T HAVE time to see Jenn's show. Not really. I had an emergency session with a new patient who hadn't slept in a week. His wife had called me in desperation. He was having aural hallucinations and she couldn't tell if it was the exhaustion or the PTSD.

I met him, wrote him a script, and didn't have a place in my schedule to see him until he started crying. A grown man. A soldier. Six feet tall and two hundred pounds of muscle, weeping in my office.

And I got upset when my husband was a little distant.

I handed the patient a tissue. He cracked his neck and got on with it. Maybe I needed to relax on Caden a little.

Deciding I didn't need lunch on Wednesdays, I fit him into my schedule. Then I got a cab to 57th Street while it was still daylight.

"Here!" The driver pulled over in front of the Kadousian Gallery.

From the street, I saw Jenn, in baggy overalls and Vans, animatedly talking to people I couldn't discern past the glass's reflection. Rows of painted masks hung on the walls.

Jenn saw me and opened the glass door. "Hey!"

We hugged, and she introduced me to her guests. Tina Molino of Mt. Sinai's Psychiatric Division, and Dylan Coda from the VA Hospital in Newark.

"I'm sorry I'm late. I had an emergency."

"I was just telling Tina she works in the same hospital as your husband."

Tina was almost six feet tall with a black bob, white skin, and red lipstick. She looked like Snow White. "I was hoping to meet you at the fundraiser. Caden St. John is quite a star around the doctors' lounge."

"Careful. His ego can get to the size of a blimp."

"You trained him well."

"War makes men humble."

"Nice segue." Jenn held her hand out to the rows of masks and began the tour. "All of these were made by vets as part of the NEA's Creative Forces program."

I WAS HALFWAY DOWN the block when I heard a woman's voice calling my name.

Tina scurried toward me. "Hey, I wanted to talk to you. Do you have a minute?"

I looked at my watch. "I have about eleven if there's no traffic uptown."

"It's enough."

We went into the little coffee shop wedged between a FedEx and an office building. We had our coffee in ninety seconds and seats on the window ledge in five more.

"Okay. Jenn told me you're an officer and an MD specializing in PTSD in vets."

"Kind of fell into it. But yeah."

"Do you like it? I'm trying to hurry so I don't keep you."

"Do I have to answer quickly?"

"Take your time." She sipped her coffee, leaving red lipmarks on the plastic top.

"I'm from a military family. I enlisted at eighteen."

"Wow."

"Yeah. It was the only life I knew. Then I met Caden, and he wanted to go into private practice. So I left the army and came here with him. I thought I'd never feel right as a civilian, and New York... my God, there's no place in the world more overwhelming."

"That's the truth."

We tapped our coffee cups together.

"Helping these men and women... they're broken, but working with them makes me feel like I'm home. I love it."

"That's..." She shook her head in appreciation. "I'm glad to hear that. We're tackling a mental health unit to serve the military and—here's the newish thing— civilian contractors. Anyone who's worked in war. We're financed by Darren Gibson, and I think I may have an opportunity for you."

Chapter Eight

CADEN

Greysen spit toothpaste into the sink. When she ran the faucet, the Thing spoke inside the gurgling water. When she took the water in her mouth and her lips tightened and moved when she swished, my inner cold ran boiling hot.

She spit the water, and the Thing dispersed into the air vents, the fogged mirror, the space between my feet and the floor. It snaked around my wife's voice when she spoke. "She wants to talk to me about creating a treatment protocol for PTSD in vets. Then she's thinking of maybe expanding it to the general population. Kids and adults dealing with trauma."

She shook excess water off the brush and popped it into the cup. I didn't know how much longer I could last.

She was wearing a big T-shirt and underpants. Her feet were bare. Her nipples were hard. She was talking about Tina's offer to design programs at the Gibson Center, which wasn't really an offer but more of a suggestion to talk more. She was overwhelmed. She hadn't been in professional life very long.

"When I was promoted before, it was all forms and steps," she said. "Now it's fuzzier, you know?"

Sure. I knew.

"I thought you had a full schedule."

"I'm thinking I can squeeze it in."

There were reasons she shouldn't. She'd push herself to exhaustion. No one was here to give her limits. There was no ceiling or walls on what she could accept. This wasn't the army.

She crawled onto the bed and flopped into a sitting position with her back against the headboard.

The reasons she shouldn't do too much were easily explainable, but if I explained them, she'd fight me. I didn't want to fight. I didn't want to get angry, or I'd lose it again and hurt her. I didn't want to feel anything. I wanted this deadness, needed it to dampen the fear and anger.

"What do you think?" she asked.

"Did she tell you the salary?"

"No, I mean about..." She spread her legs.

I'd made love to her two nights ago and had barely kept myself from hurting her. I'd had to keep my hands on the bed and let her ride me. The Thing had been watching. If I touched her now, I would tear her apart to get rid of it.

I ran my hand inside her thigh and stopped.

The sense I wasn't alone was worse when I touched her.

"What?" She pouted.

"Touch yourself."

She bit her lower lip and slid her fingers under the crotch of her underwear.

Was It watching her? Hard to tell, but the feeling wasn't as strong.

She groaned. I was aroused, but I didn't have an emotional response to this beautiful woman fingering herself.

"Don't stop." Was my voice as emotionless and robotic to her as it was to me?

"I want you to fuck me."

"Faster." I stood over her and undid my pants. She reached for me, but I swatted her away.

"Tease," she said when I released my dick and fisted it.

"Pick up your shirt."

She showed me her tits. I felt the Thing stretching at the edge of my perception, trying to get in on the action, but for some reason, without a connection between Greysen and me, the circuit wasn't closed. It could feel what was happening, but not see it, or the other way around.

Fuck you, Thing. This one's for you.

I grunted. "Let me see you come."

In another minute, she was pumping her hips under her fingers with heavy, wet breaths. I came over her, leaving my semen streaked over her body.

She moaned with a satisfied *mmm* and took her hand from between her legs. I snapped tissues out of the box and wiped her up with all the tenderness of a clinician.

"Thank you." She smiled. "Come to bed."

I couldn't. I knew I couldn't but couldn't avoid it.

I loved her, but I felt nothing. My balls were empty and my heart was dead.

My beeper went off.

"Shit," she said. "Ignore it."

I picked it up, thanking God without the actual feeling of gratitude. "Hospital." She sighed.

"Greysen." I was this close to telling her everything. If I didn't have an emergency to attend to, I would have, right then. Instead, I said, "I'm sorry."

"This is the life of a surgeon's wife."

I kissed her forehead and left without looking back.

This wasn't sustainable.

I MANAGED to stay at the hospital through the next day. I didn't know what I hoped for except this Thing would go away if I starved it of my wife's presence.

The surgery wasn't done until early morning. I showered in the attending lounge and collapsed on one of the cots. The Thing missed her. Its longing whispered through the air conditioning. I could spite it indefinitely, but I didn't know how long I could spite myself. I missed her already. We'd spent plenty of time apart, but I'd gotten spoiled. If she was next to me, she was safe. Knowing that helped me rest.

I was awake when she beeped me. I called her, still on my back on a narrow cot.

"Hello," I said. "What are you doing up? It's not even six."

"I woke up and couldn't get back to sleep." Her voice was husky and broken.

At the sound of her voice, it softened like a puppy and vibrated off the walls. It was worried about her.

"Figured I'd start working on Tina's proposal," she said.

"Don't burn yourself out."

"I won't. Are you coming home?"

"I have to check the post-op report in a few hours."

"Okay. I know you're tired."

"I am."

"We have tickets to a play tonight."

Shit. How long would it take to starve this Thing? The room was dark, but I covered my eyes with my wrist to block it out. "What time?"

"Seating's at eight."

I could fake a surgery. I could fake being tired. I could take a trip. Starve it out. I didn't know if that was even an option, but it was the only idea I had.

Tell her you have to be in the OR.

No words came. I couldn't lie. I could make the words in my head but couldn't get them out.

It wasn't that I couldn't speak. I couldn't *lie*. And I knew, as sure as I knew the boundaries of the dark room I'd gotten up to pace across, that I couldn't lie because my emotions were stuffed in a bag and sealed away. Lying meant I had to fear the truth, which I didn't, and it meant I had to create fake vocal nuance, which I couldn't.

Hiding my emotions had been intentional, but easier than ever. The process of detachment had become greased. Frictionless. I barely had to think about it. I wasn't nervous. Wasn't panicky. I was curious about my feelings, what they'd been and how they drove me to lie. Why would a person lie unless there was a reward for it?

"Okay. I'll meet you there."

"Barring unforseens."

"Yes," I said. "Barring unforseens."

"I love you, Caden."

"I love you too."

I hung up, and with the separation, the Thing became clear in my mind. Very loud. And for the first time, it had a well-defined thought I could read.

You don't love her. I do.

THE FRONT DESK had a vertical whiteboard with the rooms, procedures, and the doctors performing. I scanned it as Wilhelmina picked up the eraser.

"Looking for something, doctor?" she asked, getting up on a stool to reach the top.

"Not yet."

Checking her clipboard, she erased Dr. Everett's name.

"What happened to Everett?" I asked.

"Strep."

Nurse Bergstrom picked up the phone. "Samuelson's on call."

"I have it," I cut in.

Wil looked at me as if I'd just clucked like a chicken. "It's an assist."

"I know. It's fine. I got it."

Will shrugged and wrote *St. John* in the empty space.

Chapter Nine

GREYSEN

Caden wasn't going to make it to the play. My answering service picked up the message, and delivered it as I was putting on my shoes. He'd taken on another patient, and the patient needed pre-op monitoring.

I should have gone myself, but I didn't want to. I wanted to go with him.

He'd been worried I was going to burn out, but maybe he was the one who needed to snuff one end of the candle. And maybe this was why he'd been so distant and preoccupied.

Maybe.

People weren't always predictable. They didn't react the same exact way even when in very similar situations.

The last time I'd seen Caden under tremendous stress was during the war, and he hadn't been rigid and distant. On the contrary, even when he was closest to his breaking point, he'd been funny, even charming, as day three of his hands in men's bodies crested into day four without relief. I was giving him vitamin shots and an uncomfortable amount of amphetamine. He seemed to thrive, and yet... no one thrives when someone loses an arm or a leg on the table and you have to move to the next without a break.

He was like a carnival wheel spinning long after the barker's hand had left the rail. Spiraling on his own juice and energy, ball bearings lubricated to go on and on, he couldn't calm himself. Even after I'd given him a sedative, he couldn't sleep. I'd crawled onto the mattress with him, and finally, relieved of a single thing to do but sleep, he held me in his bed.

I knew how to be detached. My job required it. But I couldn't be. Not with him.

At first, he hadn't been more to me than the next overworked army doc. But he was the only one I'd ever let pull me onto his cot fully clothed. He wasn't the only one who had wept with me, but he was the only one I'd wept with.

Was this what it was to love someone? To have that wall of detachment crumble and be rebuilt into a bridge?

I thought so. I swore it to myself because after those hours, we were so real together no one had to ask what was going on. Caden and I were an incurable condition.

Dispassion had a place in our lives, but not with each other.

The situation was different now. We were civilians living in New York City, not soldiers trying to save people in a war zone. Maybe I shouldn't be surprised or concerned by his distance. He might be far away for a reason that had nothing to do with me or our marriage. Maybe it was him, just him.

"Is everything all right?" he asked after I'd beeped him twice. His voice was flat, as if he was asking a patient if they were in any pain and could they please describe it.

"You're not home," I said, meaning something completely different.

There's a nagging ache in the center of my chest.

"I had rounds." He had a different meaning under his answer.

On a scale of one to ten, with ten being unbearable, how would you rate your pain?

"I missed you at dinner," I said.

I want to say it's a three, but it's closer to a seven.

"I missed you too."

Here's an aspirin.

"When are you coming home?"

Maybe I can have something stronger?

"Samuelson's got strep. I have to fill in for him again."

No.

"Okay."

I'll manage then.

"I love you."

Maybe try acupuncture.

"Yeah." I hung up the phone.

Shove it.

MID-AFTERNOON.

I'd been in session all morning. I heard Caden upstairs while I was with a patient, heard the old pipes rattle in the walls when the shower went on, then saw his feet come down the front steps. I was seeing a patient in and couldn't catch Caden without disrupting the gentle flow that was part of my job.

"How were you this week?" I asked Specialist Leslie Yarrow, who liked to sit in the chair with the high cushions. She still wore her dog tags under her polo T-shirt and kept her hair very short. She'd been sent home with a shoulder injury that was healing better than her mind.

"Fine. Good." She shifted in her seat. She'd had a hard time sitting still since she got back.

"Did you sleep?"

"Some. The pills helped. Thank you."

"But not entirely?"

"Nah." She flipped it off as if it wasn't a big deal, but her eyes were ringed in pink and purple.

"Did you have the dream again?"

"Yeah."

The dream was a recounting of a child torn apart by an IED. She'd been eight and screaming in pain. When Leslie recalled the memory, she said she screamed for hours while she tried to find a medic, but on further investigation, it had been a minute and a half before the girl died in her arms.

In the dream, the girl was her daughter.

"Something this week... my wife got freaked out. She said I should tell you."

"Should you?"

"Yeah, probably."

I waited.

"When I woke up from it, I didn't know Mindy."

"How so?"

"I went into her room, and I knew the room and all the stuff. But the kid sleeping there? I was like, who is she? She was a stranger."

"How long did that last?"

"A minute... maybe ten. Molly came into the kitchen and was like, 'Are you going to wake her up for school or what?' and then I came to."

"So you'd describe it as a fugue state? Did you have the feeling you were half asleep?"

"I was... I forgot the entire thing after not knowing Mindy." She shrugged, and that wasn't a normal reaction for someone who'd lost a bunch of time.

"Is that the first time it happened?"

She looked away. "Yeah. I told Molly I really didn't want to talk about this."

I wasn't letting her off the hook. We had four minutes, and it was hers to use to talk or not. Her decision, not mine.

"When I was a kid, I lost some stuff. Few hours here and there." She shifted in her seat. "My dad used to come to my room and do things. It was... I knew he did it, but I would forget the actual *thing* if you know what I mean." She made a nervous laugh, and I held onto a non-judgmental, non-enraged, almost inhuman detachment.

"I want to pause for a second. I heard both parts of that, and if you—"

"Is it time to go yet?"

"We have a couple of minutes"

"I don't want to talk about this right now, okay?"

"Okay, but you're safe here. Any time."

She stood. "I should get going."

I adjusted her sleeping pill dosage and asked her to keep a log of any more feelings that she wasn't where she was supposed to be, or that she didn't know the people around her. She agreed, apologized profusely, and left.

I hurt for the little girl she had been, and promised myself I'd do everything I could to help the woman who came to my office.

I briefly made the connection between Leslie Yarrow's dissociation and my husband's. It was a symptom of PTSD and needn't be a personal betrayal.

That realization was my medicine for the rest of the day.

———

IT WAS dark by the time I went back up to the house. Everything was perfect. He hadn't left a crumb behind. Not a note or a rumpled sheet.

Calling got me his voice mail. I beeped him, but he didn't call back right away. I heated up dinner. Got into my pajamas. Put on the TV. Shut it off. Listened to the traffic outside. Went to the bathroom.

His clothes were in the hamper. Underwear. Slacks. A pale blue shirt that brought out the depth of his eyes. I gathered it in my hands and pressed it to my face, expecting to smell fresh coffee grounds in stale sweat.

I got something much more floral.

Feminine.

This is not cologne.

My blood took a second to boil. In that pause, I checked again. Definitely perfume.

Oh, fuck no.

No no no.

I was out the door so fast I didn't change out of my pajamas and almost forgot to put on shoes. I stuffed my feet into Keds, put on a long coat, and caught a cab at Columbus Circle.

Because, no. We had a deal and the deal included fidelity. Non-negotiable. Deep breath.

People cheated for a reason. Either it was personal, and they were just cheating assholes. Or it was situational, and a cheating asshole was in a situation where it was easy to cheat. Or it was us. And that last option stuck in my craw, because even after years of talking to people about why they found themselves betraying or betrayed, it was now me. And if it was the relationship, it was me, my fault, what I delivered or didn't deliver.

I'd come to a strange life in a strange city to be with him. Maybe that was the problem. Or maybe we didn't work as a couple outside a war zone. Or maybe he liked it hotter than I was used to.

Fuck this. It wasn't my fault.

He owed me better than touching another woman. Saying sweet things to her. Those were my kisses and sweet words.

Or maybe there was none of that. Maybe it was all warm holes and quick spurts.

The disloyalty was bad, but not knowing the exact terms of the betrayal was eating every brain cell not occupied with breathing.

My phone rang on the way. I flipped it open.

Him.

Was his dick wet with her? Or was he on his way there?

"Hi," I said.

"Hey, you called?" Flat flat flat. Why hadn't I seen it before? How blind had I been?

"Where are you? I was thinking of bringing you dinner."

"Ah, that would be great, but I'm assisting in an hour and I need to scrub in."

So that's what you sound like when you lie?

"Oh, all right then. When do you think you'll be home?"

"I came home today and you were in your office. I didn't want to bother you."

You knew I'd be in session.

"Yeah. Hey, the other line's beeping. I have to go."

"I love you," he said before I cut the call.

"Thanks for the aspirin."

WILHELMINA WAS at the front desk of cardiac. She confirmed Caden was scrubbing into an emergency open heart procedure. I told her I needed a key and he had it in his bag. I didn't like lying, but I was past sense. I was cussing up a blue streak in my head and smiling on the outside as if showing up at the hospital in Keds and a long coat was the result of an annoying misplaced key.

She led me into a row of large grey lockers and left me alone.

I tipped his padlock up to see the numbered dials. It was the same lock he'd had in Iraq, and I knew the combination.

Every marriage has boundaries, and going into his locker had a thick red line around it. My thumbnail in the grooves, I clicked the number sequence, paused with the weight in my hand.

Just ask him.

The mature thing to do would be to ask. Just say flat out, you've been different. You've been unavailable. You've got perfume on your shirt.

Fuck that.

I snapped the padlock open and slid it out quickly, before I could change my mind.

The locker was the size of a small closet. He had a suit, shoes on the floor, bag of toiletries on the top shelf, new clothes still in tissue paper in a Barney's bag, and a plastic bag of dirty things.

I picked up the dirties. I smelled it before I even opened the bag. Perfume.

"Fuck you, Caden."

I threw the bag back in and slammed the door. Something clicked and fell.

If one thing is out of order…

"I don't care."

…he'll know.

"I don't." I put the lock in the loop.

You'll never know if he would have told you the truth.

"Fuck!"

I opened the locker and readjusted the laundry bag. I couldn't find what had fallen. I tiptoed so I could see the top shelf. Next to the toiletry bag, a glass bottle lay on its side. I picked it up. It was from Lyric scent shop, where I got my perfume.

Before I even turned it over, I knew.

Scent #6512 - Greysen F.

Before I opened the top and waved it in front of my nose, I knew.

It was mine. I hadn't recognized it mixed with his scent, but once I had the bottle under my nose, it was unmistakable.

When we were separated, he'd given me one of his T-shirts. His smell had comforted me. I buried my face in it when he called, wrapped it around my neck when I slept, curled around it when I brought myself to orgasm.

When had he taken my perfume? And why? Did he know he'd be gone for days?

I put the bottle back and put the padlock back in place, touching the door with my fingertips. "I'm sorry."

Across the room, the door opened. I peeked around the lockers to find a cleaning person wheeling in a yellow bucket.

"Hello?" he called. "Anyone in here?"

"Just leaving," I said, smiling stiffly as I walked by.

"DID YOU FIND THE KEY?" Wilhelmina asked blithely, as if nothing was wrong. She could see into my heart and all was well there.

"I realized I had it."

"Ah, better watch, doctor. When the mind starts going, the body's sure to follow."

I laughed a little, but it was more from uneasiness than humor. "Do you know where he is?"

She slid a clipboard into a cubby. "I think he's in five." She took a quick inventory of my posture, my hair, my coat and pajamas, the look of emotional desperation that must have been all over my face, using a skill they didn't teach in nursing school but a large number of nurses had. "It's a viewing theater, if you want to take a look."

"Um, sure. Okay. Yeah. Yes, I'd like that very much."

I didn't know what insight I expected to get from watching him. Something was still off. My perfume didn't change that. But Wil led me to the upper floor viewing room where med students watched the procedure. I sat away from them, letting the narration from their instructor fade into the ambient hiss of the air conditioning.

From above, I saw him and the other attending move together with an efficiency bordering on grace. They cut a woman open and spread her ribs. I flinched. It was hard to watch.

But still, my husband did his job, isolating a living, beating heart.

The lead turned away from the table and looked up at the med students. Her voice carried over speakers to the little room as she spoke a language I hadn't been trained in med school to understand. My eyes were glued to my husband anyway. He was still working, though I couldn't discern what he was doing. When the lead surgeon said his name, it cut through the jargon.

"Doctor St. John here is assisting, but he's been lead on this procedure a few hundred times."

Caden looked up to salute the students.

He saw me and froze.

We didn't move as the other doctor continued. His eyes betrayed nothing. I was wrong to be here. Wrong to distrust him. Wrong to worry. He had his hands on a living heart. Of course his detachment bled over.

I waved and tried to smile.

He nodded and got back to work.

———

HE CALLED after one in the morning. I was in bed, watching the clouds cross the setting moon over the brownstones across the street.

"Did I wake you?" he asked. The vocal deadness was still there. Maybe I'd have to get used to it.

"No."

"Did you enjoy the surgery?"

"Better than *Cats.*"

He laughed a real, true, guttural laugh and I almost burst into tears.

"I'm sorry," I said. "I disturbed you."

"You didn't disturb me."

"I missed you."

He sighed. It wasn't an annoyed sigh or a sigh of boredom, but a final exhale of breath after the realization that what was started wouldn't be finished. It was an acceptance of defeat. "You know how much I miss you? I stole your perfume so I could smell you when I'm on the cots."

"You're not that far away."

"I know."

He didn't offer an explanation as to why he couldn't sleep at home, or why he'd decided to stay away for days. I was owed that.

"Are you coming home now?" I asked.

"I need to be here."

"You're pushing it, darling."

"I know, baby."

"I'll be at Jenn's opening tomorrow at five. The masks."

"I thought you saw it last week."

"It's been in previews or something. Ask her when you see her. Don't come if you want to sleep in. But if you sleep in, you sleep here."

"Is that an order?"

It shouldn't have to be an order, but I couldn't read him well enough to know if he was being playful or if he was offended at having his leash yanked.

"Consider it an order."

Chapter Ten

CADEN

There was no starving it while Greysen was in my life. The Thing hovered back in the ambience until I thought of her, then it smiled. When she beeped me, it made its presence known. And when I recognized her voice, I felt it listening.

Leaving her was not an option. Cutting her out wouldn't make me sane any more than pretending the Thing didn't exist would. I needed her. Before her, I had been made of broken glass in a padded bag. Everything looked fine on the outside, but I'd been cutting myself. She opened the bag and put the shards together.

I loved her too much to choose this Thing over her. That much I was sure of. But outside the OR, I couldn't think clearly. Couldn't create a solution or make a decision in the thick swirl of jealousy and panic. Every thought walked a razor's edge between sanity and insanity, and the edge kept moving until I didn't know which side was which.

Every day, it got worse. Even if the Thing wasn't fully present, I felt its pressure against the skin of my mind, pressing against the membrane like a fist punching a latex wall. When I woke in a sweat, the pressure increased, and when she called, it burst through. My emotions were getting sucked into the black hole of this nightmare and I couldn't shake it. The glue got stickier every day.

The treatment wasn't a cure, but I craved it.

It was a perversion.

To quell the Thing, I had to hurt Greysen. I had to fuck her like a fighter. Mark her like a vandal. Break her like a champion.

I could make her come over and over while I did it too. That satisfied every part of me and made the Thing howl. It separated me from it. Severed the tie.

If I could take advantage of that opportunity long enough to talk to her, maybe we could fix this. All I had to do was get over the humiliation of not being in control of my own mind.

I HAD a million excuses to avoid the opening and only one reason to go. The reason was Greysen. So I went.

Seeing my wife in a public place meant I could put off the inevitable long enough to change my mind, chase her away, talk myself into some other course of action. By the time I got there, I had my full mental facilities only by way of making sure my emotions were not engaged.

When I saw her standing in a little black dress and heels, her fingers curved around a wine glass, I felt something.

But desire wasn't an emotion. Possession wasn't an emotion.

I kissed her cheek, and as expected, the Thing jumped into the space between us.

I wasn't angry as much as I wanted to battle it and win.

Combativeness wasn't an emotion either. Or maybe it was. I didn't care.

"Congratulations," I said to Jenn. When I kissed her cheek, I kissed her cheek. No third party slid in on the action.

Tina approached and introduced herself, as expected. I smiled and shook her hand. Same thing as Jenn. Nothing jumped between where we touched.

"I've been wooing your wife," she said. "I hope you don't mind."

"It depends on what kind of wooing you're talking about."

"Professional wooing," Greysen said.

"Did they legalize that?"

Tina laughed. Greysen slapped my arm playfully then looped her hand inside my elbow. The Thing felt good about that but couldn't find a way in through the fabric.

"I hope you don't have to work as hard as I did," I said. "She drives a hard bargain."

Tina clicked my glass. "Thanks for the tip."

"I'm sure no one will have to work as hard as he did," Greysen said.

"Sounds like quite a story." Tina sipped her water.

"Not really," Greysen said. "My unit went to Balad to assist the combat support hospital. I had to assess their fitness—"

"She decided I was unfit."

"I did not!"

"You did." I looked down at her, checking her status. Raised eyebrows. Relaxed mouth.

I wanted to fuck her everywhere. Hard. Later. I would have to. Nothing was getting starved tonight. Not my hunger for her and not the Thing.

She smiled. If I wasn't fooling her into thinking I was all right, I was at least charming her into believing it. Good.

I turned back to Tina. "She said I was overworked. She said I needed rest or I'd make a mistake."

"Which did you do? Rest or make a mistake?"

"Neither."

"Of course," Greysen chimed in. "He beat the odds. It's what he does."

I nodded, satisfied that she thought that. Winners had an easier time winning.

Danny came by. I shook his hand. He kissed my wife in an appropriately platonic manner. "It's like a fucking hospital reunion. I try to get away from you people at night."

"Do your patients know you have such a potty mouth?" I said.

Greysen slipped her hand into mine. I took it away.

"Half of them can't figure out how to use a potty. So no." His orbicularis oris tightened slightly above his left lip. A sneer of a smirk so faint I would have missed it if I wasn't paying attention so coldly. Or maybe that was the reason for the sneer in the first place.

"We're going to look at some masks, if you don't mind," I said.

"Have at it."

I took Greysen to the side where we could see a mask painted blood red and clamped with a vise. The patient's story was typed onto a framed piece of paper next to it, but I was sure I knew it. We slid sideways to the next one. It had been painted by a skilled hand in Islamic geometric patterns.

"This is nice," I said, but had no follow-up. I usually had reasons to like things. I couldn't find one.

"You should see this one over here."

Again, she tried to hold my hand, and again, I took it away.

"Caden."

"Which one? This one?"

"What's happening?"

She had a hand on each of my elbows, but I couldn't look at her. She was too earnest. Too honest. And all I wanted to do was rip that black dress in two and shove my dick inside her. I wanted to fuck her mouth so deep she choked. Get my cock so far up her ass I—

"I think he used a stencil—"

"To us," she said. "What's happening to *us*?"

All I had to do was say, "nothing," but I still couldn't lie.

Both hands in my pants pockets, I bent so only she could hear me. "I want to be fucking you right now."

"No. No, that's not true." Her eyes filled. They sparkled so brightly when she was about to cry. She blinked. One fell.

Reaching inside my jacket, I snapped my handkerchief open and handed it to her.

She didn't take it. It was poison. Electrified. A pat on the shoulder from a clinician. A slap in the face from a stranger. I didn't have the sense or the will to hold her or whisper reassurances, because the Thing was punching through again, and resisting it took everything I had.

She brought her right toe behind her left heel, spun on the balls of her feet for a clean about-face, and forward marched out the door.

I CAUGHT the cab door before she closed it and slid in next to her, barking the 87th Street address to the driver.

"Greysen, listen to me."

"Why were you assisting on a surgery you've led a hundred times?"

I looked at her as if she was crazy, but she wasn't. Not even a little. "Kate was out sick and Eleanor needed me."

"Bullshit."

"You can ask her."

"Are you having an affair?"

"What? With Eleanor?"

"With anyone."

"No!"

"So what is it then?"

I needed to know what she was perceiving without me dropping hints. "What is what?"

"You're the same as you were at the fundraiser, but worse. You're so cold. You won't touch me. It's like you're somewhere else and I can't take it. I *can't take it*." The last three words rumbled deep in her throat. It was sexy as hell.

I let my desire for her out of its cage, and it filled me like a balloon. I thrust my body in her direction, leveraging myself on the window behind her.

"You're going to take it." I spit the words like a threat. "You're going to take more of it than you ever took before."

She swallowed. The tears dried up, but not the feelings that caused them. "It's not that easy."

"No, it won't be. I promise you that."

I HAD a raging hard-on the whole way home. When we were alone in the foyer behind a locked door, she put her jacket on the hook. Her lips were parted and I'd bet my medical license she was wet.

I let go of everything. My defenses. My armor. My rage. My fear. When I reached for her, I didn't hold her. I took the edges of the neck of her dress and pulled, tearing it open at the center seam.

She gasped. "Stop."

I had to stop. I felt something then. Relief.

I could stop.

She stood with her hands on her breasts, holding the dress up. "What's happening?"

"You wanted me to touch you. I'm going to touch you. I'm going to touch every inch of you. I'm leaving nothing on the table."

"There's no one else?" Her arms relaxed and the dress fell a little.

"No. Never."

"Why do you get like this? Like tonight? Like a few weeks ago?"

"Because I need this."

That wasn't a lie, but it wasn't the whole truth. I couldn't think about the whole truth. Not with her torn dress and her pheromones invading my mind.

"Take it."

She let her dress drop. Black lace bra. Garter. Stockings. A ribbon of underwear. She must have been expecting something tonight.

Oh, how the Thing screamed incoherently when it saw my intentions. How it quivered in fear and impotence.

I grabbed her, pressing her body to mine, mouthing her cheek, her lips, her throat, her ear. I nipped her shoulder but didn't bite. Not yet. The Thing was there in the connection, but it was scared.

"Upstairs."

I watched her go, gartered ass waving as she climbed. Alone for a second at the base of the stairs, I put my hand on the bannister to steady myself.

"You ready?" I whispered. "I'm going to fuck her so hard you disappear forever."

For the second time, the ambient hush of its voice made words.

I'll never leave her.

"We'll see about that."

I spun, a slave to my sickness, flipping from the man I was to the man I am.

To ring that throat.

To hold her high.

To own her completely.

I lost it. In a swirl of me, her, my love, my control, and the Thing I couldn't name, screaming out and away.

Chapter Eleven

GREYSEN

I had bruises on my left wrist where he'd held me down. He had been more gentle with the right side, which had never really recovered from the break I got in basic training, but the left took what was left over. I couldn't let patients see it.

The first time he fucked me with brutality, we didn't talk about it. I woke up thinking he'd been half asleep and it wouldn't occur again. Three weeks after that, he'd done it again, pushing me harder, demanding more, taking me to the edge over and over.

Last night, two weeks after the last time, he did it again. He'd fucked me in the ass, in the shower afterward, on the floor. He'd been rough, and the rougher he got, the more I came.

I wanted him to push me hard. I liked it. But this was slipping out of control. *There's a name for this.*

It was spring. Long sleeves would be too hot, and the AC in the office was spotty. I rummaged in my drawer and found a loose coil of bracelets. I slid them over my bruised left wrist. That would have to do.

I checked myself in the mirror. I looked fine. No one could see the bruises or the soreness between my legs. No one could see the aches or the pleasant, peaceful satisfaction.

Masochist.

The word shot through my mind, and for the first time, I let it. I mouthed it in the mirror.

Masochist.

"Where are you off to today?" he asked from the bathroom doorway, arms crossed over his bare chest. His pajama bottoms hung low on his hips, the waistband cutting across the V-shaped indent of his pelvis.

"Collecting data for the Tina thing." I leaned over the vanity and put on lipstick.

"Are you okay? From last night?"

"Uh-huh. Are you?" I snapped the tube closed.

"Yeah." His nod was serious. It was not an enthusiastic agreement as much as a simple affirmative.

"You seem more animated."

His arms unfolded. I'd startled him. "Animated? What's that mean?"

I faced him. "The coldness is gone." I put my hand on his chest and drew it through the patch of hair in the center, down to his abdomen. "Is something going on you want to talk about?"

"No."

I shrugged. I wouldn't normally gesture like that any more than I'd roll my eyes. Normally, I'd acknowledge his feelings without validating or dismissing them. But I didn't feel normal. I felt a little less in control, a little more impulsive. Less like a professional psychiatrist and more like a wife who knew her husband's boundaries.

"You on call today?" I asked.

"Yeah." He took my hand and kissed inside the wrist. "I'll call you."

I kissed him in a typical married-person way. A punctuation between activity. A comma in the day. I didn't get to the bedroom door before his voice stopped me.

"Greysen."

"Yeah?"

"I can't take this back once I say it."

This couldn't be good. Anything he might want to take back wouldn't be a statement to celebrate.

"Okay?"

"You might want to cancel your appointment."

"Caden. Is everything all right?"

Sucking his lips between his teeth as if he wanted to hold the words back, he tightened his jaw and tilted his head. We were frozen in his moment of decision while the currents of his courage swirled and gathered together.

"I think." Hands though hair. A pause. I stayed absolutely still. "I think I'm going crazy."

Part Two

Chapter Twelve

GREYSEN

DECEMBER, 2006

Caden's hands, what they could do, how careful they were in doing it, were always different in my memory than in real life. I forgot them every time they were out of my sight. They were always wider, more articulated than I remembered. When I saw his wedding ring on the fourth finger, tying him to me, I stood in awe of that single band taming a force so powerful.

"Hey," he said, meeting me at the desk at the front of the administrative offices of the hospital. He was crisp and showered in a suit with a textured silk tie. He always smelled of alcohol when he got out of surgery. He covered it with cologne and sex, but it was deep in his pores.

When he signed out, his gold ring wiggled with the letters of his name.

"How are you feeling? Since this morning?" I asked, remembering the taste of those fingers.

"If I wasn't fine, I'd let you know," he lied.

I let him have that particular deceit because it was to protect me. He was painfully honest in everything else. We started down the hall.

When my heels clacked on the floor, he looked at my feet. "Are you all right in those?"

I turned my calf so he could see the outline of the shoe and the stockings under it. "Do you like them?"

He walked again. "I like them over my shoulders."

Stating facts. Clear and concise. Cold because he was nervous, not because he was losing his mind. He wasn't lying about feeling better, only that he'd tell me.

"How's your thigh?" he asked when we were alone in the elevator.

"Nice contusion."

"Muscular or dermal?"

"Subcutaneous."

He nodded, hands folded together in front of him. "I'll be more careful next time."

We got out at the doctors' level of the garage, which was nicer than any of the others, and had valet. His Mercedes was waiting. He let me in.

"Where are we meeting him again?" he asked.

"Gotham."

"We should have taken a cab."

The car pulled onto Central Park West. It was the week between Christmas and New Year. Traffic was on a break.

"It was a cutting day," I said with a playful curl to my question. Surgery left him raw and potent. We usually fucked on cutting days.

"Just a quad. Easy. He was young though. So we had tertiary distress."

He made a left, crossing hand over hand, his attention always sharp, even when the streets were empty.

"You don't want to go," I said.

"To dinner?"

"To dinner with Ronin."

"I like Ronin."

"To dinner with Ronin to discuss the new protocol."

"No." He faced me when he made the denial, and for a second, I saw his raw power. "I don't want to go to dinner with Ronin to discuss this at all. Ever."

"You don't have to."

"Yes, I do, Greysen."

"You *don't*."

"Yes. I. Do. For you."

"Don't lay this on me."

"Jesus Christ. If I wrote you a check for three hundred bucks, would you listen to me for fifty minutes? We're married. I do things for you. You do things for me. We make sacrifices."

Before I could talk about agency, autonomy, and acceptance, he grabbed my hand and squeezed it. For a month, his touch outside our home had gotten rare, and it froze me.

When I squeezed back, he put his hand back on the wheel to pull the car up to the valet. My fingers were left alone to make their own sense of him.

THE HOSTESS LED us through the cavernous space. Pillars of changing light held up the thirty-foot ceiling, and the sounds of conversations and music were muffled by careful acoustics. Caden put his hand on my lower back to guide me through, and I kept pace in six-inch heels.

Ronin had finished basic and been stationed in Maryland. He wouldn't say where, but I knew it was the Aberdeen Proving Ground. He knew I knew and neither confirmed nor denied what he did for a living.

He was alone at a table in the corner, reading a magazine. In the folds, I saw half of President Bush's face. He stood when we approached.

"Colonel," Caden said.

"St. John," he replied, shaking Caden's hand first.

I envied the public touch, then I gave my own handshake and let Caden pull my seat out for me. We ordered drinks. Wine for me. Whiskey for Ronin. Water for Caden.

Ronin had been a handsome man in basic training, but his eyes had matured from simply piercing to devastating, and his conceit had ripened into confidence.

"We haven't seen you since the fundraiser," I said. "Are you still with that girl?"

He leaned back to let the waitress place the glass of whiskey in front of him. "Nah."

"I'm sorry to hear it."

"Not a big deal. It takes a certain type to deal with me." His eyes met mine, then Caden's, and he smirked. He asked about Caden's residency, my feelings about private practice. Usually we wouldn't ask about his job, but this time was different.

"I mentioned we wanted to talk to you about something specific," I started.

"You had me at 'secret.'"

The waitress came and took our order. It took forever to hear the specials. I didn't have much of an appetite, even though I hadn't eaten all day. I needed the feeling of being at a peak of tolerance.

"To old friends," Ronin held up his drink, and we clicked.

Caden looked as if he'd rather be cut into small pieces than sit at that table.

"So," I said, "I'll get right to the point."

"Please," Caden said.

I leaned toward Ronin. "I hear Aberdeen was working on a heightened sensory perception protocol?"

Ronin made no sign he was surprised. "I'm sure I don't know what you're talking about."

"To increase the accuracy of scopaesthesia. The feeling you're being watched."

"He knows what scopaesthesia is."

I ignored my husband. "For troops on the front line. If they can perceive when they're being watched, they can kill first."

Ronin leaned back, crossing his legs while he fingered his glass. "And this is interesting to you because?"

I looked at Caden, and he looked at me. This was the moment we broke the shell we'd grown around ourselves. For me. For us.

"Caden has a persistent condition."

Back to Caden. He wasn't looking at me. He was touching his water glass with his left hand, and that ring, those fingers, the way the index finger tapped once.

"He thinks someone's watching him."

"Not watching," Caden cuts in. "It's not malicious."

"It's trying to get inside him."

Ronin uncrossed his legs. "That sounds pretty malicious."

"It's—"

Caden put his cold fingers on my arm, and I stopped. "It wants to join with me. I don't have a feeling it wants to hurt me. It is, just so you know, crazy. It's not normal. It's fucking insane crazy talk and I'm embarrassed to be sitting here telling you about it."

"Having a wife will do that to you."

They shared a male moment and I let it slide.

"So," Ronin continued, "you've checked environmental causes?"

"Had the house checked for carbon monoxide," he said.

"And you've considered PTSD? I mean, your wife's a card-carrying expert."

"It's not PTSD," I interjected.

"Really? You were in Fallujah. Anyone who didn't go crazy already was."

We sat in a triangle of silence with our own memories of the blood, the screaming, the smell of gunpowder and meat. The food came. I was sure it smelled great to a person who was interested in eating. None of us were. When the waitress asked if we wanted anything else, no one answered.

I broke the silence. "It's not PTSD. No flashbacks. No disrupted sleep. No emotional outbursts."

No emotion at all. I didn't say that. It wasn't relevant, and it wasn't one hundred percent true.

"It's a nascent dissociative disorder," I continued.

"Wait, wait, wait..." Ronin threw up his hands.

"It's not—" Caden tried to get a word in.

"Have you tried antipsychotics even?"

"Yes," I said. "We've tried everything. But every few weeks, the feeling comes back. We get it under control, but it's been every week, and now it's every five days or so. It used to be every few months, but last time, we had a four-day spread."

Ronin looked from me to Caden, then back to me, twisting his hands out to show us his palms. "You do *what* to get it under control?"

I couldn't answer, and Caden wouldn't. Instead he said, "I need this protocol. We do. We need it now."

"What. Do. You. Do?" Ronin planted his flag in the ground.

Caden plucked it out by putting his elbows on the table and locking his gaze on our friend. "I fuck Greysen so hard I hurt her."

"Jesus." Ronin drained his whiskey.

"I gain control of her body and all of it goes away."

"Is this a control thing or a sadism thing?"

Trust Ronin to get right to the point.

"I don't know. But one day, I'm going to really injure her."

"No, you're not," I insisted, but I was background noise. It was all Caden now.

"Whatever this is," he continued, "it's not telling me to kill the neighbor's dog. It's not a schizoid hallucination channeling my id. It's a separate thing. It's not just distracting, it's overwhelming, and you know me. Right? You know I don't spook."

Ronin nodded. He'd been with us in Fallujah. He knew what Caden could do in the face of death. He'd seen how, when necessary, ice water flowed through my husband's veins.

"You do not spook," he confirmed.

"We need this," I said.

"I'm not saying I know what you're talking about, but let's say I did. Let's say I knew a way to heighten your feelings, including feelings of being watched. What then? It'll only make it worse."

"Only if it's real," I replied. "It heightens the feeling of real eyes. A real enemy. Caden isn't on the battlefield. There's no enemy. This could shake the entire thing loose. Ronin." I put my hand over his. "Please. Send me the efficacy report and I'll look at it with an open mind. If I think it won't help, I'll drop it."

He took his hand away and used it to hold up his empty whiskey glass for the server. He snapped his napkin open and draped it over his lap, then slid his fork off the table. "Ten bucks says this isn't even pink inside."

Caden picked up his steak knife. "You wouldn't know pink if you had your face in it."

I wasn't finished with the conversation, but they were. I picked up my fork and poked at my salad. I felt as if I'd gone to battle and suddenly, without reason, everyone had laid down arms and gone home for lunch with the wounded still bleeding into the mud.

———

AFTER SEEING RONIN AT GOTHAM, Caden and I were under the sheets in a warm bed, watching the shadows of leaves dance on the ceiling. I knew he wasn't sleeping, and he had to be aware that I was awake.

"Was it hard to tell Ronin?" I asked finally.

"Yes."

"We have to try everything at this point."

"I know. But I don't have to like it."

I turned my body toward his and draped my arm over his chest. "One day, we'll look back on this and say it was the greatest adventure of our lives."

"We're not making happy memories."

"They'll be different when they're in the rearview."

He turned to face me. His nose was a quarter inch from mine, and he might as well have been in a different room. "This won't. Not for me."

"Let's see. Give it time."

"I'm not even in my own skin. Do you know what it's like to have a brain that's not doing what it's supposed to do?"

"No."

"I'm a stranger to myself. It's torture. It's like I'm broken. Ripped up. And I can't find the wound to stitch up. When I hurt you, it's like I find it for a little while, but a new one opens. I've never been afraid before. Not really. But when it gets bad and I feel it coming, I don't know what I'm going to do to stop it, or what's going to happen if it takes me over."

I kissed him. "It won't. We have everything we need to figure it out."

"You've been saying that for months."

"It's still true. I don't give up."

"Don't give up on me, Major One More."

"Never. I'll never give up on you."

We shifted like tectonic plates, fitting the muscles and bones of our bodies together until we found comfort in the way our shapes clicked and fell asleep in each other's arms.

Chapter Thirteen

CADEN

SEPTEMBER, 2001

I was at a prestigious residency at NYU Medical Center, learning under the best heart surgeon on the planet. Roberto García had performed over two thousand open heart procedures, and he'd taken me under his wing. Everything was going fine.

On September 11th, 2001, that all fell apart.

I was on the morning shift when I was called down to emergency. Caked in filth, encased in equipment, burned, screaming, the horror of it all revealed in bones and blood. I wasn't training as an ER surgeon, but they needed me, so I became one. The nurses were spectacular. They helped me get a handle on the sudden situation. I locked off any feelings about what was happening while I did the job.

Between crises, I tried to call my parents. The cellular lines were jammed. No one was getting through. There was talk of other cities. Other planes. The entire system was shut down. Nothing flying. Nothing landing.

The world was chaos, but inside myself, I did what I had to. I cut. I sewed. I made decisions. For twenty-four insane hours, I was order inside madness.

A nurse named Lola dumped a bag of ice into the metal sink and turned on the water.

"Thank you," I said, but she was already gone.

The parade of casualties had slowed, but no one had time for niceties when the world was falling apart. My eyes were burning. My knees were painfully swollen. When the sink was full, I stuck my head in it. The cold shocked my mind clear.

When I pulled my head out of the ice water, someone put a towel in my hands. I assumed it was Lola, but then he spoke with his deep Mexican accent.

"Stay still."

Fingers on the inside of my wrist.

"I'm fine, Roberto."

He didn't answer while he counted. The bright fluorescents had a density all their own, and the sage green of the tile walls was loud against the soft blues of the linoleum floor. Outside the scrub room, staff ran past the windows. I needed to help them.

"You're tachy," he said, letting go of my wrist. "But better than I expected."

I ran the towel through my hair. Dr. García was five foot five with a head of thick black hair. He had the wide cheeks and full lips of his Mixtec ancestors.

"I'm fine. How many are in triage?"

"You need to rest."

"I told you I was fine."

"No one bathes in ice water when they're fine." I was about to argue, but he cut me off. "Go take a nap before I write you up. And then we're going to talk about your future."

He had the power to fail me out. He wouldn't, but I was tired and my face must have registered shock or disappointment, because he responded.

"You're too good at this, St. John. Cardiac surgery is a waste of your talent."

"What? Wait."

My beeper went off, startling me. I tilted it to see the grey-and-black screen. It was my parents' house, but not the code they used for emergencies.

"My mother."

"We can talk next week." García said, snapping the towel out of my hands. He tossed the towel into the hamper on his way out.

I flipped open my phone and called her. For the first time in dozens of tries, it connected.

"Caden."

It wasn't my mother.

"Who is this?"

"It's Kent. I'm your father's financial advisor twenty years now."

I scanned my memory. I'd met him. Business dinners at the house. Holiday cocktails. He'd tried to get me to buy term life insurance. "Why are you in my parents' house?"

"I have all the keys..."

"Where's my mother?" I recognized the hum of the refrigerator in the background, but only when it clicked off.

"I called from my number, but you weren't picking up." Kent Whoever had a desperate edge to his voice.

"I asked you a question. Where's my mother?"

Someone else murmured in my kitchen.

"We don't know," Kent said. "We were wondering if you'd seen them."

"*We?*" I didn't know why I latched onto the pronoun. Nothing could have been less important, but that was the most comprehensible straw to grasp, because as far as I was concerned, my father was somewhere in the city, sewing people back together, and my mother was home, on 87th Street, far away from the fallen towers.

More murmurs from my kitchen. Their kitchen. The kitchen I thought of when I thought of home. I was ten steps behind, still wrestling with taking a nap or demanding Garcia tell me what the fuck he meant about my future.

"My... we..." Kent shook the shit out of his head. "It doesn't matter. I have... I *had* an office in the North Tower."

I don't care —why is he telling me this—why isn't he dead but he's in the house...

"And I was late," Kent continued. "But your parents were on time."

"Of course they were on fucking time." I snapped up this lonely coherent straw, but that was the last one I'd get. "And you were late, so you're in their house calling me to tell me what?"

"Have you heard from them since the attack?"

"No. The lines are jammed."

"There's no need to panic."

"I'm not panicked, Kent."

"There are posters all over the city."

I hadn't been outside the hospital in thirty hours. Something was happening. Something inky black, dropping into my clear mind, was curling into the calm waters, wider and wider. Soon, there would be no discrete color in the solution. "I have no idea what you're talking about."

"Can you check admitting lists?"

"For—"

—who?

The reality of the world clicked with the state of my little life. My parents. Kent's office. The call from their house. I knew who I was checking the other hospitals' lists for, and I knew why.

"Yes. I'll take care of it." I knew how to do that. I had it under control, and if I wanted to keep it that way, I had to make it a point to look forward, not down. If I looked down, I'd be afraid to fall. "Don't worry," I said to him, but really, to me. "I'll call you if I hear anything."

"Thank you," he said. "You were always a good kid."

I hung up and let myself have hope. A shining light of a dream the good kid always had, but kept to himself because it was uncomfortable.

I hoped that my father was dead and my mother was alive.

JANUARY, 2007

RONIN'S experimental bullshit wouldn't come up until we were out of options.

The day after Jenn's gallery opening, when I told Greysen I thought I was going crazy, she canceled two morning sessions.

Before we sat down, I'd considered a dozen things I could claim I wanted to talk to her about. Moving out of New York. Having a baby. Divorce. Anything. I would rather have made up a story about cheating on her than admit I was convinced I was being stalked by a... what? Force? Entity? Ghost? Demon? A rogue piece of my own mind? And that after pushing her limits the first time, this Thing had disappeared, only to resurface until I bent her over a banquet table?

It was insane.

But I stood at the kitchen island, across from her seat, and pretended I was someone else. I said it. All of it. The way the Thing folded into the shadows and laced itself inside sounds. The pressure to get rid of it. The raging jealousy the more I sensed it wanted her. The method I'd used to get rid of it twice.

"And you're okay now? Right now?"

"Yes."

"Why didn't you tell me yesterday?"

"I didn't want to tell you in front of it."

She nodded, finishing her tea, thinking for a long time.

I hadn't wanted to tell her, and even though that last admission was the craziest, it had come more easily than the first because of who she was. Greysen accepted me at face value. She listened. Always. If she thought I was losing my mind, she didn't show it. There was no judgment in her.

Thank God for her. A lesser woman would have done so much more damage.

Finally, she spoke. "I think your reaction is very sane."

"My reaction to losing my mind?"

"Those types of phrases aren't helpful."

"Let's not do this."

"Do what?"

"I need you to not be a psychiatrist about it."

She brought her teacup to the sink. "That's hard. But all right. I won't monitor your words."

"Thank you."

"So obviously it's a form of PTSD. Is it affecting your work?"

"Not at all."

"How is that possible?" She got a notepad from a drawer and plucked a pencil from a cup of them.

"Compartmentalization, baby."

She smiled and leaned her hip against the counter with her pencil hovering over the paper. "Sure. All right. When did this start?"

I took the pencil and pad away and put them aside. "You're not doing an intake form on me."

"It helps me think if I write it down."

I gathered her in my arms and kissed her neck. "But it makes me uncomfortable. I only want to tell my wife."

She exhaled deeply in my arms. "When did it start?"

"It started soon after you got back, but I think it's been with me the whole time. Since the war. I brought it back from Iraq."

"Are you sure?"

I let her go.

"Could it be September eleventh?" she asked.

I sat on the stool and faced her, letting our legs tangle between us. "I wasn't exactly looking for it. So I don't know."

"And what is it like, this Thing?"

"It's... inside things. I hear it in ambient noise and in the shadows."

"In your peripheral vision?"

"No. Looking straight at it or not, it's there. Sometimes there's nothing to see, but I know it's there."

"Hm. So it's an it, not a who?"

"It's not a person, but it has a personality."

"Can you describe it?"

I laughed a little at myself. "I know there's no intake form, but man, it seems like there is."

"Please?" She ran her hands down my arms, giving her plea a warmth and need she wouldn't have given a patient.

"It's nice."

"Nice?"

"It's a nice personality. Not charming or interesting. Compassionate. Gentle. Kindhearted. The only person in the world it hates is me."

"Why?"

"Because you're mine. Every time you're in the room, it gets stronger. Every time I think of you, it comes out a little more." I pressed my lips together and breathed deeply. "It's making me not want to think of you, and that's unacceptable. Trying to keep away from you? I thought I could starve it out, but if I starve it out, I starve you out. I won't let it do that to me."

I laid her palm on mine. Her nails were short and clean. Unpolished, yet delicate.

"I stuff all my feelings away, because it feeds on them. You'd be sick to your stomach if you knew how easy it is for me to do that. It gets easier every day, and when I can't anymore, I fuck you hard because it hates that. It hides so it doesn't have to watch. Then there's this spinning sensation, like my mind is being flipped and spun... then it's gone until next time."

She put her hand on my face. I kissed her palm.

"I'm sorry," I said. "You didn't know you were marrying into this mess."

"Neither did you."

"I wouldn't want to go through it with anyone else, but at the same time, I'm sorry it's you. You deserve better."

"And you deserve the best, which is me." She smiled and waggled her brows.

I laughed but cut it off. She meant it to be funny, but I wasn't ready to laugh about this.

"Do you have to wait to hurt me? Wait until you're all bottled up and stone-faced?"

"I don't know. I haven't tried it."

She slid off the stool. "Do you feel it now? The Thing? So close after you chased it away?"

"It's there but hiding. I can manage it."

"Hurt me now," she said thickly.

When I'd hurt her before, I was under the influence of whatever this sickness was. I could only see one path out, and it was through her pain. Any other time, it wouldn't be right.

"Greysen." I ran my fingers along her throat, feeling the bend of her tendons under soft skin. "I can't."

"Yes, you can." She put her lips to my cheek. "Hurt me."

Her whisper turned my compassion into sex. I turned my mouth to her throat and bit it.

"Harder."

I bit harder, sucking apples off her skin. She gasped. Her face tightened. She pushed my face into her throat, and I sucked and bit her, grabbing her by the waist, pulling skin between my teeth.

She groaned, and I tasted blood. I pulled away. A red spot had formed inside deep, tooth-shaped indents. Her brown eyes were wide and her pupils were dilated.

"Are you all right?" I asked.

She put her hand to her new wound. "Yeah, I'm... did it go away?"

It had been faint before. I gave it my attention, feeling in the corners and behind the hiss of the water heater. "It's there. Same as before."

"Maybe you have to be fucking me?"

"It starts screaming and hiding before that. And I'd like to fuck you right now." I put my hand up her shirt and found her nipple.

The red marks on her neck were getting brighter and angrier as blood flowed to the site. Seeing the mark made my blood flow as well. I'd done that, and painfully. She was mine. I pinched her nipple, watching her suck in a breath. I twisted it, and her eyelids fluttered.

Drawing my hands down her sides, I pushed her pants down. "Let me make you come."

I guided one hand to the stool behind her and the other to the counter. She locked her left elbow and curved her back, thrusting her hips toward me.

"Would you stop if I said no?" I rotated my fingers, watching her try to maintain control over her questions. "While we're doing it and you were hurting me? If I said stop, could you?"

We were down to calling roughness and domination "it." I doubted Greysen missed the way we glossed it over when we weren't in the moment.

"Probably." I got two fingers into her.

"I need something... I'm so close... more definite."

Increasing the pressure, I brought her to the next level but reduced it to keep her on the edge. "I could."

"Then we should keep doing it."

"You like it."

"I do. I do. God, let me come."

Wiggling back under her shirt, I pinched her nipple again. This time, I made sure it hurt. Not for the Thing, which was too far away to perceive it, but because I couldn't believe what she'd said until I tested it with a loving heart.

But it was true. She threw her head back and rotated her hips against me. Her clit was bloated and tight with blood. The harder I pinched her nipple, the more the pain kept her from going over the edge into orgasm. She hovered in my hand, under my control with no more than a few fingers.

"I'm going to let you come."

"Yes. Please."

I slowly increased the pressure. She let out an *unh*, then jerked away so forcefully her hair fell over her face. Her chest heaved.

"Thank you," she said breathlessly, pushing the hair away.

"My pleasure."

She put her hands on my shoulders and pressed her body between my legs. "I have the rest of the morning off."

"I don't." I kissed her and stood. "So we'll reconvene tonight."

"I'm going to call some people then."

"Okay." I untangled myself from her and pushed the stools in.

"Would you like a man or a woman?"

"Excuse me?"

"Therapist."

"Whoa, there."

"You need to work with someone else. Another professional. I can't manage your treatment."

I hadn't regretted telling her until she suggested a stranger, but how could I be surprised? And how could I have avoided telling her? She was my wife and the target of my... whatever it was. Logically, I couldn't have avoided this shitty situation. I knew it, but I didn't have to like it.

"No."

"Caden. Please."

"You want me, a surgeon, to tell someone about this and expect them to let me continue working?"

"It's not affecting your work."

"I need to work. So no."

"I won't treat you. Period." She crossed her arms. "I mean it. It's not some arbitrary limit, because believe me, my instinct is to be your primary advocate. I'd step in front of anything for you. But I know, in the end, that won't serve you." She put her hands flat on my chest. "You're everything to me. Everything. I'm too invested."

Looking down at her, parallel lines of straight hair filtering one brown eye, the strands caught in her dark lashes, I accepted her love. Her professionalism was fine, but when she said she was doing it for me, I believed her.

"I don't want to tell anyone else about this. Who's not going to think I'm crazy?"

"Anyone in the field."

"I'm not going on a hundred interviews."

"I'll find you someone right away. It'll be easy."

I kissed her temple. "All right." I held her tight, resting my chin on her head.

"We're going to be all right," she said. "I promise."

"So do I."

Chapter Fourteen

GREYSEN

DECEMBER, 2006

Most non-medicinal PTSD treatments focus on desensitizing the patient to the trauma itself. They relive it endless times via sensory stimulation or verbal recall, until it's old news. The therapies can seem cruel, but the outcomes are consistently good.

Caden wouldn't take medication. You can educate a man out of his misinterpretations of data (these drugs do not effect one's ability to perform surgery) but you cannot educate him out of his pride (tell that to the person on the table).

As terrible patients went, he would be the absolute worst.

"How did it go?" I asked from my desk one afternoon in early December. He'd called me after seeing another PTSD specialist.

"Fine."

"Did you like him?"

"I don't know. I was only there fifteen minutes."

"Why?" I asked.

"I was late. Anyway, he wants to identify a specific trauma. I don't have a specific trauma."

"That may take work but—"

"I have to go."

"Okay. I love you."

"I love you too." He hung up.

I stared at the plastic receiver as if that would keep us connected another moment, then I put it back in the cradle with a sigh.

Since he'd told me about what he called the Thing three weeks earlier, I'd defined behaviors that had seemed free-floating before. In the days before the fundraiser, he'd been cold and emotionless. He was so detached and robotic in some ways, yet temperamental and snippy in others. After the dark banquet room, where he dominated my body so brutally I had to hide his bite mark for a week, he was back to almost normal. Not as normal as when I met him in Iraq, but you get what you get and you don't get upset.

As the weeks passed, he became more and more closed off. There had been three-plus weeks between the first rough encounter in the middle of the night and the banquet hall. I thought nothing of the timing except to note when he'd become alienated from his emotions.

I was about to call the next therapist on my list when Jenn called.

"I need a drink," she said.

I looked at my watch. It was five thirty already. "I've had seven sessions today and my brain is full."

"Meet you downstairs."

―――――――

THAT WAS the mood I met Jenn in.

That was how it began, really. Ronin and his classified secrets, breaking shit to fix it.

Caden had paperwork and opted not to join Jenn and me. Good. I was frustrated with him even though it wasn't his fault. Never get frustrated with the patient, even if he's your husband, slowing down before we got to a dead end. I wanted to speed up and find out what that wall was really made of.

I was relieved he didn't want to come, and then guilty for wanting a reprieve from watching him go through the motions of life.

Jenn pushed her glasses up her nose. She'd shaved her kinky black hair down to the skin, which made her features statuesque. She held up her beer glass. I clinked my wine.

"To an empty brain," she said.

"Cheers."

The Wednesday crowd was subdued. The Wall Street douches had had a bad day apparently, and the art school kids huddled over pitchers of the cheap stuff.

"So," I said. "You know anyone who can see a vet about identifying a trauma?"

"What about Warren?"

"I need someone to ID the incident so we can do CPT with Warren or whomever." Cognitive Processing Therapy was a simple reliving of the trauma, but if the patient wasn't sure what exactly had happened, or was in denial that a trauma had occurred, that was a different kettle of fish.

"Messy. What are the symptoms?"

"Patient thinks he's being watched."

"Oh, shit! I have to tell you something." She leaned forward on her elbows. "This is apropos of nothing. Ronin's working at Blackthorne Solutions."

I should have told her no right there. Should have said I didn't want anything to do with his crazy bullshit.

Instead, I raised my eyebrows and put on a face that said, "Tell me more."

"I got a test subject request from Aberdeen for symptoms relating to... check this out... a feeling of being watched." She pinched her fingers together at her forehead and spread them out, letting them flutter as they moved away from her head.

"And this leads to Ronin how?"

"It was an old form and his name was still on it."

"So he was working on that when he left?"

"I think so. Do you want the form?"

"Maryland's not an option."

"But Ronin's here..." she singsonged. "You could see what he's got going at Blackthorne."

"No."

I was too quick to deny. Blackthorne was a military contractor that took payment from governments and corporations. They sent security personnel into war zones, used mercenaries and special operators to manage power vacuums in small countries, and developed weapons for the Pentagon.

I didn't want the form, but if I really did have a patient like Caden, I'd get it.

"I mean, maybe." I changed my answer.

"Let me know."

We moved to other topics. She asked how my proposal from Tina was coming. I asked about art therapy and the NEA. We didn't talk about Blackthorne or my patient again, but I didn't stop thinking about it. Even after I found someone for Caden and he got his ass on a couch for a session, I made sure I had an updated number for Ronin.

———

CADEN HADN'T WANTED to meet Ronin for dinner. Hadn't wanted to tell him a damn thing. Didn't like him or trust him. But we were out of options, and he knew it.

When we got home from Gotham, Caden silently helped me with my coat. His fists were tight and his eyes burned. His muscles were taut under his shirt, and he smelled of need. My body reacted by sending a flood of fluid from my mouth, which had gone utterly dry, to my crotch, which was suddenly dripping.

"Greysen," he said.

He reached around me and flipped the deadbolt, then stepped away enough to frame the whole of my body in his sight. His eyes coursed over my edges and curves while he flexed his fingers.

"How do you feel?" I asked.

No answer.

"Now? Is it the Thing?"

"Yes."

"Okay." I started unbuttoning my blouse, helpless against the smile creeping across my face.

"Say yes." His fingers went from flex to fist over and over as if he was stopping himself from using them.

"Yes."

I undid the second button but never got to the third before he ripped the shirt open, sending buttons flying. He pushed me against the wall, hand under my bra, squeezing my breast.

He shoved his other hand under my skirt.

"That's right, baby."

He stripped me down and we began in earnest.

Chapter Fifteen

CADEN

Blackthorne Solutions.

The dark room was about six feet by six feet and painted black. I sat in a chair in the center, a clicker in each hand, keeping my eyes on the dot of light on the wall in front of me. To the right and left, in my peripheral vision, photos were projected in pairs at a faster and faster pace.

RIGHT: A child in a pirate costume.
LEFT: A child with a black eye.
(click left)

I answered as I was told, choosing the more violent image without forethought. The Thing didn't have a say. But it wanted one. It had opinions, and I had to think around it before I clicked.

RIGHT: Viet Cong shooting a man in the head.
LEFT: A flower with drooping petals.
(click right)

It was always there now, starting as a whisper in the shadows and growing into a scream in the darkness every day, every hour, every breath.

RIGHT: A dead fish on the shore.
LEFT: A dog with cigarette burns in its eyes.

(click left)

I was coping. I changed my methods as often as I could think of a new way to drive it away. Running out of ideas wasn't an option, and Ronin's call had come just in time.

RIGHT: The blood and guts of surgery.
LEFT: A butcher cutting a side of beef.
(click right)

The lights went on. I took the electrodes off my head. A young tech came in from the back and helped me with the wrist monitors. She was Korean without a trace of an accent. Her name was Mimi, and it belied her seriousness.

"Did I pass?" I asked.

"There's no pass or fail," she said.

I knew that. They kept saying it as if it was true.

I looked to the right, where a small one-way window hid the camera. "Ronin, did I pass?"

His voice came over the speakers. "I'll meet you in the hall."

BLACKTHORNE SOLUTIONS COULD MEAN ANYTHING. The corporate name was so generic, and its parent company's holdings so broad, you could research your heart out and never find out what was going on. But the offices took up three high floors in an expensive office building overlooking the East River.

Ronin met me by reception, dressed in jeans and a crisp white shirt. He led me to a stairway he accessed with a thumbprint. "Hope you don't mind walking up two flights."

"I think I'll make it."

I hadn't spent long in the military compared to Ronin and Greysen, but I'd been there long enough to know I was considered some kind of indolent ass for not enduring basic training.

He had to use his fingerprint to get onto the next floor, and my retinas had to be scanned to get into the back offices. Everything was white and dark gray wood, glass, and chrome. Ronin walked slightly ahead, saying nothing until we arrived in his corner office and he closed the door.

He took a folder off the desk and sat on a tweed couch, indicating I should sit in the love seat opposite him. "Do you want anything? Coffee? Tea?"

I wanted coffee, but it was late in the day. I wanted him to just get to whatever was in that folder. "Water's fine."

He nodded but didn't get up or call for anything. "So here's the deal. You heard a little about what we do here."

"You invent new ways to kill people."

"We like to call it defense development."

"How slippery."

"You expected any less?" He looked up as if alerted. "Come in."

There had been no knock, but the door behind me clicked open. A man in his early twenties brought in a tray with a coffee carafe, two cups, a bottle of water, and a glass of ice. He set them on the table between us, poured, and left without a word.

"That's a neat trick." I looped my finger in the cup's handle. If he'd gone to the trouble of reading my mind, I might as well acknowledge it by having the coffee.

"Not really." He dumped cream into his and drank.

"Greysen says you guys dated."

"We met in basic." He shrugged. "We were nineteen."

"She was eighteen," I corrected. He should have this shit down cold. "Do you have any feelings about what we told you?"

"I didn't marry her. You did."

"You're not concerned about her on a personal level?"

"Have you met her?" His question came out with a cough of a laugh. "She can handle herself."

"Then why take me on if you're not doing her a favor?"

"I didn't say she wasn't my friend. I'll do her favors, but you're also a good candidate. Believe me, I couldn't do a thing if you weren't right for it."

"Can you tell me what makes me right for it?"

"No. We're under contract with a few government agencies. The program you're looking to enter is paid for by Defense." He put down the cup. "The DoD's real particular about who we test on."

"Liability, right?"

"Right. There are some pretty risky trials running right now. What we're thinking for you isn't on that list, but there are still hoops and a very strict NDA." He pushed the folder toward me and picked up his coffee. "You might want to take it home, but if you leave it in the cab and the *Times* prints it, you could wind up in Leavenworth."

"This isn't Kansas anymore." I opened the folder and skimmed. Hold harmless. Liability release. Federal arbitration in the DC courts. FOIA clause. I wasn't a lawyer, but I'd seen versions of most of it before.

"There's one thing that's not in there because it's a prerequisite."

"What?" I closed the folder.

"You have to be active service."

I tossed the folder on the table. It landed with a slap. "That's out."

"I can probably swing it with you on reserve duty. You're IRR, right?"

"I was on a four-year MSO."

"Crap," Ronin said. "Surgeons get blown when they sign on."

"Not quite."

"You can still sign on for the reserves."

"No." I stood up to leave.

"IRR. Individual Ready Reserve," he said as if I didn't know what IRR stood for. "You stay home. No training. That's the last carrot I have."

"I'm not a root vegetable guy, but thanks."

Having refused the carrot, I left without considering the stick.

I WAS LOSING HER. I saw it happening and I'd stepped right into it.

No one, least of all a psychiatrist, wanted to live with a crazy person. I didn't want to come home to open heart surgery either.

Yet the more I tried to get a handle on it, the worse it got. And the more I let loose and tried to stop worrying, the faster the Thing came back. It was always there now, and the days between breaking her got fewer and fewer. Sometimes we'd be at it on normal days and I'd get rough and demanding anyway. But unless I was on the edge, the Thing couldn't see it.

"Did you do the test with Ronin today?" Greysen asked when she came upstairs from her last session. She'd had to take evening hours to accommodate patients with day jobs.

I held her close and kissed her. She tasted of the handful of almonds she'd wolfed down between patients.

"Yeah," I said.

"What was it?"

"Trigger test. I don't think I pass muster."

"Maybe he's working on something else." She slid away from me.

Her optimism only highlighted the fact that she was losing hope. I couldn't shatter it, nor could I bear to hear her ask me if I wanted to enlist in the reserves. I decided right then that I wouldn't tell her. All her hope would flow there.

"He's working on sending you every vet he comes across."

"I have a hard time telling these guys they can't see me." She got a jug of OJ from the fridge and gave it a hard shake. "You see the hard time we're having getting someone for you."

The fridge clicked on, and I stiffened. I was so sick of hearing a voice in the hum of technology that I got annoyed at the appliances.

"'Getting someone for me.'" I walked the length of the kitchen for no reason. "I'm a patient now. A run-of-the-mill nutcase with scheduling issues."

"Caden." She poured juice into a glass. "Don't do this."

"Do what? I'm the guy with a paranoid delusion that something's watching me."

Juice in hand, she came close to me, and I didn't want her to. Not unless she wanted my dick in her ass.

It had been five days.

She didn't take this seriously. She thought I was a case to be cured. I hadn't told her everything because I didn't want to scare her, but maybe that was the problem. She was coming at me, sliding her hand under my jacket, and with her big eyes and her perfume, it was risky. I was dangerous and she was pushing and pushing in ways she couldn't understand.

Her perfume wasn't soothing anymore. It boiled every emotion together. I didn't even know which one I was reacting to anymore.

"Did I tell you this Thing wants to fuck you?"

She stopped the glass halfway to her lips.

I continued. "It's obsessed with you. It thinks I don't deserve you."

"Caden." She was level and serious, as if she was going to lay down the law. Speak the truth. Get the true fucking facts. "This is your fear that you don't deserve good things."

"Oh, is it?"

"This is you punishing yourself."

What I'd been holding back herniated, popping past the membrane of resistance fully-formed, blood-red, and screaming. My Thing bridged days of suppression, begging for release to be the man she needed.

"Punishing myself for what?" I stepped toward her.

She didn't budge. She wouldn't. I knew her that well.

"You were overworked."

Fallujah again. The rows of bodies and the fast decisions.

"I was doing my job. For the hundredth time—"

"You're driving me away because you think you don't deserve to be happy."

"You think I'm making this up because I have *guilt*?"

"I never said you were making it up. Your experience is real, but denying this is a defense mechanism isn't helping you."

She was minimizing it, but she wasn't. She saw clearly where I didn't. She was honest and loyal. She was brave. Very brave. Because she knew there was a battle in my soul, yet she still stirred it.

"Greysen." I put my hand on her throat and slid it back to the base of her silken hair. Her lips loosened and she blinked quickly. I could take her right there. I could fuck the courage and honesty right out of her. "You're a warrior. I don't deserve you, but not for the reasons you think."

I released her and walked to the front of the house. I needed air. I needed space. I needed to avoid turning my rawness against her.

A force hit me from behind, slamming me against the couch. I bent over the arm and righted myself, turning toward her. She was red-faced, hair webbed over her eyes, teeth bared, hands up and ready to strike.

"Let it out. Just let it go," she growled, pushing me again.

She could hit much harder. For all her bravado, she was holding back.

That insight came from a cold place, and the cold place was colder than ever while the warm place where the Thing lived ran hotter.

And there we were.

Half a step toward her, and she didn't move.

"You think I'm crazy?" I said.

"I never said that."

"I'm not the crazy one." Another step. She took half a step away, then shoved my shoulder. "You're the crazy one."

"Stop running away. Face it, Caden. Face me."

She vibrated with frustration, rippling like a flag in a hurricane. She raised her fist to hit my shoulder again, but I grabbed her wrist before it hit home.

She wanted me to face her? She was getting faced.

I twisted her arm behind her and threw her over the couch, holding her wrist against the small of her back. She looked back at me with utter defiance, daring me to finish or not. I put my hand on her cheek and pushed her head into the cushions.

Leaning over, I spoke firmly into her ear. "This is me facing you."

I let her face go and pulled down her pants. Eye to eye, she watched over her shoulder.

"Tell me if it hurts and let's see if I give a shit."

Without preamble or a courtesy stretch, I shoved inside her as far as I could. I was balls deep in two thrusts and she bit back a scream, writhing. I yanked her arm back and grabbed her hair, fucking her through her cries. With every slap of my body against her ass, the whirlwind intensified. The thick, hot liquid of the unknown force watching me, and the brittle ice of who I was spun in a blinding cone of light and dark.

When I came, all the air left my body. My heat entered her and I was awake again.

"Please," she wept. "Let go."

She was really crying, and I had her right wrist twisted behind her back.

"Shit." I let go and lifted her.

Inside the sound of my wife's sobs, where wet hitch met breathy exhale, where true guilt met broken sorrow, the Thing spoke. For the third time, the whisper between whispers made verbal sense.

It had a name.

Damon.

Chapter Sixteen

GREYSEN

Caden was a star, so the Mt. Sinai ER took me right through triage. They gave me painkillers, took a scan, and put my arm in a sling. It wasn't broken, but the nerve damage I'd sustained in basic training had been aggravated. Twenty minutes ice. Twenty of heat. Ice. Heat. Ice. Heat.

It was almost midnight when we drove back from the hospital in silence. He'd wanted to tell them in fine detail how my wrist got fucked up, but I jumped in and told them I tripped on the edge of the rug and fell on it.

He tried to carry me up the stairs.

"I hurt my wrist, not my ankle."

"*I* hurt your wrist, Greysen. I don't care what you told them."

"I can walk."

At the door, he stopped before opening it. "I don't want to go in the house and act like this is normal."

"We won't."

He opened the door. We took off our coats and shoes. Observing a reverent silence, he helped me with both. I went into the kitchen before he could signal where he wanted to go. He wasn't doing this shit. Not on my time. No gently laying me on the couch or tucking me into bed. If we came at this as if he had something to make up for, we weren't going to get anywhere.

"Are you hungry?" he asked.

"I want to set something straight," I said.

"Okay." His pride was held together with spit and chewing gum.

"You're not yourself."

"That's not an excuse."

"It's not. But it's also part of the equation. Whatever's going on, it's not going to be fixed today, tomorrow, next week… maybe ever. So we either go through this cycle over and over, or we get control of it."

"Or we break up."

"Not an option."

"You're really going to take this as far as you can, aren't you?" he said with a rueful smile, challenging me. I didn't know how to walk away from a challenge.

"They don't call me Major One More for nothing."

I took the gel pack off my arm. It had gone lukewarm. I flung it into the microwave and powered it up.

"Has it occurred to you that I can really hurt you? I wanted to choke you."

"Was it erotic asphyxiation, or did you really want to kill me?"

"You're pretty blithe about it."

"Did you want to engage in risky but pleasurable actions, or did you want to commit murder but stopped?"

"The former, but that's not the point."

"What's the point then? Even when you're deep in it, you don't want to hurt me any more than is enjoyable. You're a doctor. You'll know when to stop."

"That's a shitty rationalization. You're better than that."

He rubbed his eyes for longer than a person usually rubs away tiredness. I pulled his arms down. He looked beaten.

"What do you have, Greysen? Because I have nothing."

"And Ronin's treatment isn't going to work?"

"No."

"Did he say that?"

"In so many words."

"When Ronin asked—"

"Fuck Ronin."

I tucked my free hand into his. I couldn't let disappointment grip me. It was too easy to lapse into depression over ungranted wishes. "He asked if it was a pain thing or a control thing."

"And?"

"And you never answered him."

"I don't know. Both maybe. It's hard to get a handle on it right after. Give me… at this rate, twelve hours."

The microwave dinged. He got up and popped it open before I had a chance to assert myself. Flipping the gel pad from one hand to the other while saying *hot-hot-hot*, he reminded me of a carnival juggler, starting low and getting more daring. He flipped it, spun it, tossed it from one hand to the other before whirling it like pizza dough until I laughed.

He lobbed it high, pulled the dish towel off the rack, and caught it with his hand protected by the fabric. I put my wrist on the counter, and he put the warm pad over it, keeping it steady with a firm hand.

"Ah, that's nice," I said.

"Good."

"I was thinking."

"Uh-oh."

"About what Ronin asked, and don't say—"

"Fuck Ronin."

We smiled together, and he kissed me.

"Would you be less afraid of hurting me if we tried to focus more on giving you control?"

He looked at my arm, his mouth twisted with consideration, as if he was holding his thoughts back.

"Well?" I asked.

"We could try it. But I'm warning you." He put an upraised finger between us. "You'd better be controllable, or we're going back to pain."

"Promise?"

"Promise."

He put his free arm over my shoulder and held me. I buried my face in his chest. I could hear his heart beating, red, warm, alive, and vital, home in its cage.

WITH MY ARM IN A SLING, I had to completely cancel two days' worth of sessions and truncate a full week to only the most needy patients. The painkillers made it hard to think quickly enough to engage properly, and the orthopedist had recommended a week of elevation and rigidity, which I couldn't deliver. Two days would have to do.

I spent the time finishing up my proposal for the Gibson Center. A state-of-the-art mental health facility for post-war trauma. Synergy with VA hospitals in three states. Transportation. Outreach and medication stability for homeless vets. A licensed day care center for children while their parents were in counseling or treatment.

I put ten weeks' of research into fifty pages of narrative and a general operating budget that took two weeks to write. I'd listened to the trials of the vets in my office and tried to find solutions. It was the best thing I'd ever done.

Five days after Caden brought me home from the ER, the sling was an optional annoyance and the proposal was ready. I emailed Tina.

Dear Director Molino,
I've finished the proposal. Thank you so much for the extension.
I am on reduced hours for the next two weeks, so I'll be free to preview it for you ahead of the board of directors meeting.
I look forward to showing you the project.
Dr. Greysen Frazier, M.D.

I tidied the waiting room one-handed. The pain in my wrist had gone from a dull throb to a sharp tremor that ran to my shoulder. The nerve had been damaged when I broke it in basic training. As much as my marriage to Caden was the result of the horrors of war, the best parts of my life were the result of falling on my wrist in my first week as a soldier.

The army had always been my goal. My father and older brother, Jake, were in the army. Both had commissions and careers that contained adventure and excitement inside an orderly routine. Only Colin had no interest in serving, and Mom still gave him a hard time about it. Meanwhile, she had been surprised when I signed up. She juggled surprise, pride, and an inability to understand my motivations. That was understandable, since I didn't really understand them either. Not fully.

I was going to be a medic. There was no war at the time, but that didn't stop me from fantasizing about scrambling through muddy trenches with my kit, telling wounded men they'd be all right, patching them up to be moved under enemy fire. I would be their rescuing angel.

Then I smashed my wrist in basic training. I couldn't put weight on it. Couldn't hold anything too heavy for too long. There was no way I could manage the physical demands of a combat medic. Nor could I hold a rifle for a long time, nor squeeze a trigger repeatedly. War or no war, I couldn't train for jobs I'd never be ready to do.

"You can get an honorable discharge," the army therapist had said.

He was in his sixties, and I'd never forget his name. Dr. Matt Darling. I'd been sent to him to see if I wanted to be counseled out.

"I'm not quitting." At eighteen, I was stubborn with a side of petulance.

"But you resist the assignments you're qualified to do."

"I don't want to push paper. I want to help people. This is what I'm here for."

He looked over my file. "You applied for combat medic training."

"Yes."

He closed the folder. "Have you considered nursing school? You can stay in the service while you finish." He shrugged. "The army pays. You'd be helping people."

Nursing school. Sure. I could do that. My mother had suggested it too, and at the time, I'd been irritated with her for thinking small.

"Why not med school?" I retorted.

My answer should have slapped back at Dr. Darling the same way it had her. But it didn't.

"Why not?"

I was surprised he didn't laugh at me. He folded his hands in front of him and asked me to decide what was possible and what wasn't. No adult had ever given me that power.

"Why did you become a psychiatrist?" I asked.

"Because it's easy to fix the body. The mind though? Once that's broken, it's hard to set right again, but if you do help someone set it back, they can overcome anything."

I'd thought about that for a long time. Studying for my MCATs, applying to schools and Armed Forces medical scholarships, I thought about helping soldiers like my dad and brother. Somehow, that first desire had landed me at this desk, with my own practice and a husband I loved more than life itself.

After laying the magazines in a row, dusting the shelves, and watering the plants, I checked my email.

Dear Dr. Frazier,
Congratulations on finishing. I'm excited to see the results.
Let's schedule a time to preview the proposal before the board meeting.
~Tina

I gave her a date range and let my hands rest on the desk. I thanked God for the opportunity to make a difference. Success or failure, the attempt was a blessing.

My phone rang. I flipped it open. "Hello?"

"Greysen." It was Caden, and his voice was shiny, hard stone.

So soon. Every time the days between his needs became manifest shortened, I was surprised.

"Tonight," he continued. "Now."

"The control thing?"

The flatness became derisive. "The control thing."

Pain or control? Some combination of both? We'd gone over the possibilities in fine detail, set ground rules, and waited for the presence of the Thing he now called Damon to become unbearable.

He had no Damon in his past. When he was at work, I'd gone through the list of casualties in Fallujah. No Damon. The name was a mystery to me, but personality bifurcation was a mystery to everyone. It had no real rules.

The stack of papers bent in my fingers. I loosened my grip on them and laid the stack flat.

"You know what I want?" I said. "A celebratory fuck."

"I can't deliver that right now. Not in a way you'd find honest."

"And I can't let you control me right now. Not in a way I'd find honest."

Not waiting for his reaction, I left the office and went upstairs.

It wasn't him. This was a single dimension of the multi-dimensional human I loved. Neither one of us had control over this situation. I couldn't be mad at Caden any more than I could be mad at a bird for shitting on my shoulder.

———

COLIN MET ME FOR A MOVIE. It was loud and fast. The sensory overload pushed my sadness and anxiety into a corner but didn't eradicate it.

"Wasn't that better than the depressing French thing?" Colin asked outside the theater as he wrapped his scarf around his neck.

"Sure."

"So," he said, hands in his pockets, looking up the street for a free cab. "What's going on with the man of the house?"

"How do you mean?"

"You called me for a spur-of-the-moment movie. You don't do that. If I want to see you, I have to make plans a month in advance."

I bounced on the balls of my feet, trying to find the happiness I'd earned. "The proposal I told you about? For Mt. Sinai? I finished it."

"All right! Congratulations! Are we getting a drink?"

A drink was so much more appealing than dealing with Doctor Robot.

———

THE LIGHTING WAS minimal and the patrons were all in the hippest years of their twenties. Colin had unbuttoned his coat, exposing his neck. The bartender, a young woman with the flattest, smoothest stomach I'd seen on anyone since treating Iraqi refugees, couldn't keep her eyes off it. I held my credit card out for her, but my brother pushed my hand away and held out his card. The bartender pursed her lips and eyed his hand, then his face, holding back a smile.

"Oh, for Chrissakes." My grumble was drowned out by the music.

When she took his card, she touched his hand.

"Remember when I had to be your prom date?" I asked. "You asked three girls and they all said yes?"

"You were a fun date."

"And you made out with all three of them anyway."

"You were dancing with... what's his name?"

"Everyone."

"Mom hasn't seen you since you came back."

I sipped my drink. Not bad. They didn't have wine, so I'd ended up with a whiskey and mint concoction, and Colin had gotten something with a vanilla bean sticking out of it. The bartender dropped the check in front of us with his card on top.

"I'm waiting for Dad to get back. She knows that."

Dad was in Japan, and Mom was doing what she did—wait for him to come back. It was the gender-reversed version of the life I'd avoided by retiring with Caden.

"Well, she's not telling you, but she's talking about coming here." He signed the receipt before showing me that his copy had her number on it.

"Jake was in North Carolina for how long before he saw them? Was she chewing off your ear then?"

"You're the baby girl. You weren't supposed to be in the military at all."

"I wasn't supposed to have my own life at all."

"And she's wound up about you guys being in Medical Corps. From what Dad says, the surge is still going and they're deploying doctors and nurses whether they like it or not. He said you guys dodged a bullet leaving when you did. Anyone with a medical license and a pair of boots is getting stop-lossed."

"I'm not going back. Neither is Caden. We're both done." I slapped my hands together to illustrate the done-ness of our service obligations.

"Are you all right?"

"Yeah. Why?"

"You loved the army. I thought you wouldn't be able to adjust to having your own life."

I couldn't tell him that my life wasn't my own or who it belonged to. I knew what the warning signs of abuse were, which was why I'd lied to the hospital staff about my wrist. Isolating the victim. Mercurial personality changes. Sexual demands. A rising tide of injuries.

No one would understand what was going on in my house, especially not my little brother.

"It's hard," I said. "I'm used to knowing what I'm doing every day and having this huge support system."

"That fails constantly?"

"At least when the pipes broke on base, Mom knew who to call. I don't know where the boundaries are out here."

"Is something going on I should know about?"

"No. Everything's fine. But like with the bartender here? I promise you she was eyefucking you before you handed her your card. And that's not even the thing. Sure, it happens in the service, but it doesn't feel so strange because I understand the context. Multiply that by a billion little things."

Colin finished his drink and pushed the glass to the back edge of the bar. "Sister, dear, you are the most competent person I know. That's the only reason you're doubting your competence. We doubt what we're gifted with."

"And what do you doubt?"

He smirked. "I doubt you could walk a straight line. You're swaying like a boat. Should I get you a cab?"

I finished my drink and plopped it on the bar, flicking two fingers against the bottom to slide it over to Colin's. They clinked together. "Let's blow this shithole."

"We have to talk about Mom," he said when we were outside. "If she comes, she's staying with you."

With me? Where Caden did violent, painful, intense things to my body?

I agreed to talk about it, but no more.

———

THE HOUSE WAS empty and quiet. Caden's coat was gone. A note sat on the counter.

Major -
I got a call. I'll be at the hospital. Come by the theater some time if you feel like watching.
- Captain

Short, businesslike, to the point.

"Roger," I said with a little slur on the edges, tossing the note on the counter.

Fine. It was fine. I needed to get to sleep anyway. I could worry about my husband tomorrow. I trudged up the stairs, hanging on to the banister. Colin had been right. I couldn't walk a straight line to save my life.

The empty bed was made; an accusatory rectangle with military corners and sheets so tight a quarter would bounce twice on it.

You failed him.

Having let in the first thought I'd been avoiding, the next ones came without being invited.

He needed you and you failed him.

You're the healthy one. You need to step up.

I stripped down, leaving my clothes on the floor, and put on a big army T-shirt.

You enjoy it anyway.

You need to just let go.

"I do enjoy it," I grumbled, getting off the toilet. "But not today. Not today."

I saw myself in the bathroom mirror.

"You," I said with all the authority the whiskey-and-mint drink let me muster, "you are awesome. You did a great job."

I opened the medicine cabinet, retrieved the toothbrush and toothpaste, and snapped it closed to see my face again. "No. Really. No arguments."

I squeezed toothpaste on my brush and got to work. Despite my mouth being occupied with daily hygiene, the woman in the mirror wasn't finished talking.

"Ou can 'ake a 'ight 'or-ooself. Ou did-a'ight 'hing. 'Oor no 'ood 'oo him 'essed uhp."

The woman in the mirror was right. I was useless to Caden if my resources were depleted. We'd worked out sexual boundaries and needs, but we hadn't talked about the toll his condition, or whatever it was, was taking on me.

I spit the toothpaste.

I could call the shots too. The man I'd married was going to have to live with that. The man he became in the weeks—no, days—between demanding, painful, orgasmic, boundary-pushing sex was going to have to live with it too.

Chapter Seventeen

CADEN

The lubricated slope that slid into the pit of cool detachment got wider and easier to find. I felt relief sliding down it and worried about how easy it was. Was I making a choice anymore, or was I like an addict telling myself the story of a decision I never made?

I didn't leave her alone out of consideration but practicality. Considering her earlier refusal, I wasn't sad or guilty. I couldn't register her needs as important outside my own because Damon was shouting in the desperate corners of my perception. But I knew they existed and I knew what they were. I knew feelings inside me would return and that I'd be glad they were there. Maintaining complete detachment wasn't hard, yet the consequences were exhausting.

It got worse every time.

I didn't wonder if I loved her; I wondered what love was at all.

It was getting harder to pull back.

I had control over what I did to her, but without love to set boundaries or guilt to govern my impulses, when would I start to ask myself what I could get away with?

Without the wherewithal to feel fear, I had to ask myself if I should be afraid.

By the time I left the OR in the morning, one thing had become very clear.

The absolutes were unsustainable.

Not my pattern of madness or her constant patience.

Not my unquestionable demands or her total acquiescence.

The calculation was made to my own detriment, but even in the hardest part of my heart, where the long-term decision happened, the truth of it was the single constant.

This had to end.

EARLY MORNING ON SEPTEMBER 13TH, 2001, I stopped working and started looking for my parents.

At one point, I realized they were never coming back from their morning appointment with their financial advisor. Dad hadn't been with the first responders doing triage or patching the immediately patchable. He hadn't made it to a hospital to offer or receive services. My mother wasn't in a recovery room or wandering around with amnesia.

The flyer I stapled to poles and subway walls had a recent photo of them at a hospital fundraiser. Mom was smiling. When I'd offered to take her away from Dad, she laughed at me. She loved him. She'd never leave him.

I loved him too. I didn't want to love him. He deserved to be despised, but I couldn't. I was a surgeon. And an adult. But all I wanted was to earn his approval.

It was a week before I could stomach the September eleventh videos, and that was when the narrative formed. The jumpers were falling like dried buds off an old Valentine's bouquet, dropping petals of shredded fabric, too fast to identify. Too blurred.

There was a couple holding hands on the way down. They could have been strangers. Friends. Lovers. Married. We'd never know.

The acceleration of gravity is 9.81 second squared. They fell for six to eight seconds, depending on wind shear, hitting a velocity of 132 miles per hour. They must have been conscious in freefall. Capable of thought and fear. Capable of peace. Capable of making a decision.

The couple holding hands wasn't Mom and Dad, because I decided that in the end, my mother would have come to peace and realized she was better than the way he treated her.

And Dad? Was he sorry?

Between the place where I trusted Mom had rejected him and the place where I loved my father enough to wish atonement for him, I hoped he'd died proud of me.

Which was pathetic.

I didn't find peace. I found impotence and rage. On October first, after hanging on to hope for three weeks, I signed up for the war to keep as many soldiers as possible from dying for my father, and to avenge my mother, who never got to avenge her years of abuse.

We weren't anything like Greysen's family. We didn't have a history of military service. My great-grandfather served as an army doctor in World War II and Korea. That was the extent of it.

The country was doing something. We were taking out the bases where the men who'd killed my parents trained. Even if it was too late, it was something. I wouldn't watch vengeance on television.

If I'd had a sense of duty before, it had been hidden. My girlfriend at the time was shocked. She'd thought I was crazy. Rich surgeons didn't sign up for the military. That was for white trash and brown people.

Needless to say, that relationship went down in a sputtering flame from a hundred and ten stories above.

I never looked back.

IN THE DARK LIVING ROOM, with the streetlights casting edges in blue, I waited for Greysen to come home. We had much to discuss.

The tricky part was explaining things to her as the man she'd married, not the monster I was.

I knew my face was somehow different to her when I was like this.

So I unscrewed the bulb from the front hall.

I knew my voice sounded different, because I could hear the hardness as well as she could.

So I wouldn't speak.

Damon swirled desperately in the shadows, so real I was sure I could touch him, but I didn't move. Not when she came up the stoop, carrying a binder, or when she opened the door. Not when she flicked the light for nothing or when she pulled off her coat and dropped her stuff on the chair to try the light again.

I stood.

When she turned and saw my silhouette, she jumped like a colt, then smiled when she realized it was me. "The light's busted."

I took her hand and put it over my lips. She let it linger there, and I slid my mouth to the inside of her wrist and kissed the soft flesh, letting my lips linger over the throb of her pulse.

"You're not mad," she said.

I shook my head to say no and ran my tongue over the inside of her arm, pushing away the sleeve of her blue dress.

"Good. We should talk."

"You talk." The words left my mouth like frozen stones. I wanted control, but I'd spent too much time talking. Too many words gave her space to hear the voice of a man disentangled from his love.

"I'm not sorry about last night," she said. "I wish I could be there for you every time, but sometimes I just can't."

"Mm-hm." I nodded into her skin. My lips ran up her arm to her shoulder, her neck, kissing the curve of her jaw. A wet sigh drifted from her, and her body lost its rigidity.

"Caden," she whispered.

She reached behind her and unzipped her dress. I pushed the neckline apart, over her shoulders. It fell into a puddle of fabric at her feet. The swell of her breasts in the lace bra, the curve of her belly over the panties. The shadow where her thighs met.

"Take it," she said. "Show me what you need."

She'd understood me and, in doing so, made the first crack in the crust I'd put around my emotions. I was hard. Raging. All the plans I'd drawn up while I waited for her were wiped away to be replaced with harder, more precisely cruel ones.

I tapped her lower lip with my index finger and she opened her mouth. I put two fingers along her tongue to the back, pushing against her barrier until she opened her throat. She bent under the pressure, and Damon hissed.

That was it. I had it. I had her.

I spun her and grabbed her from behind, pressing my erection against her. I hooked my finger in her underwear and snapped it. She got them down to her knees with me still holding her against me, and I wedged my hand between her legs. The temptation to get her off quickly and feel that first bite of satisfaction was in the muscles of my hand.

But the other hand wanted more. The other hand wanted to bring her to the edge of death and back again. Collar her with my body. Restrain her most basic bodily function.

My hand on her throat, I tightened just a little.

"Caden." She put her hand over mine. I didn't whisper or speak. I didn't move either hand. I just held her against me, waiting. "Breath play. You want breath play?"

I'd heard of it when a kid in my class hanged himself jerking off, but we called it something different. She was a psychiatrist with hundreds of patients telling her their deepest, darkest secrets. I couldn't do anything she hadn't heard in session. I nodded into her neck.

I waited. I could stand a "no." There were plenty of ways to control her, myself, and the act, but owning her life for even a second was the ultimate, and my cruelest self craved it almost as much as I craved her pain.

There had been something to Ronin's observation, but maybe it wasn't either/or. Maybe I needed both.

She put her weight backward, arching her neck. I felt her swallow against my palm, felt her body take in breath and release it. She didn't answer, and still, I waited.

Finally, she spoke. "I trust you."

I rubbed her clit mercilessly and gently tightened my grip on her larynx.

She jerked. I tightened and rubbed, keeping her still by those two points and the pivot of our hips. As I held her tight, she fought, grabbing my wrist, twisting away. Strong as a soldier, she flung herself away.

She pulled my arm. She was scared. That wasn't what I wanted. She needed to trust me.

"*Shh,*" I whispered because it didn't engage the ice in my voice. "*Shh.*"

With a short nod, she stopped resisting. That wouldn't last. Not as I kept her windpipe closed until her face was bulging red. Her body writhed. She kicked and twisted, knocking over the end table.

Then some of the fight went out of her. I didn't let up the pressure on her nub, but I let go of her throat. She went stiff, coming with a cry and a jolt. Her sucking breath turned into an orgasmic cry. Limbs limp against me, she came and came, toes pointing, hips jerking, spine rigid, eyes rolled to the back of her head.

We bent over the back of the couch, my body curved to hers. We breathed together.

Fuck. I did that. I'd held her life in my hands. Cathartic to say the least.

"Is he gone?" she asked.

"Mostly. Are you all right?"

"Yes. That was..." She closed her eyes and rested her cheek on my arm. "The most intense orgasm I've ever had."

I knew I could speak when guilt wound its way into my heart. I pulled back a little, steadying her on the sofa. My stomach was wet.

"Shit," I said. "I came."

She smiled. "Was it good for you?"

I laughed, or more accurately, the part of me that wasn't capable of laughing allowed the capable part to laugh because it would soothe her. The time between changes was the most uncomfortable, and it drove my unquenchable thirst for her.

SHE WAS IN MY ARMS, sleeping. Tomorrow we'd take stock of her bruising. We'd carve new boundaries and make new rules. The mostly sane man she married would be awake and verbal in the morning, and he'd agree she could say no for whatever reason.

Tomorrow, remorse would fill me like a bucket and Damon would reappear louder and stronger, sooner than ever before.

Chapter Eighteen

GREYSEN

I was woken at four in the morning when a bus with squeaky brakes stopped somewhere on Columbus. I lay still for a few minutes, letting the warmth of the sheets and the sound of Caden's breathing soak into my senses.

All of the familiar aches were present, along with complete sexual satisfaction. I turned onto my side and tucked my hands under my cheek. He looked like himself again. Even with his face slack in sleep, I could tell he was back.

My Caden.

My captain.

We'd get through this.

Something had happened. I didn't know if it was a breakthrough or the first step in a thousand, but something.

Five days since he'd needed to hurt me. If it was more, or even five again, we'd know.

In four days, we'd know if we could change the course of this thing. Maybe stop it in its tracks. Hope fluttered my heart, and I knew I wasn't getting any sleep.

I slipped out of bed, went to the bathroom, and put on a big T-shirt to go downstairs for a glass of water.

Most PTSD treatments involved sensory or mental exposure to the seed trauma. Caden hadn't landed on exactly what he needed to be exposed to, and I'd thought whatever Ronin was working on would let us circumvent the trauma that either didn't exist or that Caden wouldn't admit to.

That was down the shitter obviously, as was any help from Ronin.

But we had this. I was sure of it.

I rinsed out the glass and went through the living room to the staircase. Caden's jacket was piled on the floor. I picked it up by the collar and shook it out. An envelope came out partway.

The army seal was in the corner.

Probably a pension notice or something. I hung up his coat and took the letter to the second floor, where he kept his office. I didn't turn on the light. I knew what was there. Bookshelves with thick medical texts. A glass-topped desk with a computer. A phone. A leather chair in the corner.

I was about to leave the envelope on his desk, where he'd see it, when something I'd noticed before jabbed at me. There was no sending address or stamp.

Why would that be?

If the army had sent him something, it would be via mail, with a canceled stamp and a sealed flap. This flap wasn't sealed. The only way he'd get an open, unmarked envelope from the US Army was if he met with... who? Where?

Why?

I couldn't even imagine.

Prying into my husband's life wasn't a habit, but I wasn't snooping to see if he was cheating on me or spending money he shouldn't. I expected garbage. A fundraising flyer or a mentor request.

My expectations were lies I told myself to cover for the fact that I had no business opening that envelope or sliding out the paper. Leaning into the window to catch the light from the streetlamps, I opened the single page. It stretched like arms folded in anger slowly unbending for an embrace.

I read it once.

Then again, clutching the thin cotton of my shirt. I twisted it as if my heart was in my fist and by God, I was going to wring it dry before it killed me.

"Honey?" He was at the office door in his pajama bottoms, framed in the molding around the opening. Dark behind him. Lit with the barest window light.

He was a god and a saint. He lined my soul, and as I stood there with my shirt twisted in my fist, he was...

I held out the letter.

...the heart I wanted to wring dry.

"Greysen?"

"No," I said, not denying my name but his. His name did not belong on that paper. "This is a mistake."

Caden came into the room with his hand out for the letter, brows knotted with curiosity and concern. He didn't know what it was.

Hope kept the tears at bay. Hope was the only cure for disappointment—if it didn't kill you first. Hope stuck harder and took a piece of you when it was ripped away.

He opened the letter for the briefest moment then folded it again.

"It's a mistake," I said.

"Let me explain."

No. *No-no-no*. Hope ripped away, leaving pieces of itself behind. I was made of spit and tears, but I held on to them. "It's a mistake, Caden!"

"It's not. I mean, it may be, but—"

"It's not?"

Hope was a fish hook, barbed to leave a jagged hole when removed.

"It's just the reserves."

"Just? You *fuck*." I punched his shoulders with both fists. He didn't fall. He needed to fall so hard he'd break time. Then we could go back ten minutes, before I knew. Back a day, before the letter existed. A decade, before the war. "You fucking *fuck*. How could you do this?"

He held up both hands. "Just take it easy."

I snatched the letter from him and tore it up. "I do not accept this." I threw the pieces at him. "I love you. You are my life, you fucking shit." I punched his chest and he did not defend himself. "I break for you. Do you understand? I break every damned day and you do this? Why? You think getting away from me is going to cure you?"

"It's not that." He grabbed my arms before I could punch him again.

"What then?" I tried to yank away, but he wouldn't let me.

"The treatment. The experimental protocol. I need to be in the system or I don't qualify."

I buckled. I couldn't hold myself up. The floor was despair and I needed to melt into it, flatten myself against it like spilled water, spread and evaporate. Only his hands kept me upright, saving me and killing me with equal force.

"It's IRR. I don't have to do anything. They'll keep me off active duty. Please. Listen—"

"You're going to get called. Do you understand, you stupid, stupid man? They're going to call you back."

I tried to get away, but he held me harder. "They're not. Greysen. Listen to me. They're not calling me."

"You're going to get stop-lossed. They're going to deploy you, send you away, and I swear, Caden, you're not a soldier. You're not meant for it. They're going to send you back broken." My anger melted in its own heat, dripping away in thick tears.

That time he'd gone off-base with a medevac. He'd been so brave and strong inside the hospital walls, and it all fell apart on the front lines. He returned covered in blood, unable to function or process what he'd seen. He wasn't the same after that. His arrogance lost its edge after one time on the front lines. What if he was sent out again? How could he so blithely assume he'd survive it? "Why? Why did you do this?"

"I have to. I can't let you keep taking the brunt of my sickness. It's hurting you. *I'm* hurting you. Grey, I'm..." His face tightened as if he held back his own tears. "I'm afraid I'm going to kill you."

He barely got the last word out before breaking. He let my arms go, and I held him. We bent together, falling as if we'd been detonated, limbs wrapped together like a smoking pile of twisted metal beams, weeping for the end of the life we'd tried to live.

Chapter Nineteen

I sat on the stone wall on Central Park South and picked the pickles off my sandwich, eating them one by one. They got less and less shockingly sour with every bite.

The sidewalk was packed with the lunch crowd, and more than once, I had to chase someone away from the spot next to me. A jackhammer pounded the street somewhere. No matter what street I was on, there was always a jackhammer going in New York, as if the city had to remind you not to get too comfortable.

Ronin appeared with a cup of coffee, and I moved my bag so he could sit next to me.

"Afternoon, Major One More."

"Afternoon, Lieutenant Shithead."

"I had the feeling this was the kind of conversation I was in for."

"What you did was fucked up."

I watched a gaggle of tourists wrestle with a map. A businesswoman dug in her bag to pay for a knish. Two guys in suits walked as if they were racing somewhere and talking as if they were on the verge of ending poverty.

"I assume you're talking about Caden going into the reserves," he said.

"I can't even look at you."

"He's a grown man."

"He thinks you can keep him from getting called."

"How do you know I can't?"

I let out a derisive laugh. He'd always had a high opinion of his position.

"This war's messy," I said. "It's never going to end. Every week, it's clearer we're in a quagmire. You know it because your company is invested in keeping it going. War ends, money dries up."

"It doesn't work like that."

"Maybe not for you. For the suits on the top floor? For the lobbyists? That's how it works. And now my husband is on the army's radar. If there's pressure to send him back, you'll buckle. Your company will buckle. And if he goes back…" I took a deep breath and finally looked at Ronin. "If he goes back and he doesn't die, he'll be dead anyway. In his mind, he'll be someone else. I'm not ready to lose him. I'm not ready for my mind to die."

"Okay, let's do this." He put his coffee on the seat and pivoted to face me. "I'm going to tell you things you should have seen already."

"Don't try to tell me how much pull you have."

"I don't have the pull to keep your husband safe because he wants it. I have pull because he's valuable. He has the complete table of criteria for this treatment. He's educated, verbal, aware. If we nail this, it's going to treat PTSD on the field in real time."

"So you can send them back out."

"So we can send them back out. Imagine that though? Healthy men. Stable men. Fighting like they're trained to do. It would crack the recruitment problem wide open."

"How do I know he's not going to be the first guy you cure and send out?"

"Because he's not the only one. We have test subjects from all over who are better suited to going back to the front lines."

I sighed and turned back to the street. A plume of smoke wafted up from Sixth Avenue. Jackhammer debris. Was it possible to enjoy living in a city when it pounded your soul into compliance?

"I don't trust you," I said.

"He does."

"He barely knows you."

"Do you know him?"

I snapped back toward him. The years had rubbed away so much of Ronin's handsomeness, leaving behind a face that was a little more than good-looking, a little less than readable. When Caden stuffed his emotions away, he hid behind a mask of stone. Ronin's mask was made of intensity and enthusiasm.

"Maybe not," I said.

"You don't have to trust me, but you should. I've told you more than I'm supposed to."

"I love him, Ronin. He's my life, and seeing him like this… it hurts me more than you can imagine. If I could put myself in his place, I would."

"My guess is seeing you suffer would hurt him just as much."

"I can handle it better."

"Don't sell him short." He stood and leaned down to pick up his cup. "He can handle more than you think." When he was straight again, he saluted with his cup-hand, two fingers to his forehead. "Later, Major."

"Fuck you, Lieutenant."

Chapter Twenty

CADEN

The Blackthorne tech was a young Hispanic woman in a white coat, the picture of seriousness and detachment. She flicked the end of the syringe.

"Right arm," she said.

"What are you giving me?" I rolled up my sleeve.

"B vitamins." She gave me the shot with painful precision. I felt as if I was in the army again.

"Ventrogluteal's safer."

"I'll mention it to management." She collected her tray and left.

THEY PUT me in the same black room I tested in, which was comforting in a way. But the slide choices and the clickers were absent. In its place were a comfortable chair, a table with a soft lamp, and a bottle of water.

"Caden?" a voice came over the speaker.

"Good morning, Ronin."

"I just came by to say it's great to have you."

"Thank you."

"Lee reviewed how you do it, right?"

"In-out, in-out. Been doing it my whole life."

"The pacing is important," he said. "And the depth of the breath."

"This isn't meditation, is it?"

"Not quite."

"Because I don't have time for woo-woo bullshit, okay?"

"This is not woo-woo bullshit."

"All right then." I grasped the arms of the chair and the lamp dimmed.

Ronin was replaced by a woman's recorded voice. She repeated the same two syllables over and over.

Soo-hoo.

"This is ridiculous," I grumbled.

Soo-hoo.

"She's like a mating bird."

The speaker clicked on, and another voice came over the cooing woman. "Just try to relax."

Fine.

I would relax.

For Greysen.

I could do this for Greysen twice a week. I'd given up too much to be in that room, and half a self-conscious effort wouldn't reward my sacrifice or hers.

Soo-hoo.

I breathed in at *soo* and out at *hoo*, starting over without holding either inhale or exhale.

Soo-hoo.

The voice faded into the hiss of my breath, folding like a map into my consciousness.

Soo-hoo. Soo-hoo. Soo-hoo.

Something inside me trembled.

And shook.

And tried to break but couldn't.

On the fourth session, I came to a terrifying well of despair, but the tape stopped and the light went bright before I touched it.

It always did.

Chapter Twenty-One

GREYSEN

LATE FEBRUARY, 2007

"Thank you for meeting me," Tina said as she sat down behind the shiny conference table.

Outside, the western sky dimmed into a burning rust color. Dots of headlights crawled along Fifth Avenue, and the green of the park turned gray.

When we shook hands, my sleeve hiked up. Caden had tied me up three days before, and the bruises had just faded down to yellow.

Like a teacher who called on you for the one answer you didn't know, Tina's eyes fell on the discoloration inside my arm, safely an inch below the wrist. She couldn't know the pains he'd taken to make sure he didn't pinch the nerve. Nor could she know the most pleasurable pain didn't come from the ties.

"I had a cancellation, so it worked out," I said, ignoring the question in her eyes.

"The board's pretty interested in this."

"It's hot in here." She took off her jacket. "Do you want some water?"

"I'm good." I opened the folder and handed her a copy of the proposal with my inner wrist facing the table. "I put in your revisions. I think it's ready for the board."

She nodded and scanned the pages. "I think so too."

"HEY." I had my phone pressed to my ear as I walked down an empty stairway. The walls were bright white with black scuffs. I'd waited at the elevator, but I had too much energy. I didn't wait for Caden to greet me. "I just met Tina. She *loved* it. And I mean loved with a capital L and a heart for an O. She wants me to present it to the board and tell her what kind of position I want!"

Full time? Advisory? Did I want to stay in private practice? Any kind of hybrid? The options were overwhelming and thrilling. So many doors had opened, I couldn't count them.

"That's wonderful," he replied.

I slowed my run. He had been his one true self when he'd kissed me good-bye in the morning. But he wasn't now. It was creeping back. No one would notice but me. He sounded so close to normal, maybe a little tired, but he was in the beginning of Damon's cycle.

I stopped on a landing. There was going to be a course correction. "Where are you?"

"In my office. I just got out of the OR."

"What floor is that on?"

"Where are you, Major?"

"Between seven and eight. On the stairs."

"Meet me on six."

I hung up. My heels clattered and echoed off the metal steps and stark walls.

The door to the sixth floor slapped open, and he was there. Clean-shaven for cutting day. Collar open to the edges of the hair on his chest. Thick watch setting the boundary for the precision of his hands. Eyes of cold, dark sapphire that would get darker and colder very soon.

He reached out as I came to the last step and kissed me. Possessed me. Devoured me. I had so much to say, but I was consumed in that kiss.

"It's working," I said when I could breathe. "You're holding."

"I know. I know. We were down to eighteen hours. Now it's three days."

"Three whole days."

He squeezed me so hard I left the floor and only let go enough to kiss me again. "I just want a minute to kiss you like this. Taste you before I get taken over."

I forgot about the sleeves and the bruises. About the meeting with Tina and what she'd offered at the end.

He was in there with me, kissing my mouth and my neck like a starving man. Nothing else mattered. Nothing.

He put hands on both sides of my face and yanked himself away.

"I love you," he said through his teeth as if carving it in his mind.

"Three days."

"Then five. Then a week." I hooked my hands at his elbows and touched his forehead with mine. "I never thought I'd be grateful to Ronin for anything in my life."

"It's changing fast though."

"Tonight then." I couldn't help but smile.

"When this is all over—" He kissed my lips, flicking his tongue inside them. "When I'm normal again, I'm not going to stop."

"Stop what?"

He kissed my face between every act. "Tying you down. Spanking you. Hurting you. Pushing you. Owning you. Marking you."

"Deal." I pushed him away, and his face darkened as if the change was coming in with a tide.

"Be naked when I get home."

"I'LL BE THERE in five minutes," he said over the phone as I paced the living room. "Are you naked?"

"Yes. I'm ready."

"I'm going to destroy you whether you're ready or not."

He hung up.

My plan was to get destroyed, then before he went cold again, we would talk about my options with the hospital and my practice. I couldn't figure out how to manage the time. Many doctors melded the two; I didn't know how. The normal Caden would know what to do. The man who was coming home was a trusted keeper of my body and my orgasms, but my career was off-limits.

Passing the mirror by the front door, I stopped. My hair draped over my shoulders like a veil. I pulled it into a twist and over one shoulder.

Three days.

The time between episodes was getting longer. The crescent of light that glowed when the dark eclipsed the light had gotten slimmer and slimmer. Totality never came. The moon was already moving away from the sun.

There was a knock at the front door, and I froze. Why didn't he come in?

Did he want me to open the door naked onto 87th Street?

The satin lining of my coat was cool on my back. I checked myself in the mirror and let the collar loose so it fell over my shoulders as I clutched the placket together at my breast. I opened the door. Colin stood under the front light.

"Jesus, Colin!"

"You invited me for dinner. Where are you g—?" He stopped himself when he saw my bare feet, then he raised an eyebrow at me, a smile curling one side of his mouth.

"Not tonight."

I tried to close the door in his face, but he held it open. "Are you all right?"

I got the coat up around me. "I double-booked. Sorry. We have to get dinner another time."

"Sis. What's going on?"

"My husband's getting home for the first time after days of back-to-back surgery. I'd like to spend my evening doing what married people do, not letting my brother continually ask what's wrong, okay?"

The gears in his head turned. Behind him, people walked the street below. I was a woman in a coat talking to a man on my stoop.

What I wouldn't have done for a porch and a driveway.

"Fine, I get it. You two. Jesus." He shook his head.

"Tomorrow," I called when he was halfway down the steps.

"Sure, sure."

He opened the front gate just as Caden approached with a stride and a face stiffened with jealousy. It turned into a charming smile when Colin turned and Caden could see him. They shook hands. I went inside and closed the door but didn't lock it. When Caden came in, I was on the couch in my coat.

He locked the door. Looking at me, he tossed his keys onto the table. His beeper. His wallet. The bulge in his pants was distracting me, but not him. He was slow and deliberate, as if nothing could rush a man without feelings.

He put his jacket on a hook and came to me, rolling up his sleeves.

I shook off the coat. He undid his buckle, metal clicking on metal.

I'd never seen him like this. He was as stone cold and far away as he'd ever been. I didn't know he could be this far inside himself.

And yet, he was still the guy in the stairway. The man who was afraid he would hurt me.

He looped the belt, holding the ends in his fist. "Don't flinch."

He tapped the loop of the belt in his palm, looking between my legs. My breath picked up, getting shallower and faster.

He slapped the inside of my thigh with the leather, and I flinched before it struck, then gritted my teeth from the raw sting, twisting with my knees together.

"You're afraid," he said, "and you're turned on."

"Yes."

"You think those two things might be related? "We do this thing every time. I hurt you or I control you, then I lose it for a second, and boom, I'm back to normal until I'm not anymore. Right?"

"Yes."

He kneeled between my legs.

"What I thought today on the way here was, why do I rush to that middle part?" Then he pressed four fingers flat against his mouth and licked them. "Why? When you like getting hurt so much? What's a limit if you can't push it?"

He hit me with the belt. The pain was extraordinary, exquisite, nearly unbearable, and so was the explosion of pleasure.

My body expanded, taking up the entire room in electricity and heat, but I didn't explode. The detonator got warm but didn't blow.

"Has it occurred to you I have no significant war trauma because my desire to hurt you is trauma enough?"

"Correlation," I said breathlessly. "Not cause."

He stood over me like a tower pushing up against the limits of the ceiling. "You're saying I'm not traumatized by my own needs, but that they just happen to correlate to this disaster of a marriage?"

Disaster of a marriage?

That was an ice-cold knife in my gut. Through everything, neither of us had labeled our union as anything but a buoy in a rough sea. The one stable, invariable thing through his ever-changing mental state.

I put my legs down. "What did you just say?"

"Don't worry about it. Really, Greysen. Tomorrow, I'll wake up in love again. Ready to conquer the world with my woman. Et cetera, et cetera." He put his hands on my knees and pressed them open slowly. I resisted. "But when you look at it objectively, and really, I'm the objective one here, this is a nightmare." He jerked my knees apart with more strength than I had to keep them closed. I fell back. "And you're feeding it."

He wedged himself between my open legs and pulled down his zipper.

"Are you angry?" In this state, he usually didn't feel anything. If he was angry, it was a step in the right direction.

"No."

Seeking leverage in soft cushions, I tried to get up to a sitting position. "There's a name for this. For you."

"I've been called an asshole already."

"Not asshole. Something clinical."

"Really, baby?"

"Sadist."

"No, no. That's—"

"Your father. And you."

He thrust into me. "I wasn't like this until you." He pushed so deep it hurt.

"You were too weak to see it." I looked deeply into the firmament behind his eyes. "Sadist."

He twisted me, pinning my right arm under my own weight and my left behind my back, fucking me as though he wanted to push through me. "You made this monster. How do you like it?"

Did I create this? Did he become what I wanted?

Did it matter?

"Sadist." I squeaked it one last time before his hands found my throat.

He bent me harder, pushing on my windpipe to growl in my ear. "Is this what you wanted?"

"Yes." I was choking.

"You like the monster I've become?"

"I love it." Barely a breath.

"I knew it." His fingers tightened.

I was handing him my life and my sex and my orgasm with both hands. I'd fantasized about this since I was a girl and finally... I had only a single breath to use to stop him.

"I love you," I croaked before he cut my air off completely.

In my last gasps, the orgasm detonated. Hot shrapnel pinged off the shell of my skin, stinging my armor from the inside, fighting for life, stiffening with pleasure as I looked into two holes punched through a rigid, red face, open to the blue Iraqi sky.

And black.

Chapter Twenty-Two

GREYSEN

His face, briefly.

His lips on mine, briefly.

Then a breath like breathing charcoal.

Burn.

Breath again.

Cough.

Burn.

Darkness.

Cold.

Heave.

I got on my hands and knees, gulping air. Rolled to sitting. Shook out my bad wrist. No pain.

The lamp was still on, but the light in the sky was completely out. His clothes were all over the room—shirt on the coffee table, jacket over the fireplace grate—as if he'd stripped on fire.

If anything between Caden and I had ever been bad or dangerous, it didn't come close to what had just happened on the couch.

Was it the Blackthorne treatments? Were they stretching the time between episodes but making them more severe?

I got my coat on and clutched it closed against a coldness it couldn't protect me from. A chill from inside me. My feet were frigid against the wood. The front door was still locked. Between my legs, soreness and overuse hung like a weight. That had been the most intense sex I'd ever had. I didn't know if I'd live through it again.

"Caden?"

I flicked on the kitchen light. Empty.

Up the stairs. Lights still out. No sound.

"Caden!"

Office empty. Spare bedroom empty. Our room. Nothing.

I went back downstairs, continuing to the hall between my office and the back door.

Locked from the inside.

My eye caught the basement door. It wasn't closed all the way. I opened it, and a waft of cold air hit me. I thought of running for shoes but decided to bear the cold, creaky steps.

Halfway down, shrouded in blackness, feeling the stone walls for the conduit to the light switch, I knew he was there. I couldn't see or hear him, but I knew.

"Caden?"

No answer, but I found the switch and clacked on the light. It flickered and steadied to a flat blue with a constant buzz.

Down to the dirt floor I crept, moving the false wall to the speakeasy and turning on the lights to illuminate the crumbling boxes and mosaic floor. I didn't waste time calling his name or looking in the corners. I knew where he was. The wall with the false vase was already half open. I made my way to the safe and opened it, turning on lights as I went.

The light right outside the safe was off. I flipped it on and opened the false wall in the back, crouching to get into the concrete room.

Caden was in the bottle room, huddled in the corner, naked and shivering. His beautiful body was rendered sexless in distress.

I rushed to him, dropping to my knees.

He didn't look at me.

Putting my hand on his cold skin, I squeezed his arm. "Hey."

His eyes were open and he was breathing evenly, but he didn't reply.

"Captain," I whispered, "it's cold."

He turned to face me. His eyes were the clear blue sky, his lips were full and soft, and his jaw was strong and square.

I knew that face, but I didn't.

But I did.

"I'm sorry," he said.

I knew that face in the moments before his release, in the sorrow of the man who'd wept in my arms after holding death and pain in his hands for eight straight days. This was the face I'd loved on my wedding day and in the broken hours of night.

I put my hands on that face and said his name.

"Damon."

Part Three

BACKSTORY

Chapter Twenty-Three

GREYSEN

NOVEMBER, 2004
THE AIR OVER FALLUJAH, IRAQ
18 HOURS TO OPERATION PHANTOM FURY

NOT JUMPING.

I chanted two words to myself over and over.

Not jumping.

The Phrog's dual rotors buzzed like a swarm of bees. My knuckles were striated in white and pink, and my palm already ached in the center. I kept my eyes on my boots and focused on the pain, feeling it in three dimensions as the shooting ache ran from my right wrist to my shoulder. That helped. Focusing on pain always did.

"How you doing, Major?"

I barely heard Ronin over the angry swarm and the shouts of the paratroopers, but I couldn't ignore him. That was as good as an admission of the terror I felt. He'd use my fear as a weapon for good-natured but annoying mockery. Any woman with thirteen years in the military could take a ribbing, but none of us had to like it.

He was on the other side of the cargo bay, right next to the rear dock. I looked at him and released my hand long enough to give him a thumbs-up, but I couldn't do that without seeing the open bay door the paratroopers were jumping from.

My stomach twisted when I saw the rectangle of clear-blue desert sky and watched the marine sergeant smack a soldier on the helmet before she jumped and disappeared.

Ronin laughed. He was a loaner from Intelligence, temporarily attached to my unit in the First Medical Brigade. He was an ass, a friend, and an occasional bunk buddy since we'd met in basic.

"One day you're gonna have to jump," he shouted.

I kept my hand up long enough to give him the finger, then I clutched the edge of my seat again.

"Cork it!" Lieutenant Jackson shouted to him, her eyes intent under her thick, black glasses. Jenn was a nurse practitioner and my best friend in the unit.

Ronin smiled at her. She had a silver bar to his butterbar. He couldn't do shit.

The sergeant smacked himself on the helmet and jumped out.

Next stop: Combat Support Hospital—Balad Base.

The door was closed, and the helicopter whipped around, pressing my back against the fuselage.

WE ARRIVED AT THE CSH, combat support hospital, in the brightest part of the day. Sweat had a way of burning right off you between noon and two in July in Iraq, and what didn't burn off, the wind took away. But in November, the dusty landscape of the airbase sat in contrast to the temperate air. I was on my third deployment, and I'd seen every season in the Middle East. Fall was my favorite.

"They have eighteen surgeons." Our CO, Colonel Brogue, briefed us in the truck to base. "Six are army. Two are Aussie. Ten are air force."

We were a team of sixteen medical officers: Two general surgeons. Two doctors. Eleven nurses. And me, a psychiatrist. Brogue had gone ahead of us and come back. He'd been a medic in Bosnia and Kosovo and now ran our medical unit. We'd all been reassigned to Balad ahead of a push into Fallujah, because nothing creates an unmanageable number of casualties like a push into battle.

"Do they have their own psych team?" I asked.

"Not at present." Brogue was in his sixties with tight, white hair and a chest built from a cinderblock wall. Old school. He thought real men didn't need mental health specialists but could probably have used one himself. "It's all you, and we're headed into a major offensive. We need you focused on keeping the surgeons sharp."

Not healthy. Sharp. Welcome to the army in wartime.

"Yes, sir," I said.

I saw Ronin in my peripheral vision, nodding. I wondered what he was doing here, but he'd never say until he had to.

We blew by corrugated metal trailers used for housing and more permanent plywood structures that had been there when the base was run by the Iraqi Air Force.

As everyone got off the truck, I said to Brogue privately, "I'd like to meet the surgeons first. I'd like to have an idea of how they handle stress before the choppers start landing. Can we set up intakes?"

"Army guys, sure. Air force has to go through their command."

"Got it."

I got out of the back of the truck. We were in front of a tin hangar with tents being erected on each side. The gravity of the situation became clear with the sight of those tented areas. The hospital wasn't big enough for what was coming.

The sky was crystalline blue, heavy and thick, the only pure thing in a messy world. It connected all of us equally under its sapphire bowl.

Its presence disconcerted me, and yet there was hope under it.

MY DESK WAS two sawhorses with a slab of plywood laid across. I had a small, barely private office separated from triage by white canvas walls.

Ronin didn't have a desk. He stood at mine and handed me a metal box. "You should hang on to this."

"What is it?" I opened the box to find vials of clear liquid.

"Synthetic amphetamine."

"We have plenty of the generic." I went over the contraindications. To be used after rest, no food required, eight-hour spread.

Ronin shrugged. "Works faster and stays effective longer. One shot holds twenty-four hours."

I folded up the sheet and stuck it back in the box. "What are you doing here anyway?"

"I can neither confirm nor deny I'm even in Fallujah."

"I won't tell then."

He smiled and left to do whatever it was he did.

Fifty-nine minutes after I left post-op, Caden St. John poked his head around the canvas flap of my office. He was fully covered in camo, thank God, and he'd shaved.

"Major," he said with a smirk, as if he found my title arousing.

"Greysen's fine." I indicated the chair in front of my makeshift desk.

He sat in it, slipping off his cap, which told me volumes. A gentleman by training. Strict, traditional upbringing.

"In an emergency," I said, taking out the five-page mental evaluation questionnaire, "we may have to administer psychotropic medications before we can evaluate their safety for you. So, we do this assessment before we need to."

I pushed the questionnaire toward him. He put his elbows on my desk and flipped through it.

"What exactly do you mean here?" He tapped the pen on a question. "Forty-seven. Part B. Does jerking off count?"

Why was my neck going prickly? I talked about deviant sex acts with attractive patients all the time. Many transferred sexual feelings onto me, and I was trained to deal with it. This guy had disarmed me completely.

"Sexual activity is with a partner. Masturbation is covered in question forty-nine."

"Ah." He put the paper down and, on question 47b, ticked the box for "infrequently."

One. He hadn't fucked the entire camp, male and/or female.

Two. He'd made sure I saw which box he ticked.

I watched him move over the last page, his answers marked with Xs that went from corner to corner without overshooting the boundaries. His hand was wide across the knuckles with long fingers and had a way of moving that was like a lucid, articulate speech pattern. Every stroke counted.

Cool air came into contact with the sweat breaking out on my neck. I pretended to reread medication labeling while he finished, but I kept his hand in view over the edge of the page.

He put down the pen and pushed the papers toward me.

"Thank you, Caden."

"My pleasure."

I stood, then he stood. "I'll let you know if I have any follow-up questions."

He transferred his cap from his right to his left and held out his right hand. "Nice to meet you."

* * *

DAY ONE - 14:39:00

ENFORCING rest and nutrition was hard, especially with the surgeons. One in particular.

"I'm not changing out, eating a bag of chips, and scrubbing back in." Caden plucked a bit of shrapnel out of a pink gut and dropped it in a plastic tray. A nurse held up the X-ray against the light. He peered at it. "Let's get the one in the ilium."

The nurse repeated the order, and hands moved over the table.

"All you have to do is stand still for a second," I said. I'd scrubbed in to work with him and Dr. Indira, the other surgeon. She was generally easier to talk to.

"Really?" He squinted around the body, looking for a piece of something that shouldn't have been there.

"Really."

"Give me a little room here," he said to the nurse. "I think I got it."

"You're not afraid of a shot, are you?"

He glanced up from the wounded soldier, just a set of blue eyes over the gray rectangle of his surgical mask. "Where?"

"Dorsogluteal."

His eyebrows, which seemed darker and more curved without the distraction of his mouth, went up a fraction of an inch. "Go for it."

I got behind him and put my tray on a stand.

"Take your time," he said. "Can you clean that up for me?" he said in a completely different tone.

"I have six other surgeons with depleted blood sugar," I said, pulling his pants away from the smallest patch of skin possible. "I don't need to waste time on your ass."

I wished I could because as I estimated the midpoint between his side and the crack of his ass, quickly feeling for the curve of his bone, I decided it was the only worthy ass I'd ever touched. After swiping an alcohol wipe over the site, I stretched the skin and gave him his shot.

"All done." I covered him.

"What did you give me?"

"Glucose and B vitamins."

"Boring." Another piece of shrapnel clicked in the tray.

"We're saving the good stuff."

"I'll be here."

———

DAY THREE - 13:43:00

CADEN ST. JOHN WAS A MACHINE. The morning of the second day, we'd moved from vitamins and glucose to a cocktail of shots that included caffeine and an over-the-counter stimulant. He didn't stop. His joints were swollen. He denied any pain in his shoulders. He was lying.

They kept coming and coming.

As long as he wasn't shaking or losing motor skills, he was to stay in the OR.

And they kept coming. By truck and chopper, with flesh wounds and worse, they came. The smell of blood was now so hooked in my nostrils I didn't even notice it. The cloy of alcohol smelled clean instead of sharp, and when I went outside, the cold air seemed so hollow it jabbed my sinuses.

I shot him up every eight hours with vitamins and stimulants, and on day three, I went to the next level.

"Amphetamine?" he asked as he turned on the faucet to scrub in.

I held up the syringe in my latex-coated hand. "It's that or go to bed."

He looked me up and down with red-rimmed eyes. "Since both involve you taking my pants down, I'll pick... eenie, meenie, miney..."

"The speed," I said, getting behind him. "You'll take the speed or a nap with your pants on."

"Crank it up."

We were alone. Not that it mattered for him. It mattered for me. I didn't want to enjoy touching his bottom, but if I did and it showed, I didn't want anyone to see.

After exposing a patch of skin, I ripped open an alcohol wipe. "What's driving you?"

"The guys on the table."

"Don't lie to me." I jabbed him with the needle.

"Wow, tired, Doctor? You're a little punchy."

I wiped blood off. "I've spent two days looking at your ass. I think I deserve an honest answer. You jumped into the military after 9/11. Okay, fine. You're not the first. But you've got more defense mechanisms than the Pentagon, and you do this job like you're digging out of a hole someone's shoveling dirt into."

When he looked over his shoulder, I realized I was still wiping his bottom with the swab. I cleared my throat and pulled up his pants.

He turned with his hands pointed up at the elbows. "Gown."

I got a gown off the shelf and ripped open the package, careful not to touch the outside of the sterile garment.

"You're not winning," I said, holding up the sterile garment. "No one wins this."

He slid his hands through the armholes, and I draped it over his shoulders. When my arms met behind his neck, I identified his scent. Fresh coffee grounds and the cut grass of a suburban Saturday morning.

"My parents were in the North Tower," he said softly, as if his words needed to be padded with seduction. "Hundred and first floor. They fell for about ten seconds, reaching a velocity of almost one hundred thirteen miles per hour. Fully conscious the whole way down. And when they hit, the force transferred all the energy they'd accumulated over those ten seconds outward. They never identified which grease spots were theirs. But they did find one of my mother's shoes."

I opened my mouth to give condolences, but his lips stopped me. He didn't kiss me but put them against mine, transferring his words into my throat.

"My father wasn't a good person." I felt the scrape of his chapped lower lip as it moved. "He was a sadistic monster, and none of these kids are going to die for his sake."

"And your mother?"

We kept our eyes open as he brushed his lips against mine, running their circumference, and with every turn, my body hungered for more. A true kiss. The taste of his tongue. The flutter of his eyelids when they closed. A murmur of desire in his throat.

But he didn't offer that, nor did he attribute any of his motivations to his mother.

"Close it please," he whispered.

My face went hot with shame. I shut my mouth and tied the loops at the back of his neck. He turned, hands still above his waist, so I could close him up in the back. My heart was still pounding, and the space between my legs had gone swollen and heavy.

"You owe me a story," he said.

"Once upon a time, there was a handsome prince. He wanted to woo the fair lady, but he was a jerk, and she had no time for it. So, he moved on to someone else. The end." I patted him, done with the last tie.

He turned. "Your story."

"That is my story."

"It's not finished." He pulled on a glove as a new shift burst in to scrub.

The room exploded into activity, but he and I were in our own little world.

"How do you know?" I got a mask ready for him.

"It ended with what he did, not what she did." As he snapped on the second glove, the *pah-pah* of chopper blades rose in the distance. "No pressure." He bowed his head. I looped the mask around his neck, and he stood straight. "None of us know how our story ends. Shit, we don't even know how this mess all ends, or when."

"You always get philosophical when you're tired?"

"I like you. I'm tired enough to say that and mean it. And I want to know your story."

"That's the amphetamine talking." I put the mask over his face.

"If you say so." He backed away, hands still up.

I called out before he went through the doors to the OR. "Maybe I'll tell it to you if you're good."

Under his mask, he smiled.

Chapter Twenty-Four

GREYSEN

DAY FOUR - 16:23:00

I spoke to every soldier in recovery. Most of them told their stories with a healthy
serving of bravado and swagger. I listened for hours on end, doling out sleeping
pills, antidepressants, and when allowed, comfort. I heard a hundred war stories
told like the final minutes of a football game that was won or lost. But sadness was
not allowed. Weakness was a disease. More than half wanted to go back to the front
to join or avenge their buddies.

My father had been nineteen in 1968. He was a retired staff sergeant who never
mentioned Vietnam. Not when my brothers signed up, nor when I did. He only
talked about the years he spent training soldiers stateside, as if we didn't know why
we had to knock before we entered a room he was in or why he woke up shouting,
"They're all dying!" in the middle of the night.

And still, we joined because it was what our family did.

I'd never seen a battle, nor had I seen the back end of it until Balad. Casualties
kept coming. I got a few hours' sleep when I could, but they kept coming, and they
needed me as much as they needed the surgeons. One screaming soldier was
rolled under them as a stitched-up one was rolled away. Surgeons grabbed an hour
of sleep until the next chopper. But not Caden. He was shredding his brain, and I
was helpless to do anything for him except fill him full of vitamins and speed.

"He stopped joking around three hours ago." I peered through the window in
the OR door. "Hasn't spoken except to ask for instruments."

"You're obsessed," Ronin said from next to me.

Understatement of the year.

"What he's doing... it's not even heroic at this point. It's suicide. So, yes. I'm obsessed with stopping it."

"He has a commanding officer."

"Who wants results."

"They can get MPs in here to haul him away."

I shook my head, watching Caden sew up an internal organ cut open by bullets. No one was hauling him away. They'd work him until he was dead.

"We should break into the stuff I brought from the Pentagon. It's labeled for performance under exhaustion."

"It's also labeled to be taken after resting."

"Maybe that'll get him to rest." Ronin presented the logic like a gold-wrapped box tied with a bow. Justifiably, because it was a double-pronged solution.

Maybe it was safe enough. Maybe it would help him. Whatever we were doing wasn't going to work much longer.

"Go get it. I'm going to talk to him."

I scrubbed and grabbed a juice bag. The OR stank of shit, flesh, blood, and rubbing alcohol.

Caden glanced up from his work long enough to see me. His eyes were so bloodshot the irises were lighter than the sclerae. He didn't say anything. Didn't crack a joke or ask me if I had a shot.

I pushed the straw into the bag and held it up. He nodded, keeping his fingers in his instruments. Getting the straw under his mask, I looked down. The man's ribs were spread open, and his lungs inflated and deflated. Blood bubbled in a line across one lung. The nurse cleaned the area, and I looked at her.

Without a word, she told me she was concerned.

When the juice was empty, I took it away.

"How are you holding up?" I asked him.

He nodded.

"You're not talking?"

"Clamp this here," he said to the nurse. His voice came through as a sandpaper husk.

"You should have started hallucinating."

"Just aural," he said. "Shit!"

Blood spurted everywhere. People appeared around the table, orders were shouted, and I was in the way. I backed out the door.

DAY FIVE - 06:45:00

IF CADEN KNEW how often I checked on him, he'd think I was in love with him. Which I wasn't.

Not yet.

But as the days had worn on, my efforts to keep the simple, sweet fantasies from my mind were failing. They involved the days after the offensive. Meeting in the chow hall. Sitting together. Him across from me, then next to me, his boot pressed against mine under the table.

"Major Frazier?" Dr. Ynez snapped me out of one such fantasy.

"Yeah?"

"I have a guy who needs you." He handed me a chart.

Pfc. Sanchez had suffered a clean gunshot to the calf while running back from an IED explosion that had enemy sniper cover. Nothing twenty-four hours, a good hospital dressing, and a full course of antibiotics wouldn't fix. He was shaved bald, a proud Hispanic man with both his leg and his chin elevated.

I stood by him. "Private Sanchez, I'm Major Greysen Frazier. I'm a doctor."

"The nurse said you have to assess me before I can go back out."

"I do. May I sit?"

"Yeah, this gonna take long?"

I sat on the stool next to his bed. His left hand had a gold ring on the fourth finger and a dirty, bloodied piece of paper in the fist.

"It shouldn't if you're mentally fit." I indicated the paper. "What do you have there?"

"Nothing."

I held out my hand. "Then you won't mind if I see it."

I opened his hand and was surprised he let me. The paper wasn't really paper but more of a plastic sheet of film. It was a sonogram.

"Oh, that's wonderful. Congratulations."

"Don't take it." His voice was a dead serious command, and he glanced at me quickly before turning away again. "Major. Ma'am. This baby's not mine."

"How do you know it's not yours?"

"It's not my wife's either. Am I fit to serve or not?"

I slid the pen into its holder at the top of the clipboard. "I can't keep you from going back. But I can delay you."

"Why would you do that?"

"Because you're holding a sonogram of someone else's baby."

"This isn't your business, lady."

I raised an eyebrow.

"Major. Sorry, ma'am. This is personal."

"Keep in mind, Santa Claus didn't leave this rank in my stocking. It was earned. I got it because I know better. Now you can tell me what's going on, or I can delay your return to your unit until I'm sure you're not on a mission to right some wrong."

He pressed his head into his pillow and exhaled deeply. "It's Grady's kid. He's still there. His leg's pinned under a Jeep."

"And he's still there?"

I found it hard to believe that Corporal Thompson, a medic with a sense of duty a mile wide, had left a living man behind.

"Yes. When I tried to pull him away, his top came right off his bottom. I pulled him, and only a torso came. He was held together with like..." He couldn't find the words, but my mind filled in his spinal cord, intestines—everything must have been spilling out. Pfc. Sanchez didn't need an anatomy lesson. "He was screaming, 'Go in my pocket, go in my pocket, find my girl, find my girl.' Over and over... but the medevac was taking off, and Thompson pulled me away."

Either Grady was dead or so beyond help Thompson had had to make a hard calculation.

"He's alive," Sanchez continued. "I told him I'd come back. I swore it. But he gave me this and told me to find his wife. Tell her he loved her and the baby... I'm supposed to be the godfather. I had to run. Because the chopper was taking off. I had to leave him there. I can't hang around here while he's under the Jeep. You understand? I have to get him out."

"What happens if you go back and he didn't make it?"

"Just shut up!" He caught himself.

"It's all right."

"Please. I know you're an officer, but you really need to get me out of here."

I didn't know which was worse. Keeping him for a week to recuperate, during which time he'd be convinced that every ticking minute brought his friend closer to death, or sending him back to where he'd be forced to confront the truth under the most stressful circumstances.

The fact was the choice wasn't mine. Like every other guy who wanted to go back out, he'd answered every question on the evaluation to ensure that outcome.

So, out he goes.

DAY FIVE - 13:15:00

THE OR WAS empty except for Caden and a nurse with a single patient. I went in.

"Captain," I said.

He nodded without looking up.

"We have a break," I said. "No more casualties for a few hours."

"Thank God," the nurse said.

"You look tired," Caden said to her, tying a knot with one hand and holding the thread taut.

She snipped it. "We all are."

"Go lie down," he said. "I'll close."

"No, I have it."

"Major Frazier's scrubbed."

She looked at me as if checking to see if I knew what I was doing. I didn't.

"Shoo, Lieutenant," Caden said.

I wanted to talk to him alone anyway, so I nodded to her.

She exhaled deeply. "Thank you." The doors swung as she backed out.

"Clamp," he said.

I handed it to him. "I'd check it before using it. I'm not a nurse."

"I did."

"So, after this, how about taking a load off?"

"Probably should. How you holding up? I saw you getting an earful from a Pfc. in the recovery room."

"Yeah. It was a hard story to hear. I can only imagine how hard it was to tell."

"Really?" He sounded surprised.

"Really. Why's that hard to believe?"

"I'd think you'd heard it all."

"You never hear it all."

"Little detachment goes a long way. Can you pull this back here?"

I didn't think I could, but he was waiting, so I built a quick wall between what I had to do and giving a shit about it and pulled the organ away.

"Thank you," he said, looking at me.

I turned away before my skin went pink.

He seemed rough with the bone and gristle, as if he was working on a slab of meat, but he found a sliver of metal that had barely shown up in the scan. I bit my tongue against telling him to take it easy.

"So," I started. "The aural hallucinations?"

"I've been tired before. I can tell the difference between reality and deliria."

"They saying anything fun?"

"Jumbles of words. Had it in residency too. And in the ER on 9/11. And 9/12."

"I hesitate to mention this," I said.

"She who hesitates is... something." He smiled, joking. "Go ahead, mention it. I know you want to tell me how handsome I am under pressure."

"You've looked better."

"Swab this here so I can see what I'm doing, would you?"

It was hard to look at the inside of a man's thigh, watch the blood flow through the veins. We weren't built to see the inner workings of our bodies so clearly. We were built to die under these circumstances.

"Don't think about it too hard," he said, reading my mind. He reached under a raw piece of human meat to remove a shard of metal. "That way lies madness. But you probably know all about that." *Plink*. The shrapnel dropped into a tray. He examined the scan.

"The human mind is nothing if not surprising."

"Get in here with a sponge so I can sew up the artery."

I did it.

"Thanks. Tell me what surprised you today," he said.

"You surprise me."

"Your strategy is textbook. Stroking my ego's the best way to keep me awake." He reached across the body and took his own threader. "Just keep it clean over here."

It took a second to realize he was talking about part of the leg, not my language when speaking about him.

"I'm not trying to do either. Nothing I say is going to get you to rest, and from what I can see, the last thing your ego needs is a good stroke."

His mask stretched when he smirked. "You're doing great, Greysen." He stitched the artery. "Tell me why my ego surprises you then."

"It doesn't. But earlier today I couldn't find you in here, and I thought maybe you'd finally taken a nap. But you weren't in your bunk."

"You checked my bunk?"

"Yes. Does that bother you?"

"If I knew you were coming, I would have covered the bed in rose petals."

I willed him to not look up and see how my cheeks reddened, but he defied my silent wish.

"Let's clean this up and close. Then, since I have a few hours, I'll lie down."

"I'll alert the media."

He laughed.

DAY FIVE - 15:45

HE STOPPED JUST outside the medical tent and squinted in the sunlight as if the blue of his eyes couldn't compete with the depth of the sky. He rocked back and forth slightly, then with more curve to the pendulum.

I grabbed him under the arm before he fell.

"I'm fine." When I tried to take away my support, he put his hand over mine. "Stay."

"I'll walk you to your bunk." We started in that direction.

"I haven't had a chance to arrange the rose petals."

"None required."

"You're too easy." He shook the fog out of his head. "Didn't mean it like that."

"I know. And you're too fucked up to do anything about it now anyway."

"Most days, I'd take that as a challenge."

"But not today."

"Definitely not today."

"Good to know your limits."

His trailer was neat, standard issue with few memories of home. The air was stale after less than a week. I laid him on the bed and took his boots off as if he was a drunk.

"Can you come get me when casualties come?"

"Someone will come, I'm sure."

"I want it to be you."

I sat on the edge of his bed and took his pulse. Ninety-five. High but not a heart attack.

"What was it you hesitated to mention?" His eyes were closed, and his voice was barely a whisper.

I had to scan my memory of the past hour to recall that I had been about to tell him about the vial Defense sent. "How much I like you."

"Like you too."

"And that you're a fool for pushing yourself so hard, but I can't help but admire it."

I got up to leave, but I didn't quite make it to the door.

"Major."

"Yes?"

"Please don't go."

"I have to." But I went back to him.

"I keep seeing their faces. Then their wounds. And the screaming. I keep hearing the screams." He turned away from the wall and held his hand out to me. "I'm too tired to try anything. All this... in my head. It's just sensory overload. But it's bad. Stay. Please."

I sat on the edge of the bed, not intending to do more than that, but he pulled me down with him. My body was strong enough to resist, but my heart was weak. After days of talking to men who never admitted a need or a weakness, Caden's raw humanity touched me. He was fearless in so many things that I hadn't expected vulnerability.

I curled into him, my shoulder blades to his chest, and let him put his arms around me. Against my back, he wept from exhaustion and pain. From tension and sorrow. I had to wipe my own eyes and swallow a hard lump of sobs.

Eventually, his body stopped shaking, and he slept. I waited until his breathing changed and his arms were dead weights before I slipped out of them. Kneeling by the bed, I touched his cheek. His tears had dried, but his black lashes were still stuck together.

"You're not cut out for this, Captain," I said softly.

Maybe no one was.

I put a blanket over him and left.

———

DAY FIVE - 20:43

THE FIRST CHOPPER had come in an hour before, but we had enough doctors to take care of them. I'd kept a close eye on the time and peeked in on Caden's bunk twice. Five hours of solid sleep. He'd need another few days' worth to catch up, but he wouldn't get it. The last push into Fallujah was brutal, and they were coming faster than they could be admitted.

"Where's St. John?" Colonel Brogue shouted in triage.

"Resting," a nurse replied, getting her gloves on.

"Someone get him."

"I'll do it." I jumped up.

"Quick. We have more coming."

I ran to Caden's trailer, and when there was no answer to my knock, I went in. He was still on his back with his hands crossed over his chest. He didn't react to the light being turned on. I sat on the edge of his bed and leaned into his chest. Breathing steady. He didn't move when I took his pulse or when I let my hand linger over his before pulling away.

"Caden," I said.

No answer. He was out.

"Caden." I tapped his cheek. "Come on. Casualties."

I tapped his cheek harder. Nothing. I pinched his forearm gently, then harder.

He groaned.

"I'm sorry. They need you."

Deep suck of breath.

"Casualties," I repeated.

He swallowed.

"Okay," he said thickly, eyes clamping tight before opening.

"Let me help you."

I took his wrists and pulled him up. He was dead weight, but I managed to swing his legs over the side of the bed and get him sitting. His shoulders hunched, and his head hung.

"Wake up."

"Can't."

"I'll help you. Come on."

I pulled his arms, got him up a little, but he sat back down.

"Melatonin."

He named the hormone responsible for sleep. If his blood was flooded with it, he wouldn't be able to get up no matter how hard he tried.

"Do you want something to help you wake up?"

He dropped back until his head was against the wall. "Slap me."

"What?"

He didn't answer. His eyes closed again. I patted his cheek, but his breathing got the slow cadence of sleep again. I slapped harder.

"Adrenaline," he whispered.

He wanted me to slap him hard enough that the need to fight or run would release adrenaline, which would override the melatonin. He was using his own body like a pharmacy.

Fine. I planted my knees on either side of him. "I apologize in advance."

I slapped him hard. He grunted. I slapped him again. Deep, waking breath. The next slap was hard enough to make my hand hurt, so the next one was a backhand. That got him up. My hand was back for another.

"Stop. We're good."

"You sure?"

He rested his hands on my hips, making me realize I was straddling him. "Any more and you're going to turn me on. Oops, too late."

"A cold shower's going to cure you of two problems then."

Standing, I held my hand out to help him up. He stumbled to standing, looking around as if the idea of three-dimensional space confused him.

"Oh, man." He ran his fingers through his hair. "Okay. Let's do this."

I WAS WORRIED ABOUT HIM. On the way to the showers, he'd seemed disoriented, struggling to put together one coherent thought after another. He'd make a sharp comeback to something I said, then go silent or forget what he'd said. Waiting for him outside the showers, I called out to Ronin as he passed.

"Why are you stalking the men's showers?"

"I'm waiting on a tired surgeon."

"St. John?"

"Yeah. He's had five hours but needs a week."

"They need him."

"I'm going to use the Defense stuff."

He nodded. "I'll go get it."

Chapter Twenty-Five

GREYSEN

DAY EIGHT - 14:56

The battle took five weeks, but the initial offensive was over after eight days.

Caden had gone three more nonstop. No catnaps. No lie-downs. The synthetic speed did its job twice over.

When the last soldier was sewn up and the party had started in the mess hall, he was in no condition to celebrate. I found him standing shirtless over the linen hamper, scrubs balled in a fist, a marble statue of a man.

"Hey," I said. "It's over for now."

He opened his fist and let the scrubs fall into the bin. "I'm tired."

"Ya think?"

I reached for his hand so I could check his pulse. That was what I told myself. But when I took it and slid my hands to his wrist and down to his elbow in a long stroke and he lifted his arm to cup my jaw, there was no more lying.

He kissed me as if he'd been on hunger strike and our first kiss was the nourishment he'd been denying himself. As if he couldn't bear to not kiss me for another second.

Or maybe that was what I was feeling, because I clutched the back of his neck like a woman terrified of losing something. My mouth devoured him with the force of a catapult held in tension for too long yet sprung too fast. My hands released his neck and ran over the crests and valleys of his body.

I tried to get up, but that only drove me into his arms. God, I wanted him.

"Sleep with me," he said.

"Like last time?"

"No. This time, I'm going to try to fuck you, and you're going to let me."

LATE IN THE NIGHT, pleasantly sore and sticky where it counted, I drifted off to sleep while he stroked my shoulder in a way that was both casual and intentional.

"Why aren't you sleeping?" I asked with the last of my waking energy.

"I fell asleep first last time."

"Didn't count."

"I like looking at you."

"Mm."

He kissed my shoulder. I hoped he didn't want to fuck again. I was tired, and I was sure that if he wanted to, he'd need thirty seconds to make me want him again.

"All the time," he continued. "You're hard to not look at. When you're working with some jarhead who would rather be dead than talking to a psychiatrist, the way you listen? Even if he's got his back turned to you or he's telling you to fuck off? Like there's no one else in the world but that one guy? You're stunning. If you ever looked at me like that, I'd tell you everything."

I wanted to say, "Tell me everything right now." But my lips wouldn't form the words, and my lungs could only breathe in the rhythms of slumber.

Chapter Twenty-Six

GREYSEN

The week after the first surge, the doctors went on doctoring while the surgeons were put on rest. Casualties came in at a manageable rate for the normal rotation, which I no longer oversaw.

After our first night together, Caden had slept for twenty-four hours. Most of the surgeons had. He owned me the two nights after that. Rotation last night. And tonight? If it was up to me, I'd be his again tonight.

The army was a huge net of people with tight knots of community. The way Ronin and I had found each other from basic, to Walter Reed, back around again to a common assignment in Iraq wasn't unheard of. But Caden? He wasn't part of the net. He'd sought out a commission during a time of war. As soon as his obligation was done, he could, and would, leave to pick up his life where he'd left it.

Like a soldier who'd witnessed the unthinkable, I tried not to think about it.

"Captain Fobbit!" Sergeant "Little Red" Ryder cried from across the dusty field, a football crooked behind his shoulder.

Caden, the fobbit in question, held his arm out to indicate he was open. Ryder released the ball across the sky like a drill, cutting the blue only to have it enfold around its wake. Caden picked the ball out of the air but was tackled by Ronin and Pfc. "Salt Mine" Trona. They slapped his back when they got off him. I held my hand out to help him up.

"What's with that Ronin guy?" He grabbed my wrist so I could pull him up. "He was all over you. He think you're Jerry Rice or something?"

"Ryder usually throws to me."

He snapped the ball back to Ryder without an answer, and we headed for the line of scrimmage.

"You shouldn't let them call you fobbit," I said. "It's not nice."

"How's that?"

"Means you never go outside the wires. Means you don't know shit."

"Maybe I don't." He smirked as if he really believed he lacked a necessary piece of knowledge about anything important.

Sergeant Ryder called out the play numbers, and we fell back. This time, I got the jump on my coverage, and the ball landed right in my hands. Ronin got to me, knocking me three feet out of a run in an attempted tackle, but I wouldn't go down. He reached around me, trying to strip the ball away.

I cried, "Foul, foul," but we were both laughing and fighting to the death as I pushed toward the Humvee tire marking the end zone.

Ronin's weight was suddenly off me, and I ran for the line, where I spiked the ball into the sand.

My victory was short-lived. Caden was on top of Ronin with his knee in his back, pushing his face into the ground while Ryder and Trona were arriving to pull Caden off.

"You don't touch her like that, you hear me?"

Ronin was on his feet. "What is your fucking problem?"

"Watch your goddamn hands."

Ronin held up his palms. "I don't know what the fuck is going on here..."

"Like fuck you don't," Caden said.

Trona picked up the ball and tossed it to Ryder.

"All right, whatever. Fuck this." Ronin slapped the dirt off his hands and walked away.

Ryder and Trona passed the ball between them. Game over.

"What was that about?" I asked Caden.

"What's going on with him and you?"

"Football."

Of course, I knew what he meant. And yes, my answer was evasive. But he was acting like a child, and children aren't owed explanations for adult decisions.

"Why are you lying?"

I got right in his beautiful fucking face. "Because you're being an asshole."

I stormed off.

———

THAT NIGHT, in chow hall, he sat with the other surgeons, and I sat with Ronin. It was as if, after the bell, we'd gone back to our respective corners of the ring without even knowing we'd been boxing.

How did I know he was watching me? How did I know every time he glanced my way as if he happened to be looking out the window?

I was watching him as well.

"I got orders to go to Abu Ghraib," Ronin said.

"Are you even allowed to tell me that?"

"If I did, then I am."

I pushed corn around my plate, trying to pretend Caden wasn't there. My will was weak. When I lifted the fork to my mouth, our eyes met across the room, and he looked away.

"Well, I guess your work here is done," I said.

"The army's work."

"Yeah."

Caden got up with his tray. Why did that tie my heart into a knot? The surprise of seeing him get up? The broken string of our mutually denied gaze?

"Before I go, I want to make you an offer."

"That's intriguing." Not as intriguing as Caden leaving his tray on the pile and walking out of chow hall with one of the guys on the Australian surgery team, chatting and laughing over who even knew what. Livers and spleens.

He had no business laughing over internal organs when I felt so crappy about fighting with him.

"I've known you since the beginning," Ronin said. "Since you broke your wrist in basic."

"And you pushed me over the wall."

"Any other guy would have laid you down gently and called for help. I made sure you finished the course."

I nodded. "You did the right thing."

"I know. Because you and me? We understand each other. I need to not be tied down. You need to be pushed."

"And you have an offer to push me?"

"The offer has two parts. You can take one without the other."

"I'm listening."

"Part one. I'm going to Abu Ghraib in advance of a different kind of battle. A psychological one. We're going to be fighting the enemy using a new weapon: their own culture."

"How?"

"I can't say, obviously, but it's within the Geneva Convention protocols. It's a war of the mind. No bloodshed. No death. None of this shit." He checked to make sure no one was in earshot, then leaned forward. "You have a way with talking to shell-shocked men. You get it. And you speak Arabic. I want to talk to my command about loaning you out from your unit. Now this is up to you, and it's totally voluntary. It's a unicorn. Cherish the moment. You have a *choice* in the matter."

My ambition muscled out my patience and sense. I was interested before even hearing the details. "What's the second part?"

"It's optional."

"Okay."

"You come to Abu Ghraib *with* me."

"With?"

"Here it is. Straight out. Friends with benefits has been great, but I'd like to spend more time with you."

My ambition sat down, crossed her legs and arms, and scowled. "Christ, Ronin. Is this a unicorn too?"

"I'm not looking for a long-term commitment or anything big, but—"

"But I won't sleep with you in Balad, so you want to push me because I need to be pushed?"

A smile stretched across his face. "You get me." When I rolled my eyes, he took my hand. "In the past week, I realized I like you more than I thought. I know, I'm being a typical male, but I'm not lying. I want you, and if that means cornering you into a new job, I'll do it."

"You put the brutal in brutally honest, did you know that?"

I pulled my hand away, but it was too late. Caden had come back into the room. Our eyes met, and he was not smiling. I could hardly think sandwiched between these two men. One of them had to go away, and it wasn't Caden.

"Give me a day," I said to Ronin, picking up my tray. I wanted to get out of there before I suffocated. I needed to consider the half of his offer that wasn't wrapped in carnal payoffs.

"You want to put me second in line after Captain Fobbit over there, that's your call. He's going to put you in a cage and throw away the key."

The way he thought he knew me was exhausting enough. He couldn't have a clue about Caden.

"You're wrong."

"Give it time. He will."

"No, I mean I'm not putting you second in line. There is no line."

I put my tray on the pile and went to Caden. A string between us pulled taut enough to trip anyone that crossed between. A string of my intentions. My forward motion and his patience as I walked in his direction, my determination to tell him exactly how I felt even as I defined my feelings to myself.

I didn't owe him an explanation about Ronin or any other lover. I could do whatever I wanted with my body, and if he'd expected some kind of fidelity, he should have brought it up. I didn't owe him my time or my attention.

I owed him none of those things, but I wanted him to have them. My fidelity. My time. My attention, my honesty and respect—all given as gifts whether he wanted them or not.

My mother told me the moment a person falls in love is often quiet. It often comes in the night, or when you're paying attention to something else, but it's always in the rearview. You don't meet love in the moment. It's not an ambush. Someone chips away at the stone façade around it, breaching your fortifications, crippling your defenses, and the moment you fall in love is the moment you realize what you've built the wall around was love. You fall in love with your conqueror.

I didn't love him.

Not yet. But bit by bit, he was chipping away at my battlements.

Walking toward him, his face softening as mine hardened, I knew I could love him. One day, I'd look in my rearview and see what had been there all along.

I was two steps away. I could see the hair on his face and the set of his jaw. Another step and I could whisper to him. I still didn't know what I would say or which part of love's barricades I'd start with. I didn't know if I'd open with reassurance or a challenge, but I was sure, when I got there, I'd say the right thing.

Caden took the last two steps in my direction, closing the gap completely.

"I need to know," Caden said softly. "What's going on with him?"

"Why do you need to know?"

His eyes lit up like the end of a short fuse, getting brighter when ignited with a little anger.

"I don't want to share you."

"You're not sharing me."

"I hope you mean that the same way I do, Greysen. Because I don't just mean your body. I don't want to share your time or your heart or your happy fucking thoughts."

"Nobody owns me, Caden. Those things are given freely or not at all."

"Give them to me then."

He was getting them, but he wasn't entitled. His tone made my hair stand on end and my palms sweat. I didn't know whether to fuck him or run away.

"You can't demand any of that."

"Give me everything or nothing. If it's no, just say so now. Is it no?"

I felt cornered. Caught in the middle of a tunnel as the walls shook from an oncoming train.

"Yes or no?"

"Maybe."

"This game you're playing isn't a game to me. You can hurt me."

Again, I was caught. This time between reassuring him and telling him I wouldn't be emotionally blackmailed. Between admiring his willingness to be vulnerable and disdaining his manipulations. All and/or/but nothing.

That was when the earth shook.

"Mortar fire!" someone shouted.

A dozen doctors, nurses, and medics dropped everything and ran for the door, including Caden.

He turned for a half second to address me. "We'll talk later."

He didn't wait for me to agree but ran behind the last nurse. I was left with a newly buzzing chow hall and a list of questions.

I went outside, hearing the click of debris falling on rooftops. The mortar had fallen halfway between the chow hall and the airstrip. One of the supply sheds was on fire. The medical teams mobilized, and what looked like chaos of running and shouting was actually a well-rehearsed effort to get the wounded into the hospital.

My job was to stay out of the way until everyone was moved. Hoses came out. Fires were doused. The smoke in the air cleared. I went to the hospital to see if there was anything I could do.

Jenn was setting up an IV line. Her hands shook.

"That was scary," she said when she was out of the patient's earshot. "I was practically on top of it, but I had to pee... so..." Her eyes filled up as she put on a latex glove. "I walked over to the latrine."

I squeezed her biceps. "You're in psychological shock."

"I'm fine." She took off the glove.

"You're shaking."

"They need me." She pinched her fingers together to put the glove back on.

"What's with the glove?"

She froze, looking at it as if she didn't know why it hung from her fingertips like a jellyfish.

"Jenn, you can't hook up any more lines until you pull it together."

"Oh, my God."

"'Oh, my God' what?"

"I don't remember putting any lines in."

The hit had traumatized her, even if temporarily.

"Let's double-check what you did."

We checked the IVs and stents. She'd done it all perfectly, as if autopilot had worked even if the plane was about to crash.

"I'm not doing this anymore," she said. "Last deployment."

It was the first time she'd ever said that.

I WANTED TO SEE CADEN. I told myself I wanted to make sure he was okay, but the fact was I wanted him to tell me I was okay.

His trailer was dark, and he didn't come to the door when I knocked. He wasn't in the chow hall. Or the hospital.

"Hey," I said to a doctor in recovery.

"Hi." She smiled. "Ferguson. I'm stationed at the airfield."

Airfield surgeons went into combat with the medevac teams. Dr. Ferguson had vibrant skin and clear eyes. She didn't look like a woman who went to the front lines in a Blackhawk, but that assumption said more about me than her.

"I have an eye specialty, and they traded me," she said.

"Traded?"

"For a general surgeon, oddly, not a field doc. I was going to rush back, but they'd already left on a nine-line with him. That won't go over well."

General surgeons were too valuable to go past the wire.

"Did his name happen to be Captain St. John?"

"Yeah. Hard name to forget. He jumped right in. Volunteered like that." She snapped her fingers.

The medevacs did not fuck around with time. Caden must have jumped on the truck to the airfield, told them he was a doctor, and taken off.

Caden outside the wire. Everything could go wrong. What was he thinking?

He wanted to own me, but he didn't even know me. He didn't know my father had been eaten alive every day by regret and guilt even as he gave more and more years in service. He hadn't grown up with stories of blood and gore, rage and impotence. I had. The fact that I'd chosen to serve in a war zone didn't mean I fetishized battle. It meant I went in with my eyes open.

I wished I'd had time to open his eyes, and when he got back, I was making it my job to put away all our power games and make sure he didn't deploy again. He was going to hear about my father's night terrors, my brother's suicide attempt, my grandfather's guilt. Eight days of treating soldiers who had been blown to bits was going to seem like a cakewalk.

Caden was going home after this deployment if I had to scare the shit out of him.

I COULDN'T MILL around the airfield like a lost lamb. I kept my eyes on the dark sky and my ears open for approaching birds. I wasn't privy to what was happening, whether they'd landed under fire or at all. Nothing.

I should have told him the truth right away, without backpedaling or soft-shoeing. I was his, completely. Unabashedly. Unreservedly. Instead of enforcing my will, I should have opened myself with the same nakedness he had.

My desk was piled with paperwork. Since I wasn't going to sleep until I knew Caden was all right, and my office was close enough to the hospital to hear when they brought in casualties, I figured I'd do it.

When I pulled out my chair, I found a small manila envelope with my name on the front. I undid the string, and a dirty, blood-streaked sonogram fell into my hand. I shook it, and a folded piece of paper came out. A note.

> *Pfc Sanchez came in again. Head trauma.*
> *Said to give this to the psychiatrist.*
> *He didn't make it.*

I put the sonogram and the note back into the envelope before I started on the paperwork.

"It was Colonel Brogue out there."

In the dead quiet of the midnight hour, the staff nurse's voice carried through the wall. Brogue had wanted to get off base, and it sounded as if he'd done just that. I stopped what I was doing as a less-clear voice mumbled something.

"Little bird got them after the area was secured. All the casualties went to Baghdad. We're clear." I caught a ride to the airfield and waited, trying to stay out of the way, asking what I could and overhearing the rest.

From what I could glean, Caden's Blackhawk had landed under fire, which pilots aren't supposed to do until they do it, then they're responsible. With a full bird colonel on the ground, it wasn't surprising they'd taken the risk, but there wasn't supposed to be human gold in the form of a trauma surgeon on the chopper either.

They'd taken fire. Other casualties. Local civilians had gotten involved. They'd lifted out with the wounded when they knew a little bird was coming for Caden and the minor injuries.

The lighter *thups* of the smaller helicopter came out of the pale morning sky, and I went outside. With the sun kissing the horizon, the ground was still dark, and the airfield floodlights were necessary. The passengers were shadows in the glass as it landed. I held my jacket tightly around me, approaching into the wind of the rotors to see him, ready to tell him everything, reassure him, give myself to him, scare him out of this life.

He got out of the helicopter after the last of the passengers as the pilot slowed the whirr of the rotor. The front of this shirt and pants were solid black, as if he'd lain in a puddle of ink.

I ran to him. That particular shade of black was the result of the floodlights hitting the deep red of blood.

He didn't stop. He looked straight ahead, passing me by as if he didn't see me. "Caden!"

He got in the back seat of the Jeep, where the driver waited for him. I looked in the window. He was staring straight ahead, in a fugue state, seeing nothing.

What the hell had happened out there?

I RAN to Caden's trailer.

His door wasn't closed all the way. I knocked. No answer. Knocked again. "Caden," I said.

I respected his privacy up to a point, and I'd reached it. Pushing the door, I stepped into the dark room. A band of morning sunlight fell into the corner, catching his bowed, blood-soaked figure. I shut the door, making sure it clicked closed. No one needed to see him sitting in the corner with his arms around his knees.

Crouching in front of him, I laid my hands on his arms and looked into his face. He kept staring into the middle distance.

"Caden. I'm going to get someone in here to bring you to the hospital."

"No." His voice was low and flat, and hearing it cut open my worry enough to let out my sorrow.

I didn't know what had happened, but it had broken him. This man who had worked eight days with no more than a short rest, who had let his sense of duty guide him to do the impossible, who had touched me with his vulnerability and strength... they'd broken him.

I stormed out into the morning sun. I got thirty feet away. The Humvee tire we'd used as an end zone was at the other side of the field, another thirty feet away. My mind was strategizing who to tap for help and where they were when the mortar hit.

The earth shook, and with a sharp pain in my ears, everything went silent. When I landed on my back, I couldn't even hear the breath exit my lungs, but I felt it with the agony in my chest.

The silence was more disorienting than the rain of rocks and shrapnel.

I got my feet under me. Dizzy. Planting my feet. Breathing soundlessly with a sharp pain in my chest. I looked down at myself. I was covered in blood. When I looked back up, I realized I'd been turned around. Caden stood at his door, awakened by the blast, his blood-soaked shirt mirroring mine, crying out without a sound.

The ground rotated under me.

I was falling.

I would hit the dirt at the acceleration of gravity.

I couldn't break my fall, but I didn't need to.

A man was under me, catching me, holding me in his arms as he ran.

Deaf but not blind, I could only see the blue sky. The black smoke from the mortar bounded my peripheral vision on one side.

When he looked down at me for a second, he wasn't broken anymore. The eternal sky was captured in his eyes, deadly and comforting, alive with purpose.

Chapter Twenty-Seven

A single shard of metal had missed my heart by two millimeters.

"There's more ways to miss a heart than hit it," Caden said from beside my bed.

He'd used his R&R days to fly into Baghdad after me. The incision was small. I could have recuperated in Balad, but Caden had stepped in, making sure I was in the best-equipped hospital whether I needed it or not.

"I prefer to think of myself as lucky."

"Preference noted. They're sending you back to the CSH."

He was making an assumption that I was going back to Balad based on the fact that I was going back into the field. I was indeed going back into the field, but not to the CSH.

"What happened out there?" I asked. "Outside the wire?"

He shrugged and looked away. "The usual intense shit."

"I saw Brogue." My CO was down the hall with another injury so close to deadly it confirmed the existence of luck for me, and the existence of statistical probability for Caden's patients.

Brogue being down the hall had its benefits. I'd wheeled down there and checked on him. He was going home, but he was still the commanding officer of the First Medical Brigade. He could task me out of my unit up to Abu Ghraib to work with Army Intelligence for a while.

He'd agreed it was an opportunity to go from a specialty no one respected to something where I could move up, make a difference, release myself from the constraints of a unit for a while and decide how I wanted to work. He'd do the paperwork as soon as he could sit up in his goddamned bed.

If I went through with it, I wasn't going back to the support hospital with Caden.

"He said you saved his life and a few others," I continued. "He's recommended you for a commendation."

"I get a nice pat on the back whenever I do my job." He squeezed my hand and ran his finger along my forearm with a touch that was uniquely his.

"Why did you go out?" I asked. "There are field surgeons who could have gone."

"You asked me this, Greysen."

"And you deflected, which I let you do because I was post-op."

Four fingertips went back down my forearm with a tenderness that could only be described as worshipful. "You don't let stuff go, do you?"

"Nope."

"I want to be with you. Do you want to be with me?"

"Yes. More than anything."

"And if we are a couple, this is what I can expect? You to lock onto things?"

I didn't want to turn him off, but I wouldn't lie to him either. "Yep. But I'm also patient. I won't forget, but I'll let you tell me things in your own time."

He stared at the way his thumb stroked the scars on my wrist. "I went out to prove that I could."

That wasn't news. I could have told him that. But having him say it so plainly was unexpected and earth-shattering and a chest-spreader, exposing my heart to his attention.

"Caden."

"Greysen?"

So impossibly blue, his eyes were holes to the sky.

"I can't do better," I said.

"Well, I know that."

We smiled, and I looked away. "But you're not staying in the military, and this is my life."

"I do catch movies sometimes. Guy's off on deployment and calls his woman from base. She's always in the kitchen of some suburban house, holding the phone with both hands because she loves him. We can just switch it. You call me. I'll hold the phone with both hands."

"In a suburban house?"

"Probably not. That a deal-breaker?"

"No. Not that."

He didn't ask me what the deal-breaker was. Either he didn't want to know, or he was aware of what I didn't yet know.

There were no deal-breakers.

"I'M NOT GOING HOME," I said into the hospital phone. Jenn was on the other side of the line. I had an envelope stamped with the US Army seal crunched in my hand.

"Why not?"

"The incision was nothing. It was clean."

"You lost a ton of blood."

"I have it back. I'm replenished like a vampire."

"Well, it'll be nice to have you around."

I didn't think it would be hard to tell her, but I had to take a second to rework what I intended to say. "I'm not staying. Not for long. I got tasked out to Defense."

"Where?"

"I'm heading up to ABG."

My paperwork had gone through. Brogue was laid up and on his way home but had signed the recommendation. The approval had come in the envelope my palm was sweating on.

"Abu Ghraib? Why? For what?"

"I can't—"

"It's Ronin."

"It's Ronin," I confirmed.

"Okay, I'm saying this once, then you do what you want, okay?"

"This should be good."

"It will be. Write it down."

I laughed silently so she couldn't hear me, but I had the feeling I wouldn't need to write it down. "Go ahead."

"You do not have the moral vacancy required to work with the DoD."

"The project conforms to the Geneva Convention."

"Okay, if he has to say that, then that's a problem. And have you asked yourself what he needs you for?"

I didn't, and wouldn't, mention the second part of Ronin's offer, but my pause while I decided that was enough of an opening for Jenn to jump in.

"The medical degree," she said. "You can script and dispense."

"It's my job."

"I don't like it. It bothers me."

"You're just going to miss me."

"Yeah. That too."

Chapter Twenty-Eight

Caden wasn't able to come to Baghdad to escort me back to the CSH. Despite his commission, he was and always would be a civilian—with a civilian's confidence in his own agency. He'd always think he could make decisions, work around the rules while staying in the lines, negotiate with his superiors, charm his way through a narrow opening in his options.

On the Chinook, with my knuckles pale caps over where my fingers and my hand joined, I wondered how he would tolerate my career. Military wives had to submit to a host of indignities, starting with a loss of control over where they lived and ending with a loss of control over parenting. Their husbands were married to the military first. How would Caden manage always playing second to the army, especially when, after two deployments, he still didn't understand how little power he had?

He wanted a life with me. I was torn between talking him out of it and agreeing to everything. Was there a middle way? Someplace between him pursuing a stateside medical career in the army and me taking off my uniform forever?

I alternated between frustration and an uncomfortable feeling of validation. *Why do I have to think about this now?* soon became *Being wanted by Caden feels too good to refuse.*

I WAS as sleepy as I'd ever been, trying to make sense while wrapped in his arms.

"We'll get R&R when we can," I said. "ABG isn't far. Not from here."

"We'll be fine."

"For the deployment. After that... you're resigning your commission, right?"

"Yes." He peppered my face with gentle kisses. "My obligations are done."

"I don't want us to get our hopes up. The odds of us staying together—"

"Hush."

"They're not good."

"You're being a pessimist."

"I'm scared," I said, making fear my final negotiating point.

"Of what?"

"That you won't be able to stand the long distances or moving around or any of it." I didn't mention that I could retire my commission. Of the few commitments I'd ever made, the only one I could see myself sticking with was my commission.

"You don't think much of me."

"No, it's not that."

"I'm not a child, Major. I'm a grown man who can make his own decisions."

"And you're going to decide to have a life because you're normal."

"No one's ever called me that before."

"It's a compliment."

"So, a complimentary thing about me is something you're going to use to argue that we can't be together?"

I sighed and closed my eyes. "My brain can't get around what you just said."

"What I said was..." He kissed my nose. "Your thinking is incomplete. Your way of seeing me is limited. You need to give me a chance."

"Why?" I made a *mm* sound in my throat to stop his reply, waking up a little. "That came out wrong. I'm just... I want to. But outside dual deployment for married people, the army doesn't care about anyone's love life. There's no way we're going to be together much. Not for a while. I won't be surprised when you tell me you can't wait around for me."

"I'll be surprised."

"Okay. You be surprised. But I don't want to be hurt either. And, to quote a very sexy man, you can hurt me."

"I won't." He unraveled his limbs from mine and stood over me.

"Where are you going?"

"I have a shift." He got dressed, hiding his beauty from me one piece of clothing at a time. "You should stay here and get some rest. Think about it, then tell me you want me as much as I want you. Tell me you'd feel broken without me."

Asking that of me said more about how he'd feel than how I'd feel. Lying in his bed, sticky and sore, I was thrown by his need.

"I don't want to disappoint you," I said. "This life is hard, Caden. It's hard on women who grow up knowing what it's like. I can't imagine how it will be for you."

Above me, in the half-light, his eyes were dark and unreadable, but his body language—the deep breath, the articulated fingers asking me to hold on, the squared shoulders—spoke of preparation to say something uncomfortable and serious.

"I'm a practical man," he said. "A surgeon has to be. If you cut somebody open and you're careless, you're going to kill them. It's not bad luck. It's not bad karma. If you're casual or cavalier about germs or how you're holding the knife, you can kill somebody. That's just the long and the short of it. So, when I met you, I figured... pheromones. Early imprinting. Reproductive instinct. You meet all the standards for beauty and then some. I'm a straight guy. My brain and my spinal cord and my dick are wired to find a female of child-bearing age. My body reacts to you because my brain releases certain hormones at the sound of your voice or the smell of apples on your skin. It's all science, until it's not."

He sat on the edge of the bed and put his shoes on, continuing as if he were describing a surgical procedure. "You know I had you down for a few fucks and a friendly good-bye. Probably about the same as you had me down for. We're adults. It's not like either one of us hasn't ever had a pheromone-induced hormone rush. But it got weird. Somewhere in those eight days when you were checking on me, it became about more than the chemicals in my brain. I panicked. I went outside the wire because I was afraid I'd lose you if I didn't. And I'm on that fucking Blackhawk, asking myself what the hell I'm doing, because the way I needed you wasn't normal. Not for a man who knows how the body and the brain affect each other."

He'd never told me what happened that night, and it looked as if that wouldn't change. He stomped his foot on the floor when he was done lacing the second boot, then he leaned over me, placing an elbow on the mattress. "I don't believe in the Universe with a capital U, and I don't believe in God. I believe in brain signals and blood. But now? I'm willing to think maybe I'm wrong about everything. This is what it comes down to. You expanded my view of the universe. I don't know what to do with that. I'm not saying I believe in fate or karma or 'meant to be' now, but my thinking got bigger because of you. I feel woken up." As if he was uncomfortable with his own feelings, he got off his elbow and hunched on the edge of the bed, looking at his laced boots. "I feel ignorant and ordinary but awake. If that means we have a long-distance relationship until you retire, then that's what it'll be."

"Okay." My voice cracked in two syllables.

"Good." He slapped his knees and stood. "Do you know when you're heading out?"

"Tomorrow afternoon."

If he was shocked by the compression of our time together, he didn't show it. "Fine. I'm off work in the morning. We'll eat, then I'll take you to the air base."

He kissed me quickly, then opened the door, letting in a blast of cold air, and shut it behind him. I heard him clop down the three wooden steps, heard his boots crunch on the rocky sand and fade into nothing.

Chapter Twenty-Nine

GREYSEN

Ronin had traveled light, so by noon, he was spending most of his remaining hours in Balad helping me clear out. I picked up the sandwich he'd brought.

Ronin sat next to me and opened his. "We have a nice office in ABG."

"We're sharing an office?"

You don't get far in the army without sharing, but I was a full major in a different unit, and I might need to see patients. Or not. He hadn't told me much about what I'd be doing.

"You're on loan to Army Intelligence. We're pretty much in each other's business."

I bit my sandwich. "We're clear on the other part of this offer, right?"

"The other part?"

"The you and I fucking part."

"I figured you would have mentioned it if it was on. What's keeping you? My breath? Different cologne?"

"My availability's compromised."

"Let me guess. Cap'n Fobbit."

"He went outside the wires, so you can stop that."

"He sure did." Ronin chewed his sandwich pensively.

I wiped my mouth, choosing my words carefully. "Did you hear what happened out there?"

"Yup."

"What did you hear?"

As soon as he looked at me, I knew he could tell I had no idea. He picked a limp tomato out of his sandwich and answered, "I heard he overstepped for a Haji."

Haji was a pejorative for Iraqi civilians. Maybe Caden didn't want to tell me because he thought I'd be upset with him. Maybe the whole thing had been traumatic.

"He didn't tell you." Ronin read me like a book.

Caden appeared at the door in his uniform, cap pushed back on his head. He stood there, holding a rolled-up paper plate with two sandwiches in the curl.

"Hey," I said. "Is one of those for me?"

He stepped in. "Yeah. But you have one."

"I didn't know you guys had a date." Ronin folded the paper over his sandwich and slipped off the desk.

I took one of Caden's sandwiches. "I'm pretty hungry. Thank you."

"I'm going to pack up my trailer," Ronin said. "See you on the airfield."

"See you there."

Caden held out his hand, and Ronin shook it. When he was gone, Caden sat next to me and unwrapped his lunch.

"I'm not going to sleep with him," I said.

"I know."

"Then why do you have that look on your face?"

He shrugged. "I asked to be moved up there and got a no. Flat out. No."

"You seem absolutely stunned by that."

"I've never wanted to be anywhere but where I was before. So, it's different. That's all."

We ate in silence.

"I feel guilty," I said.

"You shouldn't." He cracked open a bottle of water and set it beside me. "I'm going to figure it out."

"One man against the US Army and the woman who won't leave it."

He opened a second bottle and tipped it toward me. "I'd rather take on the army than you."

He would. He was reckless and brave, like David running after Goliath with a slingshot.

"When you went outside the wire that time?" I said. "What happened?"

He shrugged and counted on his fingers. "Brogue. A guy from Georgia and an Iraqi lady. All patched up and sent to Baghdad. Done."

I narrowed my eyes at him as if the smaller aperture would bring the truth into focus.

It did not.

Chapter Thirty

GREYSEN

Caden carried my duffel to the tarmac even after I insisted I was perfectly capable.

"There's no chivalry in the army," I hissed as he took it from me. "That would ruin everything."

"I'm a civilian in a uniform." He hitched the duffel strap up. "Deal with it."

The Chinook's rotors were getting started.

"God, I hate these things," I said as we walked toward it.

"Yeah." He was agreeing, but he was also staring straight at the open door where Ronin waited, which explained the single-word answer.

"I'm sore," I said as reassurance, but my words were lost in the din of helicopter blades.

Caden stopped short and dropped the duffel. I reached down to pick it up, but he put his hand on my shoulder.

"What?" I shouted. "It's not too heavy."

"Marry me."

"What?" I must have misheard in the *thupping* noise.

"Marry me, Greysen. Be my wife."

"Are you serious?" I asked, knowing full well he was dead serious.

"You said it was a unicorn assignment. You said you never heard of any one you could get out of. Well, maybe if that's the case, there's a reason for that. Maybe you shouldn't go."

I was thrown. We were supposed to kiss before I got on the helicopter and write letters and then break up.

"I can't marry you to get out of going."

"Marry me because you want to. I'll be the best husband you ever heard of. I'll take care of you. I'll stay in the army, and we can dual deploy."

"No!"

His face fell. I'd spoken too soon, but it was loud and the Phrog was waiting.

"Maybe!" Trying to make it better was making it worse. I wanted him, but he'd caught me off guard. "But you can't stay." My cap almost blew off. I had to hold it on.

"I will." The clipped demand of his voice cut through the wall of noise. "They're begging me to stay. If you don't marry me, I'm redeploying."

"Are you threatening me?"

"It's the only way to stay close to you."

"This is weird, Caden." I glanced at the helicopter.

It was ready. Ronin was waiting. The pilots were waiting.

"Marry me."

My life was waiting. But this beautiful man was waiting for me too. He was resilient and fragile, made of rock and flesh, with a strength that lunged forward only to tear him apart.

"You can't redeploy," I insisted. "That's off the table."

"Marry me, and I'll do whatever you want."

Marry him. What would I have to give up? What would I gain?

This man with strands of hair trilling in the wind and his powerful voice demanding more from me than I'd thought to give. He held me there, in his gaze, nailing my feet to the ground until I answered.

I barely knew him except by his loyalty, his passion, his vulnerability, his honesty.

I knew nothing of his life, his habits, his choices.

"Marry me. Don't go with him."

"Is this about Ronin?"

"No! I just... I have a feeling. A bad feeling about you going up there."

"You're lying."

My accusation rang more false than his denial. He wasn't lying. If his demand was about Ronin, he would have said it, and if he didn't have a feeling, that would be the last thing he'd claim. I hadn't known him that long, but I knew him that well.

"I love you, Greysen." He raised his voice as much as he had to and no more. Just enough to sound serious and straightforward. "Stay here with your unit. Marry me. I love you."

I barely knew myself or what I wanted from a man.

What was I supposed to say?

"Major!" The pilot's voice lifted over the wind.

He'd be here in a moment to hurry me away from Caden, who pinned me in place with his eyes. I'd be torn apart between the two.

His lips made the shape of words *marry me* without engaging a voice that wouldn't be heard over the sound of the Universe he didn't believe in.

Did *I* believe?

With a glance at the pilot and back to Caden's eyes, the color shaded by the brim of his cap, I answered.

Part Four

Chapter Thirty-One

GREYSEN

NEW YORK, 2006

A woman in Sweden was walking with her son in her arms. He was three, and they were having a serious discussion about the shape of the clouds as they crossed the street. In the story, her upturned face was the reason given for why she wasn't looking where she was going. They got halfway across and stepped up onto the median in the middle of the crosswalk's length, but the mother did not accurately predict the end of the curb. When her foot dropped six inches she didn't expect, she tried to keep her balance by taking an extra-big step her arms weren't prepared for, and in the forward thrust, she lost her grip on her son.

The driver making a left turn had calculated his radius to avoid the woman, but the flying boy was a surprise. The toddler couldn't be avoided and wound up under the front wheel.

The mother, in an act of what's called "hysterical strength," picked up the car enough for the driver—who had exited his vehicle in a panic—to free the boy. He was crying in his mother's arms within a few seconds. Once her brain registered pain, she found she'd shattered five teeth and fractured her jaw from clenching it as she lifted the car.

The important detail in this story that no one ever misses is that the car was a Volkswagen, but the detail they always miss is that it was an old Beetle with the engine in the back.

There's only so much a person could do with what they're given. Could she have lifted the back of the VW? Or a Ford?

I'd like to think she'd have tried. I'd like to think it may have cost her a vertebra or two, but nothing would have kept her from using her body to leverage inhuman weight for her kid.

I reminded myself that my naked husband wasn't as heavy as a car. I needed to get him out of that cold basement. His eyes were open, but his body was completely slack, as if his cells and blood had lost the will to obey his mind. He recognized me, and I recognized him. He was another person. Not the man I'd married. Not the man who'd fucked me with a distant, commanding voice.

He was the man I saw in my husband's deepest kindnesses. In the rare moments of confusion. In the broken descriptions of his life with his parents.

This was Damon. I didn't know what the name meant or where it came from, but I knew who I was talking to.

"Can you walk?" I asked.

He blinked, shutting out the sky for a moment, then looked right through me. Not in the way Caden had in all the time I'd known him—not to pierce, but to caress and comfort. I was more sure than ever that this was not Caden.

"Damon? Is that your name?"

His lips parted. He caught a breath, then closed his lips again to swallow whatever he was going to say.

"It's cold," I said. "Can you get up?"

I pulled him toward me. His body was a dead weight.

"Can you move your limbs?" I asked. "Where is the paresis?"

No reply. I lifted his arms and let them drop. His legs were bent but fell to one side when his arms landed.

"Caden? If you're in there, you're suffering some kind of semiconscious catatonic state from mental trauma. I think the quadraparesis is temporary. I'm going to call someone. Can you wait here?" I leaned down and whispered in his ear, "Damon. Caden. Whoever's in there. I love you, and I'm going to take care of you."

I ran out through the speakeasy section of the basement, feeling as though I'd left a part of myself in the bottle room. I'd call for an ambulance, get him a blanket, put on some clothes.

The mental checklist was interrupted by an unintentional glance at myself in the mirror behind the bar. My eyes were bloodshot, and a bruise was blossoming on the side of my neck. I knew my voice was shredded. It was too soon to see if my eyes would get black underneath, but if the paramedics saw any such signs, things would get very complicated, very quickly.

The decision to go back into the bottle room without making a call was burdened with doubts over my lack of doubt.

He'd choked me unconscious, and unlike last time, when my husband had been trying to extend my orgasm, this time he'd been committing violence.

When I got back to the cold, concrete room, he was in the exact position I'd left him in, staring blankly into the middle distance. His beautiful body was rendered still and pale in the room's flat light. The black hairs on his skin looked like pen marks on a white paper.

I pulled him flat on his back. He didn't resist or help. His member leaned to one side like a useless piece of meat, the power removed like the magic from a talisman.

"I don't know if you can hear me," I said. "But in case you can, I'm doing a Ranger roll. Pray I have enough room in here."

Getting on the floor, I laid my upper back on his chest, placing my body perpendicular to his. I put his thigh over my shoulder and torqued my whole body toward his head. It took a few tries, but I finally got him over my shoulders and my legs under me. I got him out of the room by using my legs for strength, across the basement, and to the bottom of the steps. I sucked air through my teeth.

Go. Go. Go.

I took the first step.

He'd warned me he wanted to kill me. He'd told me he was scared. I put that into the equation. Someone I loved was sick in a way that couldn't be managed by medication or talk therapy.

Halfway up, I had to turn to make the narrow passage.

Or was he gaslighting me?

Grunting, I got up to the hallway.

If I looked like an abused wife, wasn't I? Wasn't my decision part of the cycle of violence? Wasn't my conviction that I was better than this part of the problem?

Six-foot-one. Hundred eighty. I couldn't get him up another flight of steps.

My office door was open.

I promised myself I'd alert someone as soon as I understood what was going on. I'd carefully and objectively note the signs of domestic abuse. Then I'd decide.

Bending at the waist, I dropped him on the couch and collapsed on the carpet beside him. At least it was warm in here.

THE PAIN CAME LESS than an hour later, as expected. Caden/Damon lay under a pile of blankets with a hot water bottle between his feet. I took a hot shower upstairs and took inventory of my body. I hadn't shattered my teeth, but my jaw ached, and my lower back and knees shot through with pain when I put pressure on them. I took four Advil.

Bright red bled through the whites of my eyes, and dark pink triangles formed on each side of the bridge of my nose. My neck looked okay. He hadn't put that much pressure because he knew how to cut off my air.

No energy had been wasted.

The surgeon side of my husband.

He'd recognized his name as Damon. That had been clear. What had also become clear was that he had been running headlong into this dissociation for months, and I'd let it happen. A little professional voice told me there was nothing I could have done and, at the same time, that I'd done everything I could. Neither recollection was true.

I'd done everything that pleased me because my body enjoyed it. Guilt twined around the realization like yarn around a stick.

ALL NIGHT, I sat by him. His head was turned toward the back of the sofa with his eyes open, staring at the upholstery. His vitals were good, so I let him do what I should have been doing. Resting.

My DSM V was in arm's reach. I knew what was in it, but I looked anyway.

Dissociative Identity Disorder.

DSM-5 300.14 (F44.81)

Trauma based. Correlated with PTSD. Patients suffering with mental trauma compartmentalized it into discrete personalities as a coping mechanism. The therapist had to tell each personality about the other, validate them, work toward integration (an acceptance of the condition), then fusion (merging of personalities) until normalcy was achieved.

I'd had a patient with a traumatic split in Iraq and not since. He'd watched a buddy shoot a three-year-old on purpose. This was a man he'd trusted and respected. When one CO wouldn't believe him and another didn't care, it tore the fabric of his belief system. He became Molly Jones, Grosse Point housewife, when the memory was too much to bear. His breakdown made it harder for him to convince Command that the event had happened, and he was sent home.

This couldn't be happening to Caden.

But it is.

My husband was the King of Detachment. He could lock up his emotions to get the job done.

That's the problem here.

I'd married a strong man. A rock. A man who didn't know how to fail.

Say it.

He was the calm eye of a deadly storm, maintaining his composure in the worst of circumstances.

Say it. You're getting warmer.

I'd married a man who would never come undone. I'd married strong, not weak.

Warmer.

I didn't marry a crazy person.

Jackpot.

AT NEARLY DAWN, his finger flicked, and a minute later, his hand twitched at the wrist. A swallow. A jerk of his legs under the blankets. Then his hand found mine and covered it. I held on to him, and he turned his head.

I recognized Caden's face. He looked like the twin brother my husband had never had. All the features were the same, but he was different.

"Hey," I said.

"Grey." He squeezed my hand and shifted his body toward me. Paresis done. He had his body back.

I hadn't realized how tight I was until the muscles holding worry about his body relaxed. "Are you all right?"

"Are you?" His voice was thick and slow, as if he had to remember how to speak.

"I'm fine." I cupped his jaw tenderly. "What do you remember?"

"He hurt you."

Third person. Complete dissociation. A break.

"I'm fine," I said, leaning my lips into his. He smelled like my husband. Freshly ground coffee and cut grass. "One hundred percent fine."

"Thank God."

He fell asleep.

AS A FAN of Siouxie and the Banshees and the Dead Kennedys, who wore thick eyeliner and shapeless black clothes, my social group hadn't required I play a sport. Nor had my family. Basketball, however, had its advantages. I had been athletic enough to play varsity in a few sports, but the constant motion of basketball ran me ragged, and I liked that. Besides, when Dad was around, we played in the driveway.

Colin shot up when he was thirteen, surpassing my height by the time I turned fifteen. Dad beamed at his son's new manhood and refused to acknowledge my entrance into womanhood. I understood why, but that didn't diminish my hunger for his approval.

"You know why she got the jump? Because she pushes." Dad bounced the ball with his left hand and pointed at Colin with his right. The pointing meant he was serious, and Colin, bent over his knees and panting after I'd stripped the ball from him to score, turned off the adolescent backtalk long enough to listen. "This little girl here will beat you every time because she has tenacity. When she decides she's taking what you have, she's going to work you until you're standing there wondering what happened."

He passed me the ball. I beamed with the compliment, eager to prove I could be the person he thought I was. Even though I was being used as a tool to inspire his precious son, it was the encouragement I got, so it was the encouragement I cherished.

"Push, Colin! Push!" Dad shouted as my brother covered me. "She's getting away!"

My brother avoided organized sports. I was the one on varsity. I was the one with skin in the game, but Colin was pushed to do more, be better, while I was an obstacle to overcome.

I swung low and jumped, making one off the rim. Colin caught the ball on the way down and flipped it back to Dad.

"Nice work, Grey. You..." He pointed at Colin again. "You're getting beat by a girl."

Colin's hair flopped in front of his face. He was skipping the awkward part of adolescence and going right to heartthrob.

"Yeah, Colin," I said. "I'm going to tell all the freshmen girls."

"I don't date freshmen."

"You're going to be dating a senior named Steve if you don't win the next point," Dad joked.

The fact that Colin was into girls didn't make the joke funny. Nothing would have made it funny. But we were young, and I played hard to beat him just to prove I was as good as he was.

WITH DAMON/CADEN resting on my office couch, I made a few decisions. Then remade them. Then I accepted my inability to change anything outside my own actions and decided between what I could choose and what I couldn't control.

I could decide to stay with my husband no matter what.

So, I would do that.

I could decide to respect him as a man, not a part of my caseload.

So, I would do that.

I could decide to accept this problem, whatever it was, while simultaneously helping him get better.

Acceptance was an amorphous goal. But I could commit to the process.

I was human, fallible and imperfect, but I was dedicated. All I had to do was commit to him as fully now as I had in my parents' backyard on the day I married him. With my dog tags (something old) dangling over the lace of my wedding gown and shiny army boots (something new) under the train, I'd sworn my life to him. In my mother's headpiece (something borrowed) and sky-colored socks under the boots (something blue), I'd submitted myself to a life tied to a man I loved for the qualities I'd been raised to admire.

In my frailty and humanity, I'd vowed to make a superhuman effort.

I hadn't been ready for this man.

There's freedom in being fully human. Once I admitted my own prejudices, I knew who I was dealing with. I feared my weakness. I was concerned about my sanity. I worried that I wouldn't be able to handle Caden and myself if he was in this kind of trouble.

I had come face-to-face with the fact that my husband had limits, but though I knew they existed, I couldn't see their outline without knowing what had driven him to them.

Maybe it was the house. This priceless, coveted property had been the scene of his mother's abuse. He'd insisted he was fine, that he'd stripped it of every memory. Moved the kitchen, the bedrooms, redone every detail until he couldn't recollect a single scene. But he couldn't change the outside, and walking through the door twice a day must have brought something back for him.

We could move.

We *should* move.

We could sell it and move to a smaller place. Stay in Manhattan. Maybe Brooklyn. I could take him back to San Diego.

I put my head on the desk, making constant decisions, tossing them aside, making others, justifying them in my mind to Caden, then Damon, who I didn't know. I realized there was no chance of a change as long as my husband was in this state. What one personality said, the other could undo.

There was freedom in being fully human, and there was also confinement.

Chapter Thirty-Two

CADEN

I woke up naked on the couch in her office, my legs bent and leaning on the back so I'd fit. Something damp and yielding rippled between my feet. I reached under the blankets and pulled it out.

A pale-water bottle. I didn't know how I'd gotten into the office, under the covers, or naked, much less why I'd needed a water bottle.

Greysen sat behind her desk with her head on her folded arms, sleeping in yoga pants and a ribbed tank. Her pink lips were parted, gravity pulling them slightly toward the center of the earth. She had patches of burst capillaries under her eyes. That was from losing air. I'd carefully cut her off to extend her orgasm, but I didn't think it had gone far enough to cause the darkness at the tops of her cheeks.

My primary feeling at seeing her was desire. Not normal sexual desire, but utter filth. I wanted her to wake up as I was coming on her face, then wipe it all off her with my dick so I could make her lick me clean.

It was morning. No time for that.

I got out from under the covers. My wife leaned a little in her sleep, ass getting closer to the edge of the chair. It pivoted. She was going to fall.

I picked her up under the shoulders and knees. She nuzzled me as I laid her on the couch. After covering her, I grabbed the cold water bottle and went upstairs.

Damon was gone. I'd felt exorcised of him after I'd broken Greysen before, but this time was different. He wasn't hiding where I couldn't hear or see him. He wasn't a pressure in the back of my consciousness. He wasn't a missing voice in the hiss of the shower or a potential presence from the darkness in the drain. Like a dead thing, he only existed in memory.

I was free of him, and that satisfied me.

After putting my wife under the bed covers, I jerked off in the shower, imagining the tiles I came on were my wife's face and tits. In the fantasy, I pulled her shirt on over my cum so she could wear my mark all day.

I got dressed before I checked on Greysen. She opened her eyes enough for me to see the bleeding capillaries in the whites. She smiled and patted my hand as if she was too weak for words. I'd taken everything from her the night before. Satisfied again, I went to work.

DURING THE FIRST eight days of the Second Battle of Fallujah, when I'd stopped seeing the men under me as people and started seeing them as puzzles with broken or misplaced pieces, I'd had a sense of personal authority similar to the feeling athletes describe as "the zone."

At work in New York, even though it wasn't a cutting day, the pieces of the world clicked into place according to my actions, my will, my desires. I didn't crave praise or recognition. I wanted nothing more or less than control over what I could see and touch.

Greysen, kneeling in the dark, her skin cast in blue from the streetlights on 87th Street filtering through the curtains. The dark fracture between her legs and the eggshells of her ass...inviting me to use her. Waiting for me with her forehead on the rug and her hands boxed behind her back, wrist to wrist, she was no less a lioness.

That was what I wanted.

I left a message for her. "I'll be home at nineteen hundred. Be naked. On your knees. Forehead to the floor. Hands behind your back. Be ready for me to enter you anywhere I want." I hung up.

Who would be there when she heard it? A patient? One of the military men she spoke with all day? A colleague? Would they see her blush? Would she smile?

No. She wouldn't see anyone today. Not with the bruises under her eyes. The bloodshot whites would be almost healed by now, but the rest would linger, reminding me I'd done something I couldn't remember. Something terrible. Something that had chased Damon away for good.

She'd want to talk about it. All I wanted to do was fuck her in celebration.

I could do both.

Doing the last of my paperwork for the day, I decided she was welcome to talk about it either after we were both satiated or with my dick in her mouth.

That should be more than satisfactory.

Outside, the last of the sun disappeared behind the western horizon.

Chapter Thirty-Three

GREYSEN

I'll be home at nineteen hundred. Be naked. On your knees. Forehead to the floor. Hands behind your back. Be ready for me to enter you anywhere I want.

The contents of Caden's message had been spoken clearly and without an ounce of doubt that he'd be obeyed. His demeanor was so commanding that I at once felt a flood of arousal so strong it hurt...and looked at the clock to see if I had time to shower before nineteen hundred hours.

That didn't last long. I wasn't getting on my knees and offering my body to him until we talked about the previous night. I'd had Friday off sessions as usual, but I'd had to cancel the gym and meetings to hide the way his hands had used me. I spent the day reading journals and studies on dissociative disorders. Dry, hopeless reading.

Until I knew who I was fucking, or what I was fucking, there would be no fucking.

Bottom line? I wasn't in the mood for Caden's controlling voice or his precise pain. I was tired from the night before. My back ached. Swallowing hurt. If there was going to be any sex, it had to be the kind that made me fall asleep with confidence in my heart and a smile on my face.

He arrived at seven on the dot. In the crack between curtains, he popped up the stoop with his jacket flowing behind him. I sat on the couch, under a tall lamp, fully dressed in a sexless sweater and jeans. I was a wife waiting to speak to her husband, not a woman getting on her knees for kinky time.

The door clicked shut. I heard fussing with keys, coat, a cleared throat, and he appeared in the entrance to the living room. I could tell who I was sharing the room with right away.

Not Caden. At least not the man calling himself Caden.

"Damon," I said.

"Greysen."

"What the hell is going on?"

It wasn't for him to answer. I should have known that, but it was impossible to be a trained therapist about my own husband. I wanted an answer, and the way he smiled was just that. It wasn't an answer I liked, but it was unlike anything I'd seen from my husband except when he was at his most vulnerable. It had no underlying meanings. No sexual overtones or cynicism. It was a happy smile.

"May I sit?"

I realized so much about my husband when he became someone else. Caden never asked to sit. He just sat. He identified the straightest course of action to a result and took it.

"Please do."

The person in my husband's body sat on the other side of the couch, leaving a full cushion between us, and twisted around so one arm was draped over the back of the sofa. He pressed his thumb to his upper lip and regarded me as if seeing me for the first time. Admittedly, I felt as if I was seeing him for the first time as well. A jaw that had been as angular and unyielding as his personality was now a counterpoint to a softer line of his mouth. The color of his eyes was less a challenge and more of an invitation.

"I can't believe how beautiful you are," he said.

"Bullshit me later."

The fact was I couldn't believe how beautiful he was.

"To your question," he said. "What's going on... I'm not really sure."

"I have an idea."

"Good." He nodded and waited.

"Can you tell me who you are first?"

He smiled ruefully and ran his nails along the damask upholstery. The pairing of gestures was surprisingly sensual, and nothing like Caden, who delivered answers like an automatic weapon.

"I am your soul mate." He laid his hand down and looked at me. "I'm the only person who truly fits with you. I admit I wasn't born in a normal way, but we were created for each other. Maybe there was some mix-up and the body I was meant for went to someone else?"

"There was a movie like that."

"Then it's not unheard of."

"It's a made-up story."

"You're saying I'm made up? That what I've been going through is fake?"

Invalidating a personality was dangerous territory. I was tired, aching, in a state of emotional shock, and in no condition to maintain my therapeutic detachment. But I wasn't going to swap ghost stories either. "Here's what I know—you're my husband, and you're a dissociated personality."

"No, I'm sure I'm not."

"How are you so sure?"

"I was my own person before. I had a name, and I've loved you from the beginning."

"Before last night, where were you?"

"You really want to talk about this?"

"What are the options?"

The way he looked at me told me what he thought the options were. "I've waited a long time to kiss you. I guess I can wait another few minutes."

Another few minutes? I wasn't sure I should even let him touch me, much less kiss me.

"Can you describe your life before last night?" I asked.

"I wouldn't call it a life. I saw out through his eyes. I heard with his ears, then forgot a lot of it. I wanted things. You, mostly. But getting out was all I could think about."

"Getting out of what?"

"I don't know. It was a kind of box. Or a bag around me. Tight. I think it was him. He kept me in it."

"Him?"

"Caden."

I was looking right at Caden, but he referred to himself as a nemesis. Not uncommon in these cases, but still strange. "What's the first thing you remember?"

"My name."

"Do you know where you were? Where Caden was?"

"No idea. I was blind. I could stretch the limits around me, and I could hear better. See better. Your voice." He shook his head as if amazed. "Went right through me. I couldn't always understand what you were saying, but it always called me. And when you... when he started hurting you and you liked it, that was when the bag got tight."

"Except last night."

"He almost killed you."

"And you opened the bag?"

"I didn't. He did."

Rain patted the windows, leaving diagonal lines across the glass. Caden had released this monster to protect me from the other monster. I rubbed my eyes, shutting out the sight of the rain as it increased, distorting the view.

"Greysen." His whisper reached through my self-imposed darkness. "It's for the best. I won't hurt you. You're safe with me."

A touch fell on my ankle, so gentle and tender I was comforted without wanting to be. I was faltering. I couldn't. Not yet.

But when he touched me, I knew I would.

"Where were you all day?"

He paused before answering. "At work."

I moved my fingers away, blinking the light back in. He slid his hand over my ankle, the closest piece of bare skin to him.

"Did you leave me a message this afternoon?" I asked.

"Yes."

I couldn't imagine the man on my couch issuing the short list of commands that I'd had to remind myself to disobey.

He was lying.

I could press him about the content of the message, but it could trigger a reaction I wasn't ready to defend against.

"I didn't do what you told me to," I said. "You didn't seem to mind when you got home."

"I was just glad to see you." He stroked my ankle with his thumb with the perfect amount of pressure to awaken the nerve endings. Caden always knew how to touch me, but this simple change in pressure was lateral in its difference in that it had the same effect. He shifted closer to me. "I want to kiss you."

No.

My first thought was a negative. I didn't know him or what would be too much for him. My arousal was bad enough. Letting him touch me was worse. My heart thudded like a caged madman bouncing off the bars.

This man looked like Caden, smelled like Caden, sounded like a man using Caden's voice. It was his body, his mind, just a different piece of it.

Reaching for my cheek with his ever-perfect touch, he repeated, "I want to kiss you."

Leaning forward, cut grass and fresh coffee beans, rich and sharp. Same pheromones. Same man. I countered him, meeting him in the middle until I could feel his breath.

"I've wanted to kiss you as long as I can remember."

"What was the first moment?"

He looked down at my lips. The curve of his eyelashes against the sine of his lids was so much my husband. But the hesitation was not. "Now is the only moment that counts."

Pseudopsychology frayed the rope connecting me to my desire.

"You don't remember," I said, pulling back enough to yank the rope taut without breaking it.

"I've always wanted you. That's all there is to it. Past, present, future. It just *is*. There's no starting point, and there's no end."

His voice wasn't shot through with rainbows and unicorns but with a pure statement of fact. This was what it was, and something about that tone resonated with every other voice I'd ever trusted.

What would happen if I made love to this man, this creature, this *being*? Could I get him to pack up and move out of this house? Probably. But what about the man still calling himself Caden? He'd return, and we'd unpack.

"Then you won't mind sleeping in the guest bedroom?" I asked.

"Of course not."

"Good." I slapped my hands on my knees and got up.

"What are you going to tell him?"

I knew who he meant.

"When he comes back," Damon continued, "which he will, and he's on the guest bed, what are you going to say?"

"He and I will have a conversation. Same one you and I just had."

"What if he doesn't come back?"

"What do you mean?"

He took his arm from the back of the couch and put his elbows on his knees, locking his gorgeous fingers together between them. "The contusions on your neck are light, but I can see them. You have broken blood vessels under both eyes. Your voice is hoarse from windpipe damage."

"Just breath play gone too far."

"The only reason he didn't finish the job was that I came for him. I resuscitated you. He was standing over you, paralyzed with fear over what he'd done." His voice went serious again. "When he's in the zone, he loses control."

Terror plucked the nerves of my spine, woke my glands, sending messages to my body I couldn't obey. "No. That won't happen."

"Damn right." He stood. "I'm not going to let it."

Damon hadn't seemed threatening until that moment.

"How will you stop it?"

"I can keep him from coming back."

"What if you fail?"

"He already warned you. He's going to kill you."

He wouldn't. If he'd released Damon to protect me, then something inside him didn't want to hurt me. But the man in our living room wouldn't be convinced. His whole existence depended on believing I was in danger from Caden.

"I'll take the room across the hall from ours," he said, putting his hand on my cheek. I pulled away. "Tomorrow, we can both sleep in. You can use it."

IN THE SPACE under the bedroom door, the light from the bedroom across the hall went out. He'd waited for me to turn my lights out first, but he had no way of knowing if I was sleeping, and he had to realize how impossible that was. I crouched at the head of the bed and listened to the night sounds of the city. People passing by, talking. Cars inching toward Amsterdam Avenue in the constant traffic that was Manhattan.

I had to talk to someone.

I couldn't do this myself.

I loved him, and turning him into a patient rankled that love. He was mine. We'd made promises. Vows. We were a unit. His secrets were sacrosanct.

Me.

Caden.

And now, a third uninvited person who held the same love in the same heart.

I loved him. I loved what we had together. I had to be the one to get it back.

Standing at the window in an army T-shirt and underwear, lost in thought, I watched New Yorkers do what they did best. Cross in the middle of the street, barely looking both ways as if they were protected by an invisible force field.

What if he tried again to kill me?

He couldn't. Not if I didn't give him the opportunity. I was the one who had spent a decade in military training. He was a surgeon. A well-built surgeon with a military fitness regimen but still just a doctor. I could take him in a fight as long as I was mentally prepared.

Jenn would know what to do, but she'd tell me to get out of the house. I wasn't giving up that easily. Not on my marriage. Not on Caden.

I fooled myself into thinking there was some quick solution that would bring us back to the way it had been. Some trick I could implement and boom, life would go back to normal. We'd be back on track in no time. But if I went through channels, brought in other people, spent weeks on an official diagnosis, there would be no going back.

Even as I convinced myself that was possible, I knew it wasn't. I was con man and mark. Thief and victim. A willing dupe in my own web of lies.

A yellow taxi narrowly missed a canoodling couple, honking and getting flipped the bird in response. The shock of the noise opened my defenses enough to let in a thought I'd been holding back.

I wanted Damon. I wanted his touch. I wanted him to stay long enough to convince me he was my husband by another name. Which he was. At least as much as the detached monster who fucked like an animal.

One more day, then he was on call Sunday. If they called him in, I'd block the door, and by Monday, I'd know if he could do his job safely.

I'd let it go one more day, then decide.

Chapter Thirty-Four

DAMON

Caden put up a fight at dawn, trying to wrestle past the room he'd given me, but I got away. All I had to do—and this should have been obvious from the start—was bring to mind Greysen motionless on the couch while he spurted cum down his leg.

When I showered, I couldn't help but feel the firmness of this body I'd taken. It wasn't just the realness that fascinated me, but the way the desires I'd felt through Caden didn't float free but were connected to the body. Hunger was in the stomach. Thirst was in the mouth. Wakefulness in the mind. Anxiety in the chest. Lust was deep in the balls.

Last night, I'd smelled how much she wanted me. The apples he'd always tasted on her skin went fermented with arousal, soured by hormones and the wetness I sensed between her legs. When I'd touched her ankle, her nipples had hardened under the tank top, and my tongue had gotten fat in my mouth with the need to suck them.

Stroking the erection that appeared, I let out a relieved breath. I could finally make love to her. Taste her for myself. Enter her slowly. Savor her groans. Guide her to orgasm after orgasm. Keep her safe while I came inside her.

The release weakened my knees. I knew the mind emptied with his orgasms, but the physical sensation was more than I expected. It had direction. Forwardness. It was a barrier shattered with a battering ram.

"Wow," I said, jerking out the last drops. Doing this inside her would be more than pleasurable. More than a release. It would be a culmination.

As I dried off by the bed, I heard her leave her room. I waited for her to knock. Instead, the stairs creaked when she walked down them.

I knew how to do it. I'd watched him love her, felt a facet of what he'd felt, noted her reactions. I could give her so much more than he could—and without pain or control.

The man in the mirror was hers. He'd always done his hair with quick, efficient precision. I ran my fingers through it and went downstairs to convince my wife she was mine.

GREYSEN WAS STANDING at the counter, a hand on each side of the gurgling coffee maker.

"Good morning," I said.

"How did you sleep?" She didn't turn to look at me but reached into the cabinet for two cups.

"Not great."

"Oh, yeah?"

"I was thinking about how shocking this must be for you."

"I can handle it." She poured the coffee. "I'm just worried about you."

A cup in each hand, she faced me for the first time that morning. She froze for a second, as if seeing me for the first time, then dropped her gaze to the island counter, where she put the cups.

"I've never been better," I said. "Honestly."

"You've never actually *been*." She put sugar and a pitcher of cream near my cup and took her own, sipping it black. The dark patches under her eyes were mostly gone.

"Do you have plans today?" I asked.

"A little follow-up work." Waiting for something, she watched my hand resting on the cup. "Transcribing notes. Prepping for the meeting with the Mt. Sinai board. Should be done by lunch. Your coffee's getting cold."

Right. I hovered over the cream and sugar.

Both? Either?

Why couldn't I remember how I drank my coffee?

Had she set me up?

"Is this how it's going to be?" I said, taking neither sweetener nor cream.

"How what's going to be?"

"Testing me? Would Caden wear this belt with these pants? Brush his hair like this? Does he like it light and sweet or black and bitter?"

"Milk, no sugar." She put her mug to her lips with both hands. "Straight black on deployment." Her face disappeared behind the tilt of her cup.

I flipped the top off the sugar, dropped a teaspoonful into the black coffee, and replaced the lid with a clack.

"I have an idea," I said. "Let's do something fun this afternoon."

I took a big gulp. It tasted as sweet as spite.

MY STRATEGY WAS to act sane. I knew that didn't sound like much of a plan, but she needed to imagine herself with a man who was exactly the same as her husband, but different. Better. For one, I didn't want to kill her. I wasn't a simpering child encased in a rock-hard ego.

His phone rang.

No.

I had to stop pretending he still mattered.

My phone rang. It was Danny. I flipped it open slowly, trying to recall my history with him. Nothing came to me.

"Hello," I said.

"I'm going to be ten minutes late," he said. "You can warm up."

Late. He was going to be late. It was Saturday. What did he do on Saturday morning?

Shit.

"I don't think I can make it," I said. "I'm taking Greysen out to lunch."

"Yeah. With me and Shari at the club. We switched it to today. Did you get the email?"

Suddenly, I knew the password. I hadn't even wondered about it a second earlier. "Where were we meeting again?"

"We're playing the blue ball at eleven, and the girls are coming for lunch at the club at noon-thirty."

Blue ball.

Racquetball.

The club. Got it.

"Yes. Right. I'm sorry. It's been a little busy around here."

"Are you okay?"

"Yeppers!"

"Yeppers? You sure you're all right?"

Every word was a damn minefield.

"I have to go. See you there." I hung up before I had the chance to screw up good-bye.

DANNY'S LATENESS had given me a chance to both brush up on racquetball rules and remind Greysen she was meeting us for lunch. She knew already. She was a worthy adversary, and she'd be a worthier partner once I convinced her I was permanent.

As far as racquetball went, what my mind didn't know, my body remembered enough to pass.

"God, you suck today," Danny said when I missed the final shot of the final match.

"Tired." I wiped my face with the white towel I'd found in the gym bag.

"Maybe it's finally getting to you." He clapped my back as if this was an old joke he shared with my body.

LUNCH WAS at a round table in the center of the room. Shari had dark hair and brown eyes. She laughed a lot and smiled like a kid on Christmas when Greysen asked to see her ring.

"He picked the perfect cut," she said.

"It's gorgeous," my wife replied. The room was hot, and she'd stripped down to her camisole. Her skin was going to drive me wild.

"When are you getting your wife a rock?" Danny pointed his water glass at me.

"It's not a priority," Greysen said before my surprise could register. I didn't know if she was covering for me or the husband who hadn't gotten her a ring.

Danny turned to his fiancée. "Apparently they don't have diamond rings on the front lines, and when they came home on leave for the wedding, they didn't have time to get to Tiffany."

Greysen stabbed her lettuce. I couldn't tell how she felt about it, but I knew how I felt about it.

It was unacceptable.

"That's interesting." Shari tucked her hand in her lap. "Hey!" She brightened. "I heard you're a candidate for the new mental health division the hospital's putting in?"

"The Gibson Post-Trauma Mental Health Center," Greysen recited the long name as if it was a joke, but she was beaming just enough.

I put my arm across the back of her chair. I ran my thumb along the skin between her shoulder blades. Her eyelids fluttered at my touch.

Danny kicked me. "You didn't tell me."

"I'm one of two," Greysen said. "The board has my proposal. We'll see."

"I have something planned," I said to her profile.

She faced me. "Really?"

"To celebrate. I didn't want to blow it, but it was this afternoon anyway."

"Well, well," Danny said with a smile. "You do have a romantic side."

"I do." Though my words answered my friend, I said them to my wife.

"IF A DIAMOND RING WAS IMPORTANT, I'd have one."

She sat so far against the other side of the cab she was almost out the door. A sheet of plexiglass separated the back seat from the front, where the driver patiently navigated the miseries of Manhattan traffic.

"Maybe it doesn't matter to you, but it matters to me."

She held up her hand so I could see the gold band. "This is all that matters."

I'd spent hours trying to understand what consciousness was and when mine began. I'd had to do it without a single human reference. If this had happened to anyone before, I had no access to them to ask how I should feel or what I should think. I had no way of knowing if I was my own person or another man's setback. In moments like this, when I had to define the indefinable, I was the loneliest man on the planet.

The traffic on Fifth Avenue was almost sadistic in the accuracy of its obstruction.

"I wish I could marry you in that church right there." I pointed at St. Patrick's Cathedral.

She looked, folded hands pressed between her knees. "Why?"

"It's the richest, most beautiful cathedral in the country."

"I bet plenty of people who got married in there are divorced by now."

"Before Caden opened the bag, I could sense some of the things he wanted or knew. He wanted to marry you in that church, but there was a two-year wait list, and he thought he'd lose you if he waited."

Her head snapped back to me, eyes on fire, formidable. "Why would he think that?"

She said "he," but she meant "you."

"He took you away from your family. Away from the military. He didn't know if he'd do something to push you too far. He was afraid of losing you every minute of every day."

"That's ridiculous. If I didn't want to be here, I wouldn't have come."

"I know, but he worried. In any case, one of the other things I knew, or sensed, was an emptiness around the idea of your finger. Then the notion kind of coalesced into a ring of a certain color, which I'm debating about."

"I'm confused. I don't have a preference. I'm not a jewelry person."

"He knows, but he thought a ring was important. He had a very clear idea in mind, which is probably why I could see it. Color. Cut. Size. What I'm debating about is doing anything he wants after what he almost did to you. On the other hand... it's perfect, and you should have it. Not on your anniversary. Now."

"You were going to give it to me on our anniversary?"

She said "you" this time, instead of implying it, and I had to look away. I didn't want her to see my reaction or notice her therapist's curiosity parsing my expression. In doing so, I saw a dim reflection of my face in the plexiglass. Not my face. His face. Which was my face. I didn't have another.

How could she not think I was him? I looked exactly the same.

I was the face of the love of her life.

Maybe I should accept that.

Maybe I could use it to give her everything, including her peace of mind.

"I was going to give it to you on our anniversary," I said, taking apart her reaction to the pronoun.

She wore full therapist detachment.

Like I said. Formidable.

"I'm not a creative man," I continued. "I was a little stuck on the setting. But yes, the situation with the ring was getting fixed. I just think now is better than later. It's been a rough few months."

I pulled her hands out from between her legs. She accepted, folding her palms over my hand.

"It has been rough," she said. "But we're going to get through it."

"I know."

"No. You don't. You don't have to buy me things to keep me. You don't have to worry that I'm ever, ever, ever going to leave you." She squeezed my hand. "The man I married is honorable, strong, brilliant, loving. He has a sense of duty that was never drilled into him. It's just a part of who he is, and I admire it so much that sometimes it hurts to think about. He's out of my league. If anyone should worry, it should be me."

I could only shake my head. How could such a perceptive woman not see her own perfection? How was she not the person she measured everyone else against? It couldn't be false modesty, because nothing about her was false.

"Fifth and 57th!" the cabbie called, stopping. The meter ticked out a curled paper tongue of a receipt.

I shoved a fifty into the slot in the plexiglass. He could keep the tip. The cab ride had been worth more than even a rich man could pay.

Chapter Thirty-Five

GREYSEN

Caden had talked about a ring sometimes, asking me how I felt about huge stones or special settings. Apparently it had bothered him enough to seep into Damon's consciousness.

I'd never been inside Tiffany. The store was as quiet as a church, with lighting that made everything sparkle.

The sales staff knew their jobs. They pinpointed us as big spenders inside five minutes and brought us to a lounge in the back. The velvet couches were robin's egg blue, and the walls were papered in a textured off-white. They offered mimosas and water from Antarctic glaciers in crystal glasses. Amy, our saleswoman, was a white woman in her middle years with straight, black hair and sensible makeup. The man occupying my husband's body consulted with her out of earshot.

When Caden had first promised a ring, I shrugged it off. They looked silly with camo, and they distracted patients. The simple gold band was more than enough for me. My husband was the prize. Not the ring.

Damon didn't stand like Caden. His posture was more relaxed. Still confident, less rigid. The way he moved his hands was more expressive, and when Amy spoke to him, he looked at her as if he was listening fully, not formulating an answer before she was done.

Same perfect body. Same sky-colored eyes. Same full lips.

But different.

When he'd touched me at lunch, it was the same casually possessive stroke as Caden's but with a consideration, as if he was giving me the touch, not taking it.

I liked the Damon in Caden. I had to remind myself that when the illness was peeled back, they were the same person, and he needed help.

Amy went to the back. I sipped my water as Damon came to the couch.

"I told her I want you to have it now," he said with Caden's mouth. "Unless you want something custom?"

"No. I'm sure they have nice things ready."

He took a mimosa off the silver tray. Caden wouldn't have drunk in the day. If Damon was doing it, did that mean Caden wanted to? What had held him back?

"What time are you on call?" I asked.

"Tonight."

"Damon?"

"Yes?" He put down the glass.

"Do you know how to perform surgery?"

He raised an eyebrow.

"This kind of thing... this disassociation... knowledge and expertise don't always transfer between—"

"Yes, Greysen. All that stayed with me. I can still crack a cage."

"Before the MFI?" I barely knew what I was talking about, but that wasn't important. He had to know.

"Before the myocardial infarction and after you give me an MIDI."

Myocardial Infarction During Intercourse.

"You're not old enough for that."

"I will be. And it'll be you."

The tension release felt like cool Arctic water on a hot day. We had time. He wouldn't kill anyone, and we had time. I didn't know which fact reassured me more.

As if he felt my relief, he smiled and ran the back of his hand along my arm, clasping his fingers around mine at the end. "Did you think I'd cut someone open without knowing how?"

"No. I guess not." He tugged my arm, and I laughed. "Maybe."

He smiled and put his arm around my shoulders, pulling me into him. Brushing his lips on my cheek, he kissed my earlobe before whispering, "Silly Grey."

He ran his mouth back along my cheek and stopped at the corner of my lips. Our faces were so close his eyes had merged into one window to the sky.

"You can't," I said, and he jerked an inch away. "Promise me. No surgery."

"You don't believe me?"

"I believe you. But it's not safe. If you're retaining only ninety percent of what you need to know, or even if you know a hundred percent and your reaction time is different? Or your decision-making is different? You could kill someone."

Sitting back fully, he seemed to consider it. "I don't want to do that."

"My husband loves the operating room, but—"

"I'm your husband," he insisted.

"I know. But listen to me. Look at me. Do you love it? Right now. When you think about it, are you excited? Or can you live without it?"

He thought for a long time. Longer than Caden ever thought about anything before making a decision. "I'm supposed to love it. I know I am. But when you say I can kill someone? It bothers me. It hurts me to think about it. I don't know how I'd live with myself."

"It never bothered Caden."

"Do you think that's normal?"

"He was never normal."

Isn't.

He's not dead.

If the man sitting across from me noticed my use of the past tense, he didn't show it. Nor did he react to the unacknowledged flip side of my statement.

My husband's not normal. He's exceptional.

No, the gorgeous man who'd brought me to Tiffany for a ring wasn't hurt or excited. He wasn't insulted or resistant.

He was relieved to be normal. Not worse. Not inferior. Normal.

"So, it's a promise?" I put my hand on his knee. "No surgery?"

He gathered me in his arms, and I slid close to him. "It's a promise."

"Kiss me." My demand came in soft breaths against the fullness of his mouth.

The single eye got narrow when he looked down, and I thought he might refuse me, but he tilted his head and put his lips to mine slowly and carefully, as if savoring every moment.

Or maybe that was me.

He cupped my jaw in his hands. His mimosa was sharp and sweet on my tongue, warming the effects of the cold water. Rumblings of desire shook my spine, the space between my shoulders, my thighs, and the core between them. He kissed as if he meant it. Every graze of his tongue was intentional.

The door clicked open, and Amy came in with a tray.

A SQUARE-CUT EMERALD with a deep blue cast. Army green mixed with sky-colored eyes. Diamonds inset in the platinum band. A flawless stone. No price mentioned.

"You like it?" he asked as I watched the light in the gem dance on my finger.

"I can't even believe how much."

"Good. That makes me happy."

Amy brought a leather folder to the table. The part he was to sign stuck out, but the price was hidden under a flap. He lifted it to check the number then picked up the pen.

In the moment when the pen tip hovered over the receipt, a drop of tension resurfaced.

Damon might not have the same signature.

I didn't care about taking the ring home. It was nice but not necessary. But I didn't want him to be embarrassed if they didn't let him out the door with it.

He signed. *Caden St. John.* Every stroke was perfect. Same signature.

I had to take a sip of water to hide a smile I didn't want to explain.

"LET'S WALK," he said when we stepped onto Fifth Avenue.

Arm in arm, we navigated the late afternoon traffic of tourists and businesspeople. We looked in windows, imagining each other in suits and dresses. He decided I'd look great in everything, and I admitted the same for him.

The ring reweighted my hand, making me pay attention to it. At the steps of St. Patrick's, I couldn't help but stare at the way the emerald shone in the sunlight. "I really love it."

"Good." He took both my hands. "I want to tell you something."

"Yes?"

"I think you should call me Caden."

"Really?"

"It's just that I'm your husband. I know you think of me as some kind of sickness, but I'm still the guy you married. I love you just the same, I have the same... I don't know, skills, language, history. Same voice. Same face. It's me... just a different part of the same person." His hair dropped onto his forehead when he kissed my hands.

"I don't know if I can," I said. "You're different enough. I notice all the ways."

"Please try."

"Why is that important?"

"I want you to look at me the way you look at him."

Putting my hands on his cheeks, I laid my nose astride his. "He's my husband."

"So am I."

He was, and he wasn't.

But what if the other Caden didn't come back? The sharp surgeon who weaponized lovemaking and detached his mind from his emotions at will was the man I'd married. He was the duty-bound child of a dead abuser and found salvation in saving lives.

I didn't know this man on the church steps. Not really. I liked him. I enjoyed him. I lusted for him, but I didn't know him.

But did I know Caden? We hadn't been together long, and the circumstances were intense enough to skew both of us.

And Damon was a part of him, not a different person.

"I have an idea," he said. He took the first step up and pointed at the gilded double doors. "Come."

Tourists were pouring in and out of the cathedral. We went up the stone steps hand in hand and entered the dark narthex.

"Wow," I said with my face turned to the ceiling. "So high."

I'd been raised with a simple Methodist structure of stucco and industrial carpet. This nave echoed with marble and carved stone, with pews of dark wood worn at the edges. The stained glass wasn't smooth, printed color, but solid colors cut into leaded borders.

Damon led me down the center aisle. Trusting him to guide me, I kept my eyes on the ceiling. It was caught in a ribbed web of curves.

"It's so gorgeous," I said when he stopped.

"Look at me."

We faced each other at the foot of the platform that raised the gilded altar. His hands were under mine, holding them up.

The ring glistened when he put the tops of my fingers to his mouth and kissed them. "Be my wife."

"I am already."

"Say, 'I do,' Greysen. Say it to *me*."

A tinge of confident demand edged the last word. I'd become so used to it with my husband I didn't hear it anymore. When it was gone, I hadn't known enough to seek it out in Damon's voice. But there it was, banging like a gong.

He was Caden. The man standing before me, holding my hands, was the love of my life, and the man speaking to me was as much Caden as the man who couldn't leave me in Iraq without a promise.

It was him, and he needed to know I wouldn't leave him.

"Be my wife," he repeated. "Please."

Always. Always him. Two words for him.

"I do."

He looked down as if praying, gratitude shaping the contour of his shoulders.

I picked up his face in my hands. "Be my husband."

He didn't hesitate. "I do." He swooped me up in his arms, and my squeal echoed over the chamber. "You bet I do."

He carried me down the aisle and out the door.

HE CARRIED me up the steps, refusing to kiss me until I laughed. By the time he put me on my feet inside our door, I was one giant hormonal throb. He peeled off his coat, and I kicked off my shoes. He slid my coat off my shoulders, and I put my arms around him. He picked me up under the arms until my legs were wrapped around his waist and brought me up to our bedroom.

"I WANT YOU TO KISS ME," I said in the waning light of our bedroom. "Caden."

Before I had his name all the way out, his lips touched mine, brushing against them slowly, savoring every movement. He kissed my lower, then my upper, running his tongue against the sensitive pink skin.

The kiss wasn't a kiss yet, and he owned me. Every touch was devotion and care. He took nothing for granted, and as a result, I was swept up in a whirl of his attention.

He groaned, and I was lost. Therapeutic detachment had been left in tatters at the church and was shredded with that groan.

Having sex with this version of my husband was a bad idea in every way. I had no idea how the other personality would react. It might show preference. He was sick and needed my help.

Hands around my waist, testing the skin under my sweater, he put his tongue in my mouth, using it as a tease to draw me closer.

We were teenagers sprawled on the bed, making out in our parents' basement. It felt that new and unexpected. When he unhooked my bra, he paused as if making sure he hadn't done anything wrong. Still connected with him at the mouth, I nodded, and he ran his hands around me. I gasped when his fingers ran over my hard nipples, gently bending them. He pulled away so I could see him.

And I did.

He wasn't any man I'd met before.

He was the only man I'd ever loved.

I lifted my arms, and he pulled off my sweater and bra in one move.

"Say my name."

"Da—"

"No."

I was breathless, thoughtless, broken in ways I hadn't unpacked. "Caden."

Chapter Thirty-Six

DAMON

I felt him with the first appearance of the sun. The sky was orange, and I was buried inside Greysen for the fifth time since we'd walked in the door. She rode me, leveraging her arms against my chest.

He was stronger than I expected. More powerful. A horn blast at the ear of the soul.

He was heavy. Patient. Everywhere at once. Watching me fuck his wife.

Our wife.

He didn't speak, but he was there, and I was afraid.

I spit out a hitching breath that sounded like a hard *ch*.

Greysen picked up the pace, lifting her body and impaling herself. She was looking at me. Staring past me. What did she see? *Who* did she see? Was I imagining she saw anything past her senses?

Yes, I was afraid, but I wouldn't be intimidated. Only one person mattered, and she was straddling me.

"Make it hurt," she whispered.

"Make..." I couldn't finish. How could I hurt her?

"Please. Hurt me."

I felt his desire to answer her call, but I didn't know what to do. I'd sensed what Caden did when he caused her pain, but I didn't know how he did it. Mostly, I was sickened by the pleasure he got from it.

I pressed her clit harder. "Like this?"

She didn't answer. I took that as a yes.

"Come for me, darling."

She leaned on the headboard, sweet little breasts hanging in my face. I took one in my mouth. I felt him there, in the infinitely small space between her nipple and my tongue, as if he wanted to push us apart. I dropped my head back, watching my wife come in a series of sighs and groans.

"Say my name," I said as the pressure built.

"Caden."

The sound of his screams wasn't in my ears but my mind, splitting it apart with rage. I didn't like hurting him, but I didn't have a choice. He'd shred me from the inside if he detected a weakness.

"Again."

"Caden."

I pressed her down so I could plant myself in the deepest part of her.

But when she kissed me?

He lost his mind in a whirlwind, and for the first time, I felt guilty.

IN THE MORNING, I told her I was going for a jog. She believed me, because why wouldn't she?

Between my time in the corners of Caden's mind and the night I'd emerged, most of my memory was lost. I couldn't remember any specific situations or words from when I lived in the darkness. I didn't remember places or names. I remembered loving Greysen and the feeling of being in eternal torment.

When Caden had first heard me in the corners of his mind, he didn't know that I existed or what I was. He didn't know the torture of the bag, the psychic silence that had its own physical form, the way I could almost touch certain frequencies and shades. He didn't know what it felt like to get out long enough to be heard.

But I didn't know what I'd sounded like. I didn't understand the feeling of living on one plane while being invaded by another. My reality was the exact opposite. But for all its lack of experience and sensory input, I'd known what the hell was going on.

I put in earbuds and moved the pocket radio dial between stations, picking up the bell curve of signal, with a classical station on one end, a Spanish station on the other, and static for most of it.

Going south along the park, I entered at the 79th Street transverse. I cut right after West Drive and entered the Ramble, a net of tight paths slicing through a dense urban forest. I was alone. In the earbuds, a few notes of piano turned into a few words in Spanish and back to nothing but white noise and the deep huffs of my own breathing.

"I know you're there," I said.

The static changed in pitch, then dropped back.

"Listen. You can hear me. I know you can. I was you."

Whoosh. A steady buzz blew through the space between stations.

"Right. Okay. Listen." I stepped onto a narrow asphalt strip. "This doesn't have to be bad. We can work through it."

The extra hiss was steady.

"You're stronger in the morning. Tomorrow, when the sun comes up, I want to talk. I want to broker a peace. A truce."

No change.

A skinny kid in last night's club kit walked by, smoking a cigarette. I jogged, slowing when I was alone again.

"This is about Greysen. I get it."

The sun was up fully, but it was still too low to warm me.

"I know it's going to sound weird telling you this, but it's your body too. You shouldn't be mad. She loves you, but she loves me too."

A deafening screech stabbed my ears. I yanked out the earbuds.

I stood in the dappled sunlight, holding the white buds by the cord.

When I had been locked in the darkness, I couldn't have done that.

CADEN GOT quieter as the day went on, and when the sun set, he was gone completely. Greysen came up from the office as I was making dinner.

"What's that smell?"

"Garlic and ginger."

She lifted the lid of the sauté pan and let the steam rise over her face. "Wow. That's amazing."

I took the lid away and replaced it, kissing the condensation off her lips. "Can you get wine?"

"Sure." She went to the wine fridge and pulled out a bottle. "I've never seen you cook something so exotic."

"One of us has to start experimenting around here."

"I haven't killed you yet, Captain." She clicked around the drawer for the bottle opener. I reached in and pulled it out from under a whisk. "Thank you."

She held her face up for another kiss, and I obliged. When she placed her hand on the bottle neck, the stove lights glinted off her ring.

She saw me looking at it as she cut the foil. "I'm still not used to it."

"It really suits you."

She drove the screw in, put the ledge against the rim, and pulled, but the cork didn't cooperate.

"Here," I said, trying to take the bottle away.

"Back up, soldier. I have it."

"Really, I—"

She twisted her body around so I couldn't reach, even with my arms all the way around her, while she giggled, sticking the bottle between her legs and pulling.

"Let me help you." I tickled her, but she wouldn't give up.

"Stand down!" she cried through hysterics. "Stand down!"

Pop. The cork came out.

She held her arms up, impaled cork in one hand, vanquished bottle in the other. "Victory is mine!"

"Fine." I put two glasses on the counter, feeling somehow like the cork. As if I'd put up a fight and lost. She poured while I tended to the simmering chicken.

"You going to work tomorrow?" she asked, picking up her glass and handing me mine. We clinked.

"I have to keep a roof over our heads."

What happened to her face could have been described as "falling" or "darkening," but I didn't know what I'd done wrong.

"When was the last time you went to Blackthorne for treatments?" she asked into her glass.

"I don't remember."

"So, you were Caden... the other Caden?"

"I assume."

She put her glass down with a deliberate silence. "You need to make your next appointment."

"Why?"

"I'm going to wash up. I think the rice needs attention."

She pointed at the saucepot on the back burner. It was boiling over, frothing and hissing against the stove.

IT WAS deep into midmorning when the beeper went off. Caden hadn't pushed against me, so there had been no talk of a truce. With Greysen and I twisted together on the bed after falling in and out of slumber and each other's bodies for hours, I no longer wanted to negotiate.

She sat up. "Is that your beeper?"

"Yeah."

"Oh my God, I'm wiped out." She threw herself back on her pillow, and I looked at the number on the little black box.

"I have to go in." My muscles were heavy with sleep, and my eyelids wanted to close. I rubbed fog out of my eyes. "Jesus, that... *you*. Last night."

"Mm-hmm." Her smile transformed her face.

"I think I'm supposed to get a full four hours sleep before I go on call."

She pulled my pillow to her chest and hugged it. "Just tell them you can't. They'll find someone."

"I'll go in and see what it is first."

UNSTABLE ANGINA DISCOVERED during heart failure. Four solidly clogged arteries. Relatively young and fit otherwise. I could do this. Five and a half hours, then I could crash.

Really, it wasn't a big deal.

The patient had been prepped and anesthetized with a curtain between my line of sight and his face because we liked to pretend we didn't cut open real people.

The nurses called out vitals, and the anesthesiologist called out his own stats. My assisting was an older doctor who smiled at me under his mask. I'd met him in the scrub room. He'd offered to assist because he'd heard about me and had to see my artistry for himself.

"It's a go," I said, holding out my right hand. "Scalpel."

The tool was pressed into my hand.

Careful.

The voice was my own but not. It was his, and it came in the time between the beeps of the heart monitor. I glanced at the screen. It looked fine.

I pressed the blade to the skin.

It hurts.

I stopped. This time, the voice came from the hiss of the anesthesia tank.

Not me.

I handed the scalpel back. "Can I have a new one, please?"

"Yes, doctor."

On the tail end of the last syllable of the nurse's last word, his voice came again.

When you open them, it hurts.

A scalpel was placed in my hand, and without question, the voice was Caden.

Except I was Caden.

I smiled at my assisting and put the blade to skin again. I knew what to do, and I knew how to do it, but the gravity of cutting someone open froze me.

It hurts you.

I knew what he meant because he was inside me. Cutting people open hurt the soul. It broke a man into his component parts and spread them apart so they couldn't hear each other scream.

I cleared my throat. Stood straight. Placed the scalpel back on the tray. "I need a minute."

"WHAT THE FUCK WAS THAT?" Abramson blew into the lounge like a four-star general after a lost battle. I was just coming out of the toilet. It was seven in the morning, and he stank of aftershave.

"That was me not puking on the patient."

Abramson sat on the bench, shaking his head.

I stood at the end of the row of lockers. One was mine. How long would it be before I knew what was mine and what wasn't? Just when I thought I had this under control, the simplest things caught me off guard.

"What's been with you lately?" he asked.

I'm not myself.

I don't feel well.

I'm still adjusting to being home.

Any one of those would have been sufficient, but Caden would never admit to a feeling, much less a weakness.

"Nothing," I said, knowing he would have been cleverer in his denial. "You all right? How's the family?"

"Joy of my life." His tone was flat, as if he was dismissing my question. With that, I stopped thinking about Caden's locker and let his body find it. "How's Greysen adjusting to civilian life?"

"Good."

The combination was set to zeroes, of course. And, of course, the combination was one of the things I hadn't retained.

"They're talking about making you head of thoracic."

I turned to him. Heads of departments didn't have to see patients. Didn't have to cut living people open. I could.

But first, Abramson.

What would Caden say? How would he react?

He'd think he was entitled to the promotion.

"Let me know when they stop thinking about it." My fingers knew the combination, clicking it into place and snapping the padlock open.

"When you stop bailing on quads, that's when."

"I must be coming down with a stomach virus."

I opened the locker door and was knocked over by the smell of Greysen's perfume. It was heaven on earth. A reminder of why I lived and breathed.

"And looking behind you all the time," Abramson continued. "Staring into corners. That sorta thing."

I took out the suit and considered what Abramson said. Caden must have been seeing and hearing me. I wanted to reassure my boss. That was my instinct, and again, it wouldn't be Caden's. "Am I being considered for head of thoracic or head of Not-Staring-Into-Corners?"

"They're worried you have PTSD."

I closed the locker. I didn't know how Caden would answer that, and I didn't care.

"I'd like to see one of those suits do combat surgery in Fallujah and not have PTSD." Fuck this. I didn't want the damn suit. I grabbed my duffel instead and clicked the locker shut. "Eight days." I slid the padlock back in and snapped it closed. "I stood over bodies shredded and burned, choosing between legs and arms for eight days." I spun the combination, leaving a random row of numbers. "So, yeah. Maybe I have PTSD. I'm still the best."

That sounded exactly like him. Perfect.

"No one said you're crazy."

"I'll say it then. I'm crazy. But if you need someone to lead the department, you're not going to do better than me." I slung the duffel over my shoulder. "And I'm taking a few days off to shit out this virus."

"Take the rest of the week." He pressed his hands against his knees to stand. "Whatever you got in your gut, we don't need it."

"I'd shake your hand, but..."

"Go. Please."

We saluted each other, and I rushed out as if I had a virus to manage.

On the way out, I reviewed how I'd done. I'd been arrogant and entitled. I'd said I was the best. Even when I was talking about Fallujah, I hadn't admitted weakness.

I liked being Caden.

Chapter Thirty-Seven

GREYSEN

Leslie Yarrow was finally opening up, but not about the abuse she'd hinted at in our first session. She still pretended that had never happened.

"It was like this part of me that I had to keep hidden had had enough." She tapped her thumbs together, opting for the chair opposite my desk as opposed to the couch. Most of my military patients did. "You know, she was, like, 'Get outta the way. I'm coming through.'"

"And how did she manifest?"

Yarrow was my first PTSD patient with a personality disassociation as distinct and high-functioning as my husband's.

"She started creeping up on me at night. Like she was a ghost or something. She'd get stronger and louder, then she'd go away."

"What made her go away?"

Yarrow shrugged and looked at anything but me. My mind listed questions inappropriately leading to whether she hurt her wife to get rid of the "ghost."

"Beer." She kept her face down. Drinking was as shameful to her as masochism was to me. "Lots of beer."

"And what about the beer made it stop?"

"Well, she didn't like it. It made her hide. Good Lord, I feel like I'm talking complete nonsense."

"You're not," I reassured her. "Trust me. You're not the only one."

THERE WASN'T MUCH in the fridge for lunch. I could go to the Korean joint around the corner, order in, or make something from scratch, which wasn't how I wanted to spend my free hour.

The front door opened as I was on my way out. My husband came in from the rain. I was getting so used to his face as Damon that nothing about his posture or face seemed wrong or different.

"Hey, what are you doing home?" I kissed the storm off his lips.

"I took the week off." He kissed the storm onto my neck and shrugged off his wet coat.

"Why?"

Arms around me, wet face buried in my neck, he said, "Let's go on vacation."

I wedged my hands between us, laying them flat on his chest. "I have sessions."

"Cancel them." He kissed my ear, down my neck, to the place where it met the edge of my sweater.

"I can't."

"Why not?"

"People depend on me to keep my appointments. Speaking of..." He pulled up my sweater, and I encouraged him by running my fingers through his hair. "The Blackthorne office called. You had an appointment yesterday. You missed it."

"Oh, really?" He pushed my bra up and sucked a hard nipple. This was going all the way. "I'll reschedule."

"You should tell them what you've been experiencing."

"After I take you to bed." He popped my buttons and slid his hand under my panties.

"I have forty-five minutes."

HIS TOES LEVERAGED against the mattress, holding my knees up over the bed, he went in slowly, as if savoring every inch, then he pushed deep,. That had been the pace since we got to the bedroom, and I loved it... at night.

"Ten minutes," I groaned, bemoaning the lack of shower time. I didn't want to go into session smelling freshly fucked.

He stood over me, grinding at the same tortuous pace. I jerked my hips, thrusting faster.

"Don't rush."

Don't rush? Annoyance pushed arousal to the side.

"Rush or get off me."

He was shocked at first, stopping deep, then he pulled out and thrust forward hard, tightening his grip on my thighs enough to hurt, face clenching with effort.

"Yes," I groaned, touching his jaw. "Make it hurt."

Before I had a chance to register what was happening, he thrust again, leaning on my legs until they were bent against my chest, his fingers digging painfully into my skin.

So good. It was so good.

"Greysen," he said through his teeth.

"God, yes!"

In that position, he fucked me hard and fast.

On the tail end of it, with the pain of his fingers sweeping the orgasm away, his face held me still. He wasn't Damon. He wasn't Caden. He was both and neither. Red-skinned with effort, jaw tight, eyes open but looking inward with a desperate intensity. He let go of my legs and came inside me, tensing and relaxing.

Blood draining from his face, he dropped his head. I couldn't see him. I tried to make him look at me, putting my hands on his cheeks and forcing his face up. He resisted.

"Look at me," I demanded.

He wouldn't.

Rotating my hips, I flipped him over until I was straddling him. He hadn't expected it, so he didn't resist. Once he was on his back, there was no point in pretending I couldn't see his face.

He was Damon. He'd asked me to call him Caden, but it was Damon.

"What just happened?" I asked.

"I hurt you."

"Did you?"

"I'm not doing it again." He pushed me off. "So, don't ask."

I got on my feet and pulled my clothes on. The silence between us was pounded away by the rain tapping against the windows. He was on his back, feet dangling off the edge of the bed, hands over his eyes.

"You have the right to say no," I said, pulling on my shirt. "But something else happened."

"Yeah."

No elaboration followed.

"You need to reschedule Blackthorne for this week."

"No."

"Why not?"

He took his hands off his eyes and bent his neck to face me. "Because I'm fine."

"Seriously?"

"I'm doing fine. No one can tell."

"I know no one else can see it, but I can. You're not Ca—"

"Don't say it!" He flopped back on the bed. "I'll go. Just don't say that."

I checked my watch and sat on the bed. I put my hand on his stomach. "If that's not working, then do Jenn's art therapy. But something. You have to do something."

"Okay. Blackthorne. Fine."

"Promise?" I leaned on the bed.

"Promise."

I kissed him and went downstairs to meet a patient.

WORKING in the house was great. Couldn't beat the commute. But I had to make a concerted effort to get out. During his days off, Caden/Damon walked the neighborhood with me, ate lunch, took me out to dinner. We made love in the afternoon and evening.

It was great sex.

Really.

He had as much right to consent as I did. He could refuse any sex act in the lexicon.

But I didn't have to be happy about it.

In the midst of discovering new things about my desires through my husband, he turned vanilla, flipping like a coin. And I couldn't ask him again to hurt me. No means no. But, damn. Making love had become an adrenaline rush. Now it was nice. Fine. Better than adequate. But I found myself thinking of the sex right before the change the way one might think of an unappreciated ex-boyfriend who'd slipped through her fingers.

He went to Blackthorne on Thursday but didn't talk about it. I thought nothing of it. He hadn't talked about the treatments before the change either. So, I was surprised when he asked about Jenn's art therapy class.

"Are you ditching Blackthorne?" I asked.

"No, I just think it would be fun. You know, art's fun."

"It's in Hoboken."

"It'll give me an excuse to take the car out."

"All right then."

SURPRISINGLY, Jenn had a last minute cancellation in her Saturday afternoon *Intro to Mask Making for Vets*. I stepped into crisp spring air under a clear blue sky— not quite Iraq-colored, but close. Green leaves caught the breeze.

We didn't have seasons in San Diego. I'd experienced full seasonal cycles all

over the country. I'd experienced fall while stationed in Washington and
Maryland, but New York City in the spring was magical.

There were never parking spaces on our block. It was hard to say who grabbed
them, but it was always someone. The only empty space was by the hydrant.
Sometimes drivers parked their cars there in desperation, and they were ticketed
faster than leaves fell. So, when a black-on-black Ferrari pulled into that space, I
figured the driver was an entitled prick or desperate after hours of circling
the block.

The hazard lights flashed, and Caden got out of the driver's seat.

Jesus Christ.

I trotted down the steps. "What did you do?"

"You like it?" His smile was wider than the gate he opened for me.

"What happened to the Mercedes?"

"Traded it in. It's an old-fart car." He opened the door for me.

"This is crazy," I said.

"Get in." He held out his hand and helped me in. The seat was so low I felt as if
I had to crawl to get in.

It did smell nice.

And the leather seat had a way of hugging me.

He got in, and the dashboard lit up like a woman recognizing a lover.
"Comfortable?"

"Sure?"

"The seats adjust." He showed me the buttons. "You can heat them up too. And
this baby goes fast."

"There's traffic all the way to Hoboken."

The engine roared when he started it, and he winked at me because he
obviously didn't give a shit about traffic.

What do you look like?

THE CLASS WAS A QUICK INTRODUCTION. Deep work came later in the process.
Veterans sat at long wooden tables with unpainted white masks in front of them. I
was a vet, so I got to paint my own. I wasn't much of an artist, and I didn't want to
paint one, but Jenn had teased me into it.

"Therapists are the absolute worst at getting therapy," she'd said.

"Fine."

"Just let it flow. Don't think too much about it. If y'all stay around a few
sessions, you'll make a really nice one at the end. It's cathartic."

"Well, if you're promising catharsis."

CADEN'S MASK was pretty obvious—initially.

He painted the skin tone the same as his own. He laughed with me when he threatened to turn it into a clown mask and wear it home. He poked gentle fun at the hearts I put on the cheeks of mine; one was pink, and one was blue. With a whisper in my ear, he asked which heart was his and which was the other guy's.

"You're the same person, remember?" I whispered back.

For a minute, he worked on the eyebrows. I didn't see his expression or what he was going through in that time, but something changed while I wasn't looking.

He dunked his brush in the red paint and drew a fine, straight line down the center of his mask.

I watched through my peripheral vision. He was coping with the disassociation. Obviously.

Then he stopped painting altogether.

I nudged him with my elbow. "You're either having an epiphany, or you hate painting."

"I was thinking about the rose petals."

"The rose petals?" I pretended to pay attention to my work, but his voice had gone a touch deeper, and I listened to that change with my whole heart.

"In Iraq, I promised you a bed of rose petals."

I smiled so hard I could barely move my lips around words. "I believe you did scatter rose petals all over your bed that one time."

He held up his red-tipped brush. "I couldn't find this color."

"They were beautiful. Everything I wanted."

He filled in the curves of the line as if precision was important, grabbing my hand under the table and tightening his grip as if he were falling from a precipice and our connection was the only thing saving him from certain death. "When we met, I thought I didn't have anything of value to give you. You were perfect already."

"Are you all right?"

"I want everything to be right for you." He wasn't whispering. There was nothing soft about his tone, but his quiet words were for me alone. I'd forgotten what Caden sounded like inside the split, but as soon as I heard that voice, I remembered. "You smell like apples. Roses were wrong."

"Caden, look at me."

When he turned to dip his brush, I caught his gaze and held it.

He was confident. Arrogant. As sure as shit that he had a place in the world.

And under that was the man who needed me to be that place. He was fully himself, but I didn't know for how long.

"Next time," he said, "I'm going to get it right. It's going to be apple blossoms. If I could…" He smiled and shook his head at a silly thought he wanted to dismiss but couldn't. A contradiction in keeping with the whole man I married. "If I could write my love in the sky, it wouldn't be big enough. I'd run out of room. I'd fall out of the sky trying to say it all."

"We're going to beat this," I said.

"You're inhumanly strong. If I have to go through this, there's no one I'd rather do it with. But there's no one I'd wish it on less." He swallowed, closed his eyes, taking a long blink. When he opened them, he was the man I used to call Damon. He put his brush on the towel and pushed the mask away. "Let's open up the car."

———

THE NEW JERSEY TURNPIKE was a thick, gray ribbon in a lifeless landscape. Saturday traffic was nothing to speak of compared to the city, and we were at the on-ramp in twenty minutes.

"Where are we going?" I asked for the third time.

"Driving," he answered with manic cheer, clicking his signal to get into the left lane.

Traffic was moving at the speed limit, more or less, but as soon as he was in the fast lane, he gunned it. I gripped the sides of my seat. He tailgated the car in front of us until it moved.

"Slow down!"

"What's the point of a Ferrari if you can't drive fast?"

"That's faulty logic!" I had to yell over the roar of the engine.

"It's fine. Just enjoy it." He whipped to the right to pass, coming so close I cringed.

"Damon!" I shouted.

"Not my name anymore."

He looked at me. He was Damon. I was relieved a third personality hadn't shown up, but my husband didn't drive like this. He certainly didn't take his eyes off the road to look at me at ninety mph.

"Are you trying to kill yourself?"

Eyes back on the road, he wove between cars to go five miles faster. "Nope. I'm trying to live."

I put my left hand against the dash as if that would stop me from dying in a crash. "So you think—"

He hit the gas. The car easily accelerated to one-ten. "There's nothing fun about this?" He whipped his head around to look over his shoulder and cut right again. "Come on. Let's unstuff this shirt."

Glancing at me, then my ring, he smiled. He slammed on the gas and cut left to avoid a Toyota, climbing to one-thirty. Traffic was getting heavier. What was going on in this man's mind? Who was he trying to kill, and who did I have to convince to stop?

Maybe both of them.

"You're going to kill someone!" I said to Damon. "And you're going to kill me!" I added for Caden.

The response was immediate.

He tapped the brakes.

One-twenty.

Swerved to avoid someone.

One hundred.

Slowed down again to pull into the right lane as the speedometer dropped to eighty-five.

Panting like a runner after a sprint, I closed my eyes and tried to calm myself, focusing on my breath. The adrenaline flowed away, leaving me to release the tension in my shoulders and legs.

The car stopped. I opened my eyes. We were at a light at an off-ramp, then pulling into a gas station. He put the car in park.

"What. The hell. Was that?"

"That was me trying to live while I could."

I didn't ask what he meant. I was tired of asking how he was and what he was feeling.

"I'm sorry." He played with my emerald, brushing my hand in that casual way only he could.

"Speed limit on the way home, okay?"

"Sure."

But he didn't start the car. He just pushed the ring side to side. "You should take this off."

"Why?"

Our eyes met over the distance of the car, and it was miles and miles connected by the glass-blue ceiling of the sky.

"I can't hold it anymore. I'm not strong enough. He's coming back, and he's pissed."

I DROVE HOME. The man next to me was more or less silent. His fingers brushed mine gently, carelessly, doing nothing but feeling the nerve endings of our joined skin vibrate together.

Dissociative disorders had patterns but no lines, and Caden's was as blurry as they got. His secondary personality was still a heteronormative cisgender male of the same race, age, and nationality. The amnesia extended to events before his awakening but not general, objective knowledge. And the secondary, Damon, stuck around.

But just as Caden had felt himself disintegrating before Damon showed up, I could see it happening again.

He walked home in silence and up the stairs listlessly, like a man with the flu, and dropped himself on the bed with his arms out. I pulled off his shoes, his socks, unbuttoned his pants.

"Grey," he said at the ceiling.

"Yes?"

He didn't say anything right away. I slid off his pants.

"I thought I loved you, back in the darkness."

I came around the bed, intending to swing his legs around, but in addition to being naked, he was fully erect now, and I was only human. He looked like the man I loved. He smelled like him. Spoke with the same voice. He was a part of him, and the fact was, I liked him.

I may have even loved him.

"Really?" I got behind him and pulled his shirt over his head.

"But I was wrong," he said to the ceiling. "I didn't love you then." He picked his head up so he could see me. "I love you now."

Gathering my shirt at the hem, I twisted it off and removed my bra. "I know."

He watched me lower my pants until I stood before him naked.

"And I want you to know that I love you." I took the emerald off my finger and put it into the night table drawer.

I crawled over him and kissed his lips.

"If you're ever in the darkness again," I said, "don't ever doubt that I love you."

Even if I make you stay there.

Part Five

Chapter Thirty-Eight

CADEN

I could have made a list of things about this shithole, drawn up a few examples of what it was like. I wasn't much of a metaphor guy, but I could have made some about it. It was like being in wet concrete but also glue. It was like having my thoughts popped apart at the joints. It was like a chest spreader for the consciousness used so it could be filled with crude oil.

But the worst of the worst was being unable to sense her.

When we were separated by a few thousand miles, I could place her in my mind. Call up her scent or her voice. But after I let the Thing take over, I was cut off in a way I couldn't bear.

I pushed, but I could only move him when he was weak or with his permission. I caused him pain, but I couldn't get through.

There wasn't a depressive bone in my body, but now that my bones weren't my own, it was getting to me. Darkness pressed around me. It wasn't black. Not the absence of light. Darkness was the absence of anything at all. You'd have thought things and sounds and lights would press up against you, but no. Not like this. This emptiness had its own mass and density. It pushed me away and pulled me into it at the same time. Like being crushed under a black hole's gravity, I didn't know if it would compress me into a white dwarf or blow me into a million stars.

Greysen's voice sometimes came through the nothingness. Not a word or even a syllable. I couldn't detect a mood or tone. Vowels skipped and repeated. Letter sets ran backward and over each other, but it was her. I clung to it when I heard it, pointed my attention at it and let it take me into its meaningless sense, twist, change, swirl around in a space that didn't exist into the cries of my mother in the dark.

That time.

When I'd hidden her in the bottle room with me.

The floor was sticky and warm.

The smell of copper was everywhere.

And it was my fault.

DARKNESS AND I HAD A HISTORY. The bottle room was just another part of the house. I'd followed Dad down there to get wine or wandered in while Mom or Clarita, the nanny, did the laundry. The door looked heavy, but it wasn't. A five-year-old could swing it shut really easily. The light switch was on the outside, and when Clarita shut it off to go upstairs, the darkness had a physical thickness that pushed all the oxygen to the edges of the room. It was hard to breathe deeply enough to scream. But I did, and Clarita came right away to wipe my tears. She showed me how to open the door from the inside. As long as it wasn't locked, I had control.

I wasn't alone in the dark for more than two minutes. The story told over dinner was charming and forgettable. After that, I'd tested myself by going in there and shutting the light and the door to see how long I could last cut off from everything.

Pretty long, as it turned out.

I went to med school right out of college to prove to my father that I was smart enough, careful enough, precise enough to do what he did.

I joined the army to prove to him that I loved him even though he'd fallen from the North Tower and disintegrated on impact.

I deployed a second time to prove to my mother that I could last in a dark room as long as I had to even though she'd jumped with him.

When I climbed into that medevac, it was at the end of a series of choices meant to prove to Greysen I was worthy of her. I could go over the wire into a war zone. I was at least as much of a soldier as Ronin, her old fuck who she kept as a friend and who looked at her with more than friendship on his mind.

After eight days in surgery with her watching my mental state like a mother hawk, I'd taken her to bed. I knew with the same conviction that the sun rose and set that I loved her. But the bond was new, and I couldn't measure the length of the tether that tied us.

When I walked out to the airfield, the Blackhawk's rotors *thupped* in the night. Once I was up, they wouldn't go back just because I didn't belong there.

The pilot shouted code and swung back to look at me. "You the doc?"

"Yes." I put on the headphones.

The bay doors were open as we took off into the star-splashed sky. Shit. A person could fall out and drop into the darkness at the acceleration of gravity.

"Convoy hit an IED," the copilot said into my headset. "Full bird from the CSH is down. Medics won't move him without a field surgeon."

Spine injury probably.

"I'm not a 62B," I said.

The pilot let out a cuss of frustration, and the copilot spun around to face me. Taunting them kept me from imagining the minutes I'd spend falling before I disintegrated.

"We can't go back!"

"I'm a GS." I smiled, coding that I was overqualified, not underqualified. "61J."

"Shit."

"Shiiiit," the pilot agreed.

"You better take care of yourself, buddy. You don't belong outside the wire."

I gave him a thumbs-up. If I survived the helicopter ride, I had this. Save the colonel. Easy. I'd saved dozens of men. One more in slightly more inconvenient circumstances wouldn't be difficult.

IF I COULD JUST GET out of the house, Mom and Dad would be happy.

I was sure of it.

If I went to school far away, my parents would stop fighting. I saw them kissing and laughing all the time. At least, when they didn't know I was there. They had a sweet banter full of dumb jokes, puns, and shared experience.

Mom kept telling me I was a good kid, but it was hard to believe that when I couldn't do anything right. I never lined up my shoes in front. I left crumbs on the counter. I didn't close the milk when I put it away. Little things. Simple things. Anyone should have been able to do this stuff, but I forgot.

My dad was overworked. In the 1980s, there weren't many heart surgeons who could do what every second-year med student knew how to do in 2003. People came from all over the country for bypasses under the great Dr. St. John, and he didn't refuse anyone. He was tall, six foot three, with slicked back hair that tucked neatly into a surgeon's cap, smooth cheeks he shaved twice a day, and thin fingers you wouldn't think could land a punch.

When he'd point at something like the crumbs on the counter, we had a fifty-fifty chance of getting through to dinner. I'd closed the milk and put it away. Tightly wrapped the bag inside the cookie box, tabbed the slot, and put it exactly where it went. But I'd forgotten about the crumbs. It was always something. There seemed to be a hundred things to remember, and I always forgot one. Sometimes I was the one who discovered the unwrapped bag or the open milk, but the crumbs were hard to hide.

Mom would rush over and clean them, apologizing for being such a slob when she ate cookies. Mom never ate cookies. She bought them for me even though I left crumbs on the counter.

That's love.

I swear, she'd have eaten dinner for me if she thought she could take the blame for not putting my napkin on my lap or taking more food than I could finish.

Once, I heard them talking about how small I was. I was eight, and he was worried the kids at school would rough me up for my smart mouth. I think, actually, I wasn't big enough for him to rough up, and he was waiting.

But when the milk was open, he'd slap it on the counter. If it was full enough, it splashed everywhere. "How hard is it—?"

"Oh, that was me." She snapped a towel off the roll.

"—to remember—" He slapped it again. More splashing.

"Run along, Caden," Mom said quietly to me, jerking her chin.

"—to close the God. Damn. Milk."

I was gone before he finished the last word, padding down the steps into the dark, the speakeasy, the laundry room, the safe with the false back wall, the bottle room, thick with damp and dark, right under the kitchen where I could hear everything but discern nothing.

Chapter Thirty-Nine

I left my husband sick in bed. He really did have some kind of flu and was convinced nothing could heal him except the force of his will.

Damon and Caden had a lot in common.

He had a session with Blackthorne on Monday afternoon. I had a lucky cancellation and decided to keep his appointment for him.

"You're not allowed back—" the receptionist called from behind me.

I stopped hearing her when the security guard stepped in front of me. He was a few hundred pounds of muscle under a bald head, armed to the teeth, with an earpiece and no distinguishing identification. "Ma'am, you can leave now, or I can take you out."

"You can stop with the faux manners. I need to see Ronin Stevens."

"Please turn around and—"

"Now. And don't assume I can't put up a fight."

He reached for his gun.

"Whoa, whoa!" Ronin's voice came from behind the security guard's bulk. "I got it. Thank you."

"Yes, sir." The guard got out of the way without any lingering anger or insult. A real professional. Totally detached.

"What are you doing here?" Ronin asked.

"Looking for you."

"You could have called."

"I'm keeping Caden's appointment."

"It doesn't work that way, doctor." He smirked, but his grin disappeared when he saw how unfunny I found him. "You have to check in your phone."

He led me back to the reception desk, where I signed in.

"This way." Ronin led me down the hallway, unlocking the door at the end with his fingerprint.

On the other side of the door was another hallway lined with more doors and conference rooms. Two men in suits passed us. Through another door and another fingerprint, we went into a windowless section of the building. It was more populated. More women. More lab coats.

"Welcome to Blackthorne," Ronin said. "It's a little fancier than the combat hospital."

"But you can neither confirm nor deny it's nicer than the Pentagon."

"I can confirm it's nicer."

For all the people and all the computer screens, I could discern nothing about what anyone was doing. Of course, another door and another finger pad led to a more warmly lit, wood-lined area.

"Your husband comes through the First Avenue side, which leads to this area." He opened a smoked glass door for me. His office. Big. It didn't have just a desk but half a living room set. "Can I get you something?"

"I'm fine."

"Would you like to sit?"

"What's the Kool-Aid in this place? You're the guy who kicked my ass literally—put your boot on my ass to push me across the finish line in basic. Now you're using full sentences like a docent?"

"Sit the fuck down or don't." He sat on a love seat.

I got in the chair across from him and decided to dispense with the niceties. He knew enough already. "My husband is a careful man, but he's been thoughtless and stupid."

He pushed forward, tilting toward me to signal his ever-so-grave concern. "Are you all right?"

"I'm fine. He choked me during sex, which was nominally consensual, and I'd like to think he just took it too far."

His eyebrow lifted, but he didn't interrupt. Which was good. I didn't have the time or will to explain why I'd never gotten that risky with him.

"But last night, he took me down the New Jersey Turnpike at a hundred thirty miles per hour, in traffic, after doing the mildest vets art therapy session I've ever seen."

"Wow. I'm so sorry. I saw him last week, and he wasn't showing any reckless ideation. Did you get the idea there was a correlation with his sessions here?"

I kept my face impassive. "There's so much I'm not telling you. So much."

"Okay, well, I have the length of his session to listen."

"I didn't know there was talking."

"Not much."

When nothing more was offered, my curiosity morphed into something more urgent. Partly, I was offended by the secret-keeping, but I was also afraid of what was happening here. There was only one way to prove to myself I hadn't put my husband in danger.

"Whatever you do with him, you're going to do with me," I said. "Today. Now."

"I can't do that."

"Because I'm not reserve duty. Right?"

"And you don't have any of the indicators."

"Have you gotten valuable data from him?"

"Yes."

No elaboration, of course.

"You haven't gotten anything, and if you knew what I know, you'd either pull him out right now, or you'd change everything you thought you knew about what you're doing here."

One eye narrowed. He may have known about the disassociation. He may have even known Damon and Caden were battling. Or not. That's the thing about not knowing what you don't know.

"He told me you give him a shot, he breathes in a dark room, then fills out a form."

"I can neither confirm nor deny." When he smirked at his little joke, he crossed one leg over the other so tightly he twisted to the side. Joke or no, his answer was defensive.

"Let me breathe in a dark room," I said. "Without the shot or with a lower dose."

He tapped his thumb on his knee and considered.

"I see him change every day," I continued. "It's killing me. I want to save him, and I can't because one thing that doesn't change is his conviction that he has it under control. Everything else flies out the window. He's not the man I know."

"You met him during a war."

"And it broke him. That war broke him. He had no business there, and he has no more business in the reserves. If he goes back, I'm holding you personally responsible."

"It was his choice."

"Irrelevant."

He sighed. "You want to see what's going on here?"

"Yes."

"You haven't changed a bit since Iraq. Or basic even."

"You have."

Leaning on his knees, he got up. "I'll set you up to breathe in a dark room. No more. And I'll have Joan draw up an NDA."

———

IT TOOK three minutes to give me instructions on how to breathe and when. The room wasn't dark but had a single, warm lamp by a cushioned chair. I spotted four cameras in the corners.

A soft female voice came over the speakers, enunciating gentle syllables.

Soo–hoo soo–hoo

I closed my eyes and breathed as I had been instructed. When I got a little dizzy, I gripped the arms of the chair but kept breathing.

Soo–hoo soo–hoo

It wasn't quite hyperventilating even when the *soo–hoos* got faster. I was breathing deeply, definitely getting enough oxygen.

Part of me couldn't believe Caden sat still for breathing exercises in a windowless room.

He must really love me.

Faster.

Soo–hoo soo–hoo soo–hoo soo–hoo soo–hoo soo–hoo soo–hoo soo–hoo

Dizziness turned into a sort of stability. It was hard to keep up with the speed of the breaths, but I knew Caden did, so I would. And then it happened.

It started with a lightness that wasn't quite dizziness and the heaviness of a gravitational pull from my chest. I was sitting in a room, in a chair, inside my body. I could feel the chair under me. I could feel my hands on the arms. But I was elsewhere. Everywhere. I expanded inward from a tiny planet in a dust mote of a universe into an infinitely vast space inside myself.

I still knew where I was and who I was; it just didn't matter. And not in a flip or dismissive way. My identity was as irrelevant as a fly buzzing half a world away, yet even that fly was an indelible part of that eternal space inside me.

To describe it as overwhelming would have implied I was confused or amazed. In fact, the feeling left me sane with dispassion. I was overcome with righteous awe, knowing I was part of a truth that needed no explanation. Even as I was facing it, I hesitated to say I was touching God because I believed in endorphins and serotonin, not bearded white men in the clouds. But my hesitation didn't change what happened.

The pace of the *soo*s and *hoo*s slowed, and though I was disappointed the experience was over, my lungs were keyed to breathe with the voice. My consciousness deflated like cigarette smoke curling back into the butt. I was in a chair, in a room, in a building, in New York.

The woman's voice stopped, and soft music played long enough to keep me from jumping out of my seat when the door behind me clicked open and Ronin came in.

"Well?" he said, leaning on the far wall.

"Bioenergetic breathing. I can't believe you got him to meditate."

"The trick is to not call it meditation. You've done it before?"

"I read about it as a PTSD therapy."

"So, it was positive?" he asked.

"If I believed in God, I would have introduced myself."

"Not everyone has that kind of experience.

"What's Caden been experiencing?"

"That's privileged."

"I'll just ask him." I stood.

"He won't remember. It's an incidental result of part of the treatment. And before you ask which part, it's classified."

I sat back down and rubbed my temples. "He has a distinct dissociative split."

"Another personality?"

I'd thrown him. The stillness of his expression came from a conscious decision not to broadcast a reaction.

"With another name," I said. "Can I presume you didn't notice?"

"He didn't seem that different."

"He is."

"Alternate personalities are more distinct, with made up histories—"

"I know."

"—different nationalities, genders—"

"I know, Ronin."

"—ages even."

"Are you mansplaining?"

He slid down the wall until he was in a crouch with his fingertips tenting between his knees. "He needs to keep coming."

"Because you expected this."

"In experimental medicine, you get hit with the unexpected all the time."

Fuck him and his excuses.

"He thought he was being watched," I said. "And between whatever is in the shot and the bioenergetic breathing that peels away identity, you gave form to the watcher."

"He needs to keep coming," Ronin repeated.

"Why?"

"To learn to control it."

"So it's not dissociative disorder?"

"Not as commonly understood."

"And the cure?"

He turned his hands until the palms were up in submission to his ignorance.

CADEN HAD BEEN HEARING voices before he ever went to Blackthorne, so as much as I wanted to lay the entire problem at Ronin's feet, I couldn't. He might have had this his whole life. The Caden I'd met at Balad Base could have been a single, dominant personality. He could have split at any time and held on for the two years I'd known him.

I sat on the boulder Jenn and I had climbed repeatedly and listened to the birds chirp. The breathing exercise had relaxed me in a way. I was clear in a way I hadn't been since Caden admitted he thought he was going crazy.

Assume that was a single personality of many.

Assume it was a dominant personality but not the primary one, which would be depressed and anxious.

Assume this split happened in adolescence, after a trauma with his father.

Now try to fit all of it into a clinical model of dissociative disorder, and what do you get?

A bunch of square pegs and round holes.

He was a surgeon, and a brilliant one. Split personalities were a minefield of unknowns, but generally they didn't share that kind of professional knowledge.

Captain Caden St. John of the US Army had not been a cardboard cutout. He'd been a real man. Complex. Contradictory. Sane.

Damon was not a child, a woman, or a stock white male character of any kind. He was as real as Caden. In a Venn diagram of the two men, there was a huge overlap of knowledge and desire. And if I was feeling brave, which I had to be, a Venn diagram of those desires would overlap most significantly over ownership of me.

I walked home in a fog, waiting for lights when no one else did, face cast at a forty-five-degree angle, trying to unravel this mess. I wanted to blame Ronin, or the army, or his father, or myself, but the responsibility wouldn't stick on any one thing.

He was home, sitting in front of the television, when I got there. Caden never watched television, especially not a dumb sitcom. And if he did, he wouldn't laugh. He'd sneer at it. He'd find it charming when I laughed, but he wouldn't stay to see what I thought was so funny.

"Hi," I said. "How are you feeling?"

"It's a *mycoplasma* infection. I picked up some Vibramycin." He turned away from the screen and looked me up and down. "Fucking horse pills. Where did you go?"

"To see Ronin."

"Cool." He turned back to the TV. "How is he?"

Caden always had a slight note of jealousy when it came to Ronin. He hid it under an abiding respect for me and a trust in my motivations, but it was always there, under the surface.

Damon didn't seem to care one way or the other. That was good, in a way. Also troubling because it highlighted the fact that I was having a conversation with my husband and myself at the same time, and those two conversations were in direct opposition.

"He's fine. Says hi."

"Great." He muted the TV. "I have some bad news."

I sat on the couch. "Tell me."

"I have reserve duty this weekend."

"I thought you were IRR?" The reminder that he'd signed on for the reserves was sandpaper on raw flesh. I hadn't wanted this, and I would be nervous about him for the duration he was away. "Individual reserve doesn't do specialty training."

"There's a surge. They called. What am I supposed to do? Say no?"

"Where?"

"Walter Reed." He turned the sound back on. "I can't get out of it."

The Comparison Train stopped at Duty Station to add another car. The Caden I'd married, whether he was a full personality, a primary, or some other unlikely split of the same, would never have tried to get out of a commitment. He took his duties seriously.

"We'll dig your uniform out of the basement."

He muted the TV again and turned to me. "Can you get it?"

"Sure."

I'D AGREED to go downstairs because my husband had asked me for an easy favor and I had no reason not to. He wasn't feeling well. I'd make him soup and pour him tea. I'd tuck him under blankets and put a hot water bottle between his feet. But going down the narrow wooden stairs, I realized he hadn't asked me to get his uniform because he was sick but because he didn't want to go down to the basement.

I left the box on the bar and went to the hidden safe with the false wall. The bottle room was still bare, still cold, still psychologically the farthest away from the rest of the house. I turned on the light and crouched through the door. It was a prison with concrete walls lined in cylindrical honeycombs. Just a little too short to stand straight. A little too small to stretch your arms. A hard, cold womb.

The little boy had hid here until he was too big to feel safe in it. Or was that the reason? He'd never told me why or when he'd stopped hiding here, only that he had. I ran my fingers along the dusty concrete shelf the depth of a whiskey bottle and pushed the door closed halfway so I could see the back of it.

There was no knob, obviously, since it was disguised as a wall from the other side. The sheet metal had holes in the back where a lock would have been. If the people in the bar were hiding, the lock would be on the inside so it would seal the room away from the cops. My first thought was that young Caden had locked it one too many times and his father had taken off the bolt. But when I looked at the outside, I saw something I hadn't noticed before. The lock had been moved to the outside, where it would be visible from inside the safe but not accessible from the bottle room.

That didn't make sense.

Until it did.

I PUT the box on the living room floor. My husband was curled up on the couch with the TV muted and his eyes closed. I touched his face. It was cold and clammy with a breaking fever.

"I got your uniform."

"Thank you," he said, tucking my hand under his head as if he wanted to trap it for use later.

"We should make sure it still fits."

"It will." He closed his eyes. "I'm the same."

He wasn't. Not at all.

I left my hand under his cheek and poured the rest of my body over his, feeling the rasping rise and fall of his breath under me as he slept.

Chapter Forty

DAMON

At Mt. Sinai, I managed to get out of surgery all week, but the military wasn't as forgiving when a guy felt under the weather. I had to put on the clown suit and show up.

I'd forgotten some kind of saluting protocol and done it at the wrong time. I was missing a piece of my uniform. My shirt placket didn't line up with my fly. No one yelled at me. I was an officer. But one of the nurses took me aside and told me, touching all the things that were wrong, in a voice sticky with sex. She had long, blond hair up in a twist and languid blue eyes. She didn't have a ring on her finger and didn't seem to care about mine. She laid her hands on my chest and told me where she was staying on base.

I was a handsome guy. I'd forgotten that. When I fought with Caden in the mornings, I thought of him as the good-looking one, the charming and smart one.

But when the nurse left without a promise or rejection from me, I realized I had all those attributes as well. Handsome Caden, who was usually quiet by afternoon, growled at the edges of my thoughts.

Don't.

I hadn't considered cheating on Greysen for a single second. Not until I felt his demand.

"Stay down," I said softly, "and I won't."

I SAT through horrifying sessions with new techniques for chemical burns, shattered bones, and amputations. I was sick to my stomach most of the time, but I understood and retained it all.

If I couldn't get the thoracic position in New York, I was switching to pediatrics or something less gruesome. Maybe I'd go back to school for psychiatry and copractice with Greysen. Maybe I'd leave medicine entirely.

The nurse who'd corrected the placement of my captain's bars sat two rows ahead of me and to the right. She looked around, making eye contact. Her name was Trina.

Don't.

He wasn't staying down.

In the break between training and dinner, I took a jog with my earbuds jammed in tight and the radio set to static. I carried the phone so it looked as if I was talking into the mic on the white wire.

I ran the track around base, speaking his name, daring him, prodding him to come out. He didn't come until the sun touched the horizon and I was so tired I feared I'd have to wait until morning.

Don't.

"There you are."

Don't.

The effort this took him tugged at the corners of my perception.

"Don't what? Fuck the blonde?"

I'll kill you.

The static, and his voice inside it, got louder and lower.

"How? You're getting weaker in there. Every morning I swat you down like a bug, and you're quiet all day."

I'll tell her.

"Grey? No, you won't." I made a left as if I knew the base, which I did. Until that moment, I'd forgotten I'd trained here before my first deployment. "Here's what I need—I need you to go away. I need you to die."

I stopped in front of a long building with a row of doors. It looked like a motel, but it was reserve officer barracks. Each one had a bedroom with a desk and a bathroom. Lieutenant Trina Anderson was in #434. The windows were dark. She'd be at dinner with everyone else. I stepped off the curb anyway...just to prove a point.

Stop.

He said it with a burst of static, like a nodule of deeper white noise that promised lucidity but didn't deliver it.

I stopped, planting my feet in the street. "You stop fighting me in the morning. You stay down. Forever. Because there're plenty of women in New York, and with this face, I can fuck all of them until you scream."

After a beat, my radio shut off completely, as if he was taking the signal into the darkness with him.

THAT NIGHT, after sitting across from Trina's flirtations at dinner, I lay in bed alone.

Flirting with Trina had been relatively painless. I'd done it to see if he'd come back, and he hadn't. Either he was tired from the conversation through the static, or he was doing as I'd demanded.

Could I cheat on Greysen if I had to? When he was pressing against me, I couldn't allow even a shred of doubt, but with him gone, I had to consider all the options.

Assuming I'd get away with it, assuming I'd never hurt Greysen, would I? Was crippling Caden worth fucking any woman but the love of my life?

When I'd gotten back from the medevac, having successfully moved the colonel and gotten him onto the Blackhawk, I watched it fly away toward Baghdad, and waited with a brigade unit. I had been fine up until that moment. Then there was blood everywhere. I knew blood. I knew the smell of shiny copper and glucose when it was fresh and the cloying scent of old wet pennies, rotting eggs, and curdling milk when it was stagnant in a wound. This was fresh. It was everywhere. It was dark.

Could I cheat on Greysen to rid us of him?

In the space between putting the colonel on the Blackhawk and the little bird coming to lift us back behind the wire, there was blood. I went into blackness. Copper and wet blood and darkness so viscous it pushed against me.

I must have been doing something right. I got a commendation.

But whatever I did about that blood was lost. I got back to Balad, but I didn't remember how. I only remembered choking on darkness as I tried to swallow what had just happened. I couldn't wake, and I couldn't get it down. I was going to die. I couldn't breathe. I sank deeper, throat plugged. The whistle of the mortar coming over the wire woke me.

Greysen was outside. I clawed out of the thick fugue for her. Only for her. Like a man in a dream waking in a panic, opening the door as the mortar exploded and she fell.

She'd woken me from a nightmare, but I'd never swallowed the memory. I'd coughed it up and left it behind to catch her as she twisted and fell with a piece of metal stuck in her chest.

She thought I'd saved her life, but she'd saved mine.

I fell asleep before deciding what to do.

SUNDAY MORNING. Caden didn't fight me. The threat had worked for the time being, but now I knew how to get to him.

Last day, last hours in the monkey suit. I had to demonstrate an emergency tracheotomy to a group of field medics, then I was home.

I knew how to do a tracheotomy. I explained it with words and slides, then I stepped up to the gurney, where a dull-featured mannequin lay under a white sheet. The medics gathered around.

"So, I'll do it first, then you all will," I said. "Once you've assessed that a trach is necessary and would increase chances of survival, you hyperextend the neck." I pulled back the chin. "If the neck can't be extended, you can't find the cricoid cartilage, so no trach. Locate the Adam's apple, and the cartilage should be about an inch down. You can feel it." I picked up a scalpel. "At the middle point between, make a horizontal incision."

I knew what I had to say and do. The training and the procedure were beneath me, to be honest. The eyeless thing on the table was made of plastic with precut incisions.

But when I put the blade against its neck, I froze.

It wasn't human. Not even a dead human. It was a doll.

I couldn't cut its throat as a demonstration of an actual incision in an actual living person.

They were waiting. Eight of them. Sixteen judging eyes. I'd told them I was doing it first, and if I didn't make the cut, I'd be a laughingstock. If I puked right there, which I wanted badly to do, I'd be Captain Buffoon, subject of unflattering stories.

Poor Damon.

He'd come through the door opened by my panic, slicing through the veil between us with his disdain and confidence.

"Half an inch long," I stalled.

Cut, then open with your finger.

The finger. Even if I got through this step... I cut off the rest and clamped down on Caden, tightening my thoughts into a narrow lane. I knew it wouldn't work. He was there.

"Half an inch deep."

More stalling, and they knew it. They weren't looking at the mannequin. They were looking at me. They wanted to get their hands on the procedure, but they needed to see it first.

It'll take me thirty seconds.

"Are you all right, doc?" one of them asked.

They were a haze of eyes and need. I couldn't discern which one had asked.
I wanted out of the situation.
I admitted to myself that he could fix it.
I didn't know that was an opening.
I didn't know he could get through it.
I didn't know how slippery it all was.
By the time I realized it, everything was dark.

Chapter Forty-One

GREYSEN

Caden never called me with his flight info. I had no idea what time he was coming home Sunday or Monday. That was the thing about life in the army. You were in control until they had you. At least as a full-timer, there were no illusions. You belonged to something bigger and more demanding. You submitted to that ideal, or you found another way to spend your life.

I left Caden a note on the counter in case he came home, and I went to the board dinner. I was still one of two candidates, and this was another hoop I had to jump through.

Bob Abramson had said he'd send me a car, but I didn't know he'd be in it.

"Oh, hi," I said when I saw him in the back seat of the limo.

"Fancy meeting you here." He smiled. The driver closed the door behind me. "I hope you don't mind sharing." He adjusted in his seat, crossing one shiny shoe over the other as he stretched his legs.

"It's fine. How are you?"

"Fine, fine. How's Caden? He was pretty sick when I saw him on Monday."

"Well enough to go to reserve duty."

"When is he coming back?"

"Tonight or tomorrow morning. He'll join us later if he gets in."

"Good. So, I wanted a minute to talk to you about something we're considering. I've brought this up with your husband already."

"Okay." I tried to wipe my voice of the keen curiosity I felt.

"He's on the short list for head of thoracic."

"That's great. He'd be wonderful."

"And we're… I mean, you can see… we're considering you for a leadership position in the mental health unit. You're quite a pair."

"Thank you."

"You met in the military?" he asked.

"He was a surgeon at the combat hospital. I was brought in with my unit ostensibly to help with front line trauma, but I spent more time helping the medical staff do their jobs without sleep."

"So, he was a trauma surgeon then? Why did he go back to heart surgery?"

"Did you ask him? I'm sure he'd tell you."

"He presented it as a preference."

"Ah, you're asking me if he was good at it."

"Not exactly."

Denials aside, that was exactly what he was asking.

"I'm a psychiatrist. I can't tell one thing from another in the OR. But I'll tell you what I witnessed. The first offensive filled the hospital for eight days straight. He was…" I shook my head with the memory of him, hour after hour, with the wounded coming by the dozen, a blur of blood and burned flesh. "I've never seen anyone work like that, one after the other. Day after day. He got a commendation for it. He also got me."

"I don't blame him for not wanting to do it again," Bob said.

"That level of dedication and sacrifice… he brings it everywhere with him." I wanted to brag about Caden for another hour, and I could have, but we were close to the restaurant. "He went outside the wire."

Surgeons weren't supposed to go off base. It wasn't safe, and they were too valuable. But after the first offensive, while we were dancing around couplehood, he'd jumped on a medevac when Colonel Brogue's convoy hit an IED. He'd come back bloody and never talked about what happened.

"What does 'outside the wire' mean?"

"Off the base. Ask him about it. I wasn't there. I was just…" I let the sentence melt into a smile. "It was a war. Everything was haywire."

Our love had been forged in military routines that offset the hazards of flying mortars and sniper fire. The trouble we were having now, inside a stable civilian life without routine or danger, was the exact opposite of the world we'd met in. We'd have been crazy to not have problems.

———

"TINA'S ON HER WAY," Bob said as we got in from the cold. "Five of the board will be here in fifteen minutes."

"Two missing? Milchenko and Karlsson?"

"How did you guess?"

"They both live overseas."

Before I had the last button undone, Bob moved behind me and took my coat.

"Thank you," I said as he gave it to the maître d'.

I heard Bob's voice say something nice, but the words got pushed into a perceptual border framing a man standing in the doorway. He wore a navy suit with a wine tie and crisp white shirt. He was pressed, fit, straight-shouldered, and proud.

I choked back a throatful of spit, losing control of my emotions.

"Dr. Frazier?" Tina spoke my name from a few light-years away. She must have shown up when I was lost in the vortex of my husband.

I stepped toward my husband to make sure I was seeing what I thought I was seeing. He pulled me forward, holding me up, moving my legs with his intensity. Only one man could do that.

By my last step, I knew I was right. It was him.

"Caden." The name was thick with tears I held back.

"Greysen." That voice. How could everyone within earshot not do his bidding?

"I missed you."

He cupped my jaw, and I leaned into his hand like a kitten. I didn't care who saw it or what they thought. He was home. I was home. It was over.

I blinked, and a tear fell onto my cheek. Wrong place and time. But I had no control. I didn't sob or blubber, but that drop needed to fall.

Caden ran his thumb over it, making it disappear as the other eye let one go. "Later. You'll cry again."

"Promise?"

He nodded ever so slightly and then changed.

I didn't understand why the change happened, but it was unmistakable. The hard line of his lips softened. The cold calculation in his eyes turned compassionate. The precision of his posture turned relaxed. A line of concern appeared between his eyebrows, as if my tears upset and confused him.

At the speed of thought, he went from king to vassal.

Like that, Caden was gone.

"WHAT ARE YOU DOING?" he asked as I frantically yanked clothes out of my dresser and threw them on the bed.

"I'm not calling you Caden. You're not him."

"Hang on, hang on."

I went into the bathroom for my toothbrush without letting him tell me what to hang on about. I'd gotten through dinner and the cab ride home. I'd gotten up the damn steps and into the bedroom without saying a word. I wasn't hanging on another second. Not until he blocked my way out of the bathroom.

"Talk to me," he said.

"No."

"Why not?"

"Get out of my way."

"Tell me why you won't talk to me."

"Because I don't know who I'm talking to."

He put his fingers to his chest. Left hand. The one with the ring. Damn him. "Me. You're talking to me."

He reached for me, but I put up my hands. "Back up."

"Okay, I—"

"What have you done with him?"

He shot out a laugh and rubbed his eyes. "That's hilarious."

"I fail to see the humor."

"Yeah, I know you fail to see it. He is me. I am him."

"Bullshit."

"You should see him. He's losing his emotions. They're draining out of him and into me."

"But I thought you were the same."

"We're both half a person. But this half?" He tented his fingers on his chest. "This half is the human half."

I put the toothbrush down and crossed my arms. "We have to get out of this house."

"Why?"

"I don't think you've been completely forthcoming about what happened here. With your parents."

He looked confused.

"Your father," I said. "You said you hid from him in the bottle room, but the lock's on the outside."

"It was always that way."

I couldn't tell if he was lying or if he believed what he wanted. What I knew for sure was that if I wanted the painful facts, the bathroom in the middle of a fight was the wrong place and time to get them. "I think coming back to this house broke you apart, and if we don't leave, it's going to break us apart too."

"I don't want that."

"I don't either. But it's happening." I gathered my things from the vanity. "We never had a honeymoon. We had a few good weeks in a war zone. I fell in love with you in the middle of a crisis. I committed to you, and I take that seriously. But I didn't marry half a man." Pushing past him, I went back into the bedroom, where I picked my clothes off the bed.

"We should take a vacation," he said. "Let's see what happens outside the routine."

"No."

"Why not? I read this article about sky diving in the Grand Canyon—"

"Are you fucking kidding me?" I stood with an armful of clothes.

"What?"

"I'm terrified of heights, and so are you, by the way."

"I am not."

Was this his way of getting back at Caden? Setting up a nice relaxing vacation doing the one thing that would freak out his other half?

"I'm too busy for a vacation right now." I brushed past him.

"He's coming back," he said from behind me. I turned before I walked out. "I can't hold him anymore. We've negotiated a sort of truce. An uncomfortable cease-fire, I guess. He'll be back."

Caden's body leaned against the doorframe. Captain St. John didn't lean. He stood straight. Even near collapse after eight days in the combat hospital OR, he'd shouldered a confidence bordering on arrogance. I'd carried him through tragedy in Fallujah, but standing in his family home in Manhattan, he seemed weak and beaten. Still beautiful. Still perfect. But altered, like the same sentence spoken in a different language.

"I'm sleeping in the guest room."

"I love you," he said.

I saw it for what it was. Manipulation. He wanted to tie me tightly to him with his words. He wanted to use my response to relieve his sense that I was untwisting the knot.

There was no reason not to soothe him, but I wasn't feeling predictable or pliable.

"Yeah. I hear you."

Without another word, I crossed the hall into the guest room.

I DIDN'T SLEEP. I kept staring at the blinking red dots of the clock, wondering what the fuck I was doing.

Myth number one about therapists was that we were any better at managing our personal lives than our patients. I had tons of words and advice. I could listen to people for hours. I could hear underlying motivations and detect falsehoods even when the patient believed them. I could see a situation from all sides unless I was one of the sides.

Detaching myself from the situation, I could deconstruct the factors driving Caden's affliction.

An abusive father...

...who had lived in the house he now occupied....

...after a traumatic stint in the military...

...exacerbated by an experimental therapy...

...and a new wife.

Did the last two help or hurt?

And where did his father end and his mother begin?

And was I making it worse?

I couldn't complete a thought without a stab in my chest where I missed the egotistical jerk who'd shocked me with his vulnerability. That surprise was the location of his split.

The light in the room went from blue to gray as the sun lightened the sky.

There was an insistent double rap at the door. I turned around, but before I could grant permission, it opened.

Caden stood in the frame, bare-chested, feet set apart, his shape crossing the corners of the rectangle. "Why are you in here?"

I bolted upright at the sound of his voice. "Caden?"

He entered with an erection growing in the morning light. "Did we fight?"

He didn't remember. Whatever happened with Damon was hidden from Caden while he was in the bag. The correct therapy for a dissociative disorder was transparency between personalities, but this wasn't a normal break.

"I had a cough, and I didn't want to wake you."

He stood at the edge of the bed, pressing his right thumb into his left palm as if massaging it. "You looked beautiful last night," he stated matter-of-factly, slipping the sheet off me. "I can't believe I didn't come home and destroy you."

"It's early. We have a few hours."

He looked my body over, as if deciding where to fuck me first. Leaning on the bed with one hand, he used the other to pull off my underpants. I closed my legs so they came off easily, and he opened them.

Oh, Lord.

He was here—inside this not-Damon half Caden.

This wasn't safe, but I wanted it so badly I could taste the sweet sting of danger.

Lifting my shirt over my breasts, he ran his fingers over my hard nipples, then along the silver scar over my heart.

"Don't come until I tell you to."

He went to the bathroom. I straightened myself on the bed. He came out with a hot washcloth. He folded it twice and placed it between my legs. The rough, warm cloth felt good against me.

He kissed me, and I wrapped my legs around him. We had so much to talk about. Leaving the house. This other person he'd been. The changes between them. But not yet. Not while he was pushing inside me, fucking me all over again. Not while the hot, rough cloth was wedged between us.

He went slowly, grinding deep.

"Caden," I whispered.

"No coming. Not until I say."

"Yes, okay."

Slowly, gently, he fucked me to maximize the friction of the cloth.

"I'm close," I gasped.

"Not yet."

"Okay, but..."

"Hold it."

His strokes got faster. I was going to burst open. I needed to.

"Take the washcloth away, please," I begged.

He came inside me with a satisfied grunt. I was so close, but he was pushing too shallow now, and when I shoved my hips against him, he jerked away. He got up on his knees, dick still hard and slick.

"Caden. What—?"

"Hold it until tonight, Major."

"This is bullshit."

"You wanted to try control."

I lay there with my mouth agape and my T-shirt pulled over my breasts. He smiled as if my frustration was entertaining.

<hr>

MY SOUR MOOD when he got downstairs was probably exacerbated by the ten pounds of unreleased orgasm I was holding between my legs. I got him a cup out of habit, but when I heard him behind me, I wanted to shove it up his ass.

"I don't know what you two share with each other," I said, not looking around.

"Us two?"

Still Caden, but in the quiet kitchen, with only my annoyance to interpret his tone, he wasn't Caden either. I looked at him, dissecting the pieces. Was this a third?

No. But the primary person was changing somehow.

Annoyance turned to fear, and fear turned into exhaustion.

"I want to get out of this house," I said.

"Why?" He acted as if I'd lost my mind, as if he hadn't heard the request before. He and Damon weren't communicating the nitty-gritty.

Now I had to say everything twice. I'd probably have to describe what I wanted twice, argue twice, explain twice.

"Forget it."

I went to leave, but he grabbed my arm. "I'm not going to forget it."

"You should. And you should start by letting me go."

"No."

I jerked my arm away. "You can't just waltz in here and start demanding my time, my attention. You can't do what you did this morning. I'm not a fuck doll."

"If you think this morning was me treating you like an inanimate object, you have no idea what that means." He was calm, too calm, in the face of my simmering heat. That alone took me back a step. "If you were a toy, I wouldn't bother with your pleasure. You wouldn't have the option to say stop."

He talked about rape like a sniper talking about bullets. Everyday instruments of death.

"This morning's game?" he continued. "It was designed to push you." He sipped his coffee black, without blowing on it. "I found your limit. You still haven't recognized it."

He threw back a big swallow of coffee. I knew it was scalding. He shouldn't have been able to do more than blow and sip.

"Who are you?" I asked.

"What do you mean?"

"What's your name?"

I recognized his smile. The right side stretched first, and the left caught up. I recognized the little nod of assent, as if he and I got the same joke.

"Caden Kevin St. John. Captain. First Medical Brigade. 065-43-0987."

"You're not the man I married."

"You didn't marry a man."

"What?" The alarm in my head came out as a whisper.

He stood over me, close enough for our clothes to touch. I didn't step away. I wouldn't show fear.

"You married the army. Your plan was to consummate it by making a family with another soldier, but instead, you chose me. Admit it. You miss your husband."

I got his point, but all I heard was the content of the last sentence. "I do," I said with a quivering chin. "I miss him so much."

He brushed away my tears. "I don't like it when you're sad."

I pushed his hand away and wiped my own tears. He didn't like it when I was sad? Jesus. Caden was a passionate and protective man. Caden wouldn't see my sadness as one of many menu options.

"I watched my mother give up control to the military," I said. "I watched her get dragged all over the country because Daddy had to be somewhere. And when he deployed, I watched her sit there crying because no matter how you sliced it, he'd betrayed her. Every time. He betrayed her for the army every damn time. So, I decided I wasn't marrying a man who would betray me. I would beat him to it, whoever he was, by enlisting. I was taking the mistress first. But... look at this. Look at us. The army broke you and handed me the pieces."

He laughed. "I'm not broken."

I crossed my arms. He was so cocky. So sure that between us, he was the healthy one. He was intolerable like this, and all I wanted was to take him down a notch. Cut him at the knees.

I should have thought about it as a therapist, not a wife, but like I said, I was sour.

"Where were you yesterday?" I asked.

"Reserve duty." He said it without the disdain Damon had. That was my Caden. Finishing what he started was to be done without complaint.

"How much of it do you remember?"

"Everything." He sat back down and took his coffee as if he'd won the argument and could move on with his day. "I trained medics in an emergency trach. Came home American Airlines flight 45 into JFK. Plane was three minutes early. I came home, changed. Met you for dinner with the Mt. Sinai board. Had a few hours' sleep. I fucked you. Anything else?"

"Before this morning, when was the last time you fucked me?"

"You doing an intake?"

"What day of the week is it?" I snapped an amber bottle from the corner of the counter and placed it in front of him with the label facing away.

"Monday. Why?" He wasn't agitated. He seemed more thrown off course and trying to correct.

"Patient is male. Late thirties. One eighty and change. Symptoms include low-grade fever, persistent dry cough, chest pain. General fatigue."

"Blood tests?"

"*Mycoplasma.*" I hoped I'd gotten it right. I was an MD but not a GP.

"Okay. Walking pneumonia. I'm really curious what you're trying to prove."

"What do you prescribe?"

"Any allergies?"

"None."

"Ten-day course of doxycycline. Preferably Vibramycin."

I'd piqued his curiosity, and I understood my risk. If he had a flawless memory of his time as Damon, he'd laugh at me. If he didn't, his reaction could be anywhere between mild amusement and deadly rage.

Worst course of action ever.

I'd try to talk a patient out of it.

Not recommended.

Doctors make the worst patients.

"Agreed," I said as I turned the bottle until the information faced him.

He picked it up, rolling it between his thumb and middle finger to read the label.

I waited. He read it again. Checking the date, maybe.

"I have a busy day," I said. "You think about where your week went. Take a deep breath and tell me how you feel. You try to remember taking five of those and leaving the rest when you went to reserve duty. You, Caden St. John, MD, didn't take a full course of Vibramycin because the pills are big and you didn't like it. We'll reconvene over dinner to talk about what's broken."

He put his arm in my way when I tried to pass him.

He wasn't angry. He was something. But anger assumed some kind of passion. This version of Caden didn't have passion. He had facts and realities, and this was the reaction he had when one of his realities was challenged.

Driven, maybe. Compelled. Motivated to correct the incorrect.

"Let me go." My voice had been drained of hysteria, matching his emotionless state. The tone was the only nonimpulsive action of the morning.

"Before this morning," he said, not moving his arm, "when was the last time?"

"Friday. I was on top."

The effort to muzzle his reaction was betrayed by a blue fire in his eyes.

"You ate my pussy like a champ," I continued. "Then you put your dick in me real slowly. You were gentle and sweet. We flipped. I straddled you and fucked you. You wanted me to come, but I couldn't ask you to hurt me since it upsets you. So, I dug my fingernails into my palm until it bled. Then I cupped your balls while you came."

"You made that up."

"Did I?"

"I have him under control."

I slid the bottle toward him. "Count the days."

"Greysen." He stretched his leg out and leaned into me. Even sitting on the barstool, his posture was so straight he was close to my height. "You're mine. Mine. I own your body. It's the only thing I have that I care about."

"Nobody owns me."

"Since you retired your commission, I own you." He stood, crowding me against the kitchen bar. "I own your orgasms, your pain, your pleasure, your hunger. I've put my fingers on your heart and felt it beat. It's mine. I own this body. Every inch of it. Every bone. Every organ. Every drop of blood."

"I'm not a fuck doll."

"You mentioned that. And maybe I wasn't clear. If you were a compliant object, you wouldn't be worth owning. Only me. Not him. Don't be confused, Greysen."

"He's you," I said.

"He's not me. I won't tolerate him inside you."

The ultimate betrayal is the self against the self.

He was growling against my neck.

Mine, mine, mine.

Chapter Forty-Two

CADEN

The pleasure of making her submit to an orgasm after denying her one was matched only by the gratification of doing a complication-free quad.

After the disconcerting discussion preceding her surrender, I was left with the knowledge that he was still there even if I couldn't feel him. He'd stolen days from me. He'd stolen her body. Her pleasure. He'd steal everything if he could.

That idea was insulting enough. He was weak. Emotional. His thinking was imprecise and fractured, yet he'd managed to overtake me, and this fact was the most galling.

After the quad, I was listing his weaknesses in my mind, placing his inability to cut into a plastic doll at the top of the list, when I froze, bloody gloves over the bin.

Days and days had been stolen from me. The man everyone knew as Caden had done things I couldn't remember, and I'd just stood in an operating theater, over an open rib cage, as if I had a right to do a quadruple bypass.

What if he engulfed me during surgery?

What if I'd gotten information yesterday that I needed in the OR today?

I dropped the gloves in the bin and let the lid close.

What happened that I didn't know about when he fucked her?

THE SHOWER IN THE DOCTORS' lounge had gone cold, but that would help the swelling. I unwrapped the towel from around my left fist and flexed my hand. Pain jolted me from the second knuckle down to the wrist. Strained palmar ligament. Grade one sprain.

Did I need a grade two? I was under no illusions that Damon would be gone in a week, but I didn't want to risk permanent damage. I turned off the shower, and the pressure sent a shot of pain up my arm.

I hadn't punched a tile wall impulsively. I'd done as much thinking about it as I'd needed to do. I didn't want to kill anyone, but if I reported my decline in functioning, I might never be allowed in the OR again. A sprain would give me a chance to fix this before it ruined my life.

The pain jolted my every move. Toweling off. Getting dressed. I wrapped it and closed the bandage with butterfly clips.

That was that for now. I reported the sprain. Wilhelmina asked how I'd injured myself, and I told her I'd slipped in the shower. She *tsked* as she took me off the schedule and joked that I should sue. Someone would be put out, but no one would be dead.

I had two weeks to fix this mess but no clue how to do it.

Mental brute force didn't work. Switching between who I really was and Damon—who I wasn't—was going to kill my career. Even if I got the position in thoracic, I'd need to remember case details if I wanted to advise correctly.

With an hour before my Blackthorne appointment, I walked to clear my head.

I had two things.

Greysen and surgery.

He threatened both.

This Thing could ruin me.

But Greysen had been right. She'd said it before, but I'd gotten more analytical in my approach and I was ready to hear the truth. He was me. The illusion that the Thing was a separate entity in the corners and white noise was gone. It was me. My mind. I'd cracked and split. I couldn't battle a man named Damon any more than I could wage war against myself and win.

Why hadn't I admitted it before?

I stopped at a store window on Fifth Avenue to consider a necklace for Greysen. It would drop between her tits just so. I could engrave it with my name. It would mark her as mine.

In the reflection, behind my face, stood St. Patrick's Cathedral.

We'd never had a real wedding. We'd run to San Diego, taken our vows in her parents' yard, had a party, and gone back to Balad. We went back to our lives as if the wedding was a private affair.

I knew Damon was the same person I was. The fact that I was crazy didn't mean I didn't have common sense. Yet I wanted to publicly take her as mine, not his, even if he was me.

Walking again, I tried to piece together a strategy. My sense of self was crashing around me. I should have been depressed. Despairing. My fundamental realities should have been shaken to the core.

I felt nothing but a need to solve the problem.

And when my mind made the words "I feel nothing," I meant it literally.

Besides a need to own my wife, a sharp pain in my wrist, and a motivation to fix what was broken, I felt nothing.

THE BLACKTHORNE APPOINTMENTS went like this:

The elevator took me up to the forty-fourth floor, where double glass doors led to a carpeted reception area. They'd decorated it in light wood and alabaster tile. I never waited. A receptionist, sometimes male, sometimes female, always young, led me through a door with a code into a room with tiles and furniture that was slightly darker. Everyone wore strict business attire. The next door used retinal ID scans on both of us and unlocked to a dim hallway with dark brown paneling. Anyone walking around wore a lab coat. The incongruity of the coats against the hotel-like hallway was mitigated by the person I was passed off to, who usually wore something more formal.

I was led to a different office by a different person every time. They asked about my week. They asked about any illnesses or injuries. Travel. Medications. I mentioned the wrist and the antibiotics. I got a shot they identified as cyanocobalamin. A.k.a. B12. Improves mental state, concentration, nerve cell health.

They never asked about my mental state except to ask if I was improving. There was no follow-up when I said I wasn't. Those questions came in the form of a post-session questionnaire that I usually finished quickly.

"This isn't helping," I said in the black room as someone whose name was irrelevant took the sensors off my head. "It's actually a waste of time."

"Your scans are improving," she said.

"I want to see the scans."

Somewhere in the back of my mind, I was convinced they'd show my brain bifurcated as the solution to the problem.

I CHECKED MY WATCH. I'd been in the dark room for an hour. It had felt like five minutes. The exercises were getting longer, and my perception of them was getting shorter. Maybe I was achieving a facility with them, or maybe I was getting muscled out by a little wife-fucking worm.

We were intercepted by a tall blonde in a business suit. "Dr. St. John," she said, turning to the tech once we stopped. "I have it from here."

The tech nodded and went through a nondescript door.

"Yes?" I asked.

"Our director would like a moment."

"Do I know them? I've never seen the same person twice."

From her deliberate nod, I knew that was by design. "I believe you've met Mr. Stevens."

RONIN SAT across from me in the same spot as our first and only meeting. A manila file sat on the table between us. I flexed and released my hand to work out the pain. Closer inspection revealed abrasions as if I'd punched a wall.

"How are you feeling?" he asked.

"Fine, thank you." I didn't want to talk to Ronin about my problems now any more than I had when I let Greysen talk me into meeting him for dinner.

"What happened to your hand?"

"Fell on it."

A woman came in with a pitcher of water and lemon and left without a word.

"I'm told you want to see your scans?"

"I do," I said.

He nodded and poured water into two tumblers. A lemon wedge blocked the pinch in the lip before tilting and landing in my glass with a splash. "Well, here's the problem: your scans are classified."

"My scans are...? It's my brain. How can the scans be classified?"

"All materials from this project are classified."

"What are you doing here, Ronin? Building some kind of super soldier or something?"

"There was a movie about that." He smiled. "It sucked because it wasn't believable."

"That would explain why this shit isn't working."

"How do you know it's not working?" he asked.

"The problem we came to you with isn't fixed."

He took a sip of water. I left mine alone. I didn't need the dramatic pause.

"You've noticed we don't ask you deep questions about your life."

"Yes."

"That's by design. We're observing changes in the way the brain works so they can treat PTSD without therapeutic interference. It's quicker and more effective."

"And has mine been changing?"

"Yes."

"It's getting worse," I said.

"How do you mean? Your questionnaires are vague."

I never knew if he was reading the post-treatment surveys, but I had been vague on the off chance he did. Good choice. "I mean there's no change. I'm learning to live with it. That's all."

"Your last two sessions were different apparently."

"When was that again?"

I earned his suspicious look. I was fishing, and he knew it.

"Last two Thursdays. You were more forthcoming than usual."

"I wasn't feeling well." I held my hand out for the file even though I could reach the file myself. "Let me see it. It'll refresh my memory."

Ronin handed it to me. "I hear you had reservist training this past weekend."

"Yes." I opened the folder. The standard pages were there but filled with my handwriting. Flipping to the previous session, I recognized the one-sentence answers.

"How was that?"

"Uneventful."

Back to the previous week, with Damon's puling and complaining. Jesus Christ. You'd have thought the flu was going to kill him. And he went on and on about the effects of the breathing. How he'd felt *happy*.

Happy.

If feeling like the king of the world with all the uplift of power and weight of responsibility was *happy*, then I knew less about him than I thought.

He is you.

He reported a marked improvement in the feeling of being watched and complimented the treatment as if he'd been delivered an unexpectedly delicious meal.

He wants out of the sessions.

With every passing answer, his desire to stop coming to Blackthorne became clear.

At least to me.

Because he's you.

Why did he want to stop? Was he afraid of losing? Was he running scared? Or was he sure that he'd won already?

I had a flash of... I couldn't call it a thought. A flash of a thought process that was unlike anything I was capable of. The process was nuanced in webbed layers of connections. It was like seeing the fourth dimension. It did not have a decision at its end, only a path that wound between who I was and who Damon was.

The course of it was a series of questions and unactionable conclusions.

You invented Damon.

You are not you.

Don't hide.

You have a problem.

You didn't know she was pregnant.

I'm not hiding anymore.

I closed the file.

The enemy is you.

"Thanks. I think I was running a fever."

You're crazy. Shitbird crazy.

That awareness, like the ones before it, opened up to new paths where emotion crisscrossed sense, sending my thoughts in a direction before I could identify which one I was on.

Greysen deserves better than crazy.

And with that, a cluster of thoughts between the two personalities, all shaped like fear.

"Our team would like to do another assessment," Ronin said. "Like the one you did before we started. To measure against the benchmark."

The nuanced, complex thought process shut down steadily, strand by strand, until everything aligned into tight, sane little rows.

"Not today."

"You can set up an appointment for whenever you'd like."

"Fine," I said. "That's fine."

We shook on it.

Chapter Forty-Three

After I finished my last session, I could have stayed home and cooked dinner. I could have waited for my husband just to see who showed up.

Instead, I called Colin. He wasn't around. I left a message and made plans to meet Jenn. As a result, I wound up at Jenn's place in Williamsburg, Brooklyn, waiting for Colin to show. She had a loft on the second floor of a brick townhouse. The only things that made it a loft were an open floor plan, high windows and ceilings, and concrete pillars where walls used to be. She shared it with two active duty nurses who were on short deployments and had it all to herself for the time being.

"Who did this?" I pointed at a huge canvas above the low bookcase. It was an abstract with a yellow chevron pattern exploding inward on a blue sky cracked with blood red.

"Me."

"Wow."

"You like it?"

"It's really powerful. I can feel it shaking."

"It's me after the mortar hit."

My silver scar ached as if it had been called out from oblivion. I touched my chest as if that might soothe the memory of the blast, the dead silence after the shattering explosion, the intense ringing in my ears as Caden carried me to the hospital, the pain in my chest with every step as the shard of metal got closer to my heart, piercing my lung, leaving me gurgling blood.

"That was bad," I said.

"It was nothing compared to what the medevacs were bringing in," she replied. "I felt guilty for having PTSD over it."

"The mind does what's necessary for survival."

"Ain't it the truth."

There was a knock at the door. I went to the stove to stir the pasta while Jenn answered it. The penne had floated to the top of the water like soap suds, crowding together in a herringbone. I stuck the spoon in and stirred, forcing them to swim to the bottom before they fought their way back up.

The mind did what was necessary for survival.

A boy locked in a concrete box underground might invent a story of his own strength and detachment, which he has to believe in order to survive.

A war might break that detachment, or it might drive the wedge deeper.

Pushing the spoon down, I drove the penne to the bottom only to watch them pop stubbornly back to the top. Every one a survivor.

And what had happened the day Caden went outside the wire? Why had he returned so soaked with blood I'd thought he was shot? Had that broken him? Was there an instant before and a life after?

When did a man break?

Why did I insist there was a single moment?

How did I not know better already?

"Oh, Caden," I said into the hot steam. "I'm failing you."

The tears came hot and fast, salty as the water I stirred, lost in the scalding vapor. He needed me, and I'd failed him over and over, treating him like an adversary instead of a human soul who needed my unconditional love.

"Grey." Colin's voice came from behind me. "Grey!" Closer now.

I wiped my cheeks but not in time.

He leaned over the counter to face me. "Why are you crying?"

WE'D PUSHED the half-full plates to the center of the kitchen island long ago so we could take the wine more seriously. I'd lost my appetite completely once Colin sat me down. Once I was outed as crying, I buried my face in his coat, blubbering like a fucking baby. He didn't complain about the streak of snot I left on it. He was a good brother.

"Right before my eyes," I said as Jenn filled my glass again. "He changed standing there, staring at me. No trigger. Nothing happened. Just bam." I snapped my fingers. "Like that. Then we had dinner with the board."

"Did you get the job?"

"The what?"

"The Gibson Unit?"

"If I'm reading the tea leaves…" I put my glass in front of my face to hide my smile. "It looks like I got it."

"All right!" Colin cheered. "Took long enough."

We all clinked to my future, which was unsure at best but looking up at worst.

Jenn leaned over Colin to fill his glass, and when he turned his head to thank her, he took a deep breath and closed his eyes a second longer than a blink.

"Thank you," he said.

She looked down and smiled. You couldn't see a blush on skin as dark as hers, but the way she tried to not look at him too long but couldn't help herself at the same time? Well, I'd seen that before.

"And after dinner?" Colin asked, tapping his fingers together as if he was counting something.

"Same until the next morning." I didn't tell them about the tone of the sex or how hot it was for me.

"Then he was cold Caden?"

"Yes. Ever since he got back from reserves, he's been switching."

I didn't tell them about the name Damon either. I didn't want either of them to slip in front of him.

"So." Jenn sat when her glass was full and the last drops had spilled out of the bottle. "Cold Caden is demanding, possessive, competent, and precise."

"Dutiful. Honorable. Confident," I added one for each finger. Naming their traits had been soothing. It forced me to face the differences between the two personalities and hold them both in my mind.

"Warm Caden is emotional, romantic, devoted?" Jenn wasn't holding a pencil, but I knew she was taking mental notes. "Impulsive."

"And manipulative," I added.

"Sounds like him," Colin said.

"Which one?"

"Both," Jenn and Colin said at the same time.

I sipped my wine. "I feel like shit for telling you this."

"You weren't doing yourself any good holding it in," Jenn said. "I mean, come on, how many studies do you need? How many ways do you have to hear getting it out is better than keeping it in?"

"You're a psychiatrist, for fuck's sake," Colin mumbled.

"Oh, fuck off." I kicked him. "I was trying to protect someone I love."

"And killing yourself in the meantime." Jenn reached across the island and squeezed my arm. "If it was just about him, I'd say you need to shush it, but it's eating you alive."

"It is." I put my head against the cool stone of the counter. The room was spinning, and my thoughts were butter-thick. "I don't know what I'm going home to."

"Depends what time you go home," Colin said.

I picked up my head too quickly and braced myself against the edge of the island. "What do you mean?"

"It sounds to me, if I heard you right, that he changes at sunup and sundown. Cold Caden is awake in the day. Warm Caden is awake at night. Your dinner probably started just as the sun set."

"Oh, my God." I stood. Stumbled.

"He's a vampire," Colin added glibly.

"This is not funny!" I shouted, thrusting every ounce of sobriety I had left in his direction. "I'm not living in some movie. This is not a book. This is not a teenage fantasy. This is my life, and it's not funny. My husband, who I love more than anything... who I gave up everything..." I couldn't finish the stupid, selfish thought. "He's not a pop culture monster. He's sick. And I have to help him."

I laid my hands on the counter to steady myself, but the counter moved. Jenn got under me before I fell.

THERE WAS A HEADACHE, and the headache was the alpha and omega. It hurt when I moved, breathed, or had a thought. I hadn't had that kind of headache since the morning I left for basic training. My friends had taken me out to a goth club and tried to talk me out of enlisting, but it had already been too late. I was committed, and there was no going back. But I drank to their efforts and went to Fort Jackson with a knockout of a migraine.

I had a bottle of water lodged under me and a bottle of Advil in the hand that fell over the side of the couch onto the hardwood.

I wanted to know what time it was, but more importantly, I had to get the Advil bottle open.

The arrow on the top and the arrow on the rim were already lined up. I popped it off with my thumb then wiggled the bottle from between the cushions and my rib cage. The seal had been cracked.

Jenn was a good friend, but that kind of attention to detail was all Colin. I took three Advil and put my watch in front of my face. Blinked. Arranged my thoughts around the spike in my head. Blinked again.

07:21 hours.

First session was at 09:30.

I could make it.

Jenn came in from the hallway in a yellow robe with a towel on her head. "Good morning, sunshine."

"I have to go." I got up. No, I didn't. A sledgehammer hit my head, and I sat back down.

"Take it easy. Have coffee and let the Advil do their thing."

"I can't believe everything I told you last night. You're never going to be able to look Caden in the eye again."

"I just did." She handed me a cup.

"What?"

"He's waiting outside."

"How—?"

"You think I'm going to put you on my couch for the night and not tell your husband where you are? I will not be party to breaking you guys up."

"But you think we should?"

"No. No, no, no." She sat on the edge of the couch. "Don't put words in my mouth. I never said that, and I never thought it. He loves you. He's fucked up from the war, and he loves you."

"Not just the war." The coffee scalded my tongue, but I drank it anyway. I didn't think I'd told them about the bottle room, but I wanted to make sure.

Jenn shook her head and looked into the middle distance, holding her cup with both hands like a safety blanket. "Yeah, well, it's rarely just the war. Anyway. Listen. If I had someone to send you to, would he go?"

"What's the specialty?"

"Dissociative disorder."

"It's not that. Not textbook at least."

"I'm not pressuring you. Just tell me if you want the referral."

"What's with you and Colin?" I changed the subject.

"What do you mean?"

"Are you obfuscating?" I managed to sit up. "Or do you really not know what I'm talking about?"

She shrugged. "I'd rather not talk about it."

"Did he—"

"No. Not Colin. He's fine. And no. There's nothing. We're friends."

That was a bald lie, and the twist of her mouth after she said the word *friends* proved it.

"And you don't want to talk about it?"

"Right."

"Didn't you spend all of last night raking me over the coals for keeping things in?"

"I did. And it was fun. But you have a husband downstairs waiting for you, and he's the cold and possessive one. So, for him to give you enough distance to wait out there instead of in here? You gotta respect that by moving your ass off my couch."

She slapped my leg and held her hand out to help me up.

I WAS BORN in May of 1974, the middle of three. The only girl. My father was twenty and in Vietnam when my mother had me in a base hospital. When she cried out in labor, the nurse snapped and told her she was disturbing everyone. It was time to stop crying like a baby and grow up.

She did both.

My father didn't hear about the nurse until I was eighteen months old and my mother mentioned it in passing. He was home from the war, but he'd brought the war back with him. We were still living on base, which meant my dad could grab his rifle and storm to the hospital maternity ward where, before the era of viral clusters of mass shootings, there were no guards.

He didn't point the rifle at anyone and he didn't find the exact nurse who'd said the exact thing, but he gave the entire staff a good talking to before he was hauled away to spend six months in a white room "getting better."

I had to break my wrist to consider a career in mental health. Maybe it was avoidance. Maybe I had to shed a crust of ideas about what being a soldier meant. But really, it should have been obvious I knew the effects of a war on a man's soul.

One night, while studying in the med school library, exhaustion twisted a menstrual cramp from an uncomfortable ache to a stabbing agony. As I laid my head on the carrel desk, trying to breathe through it, I told myself to stop crying like a baby. It was time to grow up. For the first time in years, I thought of that nurse and wondered if she'd been in Vietnam. I wondered if my mother's cries had triggered a memory or flashback. I wondered if she'd actually given the best care and advice she could have under the circumstances.

EVEN THOUGH THE Advil swathed the sharp wedge in my head with cotton and gauze, moving exacerbated the pain. Freshly showered and wearing my best friend's clothes, I took the stairs slowly to find Caden on the sidewalk, waiting.

"Morning," I said at a volume designed to maintain equilibrium.

"Good morning." He laid his hand on my lower back and guided me to the Ferrari parked at a hydrant, its hazards flashing.

"Sorry I made you wait."

"I don't mind." He opened the door. "I'm sorry about this stupid car."

He helped me lower myself into the asphalt-scraping seat, shut the door, and got into the driver's side, stopping before he turned on the ignition.

"What happened to your hand?" I pointed at his left wrist, which was wrapped in an Ace bandage.

"Sprain. I fell on it. It's nothing." The car roared when he gently pulled out of the spot. "Please tell me he bought this without telling you."

"He bought this without telling me."

He looked at me as if asking whether I was honoring his request or telling the truth.

"Seriously. You just showed up with it."

"Are there any other large expenditures I should know about?" he asked.

"A ring."

"A ring?" He held out his fingers. Nothing but the wedding band half-covered in bandage.

"For me." I held out my hands. Nothing but the wedding band. "An engagement ring. It's home."

The car jerked when the light turned green. "Is it nice?"

"Very nice."

"Do you like it?"

"I love it, but I don't need it."

"No, you do," he said matter-of-factly. "I should have taken care of that a long time ago."

The car roared like a stallion chomping at a bit, protesting any kind of safe driving.

"It goes really fast when you open it up."

"It's rush hour." The car rumbled over the Williamsburg Bridge.

"In New York," I agreed.

"What a dolt," he mumbled.

I put my hand on his knee. He was the dolt, and he wasn't. "Thanks for picking me up. I needed a night without... you know. It."

"This has got to be stressful for you."

"It's fine."

"I'm sorry I'm doing this to you."

I gave his leg a squeeze, but he didn't look at me. He looked straight ahead with his right hand on the bottom of the steering wheel, left arm bent against the window.

"Goes fast, huh?" he said as we coasted along the off-ramp. Space opened up in front of us.

"Gets quieter the faster it goes."

He let the car slow even more. "Really?"

"Yeah."

The light turned red up ahead, but the three cars ahead of us ran it to make a left.

Caden hit the gas and the car took off quickly and smoothly. I screamed. Half a block of pure inertia-defying, door-clutching, back-against-the-seat acceleration. He slammed on the brakes for a red light. Tire smoke surrounded us, and my heart pounded like a jackhammer.

Then I laughed. "You asshole!"

For the first time as Caden, he laughed too. "That's fucking fast!"

We were in hysterics all the way home.

THE HEADACHE SUBSIDED, but the cloud of guilt over having a ring I hadn't told him about clung to me. Even though he was him and he knew... but didn't.

After work, I went upstairs. On the way to our bedroom, I passed him in his little office on the second floor.

"Hey," he said, standing by the desk and slashing open an envelope. "I'm stopping Blackthorne." He flipped the paper open, scanned it, tossed it onto the desk, and picked up another.

"Why?"

"It's not working, obviously." Slash.

I went into his office. "I went there the other day when you couldn't make your appointment."

"Oh, yeah?" He blew open the envelope. "What did you think?"

"It was fun but had the distinct odor of bullshit."

He let out a short laugh and pulled out the letter. Tossed it. "Yeah."

"We need to see a specialist."

"We, huh?" He continued through the mail. Slash. Blow. Open. Toss. Slash. Blow. Open. Toss.

"You can go yourself. But we can't do nothing."

"Anything else you'd like to prescribe?"

"I mentioned leaving this house."

"Was that his idea?"

"No."

"No. Just the ring was his."

"He said it was your idea."

"I'd like to see it before I let him get away with that."

I went to the bedroom and returned to the office with a box the size of a fist.

"Tiffany," he said when I handed it to him.

"Open it."

He opened it.

"Is it what you envisioned?" I asked when he took out the ring.

"Close. Why aren't you wearing it?"

"I didn't know what you'd remember. I thought you'd freak out. I don't know."

He placed the ring back in the box and put it on the desk. "You know how much I love you." He tapped the desk surface in front of the open box. "When you were too close to that mortar and you started to fall... the thought that you might be dead... it lifted me out of myself. I wasn't important without you. I didn't even exist if you didn't. When I opened you up to take that shrapnel out..." He touched the left side of my sternum, the scar under the fabric, as if he was so intimate with its placement he didn't need to see it to know where it was. "You're the beating heart of my life. You're the blood in my veins."

"I love y—"

"Did he fuck you after he bought it?" He cut me off as if the last question was the whole point of the previous speech.

"You did."

He kept his eyes on the emerald, pushing his jaw forward as if he could hold back his rage only so long. I put my hands on his, pressing down until the box snapped closed.

"God *dammit*, Greysen." He pulled away, body rigid as if he had to hold back from hitting something.

"You cannot be jealous!"

"It wasn't me." His growl came from the deepest part of his chest.

"It was!"

With his good hand, he took me by the jaw and squeezed just enough to keep me still. "Did you like it? Did he make you come?"

Cold Caden was detached except when laughing about speeding to a red light or demanding I not fuck him when he wasn't him. Cold Caden was Hot Caden when he was mad, and my body went limp with desire.

"Yes, you did," I spit, unable to get my mouth to move around his hand.

"How many times?"

Did he want the play-by-play? Was I supposed to write it down and have it notarized? Because fuck him. Fuck this. I had two unpredictable halves of a single sane husband. Nothing was what it was supposed to be. I hadn't signed on for any of this.

"So. Many. Times." Giving in to my impulse to egg him on was the only satisfying thing I'd done in weeks. The power of my agency was a drug. Pushing him and myself made my blood hot with challenge.

He raged with betrayal, and the fact was I raged for the same reason. He pushed me back until my spine ground against the edge of the desk. He could hurt me, and the realization didn't frighten me as much as it thrilled me. His power… unleashed on my body.

"I don't want you fucking *me* when *I'm* that way," he said an inch from my face. "Did I say that with the right words?"

I pushed his hand off my jaw. "I heard you." I shoved him back by the shoulders. "And I'll fuck you any time I want."

Now. Now would be a good time.

A conflict flickered across his face. He didn't know what to do.

"Don't test me," he whispered.

"Pick up your pencils, class. Question one: who can your wife fuck any time? Answer: her husband."

"I don't want to hurt you!"

"Yes, you do!"

My agreement was permission, and he knew it, grabbing a fistful of hair and pulling me close. "Tell me to stop."

"No."

"Say it!"

"Any. Time."

He reached under my skirt, fingers limited in their movement from the wrapping, and ripped through my stockings. "I'm going to fuck you now. *Now.*"

"Yes."

"You're not going to like it." His fingers drove roughly under my panties.

"Try me."

He spun me and pushed me face-first into the bookcase. Heavy medical textbooks fell around me. I grabbed a shelf as he yanked my skirt up and my underwear down to mid-thigh, restraining me and exposing me at the same time.

"You knew I wouldn't like it," he said, grabbing my ass with a painful grip. "And you did it anyway."

"It's my *right.*"

With a *thwack* and a stinging sensation, he slapped my bottom so hard my knees buckled. He pulled my hips toward him, forcing me to bend deeper and grip the shelf harder.

"You can't just leave me to explain to the other guy that I can't have sex with him," I said.

"So, you don't want to?"

"I do. I like him. He's not perfect, but he's nicer."

I got a hard slap.

"Since when do you like nice?"

"Sometimes. And you were nice. You were. You were sweet and conceited and rough and sincere. You were everything. Now you're just someone else."

His belt buckle clacked. I looked around to watch him get his dick out.

"Face forward." He slid the belt out of the loops. "Don't look at me unless you're telling me to stop."

I turned back to the books. *Essentials of Surgical Medicine. Post-Operative Technique.* "You were so real. You wanted me to be happy. You were so dominant but so confused by what you felt for me. And just impulsive. But remember when you asked me to marry you? You freaked you out."

A sharp pain burned my ass. I gulped and cried a clipped vowel at the same time.

The belt. He'd used the belt. Without a moment to breathe, he did it on the other side, searing the skin under the leather.

"That's enough, Greysen."

"I was reassigned to ABG, and you were staying at the combat hospital. Right on the tarmac, you threatened to redeploy if I didn't marry you."

He swatted me hard enough to make me grunt. He'd have to gag me to shut me up.

"I realized," I choked through tears. "You were so desperate, I realized if you redeployed, it would break you. I could save you and keep you at the same time."

Two hard thwacks stung me.

The sensible part of me wanted him to stop. Caden was trustworthy when he was whole, but who was this? Could I trust him? The insensible part of me did trust him. That part was an animal. She wanted to see how far he'd go because the animal was stupid, and the animal had something to say.

"I miss my husband," I spit out.

The animal was exhausted.

She wanted fight and pain.

She was so strained, so tired, so bottled up keeping it all together.

The animal was aroused by surrender and subjection.

She wanted to break.

I gave in to myself before I gave in to him. Sensible had surrendered to the animal by the time the third stroke hit even harder on already-enflamed skin. He grunted behind me for the fourth, and I bit back a scream.

If I screamed, he might stop.

He moved to the side, and I turned my head away so I wouldn't look at him.

The bandage on his left hand was rough on my lower back when he pressed it down. "Put your ass up where I can reach it."

I heard the *whoosh* as the belt cut the air and landed over and over across the tender backs of my thighs. The pain was its own thing. It pushed out worry. Muscled past responsibility. It had weight of its own, a density to its throbbing need, lasting even after the blows stopped.

"Stand up."

I straightened my back, cringing from the burn where he'd beaten me. He took me by the chin and made me face him, but I averted my gaze.

"You're crying."

I didn't say anything. I was crying with a sort of relief I'd never felt before.

"You want your husband."

I nodded, unable to speak.

"You have him."

I shook my head, denying his truth.

He took half a step back. "Tell me to stop."

"No."

"I'm going to use you like a piece of meat if you don't make me stop."

I met his gaze then, and again I saw that flicker of wholeness. But though I tried to hold everything still, it was gone in a breath. "Use me."

"On the desk. Move."

Like a good girl, I pulled the chair out and sat on the desk, bottom burning when it touched the wood. My ripped stockings were mid-thigh, and my skirt was pulled over my waist. My hair was half out of its ponytail. I was a wreck, but Caden's eyes burned bright blue with a desire to tear me apart.

God, I wanted to be shredded.

He unceremoniously pulled off my stockings and underwear and jerked my legs open so violently I fell back on the desk with my knees up. He bent them back and ran his eyes over my bottom and thighs.

When he touched the raw skin, it burned all over again. "Hurt?"

I nodded, biting my lower lip.

"You know what to do if you don't like it." He swatted me hard, sending a shear of pain through me, then waited for my objection. "Fine."

He slid in with no resistance.

He leaned over me and whispered, "I don't care when or if you come."

I didn't have time to be insulted because he started pounding me mercilessly. He ripped my shirt open, put his lips on my breast, and sucked on the skin, clamping his teeth together in an agonizing bite.

He took me as I fingered myself to orgasm, coming inside me with a grunt. He bent over me, breathing in my ear, and kissed my cheek.

"That's going to hurt tomorrow," I said softly as he popped out.

He opened his mouth to answer, but as if the Universe was out to prove me right, the last of the sun fell beneath the horizon. Before he got a sound out, he blinked and was changed.

"What's going to hurt?"

Chapter Forty-Four

DAMON

I entered consciousness in my office with her crying beneath me. There were books all over the floor, and my belt was out of the loops. She was on the floor, sobbing. I tried to pick her up, but she ran to the guest room and crawled onto the bed.

He'd beaten her bottom raw. As she lay on the bed, still sobbing, I soothed it with a cream even after she told me to get away from her.

She excused what he'd done to her with my body, saying she'd liked it. She'd wanted it. She'd asked me to hurt her in bed, but I didn't understand how she could have meant what I saw.

Once she was asleep, I scrubbed every inch of myself so hard I exacerbated the wrist sprain I didn't remember getting.

Was he sending me a message? He could bruise her and harm her. He could leave her broken for me. This must have been his response to my threat to use our body with other women. The soulless fuck had taken it all up a notch. I admired and feared his callousness.

He'd be back when the sun came up. He'd do it again to spite me. I couldn't cut off his desire for her, but I could make sure he couldn't act on his desires. He wouldn't hurt her tomorrow, or the next day, or the next. Not if I could help it—and I could. I had weapons in this war.

I wrapped my hand around our dick and jerked off.

Two could play at that.

THREE IN THE MORNING. She woke when I crawled into bed again.

"Hey," she said sleepily.

"Hey. It's early. You can go back to sleep."

"I wanted to talk to you." She sat up. I tried to ignore her cringe. "I want to see a specialist."

"In what?"

"Dissociative disorder."

"Ah."

How could I refuse her after what she was going through? But how could I agree to what would be my own destruction?

"It'll mostly be in the day, but I'm letting you know." She squeezed my hand. Her lips set in the dark as if she was about to say something difficult. "This is not optional."

I cupped her face, running my thumb under an eye still swollen from tears. "All right."

She curled into my arms. I kissed her head and looked out the window, wondering how to save her when she was trying so hard to save me.

"Thank you," she said with her hand on my chest. She was wearing the ring.

"I'm sorry about what I did."

"You apologized already, and there's nothing to apologize for." Her hand drifted down my chest and to my waist. I stopped her.

"Let me take care of you," I said, rolling on top of her.

"No, stop, don't," she said with a smile, but I straightened to get off her. "Joking. I'm joking."

"Good."

I kissed her face and neck, lifting her shirt to caress her breasts with my lips. I slid off her underpants and kissed inside her thighs, running my tongue along the soft skin, careful to avoid the places she'd been hurt.

I kissed her sweet pussy, demanding nothing but her acceptance of my tongue inside her, gently guiding her to orgasm. She pulled my hair, pushed me into her, dug her nails into my shoulder as she bucked and groaned.

When she was done, I wiped my mouth on my sleeve. She took my face in her hands and kissed me.

"Your turn."

She reached for my dick, but I guided her away. "I'm tired, and so are you."

I took her in my arms and stroked her arm, kissing the top of her head until her breath fell into a soft, steady rhythm.

When she was asleep, I went into the bathroom.

"Gah!" He cried from the bathroom. "What the fuck?"

I tilted toward the door. "Caden?"

No answer. The medicine cabinet clicked open, then closed. Drawers went *slide, snap, slide, snap.*

The door opened suddenly, leaving me too close to the threshold. We were face-to-face. Caden was in a T-shirt and shorts, looking through me, then directly at me as a barrier.

"What's going on?" I asked.

I didn't move out of the way, and he didn't reply. I took in his form, looking for a reason for his dismay, not expecting to find one painted clearly on his body.

My expectations were defied by a tiny dark spot that soaked through the fabric of his shorts. "You're—"

"It's fine." He pushed past me.

"Is the blood *from* your dick or *on* it?" My snappish, accusatory tone was meant to stop him, and it worked.

He froze before leaving the room and looked over his shoulder. "What do you think?"

I didn't know what to think, but it didn't take long to dismiss my immediate paranoia that he'd run out and had sex with a random, menstruating woman. I held the possibility of relief from my worst suspicions and their confirmations in my heart.

"I think there's a part of every person that wants to have sex with multiple partners, and I don't know if that's attached to your Damon part," I said. "Or if Damon has the will to act on it. But I think you're surprised you're sore."

"I'm irritated."

"I'll forgive the pun."

"Where were you?" His words carried a tinge of accusation. "He wasn't fucking *you*?"

I went toward him and laid my hands on his body. "Would I lie?"

He nodded with an understanding that cut through assumption.

"I hate him." He growled deep and low.

"What did he do?" I asked, newly alarmed.

"Made sure I couldn't fuck you." He whipped open the tie on the drawstring and lowered his waistband below his dick. It was hot red, with a spot under the head so raw that spots of blood soaked through the mesh of skin to form a heavy red drop.

"What the—?"

"Punishment." He pulled his pants back up. "He jerked his own skin off to punish me for hurting you. Maybe he's punishing you too."

"He knows I liked it."

He?

You was the correct pronoun. I kept treating them as two separate men when they weren't. It was all Caden. He'd penalized himself for his kink, then turned it on me because I encouraged it. Comforting daytime Caden about it only enraged the other.

What was next? Were these two personalities going to torment each other day and night? What kind of damage would he inflict on himself?

"You can't do this anymore," I said.

"I'm going to get this under control."

"How? By proving your dominance over him? Over me? No, you've tried to get this under control. I can't watch this escalate. I won't be a weapon of war."

I met his gaze, the blue Iraqi sky, remembering the man I fell in love with. All his inner conflicts, all his grace and dignity, they were all there, and none of it worked in pieces. He only worked as a whole man.

"I want you back," I said. "I want that dominant, loyal, devoted, loving, careful man back."

He leaned back a few millimeters, enough for me to discern I'd said something unexpected. I'd mentioned traits he knew the other side of him had retained.

"I have limits." I took a breath before saying something that couldn't be taken back. "You're going to lose me. Maybe not today or next week. Maybe not next year. But you're going to lose me if you don't engage in a sane way of fixing it."

"You want to sell this house?" It was a challenge more than acquiescence.

"Move out. Rent it. Leave it empty."

"No. We sell. If we're doing it, we're doing it."

"Strategic therapy. A specialist who can help you merge these two personalities."

He hesitated. I reached for his dick, and he pulled away from the pain.

"What's he going to do to it next time?" I asked.

"Nothing." His authority would have convinced anyone else, but I knew how little agency he had once the sun went down.

"What's he going to do to *me*?"

Anger saturated his blood, flowing to his face. His expression was one of revenge for a crime not yet committed.

I knew he'd agree before he did. The battle was won, but the war was just beginning.

"HEY," he said from the doorway, in jeans and a tank.

I was under the covers in the guest bedroom, reading a PTSD study Jenn had sent me. It was night, so I knew who I was talking to.

"How's your dick?" I said without preamble.

"So, you've seen it."

I put down the papers. "That was childish."

He sat on the bed. "I hurt myself to keep him from hurting you."

"All you did was guarantee I sleep in here from now on."

"Bed's a little hard for me, but I can manage it."

I folded my arms.

"Greysen, listen—"

"No, you listen. This is hard enough, worrying about your mental state all day and night. Now I have to worry about your body?"

"And I have to worry about yours!" he growled. "I will not ever, ever see you get hurt like that again. I will throw this motherfucker in front of a freight train first."

It wasn't like Damon to speak like that, and I was stalled with surprise.

"I'm sorry," he said, reaching for my hand. "I mean what I say, but I'm sorry I said it like that." With his thumb, he pushed my ring from side to side. "This all... it's very stressful."

"Really?"

He looked at me and gave me a rueful smile. "You'd know."

"I'm going to lay down some ground rules. And actually, I'm repeating them." I flipped through the journal Jenn had sent and found a piece of paper. I unfolded it and passed it to my husband. It was a list, and he'd already signed the bottom.

"One, you've agreed to sell the house. Two, you've agreed to see any specialist I think is best, and you've agreed to be enthusiastic and constructive about it. Three—"

"I can't agree to three."

"It wasn't on the table until you jerked yourself raw."

"How long are you going to go without sex?"

I took a pen off the night table and plopped it on the paper. "Sign it."

"This isn't legally binding."

"Thanks. You've saved me the trouble of getting a lawyer." I pushed it an inch closer to him. "You—meaning those eyes—will see in the morning that it was signed a second time after sundown, and I won't have to argue about who agreed to what. This is for me, so I can sleep at night. So I can have a life. This does more to protect me than your heroic string of masturbation sessions."

He snapped up the pen and tilted it in my direction. "It was fucking heroic." He signed. "I'd cut it off to defend you."

"That's what I'm afraid of." I snapped the paper away.

He crawled onto the bed and over me, placing a kiss on my forehead. "How long can you go?"

"Long." I gently pushed his shoulders.

"I don't think so."

"Back up."

"I'm going to take you away." He kissed my cheek before backing away just enough to satisfy me. "I got us a week in Hawaii."

"When?"

"Whenever you want. I don't know what to do for you to make this all right. I thought this would be a step in the right direction. If you want to leave me here and take Jenn, that's fine. But"—he held up a finger—"if you take me and that other guy, I get the sex."

"You're..."

Out of your fucking mind.

He was thinking of me. Caring for me. He saw how hard his split was on me and did everything he could. It was inadequate and wrong, but at least he tried.

"You're all right," I finished.

"I love you so much." He grabbed my hand again. "So much that when you hurt, I hurt. When you're stressed, I am. I hate that I'm doing this to you. You're my life, and if anything's breaking you, it's me. I should be the one suffering, but I'm just inflicting it."

I squeezed his hand. "It's not your fault."

"Whose fault is it?"

"I don't know, but starting now, we find out."

He nodded and kissed me gently at first, then went in for more.

I pushed him away. "I'm tired. Get outta here."

"All right."

After one last kiss on the cheek, he left, closing the door behind him.

I WASN'T HAVING any kind of sex with my husband, day or night. It took all my strength to sleep in the guest bedroom. Seeing him in the morning with his cold, rigid expression and his bedclothes stretched across his beautiful body was as hard as seeing him in the soft lights of nighttime, over dinner, at a party, with a gentle touch I couldn't walk away from.

"Just once," he whispered in my ear at the tail end of a dinner with hospital administrators. "I'll just make you come."

We were at Bob Abramson's penthouse on the Upper East Side. An inappropriate and somehow arousing place to flood my underwear. I was a mess of frustrated desire, but I shook my head and sipped my wine. He ran his fingers along the back of my neck and down my shoulder as if he thought he could wear me down.

He didn't know who he was dealing with.

Tina was on my left. Over dessert, she leaned into me. "Is now all right?"

"Now is great."

Tina stood and clicked her teaspoon against her water glass. "Ladies and gentlemen. Doctors. Paper pushers." Laughter. "As you know, we've done an exhaustive search for someone to head up the military division of our mental health unit. I'm proud to announce that from a field of highly-qualified candidates, we've convinced Dr. Greysen Frazier to join us."

Applause. Caden took his hands off me to join them.

Tina spouted my qualifications, but Caden held my attention because for a flash I may have imagined, he wasn't half a man. He was fully himself, and when he looked at me, he did so with a deep admiration that was more than the sum of two broken parts, a synthesis of everything he was, everything I married and everything I loved.

Then it was gone.

MANY OF THE patients I had in private practice could move to the hospital practice. Some were referred to other providers. Some didn't need me anymore.

The phase-out would be gradual for my practice but hard on my schedule. I'd have to work weekends and nights.

Caden was in his office. I hadn't seen the dominant side of him in a week, but there he was, in a jacket and open shirt, slashing open an envelope with a confidence that was code for fuckable. The ACE bandage was off his wrist.

"The realtor came by today," he said before blowing into the envelope. "If the house had a leg, she would've humped it." He opened the paper inside and tossed it in the correct pile.

"Did you call the specialist?"

Slash. "Yes." Blow. The single syllable carried a fifty-minute hour's worth of irritation. "She wants me for an afternoon appointment." Open. Toss.

"Can she see you this week?" I leaned on the arm of a chair.

The second to last envelope was on top of a big Express Mail envelope. Slash.

"Sure." Blow. Open. Toss. "I'll tell her I'm the Jerk-Off King of 87th Street."

I laughed. He picked up the Express Mail envelope and smiled as if he got the humor but wasn't inclined to find it funny. He ripped the tab.

"The question is…" He took out a smaller white envelope. "When am I getting inside you again, Grey? How much longer?"

"I don't know."

"I've done everything you asked."

"I'm not trying to bribe you into doing what I want. I'm trying to protect you from yourself. Literally."

"I know you're not sleeping with him. You know how I know?" He flipped the envelope around. The front had the army seal on it. "You haven't been satisfied in a week and a half. When I touch you, your body hums. You lean into me. Your breath gets quicker, and blood flows to your cheeks. You want it so bad I'm starting to think refusing me is your way of getting control." He poised the opener at the edge of the envelope, tucking it under the flap. "Look at you now. You're wet."

Slash.

I was hard and raw and aching for him. I didn't know how much longer I wanted to stay away. Every part of me longed for every part of him. I watched his hands on the letter opener as he placed it on the desk. I remembered the way he put those fingers inside me, the way they tasted in my mouth, the way they squeezed the pain out of my skin.

"Open your legs," he said, then blew into the envelope with a mouth that kissed and sucked and bit.

I hadn't walked into the office to release my pent-up desire, but I found myself resting on the arm of the chair, setting my feet apart, hungry for his approval. "Like this?"

He put the envelope down and stood in front of me with his crotch at eye level. "Like that." He put a hand on my jaw, and I leaned into the caress. "Greysen. I don't feel much. But without you, I feel nothing. You're the only thing keeping me human."

His thumb ran over my lower lip, and without thinking, I opened my mouth to suck on it. My body obeyed a part of my mind running on fumes and heat.

"I've lost everything," he said. "My family. My house. My sanity. I'm drawing a line around us, and we're staying inside it. Outside the wire is madness."

I let his thumb go, and he drew a wet line across my cheek as I looked up at him.

What about that moment convinced me it was time to stop withholding? Was it the sweet scent of coffee beans? The low timbre of his voice? The promise that his humanity breathed because of me? Or was it his eyes, blue as the noon sky when the rest of the world lived in twilight?

All of it. The package. All the traits that gave me pleasure stood over me, and right then, my body didn't give a shit about anything else.

"It's us, Captain. You and me."

"And him."

"There is no him."

He bent over and put his nose to mine. "As long as you're having orgasms I don't remember, there's a him."

"I give myself one every night thinking of you." Our lips were kiss close, brushing against each other when I spoke. "Our wedding night. I hadn't seen you in months. You spread my legs like you owned me." Remembering that moment, I shuddered.

"I do own you." He put his hand up my skirt and fingered past my underwear. I was engorged with suppressed needs.

"Take what's yours," I groaned.

Hooking his fingers on the crotch of my underwear, he pulled them off.

He kissed me and picked me up before he got on his knees with my legs wrapped around his waist. Placing me on the floor, he ran his head along me and thrust in.

I was so needy I nearly came, pushing into him as if I could force him through me. Three thrusts, and he was buried inside me. He put his hands on my shoulders, putting his weight on them so he could hold me down and hold himself up at the same time, pumping his hips to mine. Immobilized, legs spread for him, I didn't need pain when I was this fully dominated. Every muscle submitted to him, relaxing into pleasure.

"Give it to me." His words were hard breaths. "Come. It's mine. Give it."

"Take it," I croaked before going rigid under him. I bent around the orgasm, twisting and crying as he held me still. At the height, my limbs went slack, and my legs bounced with his thrusts.

"Stay still." He came with an exhale. His hands slid off my shoulders and he rested on top of me, his orgasm going on as he drove deeper.

"Thank you," I said when he picked his head up to kiss me.

"Sun's almost down."

He was correct. The sky was turning deep orange at the horizon.

"I don't want a fight."

He looked me in the eye. I was afraid he'd want to get scrappy all over again. Leave a trail of evidence behind to prove his ownership of me. I feared we'd gotten nowhere, and I'd just succumbed to my desires out of weakness.

"Let's put everything in its place then," he said, getting up.

He held his hand out to me, and I took it. We got dressed as if my parents were pulling into the driveway. I was leaning on the chair again when he tucked in his shirt.

"Thank you, Greysen."

"My pleasure."

As the sun disappeared, he picked up the envelope and blew into it, changing with a breath.

Every day, it was amazing how fast it happened, how subtly, and how definitively. He stood still with the envelope in one hand as he steadied himself with the other.

"Welcome back," I said, turning on the lamp.

"Hi. How are you?"

"Fine." I walked to the standing lamp and turned on that one too. "Busy."

"What did we decide?" He opened the letter. "About Hawaii?"

Had we been talking about the vacation? Maybe. I distinctly remembered putting him off, but the Damon side had his own way of being tenacious. He had a pit bull's tenacity and a dachshund's bite.

"How about Christmas break?"

He read the letter and tossed it in a pile. "Sounds good."

I snapped my head around so hard I thought I'd break. He was out the door with his back to me. He stood straight and tall, with an arrogant hauteur a man can acquire when he's beautiful and brilliant.

"What did you say?" I asked.

He went upstairs with a deliberate, precise footfall on each step.

I didn't chase him. Instead, I picked up the letter. My eyes blurred, and my hand shook as if my body wanted to defend me against what was on that paper.

—*United States Army*—

—report for duty—
—immediate deployment—
—rank of O-4 pay grade MAJOR—

"I knew it," I hissed, dropping to my knees. "You fuckers." My voice got louder. "I knew you'd do this."

I yelled upward, to the blue-eyed sky, "*Caden!*" extending the E in a long scream. I called him again, letting the vowels run to every corner and crowd there, until he came to me.

Not sweet, misguided, impulsive Damon who would get crushed in the military.

Caden came. The surgeon looked down at me with his emotions signed, sealed, and sent away.

I called as if he was still far away. "*Caden!*"

The last sound ended in a sob, and still, he stood over me.

"Why are you shouting?"

"They can't."

"Oh, but they can. And they have."

I leaned on his legs, letting my tears fall on his trousers. "We have to fight it," I sobbed.

Finally, he got down on his knees with me. "Greysen." He took my hands, and we looked together at where we touched, at the glimmering gem his love had broken away and purchased. "I can handle it."

"No. No, you can't. It broke you. They broke you, and they're going to keep breaking you."

"I have to pack, Grey. I leave tomorrow."

"And if we tell them. If we explain. If we tell them about Damon."

"He's gone."

"They don't want you like this. Do you understand?"

"I do understand, Major." He caressed my cheek. "They want me exactly like this."

His eyes were distant and cool, yet there was compassion in them. The sky was the same color no matter who cried under it.

"I can't..." I was barely coherent through my blubbering. I couldn't lose him. Not again. Not ever. "I can't do this. I can't do it."

"Hush."

"I won't. I. Won't."

He shook his head and looked me in the eye with unimpeachable steadiness, taking my face in his hands to share his balance. "It's time to stop crying."

"No," I whispered, laying my hands over his.

"Wipe your tears." He spoke with kindness. "It's time to grow up."

"I won't let this happen to you."

"I love you, Greysen. I love you more than I love anything, but this isn't about what you want."

My husband walked out and back up the stairs with deliberate, almost-surgical precision.

Part Six

Chapter Forty-Six

GREYSEN

NEW YORK - MARCH 2007

Before he left, he made sure I was set. Here was the property tax bill. Anthony would pay it when he paid the utilities. Here was the water filter system. It needed to be changed in six weeks. He'd have called Franco to do it, but the number was on the—

"You can't go."

We were in the laundry room. Its base functionality seemed absurd against the backdrop of my husband going to war. How dare the washing machine be white when this was happening. Fuck you, dryer, for being half an inch higher. The basket of clothespins was a slap in the face, and the steady hush of the water heater was a mockery.

Caden looked green in the fluorescent light, and his eyes were flat gray. He looked as if he were dead already. "I knew I could get called."

"You were tricked."

He smiled ruefully. Even green, he was beautiful. Too brilliant to be conned, too loyal to go back on a promise. He put his hands on my shoulders and slid them down to my biceps. "I'm going to be fine. They're giving me a nice bonus."

"Because I care about money."

The smile went from rueful to pleased, and I had to admit he'd been more himself in the past day than he'd been since his alter ego had appeared.

"Did you tell them about Damon?"

"I took a battery of tests."

275

"They'd never send you if they knew."

"As soon as I read that letter, as soon as *he* read it, he crawled back into the hole he came from."

"He's gone?"

"Are you going to miss him?" he teased.

"Are you?"

"If I deploy, he's staying gone." He gathered my hands in his. "I won't miss the little chickenshit."

"He's the cowardly side of you."

He got close to my face and put up his finger. "I don't have a cowardly side."

The way he looked at me, I could kind of believe it. He was so strong, so clear, so commanding, even with a part of him stuffed into a dark bag. If I hadn't known better, I would have forgotten to worry about him. I would have overlooked the broken pieces for the sake of seeing the man in front of me.

"We all have a coward in us," I said.

"You don't."

"I do. She's scared of heights and spiders. And she's so scared of losing you."

He took my chin and pointed it up to face him. "I see that look on your face, Major."

"What look, Major?" I had to smile at our equal footing.

"You are not to walk into the AMEDD recruiter."

"I was going to stay in the military for life anyway. It's easy for me. We can get a dual deployment. They'll station us together."

"Maybe. Or they can put us half a world apart."

"It's a risk, but I'm willing to take it."

"I'm not willing." He put my hands against his chest. "You're going to run the PTSD unit of Mt. Sinai Hospital. You're going to do what you were meant to do with your life. Help people after they get back. All you'd do on active duty is manage to get a revolving door of soldiers honorable discharges. They'd come back fucked up with no one to help them because you're on the other side of the wall."

I looked away from him at the way our hands wove together against his chest. "You think a lot of me."

"The world needs you."

"What about you? Do you need me?"

He unwove our fingers and put his arms around me, squeezing me so tightly it hurt.

"I need you," he said with his mouth pressed to my scalp, inhaling the scent of my panic. "I need you safe. I need you here. I'm a selfish and greedy man. I need you to stay here and do your work so I can keep it together. You're the only thing in this world saving me from going insane."

"What if he comes back?"

"He won't."

"He will."

"Well, then they'll send me home in disgrace. Maybe he'll buy a Maserati to make it up to you." He pulled away enough to meet my gaze. "But if you're deployed, you won't be here to make him sell the Ferrari first."

I laughed. He smiled with me, brushing a ribbon of hair off my cheek.

"I'm going to drive it when you're gone."

"Drive it now." He closed the panel door of the water filtration unit. "It's got a lot of kick."

"You're almost back to your old self."

"I think he needed a shock to the system. He's terrified of going back, and when the letter came, he wanted no part of it." Shrug. "War is his limit."

"You were forced to face your worst fear."

I saw his sharp glance behind me, to the false safe. The door was closed, but behind it was the bottle room and a darkness that had its own density. He looked back at me, his stare hard and locked as if he wanted to make sure I was there.

"Definitely the worst," he said, grabbing me and pulling me to him. "I can handle anything now." He kissed me, and I moved with him as he pressed his growing erection against me.

"We have about twenty-four hours," I said. "Can we spend twenty of them fucking?"

"What are we wasting those four hours on?"

"Sleep?"

He picked me up. I wrapped my legs around his waist.

"You'll sleep when you're dead."

We kissed as he carried me, clanking and banging ankles and elbows, kissing between ows and ouches, laughing all the way up the stairs. We wound up rolling on the carpet between the back door and the door to my office, peeling off as much of our clothing as we needed to get his dick inside me.

I braced each foot against an opposing wall as he pushed into me until he hit the end, and with another thrust, he found my limit but kept pushing.

Yes, it hurt. And yes, he knew it.

He did it again, and while he was buried deep, he yanked up my shirt and bra.

"I'm going to miss these tits," he growled right before getting his mouth under one and sucking the skin, closing his teeth against the flesh in a long, painful bite.

I fisted his hair, pulling his mouth against me, begging for the hurt. He bit and sucked, thrusting hard and slow, rotating his hips when he was rooted in me.

"I love you," I cried when I was close. "Caden, I love you."

In response, he bit me harder, and I came right into the pain.

Chapter Forty-Seven

CADEN

Greysen passed out at one in the morning after I'd bathed her, laid her on the clean sheets, and taken another of her orgasms. She was sore. I could taste the raw skin when I licked her cunt, sharp with open nerve endings and the threat of blood.

But I couldn't sleep for the allotted four hours. There was too much to do. As I went about preparing the house for my absence and making Greysen's world as easy as possible without me, I felt as right as I had in a while. At least as right as I'd felt since Damon had ruptured my mind.

He was in the corners again, but I knew what he was now. He was my fear. He'd always been there, and when I faced him, he went away. My relief didn't last. Neither did my control.

Damon fled at the thought of war and danger, but something else had been born. It didn't hum in the white noise. It was a hard buzz, like the approach of hornets. I told myself it was just Damon and I had him in hand, but it wasn't. I knew it, and I decided not to know it at the same time.

I went back into the laundry room to check on the circuit breakers. I'd be gone a couple of summers. The HVAC unit that had been installed while Greysen was still deployed was newer than the electrical box.

With a roll of tape around my wrist and a felt-tip pen behind my ear, I opened the metal panel. The black switches were labeled with masking tape in my father's handwriting, and since the new unit had been installed, many of them were wrong. I knew which was which and had never bothered correcting them.

I'd talk her out of selling the house for now. I wanted her to have a place to live in or sell if something happened to me. I'd pitch her the idea that since I wasn't here, there was no need to worry about me getting triggered by the fucking moldings or whatever she thought had prompted my split. We could sell when I got back.

Peeling off the first swatch of masking tape, I realized how neat my father's writing had been. He'd made a lie of the cliché about doctors having sloppy handwriting. He'd made a lie out of a lot of expectations.

I ripped off a piece of tape and put it by the switch. My edge was straight but ragged from the tear. My father had used scissors, of course. And when I wrote "Dining Room" on the tape and it was a mess, I realized he'd written the label while it was still flat on the roll.

I peeled it off and started over.

<hr>

CADEN - NEW YORK - 1981

TWO PAIRS OF SCISSORS.

My favorite T-shirt.

My most recent algebra test.

Three pages torn from an old *Hustler* magazine.

The shirt was still crisply black, and the three digitally-styled symbols, one for each band member in the Police, were still alarm-clock red. It was laid out on the shiny dining room table without a wrinkle.

My algebra test was lined up parallel to the edge of the table.

The *Hustler* nudes were spread above that, pages creased, with corners curling and the pinkest parts faded with age.

Dad sat at the head of the table. When I saw my mother kneeling at his feet, I dropped my bag. It was open. A pencil rolled out.

"How old are you, Caden?" my father asked as if he'd ever forget the day the mess was born.

"Eleven, sir." I tried to make eye contact with Mom, but she was bent toward the Persian carpet.

"Come here."

I stepped toward him, close enough to hear my mother's ragged breaths, and with the new angle, I could see that he held the end of a belt. The other end was looped around Mommy's neck.

"Describe what's on this table."

I took my gaze away from my mother and looked at the table. "Two pairs of scissors. My *Ghost in the Machine* shirt. My algebra test. Three—"

"More on the test, please. Finish the job."

Mom coughed. I started to sweat. He wanted me to be specific, and I needed to pay attention.

"It's from last week. Wednesday. There's an eighty-six in red at the top, and under it is the word 'good' in script with an exclamation point. The magazine—"

"You're not finished with the test. What's in the left corner?"

"Your signature, sir."

Mom gasped. I couldn't look. I couldn't watch him making the belt tighter, and I knew he wanted me to keep my eyes on the table.

"Did I make that signature?"

"No, sir."

"Who did?"

"I did, sir."

"Why did you do that? And be honest, please. I don't want this to be harder than it has to be."

"I thought you'd get mad that it was a low grade."

"I would get mad. I didn't fight for you to be in eighth grade math so you could get fourteen percent of the questions wrong, did I?"

"No, sir."

"And what about the magazine? Where would an eleven-year-old boy get pictures like that?"

"Brian Muldoon's brother." Brian was Irish. He had six brothers and sisters. The *Hustler* was a third-generation hand-me-down.

"All the Irish do is fuck and have babies, Caden. Don't forget it."

"Yes, sir."

"Can you tell me what you think you're looking at?"

If I hadn't been sweating before, I was when he asked me to study the photos.

"A motorcycle." Mom heaved a breath. I was shaking. "A naked lady on a motorcycle."

"What's she doing?"

"Showing her... thing."

He yanked Mom up to her knees. Her hands clutched the belt, and her eyes tried to tell me everything was all right.

"Your mother was hiding these with the test when I came home. Do you think she'd bother hiding a meaningless *thing*?"

"No. Yes? I... I don't know."

"Don't know what? The real name?"

He must have wanted me to not call it a "thing."

"Puh-puh-pussy."

"No." He denied my answer, but it satisfied him enough to let Mom back to the floor. "These 'things' have *names*."

I swallowed. My mother didn't make a sound. Her silence was for me. I was old enough to know that but too young to forgive her for it.

"Vulva," I whispered.

"Louder. Like a man."

"Labia minora."

"Better."

"Labia majora." Tears streamed down my face, but I spoke clearly around the sobs. "Urethral meatus. Clitoris. Vestibule. Introitus."

"Very good. You're qualified for a career in gynecology. Now. You have two pairs of scissors. One is for fabric. One is for paper. Cutting paper with fabric scissors dulls them. Paper scissors cut fabric inefficiently. You use the right tool for the right job. When you're done, your mother will start dinner."

I picked up the heavy fabric scissors and sliced my favorite shirt in half. After I'd shredded it to rags, I switched scissors and started on the test. Last, I cut up the motorcycles and the women on them, hoping he wouldn't notice that I'd left their delicate parts intact. I couldn't bear to slice those. It hurt to think about.

When I was finished, I was sent into the bottle room until Mom finished making dinner.

Chapter Forty-Eight

GREYSEN

I kept walking around the house.

I'd seen him off to a week of training in Fort Bragg, after which he'd be sent to Iraq as part of the troop surge. He'd kissed me at JFK, and I'd breathed him deeply, smelling fresh coffee grounds and the laundry detergent we'd washed his uniform in. The taste of my pussy was faint on his tongue, but once he brushed his teeth and showered, I'd be erased from his body despite his claims of a marital vascular infection. Vitamin G.

He'd said a lot of things in our last day together, and I believed he'd meant every word. When I stopped overthinking everything, in the nether state where wakefulness won't leave and sleep won't come, I knew they were all true. He and I were bound together by something more than shared history and compatible pheromones.

I knew him. My instincts felt his presence in the world. He'd meant what he said, but he was torn apart. Pulled away from his feelings, his passions, his doubts. Damon had been forced back into the bag, along with half of what I loved about him.

And his feelings for me? They were locked away even if he said they weren't. I was a feeling he knew he was supposed to have, a love he believed he had but didn't understand.

Without him in it, the brownstone was a fancy hotel. I smelled him in the sheets, in the shirts hanging in the closet. His love was in the furniture choices in my office, soaked in the linens, in the things I liked that he'd left for me in the refrigerator. But soon, those things would be gone.

I walked the house in the dark, exploring closets and corners built in 1821 and saturated with the aches and triumphs of the five families that had owned it. In an unused room on the top floor, a window seat held a stash of old *New York Times* from World War I. The brown paper flaked to the touch, and the pictures were muddled, grainy blobs inside rectangles. I tried to read them, but without the exhausting detachment I showed at work, I couldn't concentrate. There was no point anyway.

Different time. Different war. Different soldier.

I threw the papers back and wandered again, looking for answers to questions I couldn't articulate. Loneliness and loss weren't wandered away.

I ended up in the bottle room. It was bare, flat concrete down to the corners.

I shut off the light and closed the door. The darkness was complete. Heavy. Thick. It partnered with the silence to press against the senses.

Feeling for the wall, I leaned against it, crouching to the floor. Nothing to see, hear, taste, smell. I touched the cold floor to get a sense of my space and reality.

The compulsion to leave was so strong I sucked in a breath and stood without willing myself to. That deep breath, coming after the smell of nothing, brought a new scent so faint it would have disappeared in any other room.

Copper. Iron. Meat. An operating room without the sting of cleansers.

Blood. It was blood.

I turned on the light and inspected the floor. It was spotless.

Eventually, I gave up and went back into the laundry room, where I smelled nothing but fabric softener and dust.

He was landing in Fort Bragg, and I was desperately worried.

"LOOK," the AMEDD recruiter said. I'd finally called. It was the same guy who'd signed him the first time. "Anyone who's been on a previous deployment gets a battery of psych testing. If he passes, he goes."

"What tests? Specifically."

"ASVAB, TAPAS, MEPS. MMPI for meds. Plus an interview. If he had PTSD, we would have caught it."

"Are you sure?"

"Trust us. We've done this before."

And that was that. Caden was going to do what he did, and the army would do what it did. It was out of my hands.

Soon after I hung up and went upstairs, the phone rang. It was our first night apart. Had Damon punctured the curtain that detached the doctor from the man?

Had he freaked out? Was the call from Command telling me to come get this un-soldierly mess?

I ran down the stairs like a woman on fire.

"Honey?"

My mother.

"Mom?"

"Why didn't you tell me?"

I stared into the sink. It was bone-dry. "I don't know."

I knew, but it was too awful a reason. I hadn't wanted to tell her I'd lost. My battle to not be like her had been won only briefly. In the end, my husband had gone away and left me home to worry and wait.

"Your father says it'll be fine."

My father's brusque voice came on the line. "He's a doctor. He's not getting shot at."

"I'm not worried about him dying, Dad." I regretted saying that before I was done with the sentence. They'd ask what I *was* worried about.

Thankfully, my father had a point to make that superseded mine.

"Besides," he continued as if I hadn't said anything. "It's not like it was. Now it's all tactical strikes. It's not as messy."

Sure. A clean war. Because if a foreign army came down Main Street, USA, in an orderly fashion, everyone would be calm and the battles would be bloodless.

"He'll be fine." I leaned over the counter, flicking a grain of sugar off the marble.

With a click, my mom got on the other line. "You should come stay with us."

"She has an important job now, Louise."

"Then I can go there." Mom sounded as if she'd tried to make this point a few dozen times.

"I'm fine," I said. "Really. Maybe I'll come out for a weekend."

"Bring your brother," Dad huffed.

"Charles," my mother said, "I'd like to speak to my daughter."

"About what?"

I smiled and rubbed my eyes. My persistence had been handed down in my genes.

"Woman talk."

Dad grunted and hung up the phone.

"Mom, I'm fine."

"I know you are. I'm not worried about *you*. I'm never worried about you. It's Caden. You always said he was a civilian in uniform."

I bristled. I was allowed to say and think that, but I didn't want to hear it from anyone else. "He's more than qualified, and if you'd seen him in Fallujah, you'd know that."

"Yes, I understand."

I could almost hear her smile, and I knew why. I was being unreasonably defensive, and she knew it. I sounded like a loyal army wife, which I'd become in spite of all my efforts.

"But, yeah, I'm having a hard time."

"Come home for a weekend," she said. "We can talk."

Chapter Forty-Nine

CADEN

BAGHDAD - APRIL 2007

Baghdad was different from Balad and much the same as I remembered from Greysen's injury three years before. The facilities were permanent. I had a room, not a trailer. The docs shared a personal computer with spotty, expensive Wi-Fi. I'd been inserted into an established unit as a replacement, and I hadn't even met my new CO before I heard the first of two Blackhawks drop onto the landing pad.

The buzz dispersed like hornets in a high wind.

And suddenly, I knew what I was doing. A butterbar who went by the unexplained nickname "Toadie" was showing me around when I heard the *thup-thup* of rotors. I must have snapped to attention like a man waking up from sleep.

"It's all right," he said. "We're staffed."

"I want to see triage."

EIGHT AT ONCE. IED. The madness and noise of triage had an orderly pattern. Toadie fell away into his own job as I entered into mine, following the last injured man. He was gurgling. Color was bad.

"St. John. 61J." I gave the medic the code for general surgeon. "What do we have?"

"IED. Fucking mess. Chest wound. Lungs filling up."

She gave me his vitals as I opened his shirt. Fucking mess was right, but I'd managed worse in poorer conditions.

"Get him prepped for the OR."

"Hey, what are you doing here?" Male voice from behind.

I turned. White guy in scrubs. Six-three. Bald head shaped like a wedge. I stuck out my hand. "Cap—Major St. John. I'm your new GS."

He shook. "Captain Quinn. Ortho. Call me Boner. Glad to have you. Scrub-in is third on the right." As I walked down the hall, Boner called, "Six tonight!"

I turned and walked backward.

He continued. "The roof. Thursday is Beerday."

I gave him the thumbs-up.

———

I PUSHED into the scrub room. Three surgeons were getting their blues on over their clothes. The fourth was in the process of stripping off a blood-soaked uniform. When she saw me, she paused, clearly unashamed of her mismatched bra and panties.

"You must be the new 61J," she said, hands on the curve of her hips, ignoring the nurse who held out a gown for her.

She was daring me to look at her body, so I didn't. I stayed focused on her ochre eyes. "St. John. Caden."

She held her hands out for the gown. "I hope you live longer than the guy you're replacing." She turned around to give the nurse access to the back of the gown.

"Lt. Cash," a female nurse introduced herself. "Call me Aretha. Sink's here..." She quickly showed me the layout of the room, and I got to work.

I tried not to think about how the last guy had exited his job. If I died in Iraq, Greysen would find a way to bring me back to life so she could personally kill me.

Thinking about her raging doggedness, I couldn't help but smile.

Even with thousands of miles between us, her tenacity made me strong.

———

I FELT GOOD, working on that first chest wound. In control. Sane, mostly. I knew sanity was a slippery concept, but Damon was gone, replaced by a buzz I didn't know well enough to fear. I didn't have time to attribute it to the pace of the work or even pure necessity. I only had time to get pieces of metal from a guy's lungs.

"Need help?" Female voice.

I looked up. It was the half-naked woman from the changing room.

"Almost done."

"How's his love muscle?" I must have reacted because she smiled under her mask. "His heart."

"Little nick right here." I pointed. "We got it in time."

"Good find." She met my gaze over the table. "Those are some pretty eyes you have there."

"Thanks." I put my attention back on the patient. "Got them from my father."

"He must be a handsome guy."

"He was an asshole, if that matters."

To my relief, she walked away without answering.

THE DOCS HAD SET up chairs in front of the rooftop stairway structure. A thick layer of clouds hung over the sky. At Boner's feet sat a specimen cooler full of half-warm beer cans. A doc with a flat top and a diamond earring on the left handed me a can.

"This is Captain Jackson," Boner said.

"Call me Stoneface."

"Thanks." I took the can of Miller Lite and shook his hand.

"Major McDonnell over here. He's a fucking star."

As I shook the hand of the man with curly red hair and boyish cheeks, McDonnell said, "Agent Orange. And I'm no star."

"You guys and the names." I cracked the can and tried to catch the foam before it made a mess.

Without warning, the air was filled with a plaintive voice singing in Arabic. It came from a thin stone tower that rose above the rest of the city. The voice hopped from octave to octave, calling all Muslims in earshot to prayer.

"You get used to it." Another white guy with an all-American haircut and clean cheeks transferred his O'Doul's to his left hand so he could hold his right out to me. "I'm Timothy Eberhardt."

"Let me guess yours," I said as I shook. "Boy Scout?"

"Good guess, but it's Heartland."

"Nice one. Who gives these out? So I can avoid them."

"Harpy," Boner said. "Our CO."

"Harpy?"

"Colonel DeLeon," Jackson said. "She's all right. You'll like her."

"I think I met her in the OR." I wasn't shocked or dismayed that a woman was running the unit. I wasn't concerned with *what* she was but *who* she was.

"Smart mouth?" Eagle asked. "Light-brown hair with eyes to match?"

"Body like a—" Agent Orange stopped himself and sipped his beer.

"Yeah. That's her."

"A real firecracker," Heartland said.

"She'd get along great with my wife," I offered. "Same set of brass balls."

I loved Greysen's balls, and truth be told, I loved bragging about them.

"Where's she holding the fort down from?"

"New York."

"Civilian?"

"Resigned her commission last year," I answered. "But she's from a long line of military, so she gets it. Her father was in the 101st Airborne. Plane jumper."

"Badass." Stoneface tipped his beer in respect. "Mine's military too. She's nearly snapped my neck between her thighs a few times."

"Probably because you eat pussy like a dog lapping a bowl of water," Boner said.

"What do you know about pussy, cocksucker?"

"Spread your legs, and I'll show you."

We all laughed at the final insult. Boner and Stoneface tapped their cans and drank.

The singing stopped, leaving the whipping wind to fill the soundscape.

It was there. The buzzing. The new Thing.

I heard it in the white noise, breathing in my ear like an angry parent. Not weak like Damon, but strong and chaotic. Unfocused. Wordless. Without intention. But there.

I didn't have Greysen's willing body to keep me together, and I wasn't convinced that was a good thing. Damon hadn't wanted to hurt her, and I'd used his fear and distaste to frighten him away.

This new Thing wanted her pain like a thirsty man wanted water. Damon was gone, but I was still broken in two.

Disappointment became resentment. I walked away to suppress it. These guys didn't need to see me all wound up. But as I got to the edge of the roof, a hand locked painfully onto my bicep. It was Stoneface. I understood then where he'd gotten his name.

"We stay on this side of the stairs." He pointed at the concrete structure, then out at the tower where the voice was being projected from. "They have snipers in the minaret."

From there, they could have picked me off like a duck in a shooting range. Shoot out the star for a prize. I was less than human and more valuable for it.

I joined them in the circle of chairs.

On cue, after prayers ended, the bombs started in the distance. I remembered the sound of mortar fire all too well. So did the Thing I wouldn't call by name.

"Ah, shit." Agent Orange took his beer from his lips.

We peered out from behind the structure at the plumes of smoke.

"The Blackthorne guys were talking about a convoy out that way," Boner said.

Blackthorne. They were known for military contracting, not medical research. My blood chilled at the mention of the name anyway.

"Who's on the medevac?" Stoneface dropped his half-full beer back into the cooler.

"Catapult." Agent Orange looked at me. "The 61Js go out when the field surgeons are short."

"And they're always short," Heartland added. "Better get down there."

The Thing disappeared at the thought of going into the Red Zone, leaving nothing but fearless clarity. It wasn't afraid. It was satisfied.

Fucking Greysen hard was the way to get rid of Damon. This new Thing craved danger.

Chapter Fifty

GREYSEN

APRIL, 2007

Caden wasn't the only one with professional detachment. My work at the hospital went on as planned. When people asked about him, I told them he was deployed. I told them I was proud of him, and I was. He'd ripped himself apart to keep his promises. Who wouldn't have stood in awe over such a thing?

"I'll be in California Monday of next week," I told Leslie Yarrow. With a phone call and a credit card, I'd turned Damon's Hawaii trip into a flight to San Diego.

"I was going to mention this at the end," she said, rubbing her hands together as if she was nervous. "I've been stop-lossed."

"Oh." I was surprised. Troops seeking mental health care weren't usually sent back. "When are you leaving?"

"Tomorrow morning."

"Are you going to be all right?"

"Yeah. I really think I am. I have this. I feel like I can shut a lot of this off now."

She was the last patient of the day, and it was my second week without Caden. We'd had an unsatisfying call from Fort Bragg. He'd be in Iraq now.

I missed him.

The last months had been stressful. Damon's appearance had thrown me, and the months before that, with the unexpectedly rough sex and the more unexpected reason for it, had been a slow crawl of emotional tightness that unwound just as slowly without the day-to-day chaos.

In the unwinding, my own feelings were freed. Disappointment unraveled to reveal anxiety, which dissolved into a puddle of worry that boiled with anger that steamed into sadness before soaking into resentment.

With the coil of emotions unwound, I was left with a deconstruction of everything that overlaid the only thing that mattered.

Caden. Me. The love that bound us together wasn't connected to the skein I'd built around it. It stood discrete. It was at the heart of every decision I was about to make.

As an officer, Caden was allowed a cell phone, but the service was spotty and he had it off so often I never got through.

When Yarrow told me she'd been stop-lossed despite her issues, I had to talk to him. His voice would take this spinning feeling and pin it down.

I started the calls in the afternoon. The AMEDD recruiter gave me his stateside unit contact, and from there, I knew enough of the right things to say to get me a number to the Baghdad CSH office. After midnight, when the sun was rising over Iraq's capitol, I sat at the edge of our bed and punched the numbers in the night table phone.

"He's off base," the nurse said after he'd looked at the chart.

"I'm sorry?"

"Probably be back in a few hours."

"Wait, Lieutenant, hold up," I said. "He's outside the wire?"

"Yes, ma'am."

"Is he in the Red Zone?"

"Everything outside the green is red, ma'am."

I had to stop myself from asking why he'd gone or if it was the first time. I thanked him and hung up.

<hr>

HE SENT me an email with Skype names.

I was sure any emotion that weakened him was still locked away, but I was glad that hadn't affected his sense of humor.

According to the email, the docs had chipped in to share an old computer and prohibitively expensive and totally crap Wi-Fi. I needed to dial in at two in the morning EST on Wednesday. The connection was terrible. It dropped three times before I heard him.

"Grey?" His voice came over the speaker.

The screen was black with a little red phone in the center and a slash through a video icon. I saw myself in the little rectangle on the lower left.

"I can't see you," I said.

"The camera on this thing doesn't work. I can see you. You look beautiful."

I patted an errant length of hair. I'd become a connoisseur of my husband's vocal inflections. He sounded like himself... mostly. Not like Damon, but not without a certain edge.

"You look like a little red camera with a slash through it."

"New uniforms."

I laughed. Sense of humor intact.

"How are you?" I asked. "I tried to call, and the nurse at the desk said you were off base?"

"It's different now. And Baghdad is different. We're in a permanent building. Not trailers."

He was changing the subject.

"Where did you go off base?"

"Not far."

I was embarrassed I'd asked the question. He wasn't allowed to give me any locations, and I was asking what any self-respecting army wife knew not to. "I'm just worried."

"You think I went to a brothel?"

"You wouldn't do that unless you wanted me to fly there and start burning shit down."

"You could put an end to the entire war."

"All you have to do is cheat on me."

"This war's going to go on a long time then."

"Yeah." I swallowed and tried not to think about it. "Have you heard from Damon?"

"No. Can you tuck your hair behind your ear? I want to see your throat."

My neck tingled from the attention. I pulled my hair away, watching myself in the little box as I showed him the pale length of my throat.

"Pull up your shirt."

Naively, I hadn't prepared mentally or physically for Skype sex.

I pulled the hem of my T-shirt up over my bra.

"Your tits, Grey." He sounded like a teacher I'd handed the wrong assignment. I pulled the sports bra over my breasts, showing my hard nipples to the little box that was my mirror and the black screen that was his window. "Yes. I want to mark those too."

"Where?"

"Underneath."

I ran my hand over my nipples to the soft skin underneath. "Here?"

"There. I'd bite you until you screamed."

I pinched a bit of skin and twisted it, cringing when it hurt, then pushing myself to twist harder. He didn't speak until I whimpered.

"Stop," he said. "Show me."

I pulled my shirt and bra off in one motion and stood for the camera. The red mark was angry and raw. It wasn't finished either. It was going to blossom into a nasty bruise.

He sucked air through his teeth. The idea of him jerking off to my pain was arousing and sickening at the same time, with the arousal being fed by the aversion.

"Pants off. Everything off."

I slid my pajama pants and underwear down, stepping out of them as he said, "Show me. Open your legs and show me."

I angled the screen down so that when I sat with my feet on the desk and my legs spread, the little box in the corner centered around the space between my legs.

"I'm so turned on," I said, sliding my hand into my seam. "And I can't even see you."

"I'd bite inside those thighs and make you stay still for it," he said with a rumbling depth. "I'd bring you to the edge and give you enough pain to pull you back, then start over until you begged for me to finish you."

"You'd do it like this?" I tugged on a pinch of flesh inside my thigh, squeezing and twisting until it hurt, then doing it harder. "Leave a mark," he said, and I twisted into exquisite agony. The leash frayed but held.

"It hurts," I groaned as the pit bull bucked against her restraints.

"Like that. Come like that."

Deaf inside my own experience, I didn't hear him come. I only heard his sigh at the end. I threw my head over the back of the chair and moved my hands away.

"Ow," I said.

"That's going to leave a bruise."

I bent as far as I could to see between my legs. "Yeah. No bikinis for me."

Slowly, I lowered my legs off the desk.

"I want to watch you get dressed," he said.

I pulled my shirt down, grimacing when I touched the spot I'd bruised under my breast.

"That's mine. Think of me when it hurts."

"Do you have any more time?"

"Five minutes."

"What's it like? Your day? Just talk to me. I wonder what you're doing all the time."

"The surge isn't the same as Fallujah when we were there. Casualties are spread out. We haven't had anything like those eight days."

"I hear the Red Zone is constant guerilla warfare."

"Yeah. Less of a front line. More of a huge, very shitty neighborhood."

"And you're safe in the Green Zone?" I smoothed my clothes over my body.

"It's like a regular neighborhood, and I'm some asshole doing my job."

"When I called, they said you were outside the wire."

"It's different here, baby. You have nothing to worry about."

The bruise between my legs shot through with pain when I sat in the chair again. It would get worse before it got better, and that seemed exactly right.

"SURPRISE."

At nine thirty at night, two days after I'd bruised myself for Caden, Colin stood at my doorstep with a droll smile and a suitcase at his feet. My mother pushed past him with her arms out, and Dad came right behind her until I was crushed in a hug.

"What are you guys doing here?"

"Your mother—"

"I said I was coming with him or without him." Mom picked up her suitcase, but Dad shot Colin a look until his son took the hard-sided case.

I got out of the way and let the three of them in. "It's a bit of a mess. I can't believe you came."

"You sounded so sad," Mom said. "I couldn't wait until you came to us."

"This is quite a place," Dad said, letting himself into the living room. He was checking out the furniture and woodwork.

"Priceless, apparently," I said. "I haven't set up the guest rooms, but—"

"We can get a hotel," Mom said.

"No, no—"

"It's all right," Dad chimed in. "The city's full of them."

"They haven't seen the prices," Colin said.

"Yeah." I picked up the suitcase. "You're staying here. This house is huge, and honestly, it's wasted."

My parents jumped at the opportunity to reduce waste.

AFTER A TRIP to the linen closet for sheets and towels, I settled them into the guest bedroom. With military efficiency, we made the bed and got the clothes in the drawers. My father closed the closet with a definitive *click*, and I took a deep breath.

"I'm so glad you came," I said.

"We're always there for you," he replied.

"I just... I thought I had this, but now that you're here, it's like I didn't realize how much I wanted to be near people who understand."

"That was the thing your mother always had on base. A community. You don't have that luxury in the shitstorm city like this."

I'd always considered that community oppressive, but I'd only seen it from the point of view of a disaffected teenager.

"She woulda died of loneliness without those magpies," Dad continued as we walked downstairs. "But everywhere we went, there was a group of women who didn't look at her funny or exclude her."

"What are you telling her?" Mom had made herself right at home in my kitchen. The teapot was warming, and she'd cut cheese slices I'd left in the fridge into bite-sized pieces. They were fanned out along the edges of a plate, a stack of crackers in the center. Little bowls of olives and pickles were set out on the island.

Colin was tapping on his Blackberry.

"I'm telling her you weren't miserable." Dad slid onto a stool and popped an olive in his mouth. "You might wanna back me up."

She shook her head. "I don't wish that life on you," she said to me. "But it could've been worse. Cracker?"

Nothing like being offered your own food in your own house. I took a cracker and put a piece of cheese on it.

"Have you spoken to him?" Mom asked.

"We had a Skype call."

"How is he?"

"Fine."

"Why the fuck did he go in again?" Colin got right to the point once he'd put his Blackberry down. "I thought he was done."

"He was." I pressed my fingers to the counter to get the crumbs up.

"So, what was he thinking?"

"Colin!" Dad scolded. "Just because you don't understand a sense of duty doesn't mean it doesn't exist."

My brother rolled his eyes. My father wagged his finger twice. This was such an old argument between them that they could get into it and out of it without actually having it.

"What are you guys going to do while you're here?" I asked. "You going full tourist or just hanging out?"

"Whatever's easy for you—"

"No," Colin interrupted. "Why, Grey? You won't answer me when I ask you, so maybe you'll answer in front of Mom and Dad. Why did he sign on again?"

Our parents would try to deflect, but the question would remain. In Colin, the family tenacity had manifested in curiosity. I'd have to address it at some point.

"He did it for me," I said, glancing at my mother, who was frozen with a pickle halfway to her mouth. "I wanted him to take part in something, and he had to be in the reserves to do it."

"Something?" Colin raised an eyebrow.

He knew about Day Caden and Night Caden. Was he being intentionally thick, or was I being too cryptic?

"I told you he had PTSD, Colin."

"Ah!" Everything must have clicked for him because he picked up his Blackberry again.

Dad held up his hand. "Wait, wait, wait."

"He's fine," I said. "He had to be in the reserve system for the treatment, and he got called. End of story."

As if to punctuate my reluctance to speak further on it, the teapot whistled.

"Well," Mom said, turning down the heat, "he's a good man. I worried about you with men."

"Mom. I'm deeply offended. I didn't have a ton of boyfriends."

"Two words," Colin said. "Scott Verehoven."

"Hey!" Dad snapped. "We don't mention that name."

"What? Why?"

All three of them started talking at once. Colin called for Jesus Christ. Dad cursed. Mom *tsk*ed.

"That boy." Mom shook her head, pouring tea for Dad.

"Douchebag," Colin mumbled. My brother had been at UCLA the same time as me, though he hadn't been in ROTC.

I shrugged. "Everyone dates a douchebag at some point."

"When he called you a dyke in front of your entire patrol," Colin said, "and all his friends thought it was hilarious?"

"There's nothing wrong with being gay," I said, taking my teacup. I'd gotten a haircut, and yeah, there was nothing wrong with being gay, but he'd meant it as an insult, and it had hurt my feelings. He was supposed to be my boyfriend.

"And the diving board." Colin went to pick up his Blackberry again but just flicked it across the counter. "Asshole."

"Platform," I said. "It was the platform."

———

LOS ANGELES

MAY 1994

THE NIGHT SCOTT called me a dyke was my twentieth birthday. My patrol had told him to shut the fuck up. Even Nancy, who was indeed a lesbian, told him to go pound sand up his ass or she'd do it herself. He left in a huff.

At midnight, I slipped away to find him. The gate to the high dive was open. He was a star and had the key so he could start practice at four thirty in the morning. His body landed in the water like a knife, a dark blade against a darker backdrop.

"Hey," I said from the edge of the pool as he surfaced. "Sorry about Nancy."

I shouldn't have apologized for my friend. She was wonderful. He was an asshole. But I was newly twenty and continually insecure.

"She knows I can't do anything to her." He bowed his back and went underwater. The muscles of his back were molded in the moonlight, shaped like the surface of the water.

We'd only made out and done some groping in the six weeks we'd been dating. He acted as if he'd put all this work into grooming me and gotten nothing in return. I should have dumped him. He was beautiful to look at, but he never made an attempt to be a nice person. I stayed with him because I liked the way other girls looked at me when we were together. The ROTC uniform made me look like a dumpy asexual. Having those sexed, free, powerful young women look at me as if I could be one of them made me feel sexed, free, and powerful too.

Scott got out of the water. Compared to most of the country, Los Angeles nights were warm in May, but his nipples were hard and his pecs were pulled into tight mounds.

"You coming in?" he asked, taking stock of my body in modest civilian clothes.

"I can't dive." I couldn't swim well either. And I wasn't great with heights.

He shrugged and headed for the ladder, his shoulder blades sharp wedges under his skin, wet shorts falling just below his waist to reveal a perfectly formed Adonis belt.

Beauty aside, he'd challenged me by climbing up that ladder. I kicked off my shoes and stuffed my socks in them. I didn't have to dive if I didn't want to, right? I peeled off my jeans, folded them, and put them on a chair with my jacket.

"Come on then." He was past the lower platform already.

In my underwear and T-shirt, I went up the ladder.

"I REMEMBER the look on his father's face," Dad said in my kitchen fourteen years later, smiling with the inner satisfaction that comes from reliving a great memory.

"When?" I asked.

He and Mom exchanged a glance.

Scott's father had blamed me for the fall, complaining to the dean that since I wasn't on the diving team, I had no business by the pool at all.

Dad shrugged. "You got any sugar for this tea?"

"It's right in front of you. When did you meet Scott's father?"

Mom tapped her foot. "Might as well tell her."

"Yeah, Dad," Colin said.

"Well." He stirred sugar into his tea. "Jakey and I met up with him on this little street in Palisades and had a talk with him."

"A talk?"

Colin chuckled.

"These pussy Hollywood types spook easy." He waved off the gravity of whatever it was he'd done. "They see a rifle and start praying."

"What?"

"We just talked, Grey." Colin waved it off.

"You were there? You were barely eighteen!"

"I had a driver's license."

Dad laughed. "He drove him off the road. Scared the hell out of us."

"What?"

"I stayed in the car," Colin protested from behind his cup. "I didn't get to put a rifle butt through his windows."

I couldn't believe what I was hearing. It was so outrageous I couldn't speak.

Dad took that as permission to find humor in the story. "He was shaking so hard I thought he was going to create his own weather pattern."

"What did you say to him?" I was stunned. I couldn't imagine that ending well.

"Not a word. Jake just kept grunting at him. He's a funny kid. Laughed the whole way home."

Colin—my refined, intelligent brother—smirked at the violence. "They just broke his windows and his cell phone. Words would have been superfluous."

"Jesus Christ, guys."

"He'd come a long way from going to the hospital with a rifle." Mom sipped her tea.

"You knew about this?"

"Of course. Can you eat the cheese you took, please?"

I picked up my cheese but stopped it on the way to my mouth. "I don't know whether to yell at you guys or thank you."

"Don't thank me," Dad said. "You thanked me by graduating and getting a commission. If you want to yell, you're a grown woman. You can yell if you want."

I ate the cheese and chewed pensively, realizing I wished I had been there to smash Mr. Verehoven's windows with an assault weapon just to see his fear create a weather pattern.

I'D NEVER TOLD my dad I was afraid of falling. He was in the 101st. It was his job to jump out of planes. I didn't want him to be disappointed in me. After hearing about the broken car windows, I was even more glad. Who knew what he would have done if he'd had any idea how terrified I was of falling from a height?

With Colin gone and my parents tucked in, I couldn't sleep. The memory of getting pushed off that ten-meter diving platform haunted me. I had been convinced I was going to die, and inside the conviction had been a clarity that expanded time. From the high platform, a diver spends about 1.42 seconds going straight down.

The water had had a misleading gentle turquoise glow from the underwater lights. The surface—I knew—would hit my body with the force of concrete if I landed flat.

My neck would break.

Near-death lucidity was a very real phenomena. It expanded time and mental capabilities. It allowed me to hold my breath. It gave me time to turn just enough to tuck my arms to my body and protect my neck so I only devastated my shoulder.

I lived a full life in a second and a half.

My terror of heights didn't come from the injuries. It came from the second and a half of clarity. Feeling, seeing, hearing everything. Elongating the string of time into an elastic band the exact length of the rest of my life.

Near-death lucidity was my limit. A hard no.

When Scott had half apologized at my hospital bedside, admitting to no more than clumsiness, I thought he'd had a change of heart. I hadn't realized my family had gone full military.

Not that it would have mattered. I'd told Scott to go fuck himself. I hadn't trusted myself with men for a long time after that. I dated on my terms and had sex on my terms.

The night Dad had admitted he'd "facilitated" the diver's exit from UCLA, I stared at the ceiling with my arms folded over my chest, listening to the soft, irregular hum of traffic and trying to feel remorse or guilt. I had none. Scott could still go fuck himself.

I'd kept myself in complete control until Caden.

I'd chosen wisely. He was worth my trust.

Chapter Fifty-One

CADEN

BAGHDAD - APRIL 2007

The first time I'd gone outside the wire, in Fallujah, it had been a mess. I didn't talk about it. Ever. I hadn't even told Greysen anything more than "Everyone lived, no problems." After filling out the report, I'd shoved the incident into the back of my mind, where it died a quiet death so that I could live.

My first trip out in Baghdad shut down the Thing before the Blackhawk even got off the ground. We circled over a patch of road with the median blasted out. The injured was lifted onto deck, and I treated him. We went back to the Green Zone without touching the ground.

The Thing came back as soon as I got off the helicopter.

Was it the idea of danger that ran it off the road? How shitty did it have to get before it gave me some space?

I'd had a call with my wife that night. She'd done to herself what I needed to do to her. The Thing was gone. That space in my mind was filled with Greysen, and it was strong.

COL. DELEON—NO one called her Harpy or even Karen to her face—threw herself into the chair next to me. There were two adjacent desks in the tiny office, each with a beige computer we all used for notes, reports, and requisitions.

"How you holding up, Asshole Eyes?"

That, apparently, was my nickname. My father had been an asshole, they were his eyes, and bang—nickname. Could have been worse. She'd called me Pretty Boy once, and I'd given her a look that made the buzz in my ears even louder. She knew enough about leadership to back off. I appreciated that.

Not looking away from the computer I typed notes into, I answered, "Good."

She tapped her password into the other machine. "Heard you were at Balad for the first few days of Phantom Fury."

"Yeah."

"Eight days straight."

"More like seven and three quarters."

"Impressive."

"Not a big deal."

"You speak Arabic too?"

"I understand enough. My wife speaks it."

Mentioning Greysen was completely unnecessary yet critical.

We worked for a few minutes, then she twisted her chair to face me and crossed her legs. "Why'd you resign your commission?"

"Personal reasons."

"It seemed strange," she said, blowing right by my answer, "because you're really good at this. You belong here."

Finished, I logged out and turned to her. "I'll take that as a compliment."

"It is."

"Thank you."

"You don't like me much, do you?"

"Are you here to be liked?"

"Hell no." She smiled and crossed her arms to match her legs. "It's not about you learning about me. It's about me learning about you. A lot of guys take issue working under a woman, and I need to know where you stand on that."

"I'm fine with it."

"I know. You all are. But some of you have a little voice inside you that's bothered by it, and it's my job"—her voice got very feminine and seductive—"to tease out that tiny voice, little by little, so I can *crush* it." She said "crush" with a growl and a clenched fist.

I laughed. I couldn't help it, and neither could she.

"My little voice has been crushed," I said, holding up my hands. "Trust me."

Her eyes fell on my wedding ring, then on my asshole eyes.

WOMEN FLIRTED WITH ME. I knew it when I saw it, but I wasn't particularly good at it. When I made an innuendo or expressed a desire, it was because I planned to follow through. Promising sex without the intention of delivering it was a waste of everyone's time.

I was sure I hadn't given DeLeon reason to believe I was interested in flirting or fucking. She'd seen my ring. I'd seen the fact that she didn't have one. Not that it mattered. Married people fucked around all the time. Just not me.

But I had a problem. I was back to square one with a new Thing. It was in the sounds and the shadows. In the midnight chanting from the minaret and the muffled voices behind doors, it buzzed. It wasn't frightened away; it was satisfied away, like a noisy cat being scratched behind the ear. It was quieted by danger, surgery, and Greysen's pain.

Danger came when it did, and surgery was regular but unplannable. Without Greysen's body, I didn't know how to stifle the presence. Without access to her pain, I couldn't placate it.

"Eyes!" Heartland ran up behind me as I checked the charts. He refused the word "asshole" like a vegetarian refused meat. "Nine-line. Boner's in OR."

"I'll go."

AS THE BLACKHAWK LIFTED UPWARD, inertia tried to pull my stomach downward. I usually took this as a sign of my discomfort in the air, but with the reappearance of the Thing came the slippery shaft I pushed my emotions into. Fear went right into the locked box.

We arrived over a rocky dry riverbed in four minutes.

"Aw, shit," the pilot said in my headset.

I looked down, something I would have struggled to do without my personal emotional sponge, and took in the scene.

An overturned truck. Two stopped but upright. A plume of smoke. A perimeter of men on their stomachs protecting the center. A man waving a sign for sniper fire. Two men crouched over another lying on his back. The pool of blood enclosed him in a huge, black comma.

They weren't military.

"We can't land under fire," the copilot, Gangrene, said in my headset.

"That's a lot of blood," I replied.

"Fucking contractors," the paramedic grumbled.

"He's going to die," I said, turning to make eye contact with the medics, then the pilot and copilot.

"Fuck!" the pilot barked. "Are we in or not?"

"I'm in." If the doc answered first, it was easier for the other guys to agree, and I knew they wanted to.

They chimed in their agreement, the contractor-hating paramedic consenting last.

The Blackhawk whipped around and swooped down.

Trapped in a speeding tin can, hurtling into sniper fire with the angry Thing boiled into adrenaline, I'd never felt so free.

Chapter Fifty-Two

It was eight thirty in the morning in Baghdad when I called. Army lunchtime.

"Corporal Lorben. How can I help you?"

"I'm looking for Dr. St. John. This is his wife."

"He's not here. Do you want to leave a message?"

No, I did not want to leave a message. I wanted to hear my husband's voice.

"When is he on duty?" I asked.

"I think he's on his way back from a medevac."

What?

"No, that's…"

Not possible.

Not right.

Not allowed.

Stop acting surprised.

My hope that his last trip out had been a one-time deal got shot out of the sky.

"Ma'am?"

"Let him know I called. It's not an emergency."

IF SLEEP WASN'T HAPPENING, I could at least go to my office and get work done. On the way down, I heard my father making his "night noises." Huffs of fear. Startled jumps. As I passed, he made the *uh-uh-uh* that could go on for minutes.

The PTSD never left him, but he'd never admitted he had it. Mom had stopped nagging him years ago.

Don't let Caden become like Dad.

I hurried downstairs, banishing the thought. Keeping busy was the trick. I packed up the files of the patients I'd referred out and the ones moving to the hospital practice.

Decisions are made before they're made. The seeds are planted and watered, growing invisibly under the surface until the sprouts show, and even then, with those first two spear-shaped leaves, we can't identify the fruit they'll bear.

But a seed had been planted. I just couldn't see it in the noise of daily life. I had bills to pay, a business to wind down, a dream job to ramp up, and patients who needed care.

As I went through the files, I noticed where they'd come from. Some of my first military clients had come from Jenn, but even more had come from Ronin.

I'd stacked the files in order of where they were going, but I restacked them according to where they'd come from, then I looked at the names.

I knew them. I knew their problems, their struggles, and the details of their PTSD.

I wrote down the names of those who had described feelings of dissociation. Most were mild and had shown improvement. One had gotten worse, but he'd been stop-lossed two weeks before and I couldn't check on him.

Weird.

They weren't supposed to stop-loss troops with PTSD. Maybe Caden hadn't been an exception.

But in a way, Caden was part of a larger pattern.

All of the dissociative cases had come from Ronin.

"COINCIDENCE," Ronin said casually. His body was turned to the side, and his legs were stretched out while his elbow rested on the table as if he wanted to be fully present but also needed to be able to leave the coffee shop quickly.

"Were any of them getting the same treatment as Caden?"

"You know I can't tell you that."

"How did you expect me to help these people if they weren't forthcoming about what other treatments they were receiving?"

"Nothing you prescribed interfered with what we were doing." He was such a baldly self-involved ass that I didn't have an immediate reply, which gave him room to wedge in more excuses. "Overall, did your PTSD patients have a normal ratio of disorders or not?"

"The problem is that they all came from you."

He shrugged. "Your sample is too small to determine that I'm the problem here." He turned his body around to face me fully. "What we're doing is important work, and it's safe work. It's for us. For the country and for the life of every soldier in the field."

"You going to vomit stars and stripes now?"

"You're looking for a reason your husband broke. The fact is there is no reason. It just is. Some people break, some crack, some are fine. Look at you." He put his hand out as if presenting me on a silver platter. "You're fine."

Was I fine? Maybe. I slept. I ate. I loved.

After the carnival where I'd stared down a fear of mortar fire, I didn't jump at whistles or booms. My mind had snapped back like a new rubber band. I hadn't identified any triggers that changed my mood or caused a sharp negative reaction.

So, I was fine. I was the end of a long line of soldiers.

I had been born for this.

"I want you to send me back," I said.

"Excuse me?"

"Blackthorne's contracting security in Iraq. I want to go back. Hire me."

"Wait, wait, wait…" He shook his head.

"A psych on staff can reduce your liability when your teams come back with PTSD."

"We have no liability."

I wasn't ready to blame Ronin or Blackthorne for my husband's condition. It had started before the treatment, and it had gotten better under it. But he'd been sent away because of them and they owed me. "Hire me."

"It doesn't work like that."

"Tell me how it works and make it happen."

"Why don't you just sign on for another commission?"

"Because they'll put me where they want me. I could end up in Korea. Blackthorne will put me near my husband."

"I always thought you were crazy." He stood and placed his hands flat on the table so he could lean close to me. "You're still gorgeous, but you're still out of your goddamn mind."

"I'll get on a plane to Jordan right now and walk to Baghdad. If I have to do that, Ronin, if I have to go as a free agent, I'm talking to every left-wing, contractor-hating journalist who'll listen."

"About what exactly?"

"All I have to do is make them curious about what you're doing here. They already hate you because of Abu Ghraib. Hire me, station me where I want to go, and you'll have your NDA."

He stood straight and buttoned his jacket. "It's been great catching up."

"I'M NOT EXACTLY WALKING across Jordan." I whipped a pair of thick cargo pants out of the drawer. "That was just a manner of speaking."

Dad sat in the bedroom chair. "You have no idea what you're doing."

"No one does until they do it."

"I mean those clothes. It's in the eighties in Baghdad. You want to sweat your skin off?"

"Oh, right." I pulled a pile of underpants out of my drawer and threw them on the bed. "I'll wear my gym shorts and a rib tank. Should I bother with a bra?"

"You were always a wiseass."

"It's a defense mechanism." I rolled up the pants and tucked them into a corner of my duffel bag.

"Defends you from listening to common sense."

"I'm uncommon." From my dresser, I picked up a small photo in a silver frame. Caden and I in our wedding gear. Tux and white gown, on the beach in San Diego. Faces full of sand. We'd stopped in the middle of the photo shoot to build a sand castle. "I make uncommon decisions and do uncommon things."

"Like show up in the Green Zone to see your husband."

"I'm devoted." I put the picture back. Baghdad wasn't the place for sand castles and wedding gowns. "What can I say?" The front doorbell rang. I leaned out into the hall and called down the stairs, "Ma? Can you get that?"

"All right!"

Dad continued as if uninterrupted. "How do you think he's going to react to you going there?"

My mouth tightened into a wry smile, and I shrugged, picking up a hoodie and rolling it into a log. "He's going to be pissed."

"Why's that make you smile?"

"I don't know." I jammed the hoodie in the bag and reached into my underwear drawer. "Maybe because if I was a boy and I traveled over the surface of the earth for a woman, you'd give me the same advice but you'd be proud I took some initiative."

"That is not true."

"It is true. I love you, but you never understood me. I never acted the way you thought a girl should."

"No, I mean, I am proud of you. I can be proud of the decisions you want to make and think they're stupid at the same time. You want him back? You have access to all the channels you need right here. You tell them he's got PTSD, and they'll put him on a plane so fast it'll give you whiplash."

"And the divorce will come right after."

"Better divorced than dead."

"Yeah… no." I zipped the bag. "You have those in the wrong order."

"Greysen?" Mom stood in the bedroom doorway and handed me a manila envelope.

There was no address. Just my name printed onto a sticky white label and a red stamp. CONFIDENTIAL. Once I took it, she started wringing her hands.

"They still deliver death notices personally, Ma." I tore open the envelope.

"I know, I know."

The cover letter slid off before I could read it, revealing the first page of a contract.

NONDISCLOSURE AGREEMENT between

BLACKTHORNE SOLUTIONS INCORPORATED (the Company)

And

DR. GREYSEN FRAZIER (the Independent Contractor)

"YES!" I threw my arms in the air, but my parents didn't share my enthusiasm.

MY FAMILY WORKED hard to talk me out of it, but they'd tried to talk me out of everything I'd ever wanted. Military service (too restrictive for my personality). Med school (too expensive). Voluntary deployment (too dangerous). Everything except marrying Caden. I'd stopped holding their objections against them long ago. They loved me, and they'd always tried to talk me out of things that made them proud.

Everything would be fine. The thought of taking this problem into my hands outweighed their opposition by a few metric tons.

I had work to do, and that made me happy.

THE GRAY DOT TURNED GREEN, and the red camera with the slash through it disappeared. I thought the thing was broken and I was going to have to reconnect. But it wasn't.

His face.

He took my breath away.

I think I gasped. I was sure a high-pitched sound escaped my lips. I covered my mouth.

I must have looked shocked or displeased, because he ran his fingers through his hair, and I took mine off my mouth to touch the screen. It prickled with electricity, smooth and cool to the touch. Nothing like him. He was rough and warm. If I could have run my hands over the T-shirt that clung to him, his skin and muscles would have yielded only so much, and the dog tags that dangled over his chest would have clinked softly when they moved.

"Are you all right?" The sound was a split second behind the movement of his lips.

"I forgot."

"Forgot what? Are you sick? What happened?"

When I got close to the screen, he broke into tiny points of light. His skin color was pale yellow from the monitor. He'd lost weight. I preferred a little scruff on his cheeks to the clean-shaven, boyish look. His hair was too short, and the webcam stole the sky from his eyes.

"I forgot what you looked like."

I must have been clenching my fist the entire time he was away. Muscles I'd learned about in anatomy, but never used, uncoiled and melted into warm relief.

The morning I'd woken up from the nightmare that I was marrying the wrong man, I'd felt the same release. Everything would be all right as long as Caden was with me. The relief didn't come from my lungs or from my heart, but from cell and tissue. This was the man. He was mine. He was imprinted onto my neurons, triggering a hum and flash in my brain when the planes and angles of his face appeared.

He was beautiful. His smile was the answer to questions I hadn't even thought to ask. And the response was always yes.

I was more sure than ever that I was doing the right thing, and in that whirl of optimism, I forgot that we were separate people. I let go of all my plans to tell gentle half-truths or guide him through my maze of intentions.

"I'm coming!" I shouted, imagining his skin under my fingers. His voice, his scent, his presence with mine. I could barely contain myself. "I'm coming."

He blinked, tilted his head a little. The muscles around his left eye tightened. "I didn't even start."

I laughed. The English language had really fucked it up by making homonyms of an orgasm and an arrival. "I'm coming to Baghdad!"

"You're… when? For how long?" I knew he was calculating how long he'd need to get an R&R request in. I was about to free him from that, but he got more words in first. "You just started the new job. It's not going to look good if you take a vacation right away."

"It's not a vacation. It's—"

"I'm really confused here, Grey."

"I got another job. With Blackthorne. I'm heading out to you."

I should have expected that to go poorly, but the sight of his face had sent me over the side of the road.

"I'm sorry." He tried to make some kind of sense out of what I'd said. "You lost me."

"I'm working on a deal with Mt. Sinai. It was really the plan they wanted; anyone can implement it. I—"

"Anyone can implement it?"

"It's connect-the-dots. I'm not special."

"Like fuck you aren't!"

I rubbed the sweat from my palms. All my arousal and excitement curdled into sour clusters.

"What are you thinking?" he asked. "What's going on in your mind?"

I miss you.

Those three words took up the bottom line.

I was worried about him. I wanted to check on him. I was the only one he trusted, and I needed to be there if something went wrong with the dissociation, but the last words on the matter were longing and desire.

I missed him.

"It's going to be all right," I said. "I'm not providing security. Just tending to the mental health of the contractors."

"Let me get this straight." He leaned on his elbows, getting his beautiful face closer to the camera. Since my camera was on top of my screen, he couldn't see when I touched the bottom of it to caress his glass chin. "Ronin hired you as a private contractor because Blackthorne gives a shit about the mental health of their security guys?"

"It's single site inside the Green Zone."

"You expect me to believe he came to you with this and you left a job you've been working to get for months to take it?"

"Yes."

"No." He leaned back, and his body slid away until my fingers touched the glass of his stomach. "No, no, no."

"You think I'm lying?" Typical defense mechanism. Assume the worst. Force them to say no. Say they're sorry. Backpedal just a little.

"Yes. I do." Caden didn't take the bait. I hadn't married him because he was easily manipulated.

"Great. Thanks."

"First, you're lying to yourself."

"I wish I'd never sent you that webcam."

"Dane's wife sent one first. Yours hasn't gotten here yet. And that's another lie."

"You don't want me to come."

"No fucking shit, baby."

"You don't think I can handle myself?"

He slapped his hands on the table. "Why is everything a fucking pissing match with you?"

Don't cry, Major Frazier. "What—?"

"You can handle yourself, okay? If there's a person in the world who can handle herself, it's you. But admit it to me, your husband, that you want to be here because you never wanted to leave the army in the first place."

Don't you fucking cry. "That's not why."

"But it's true."

"It's true, but it's not why."

"So, you sold your soul to a company of douchebags to pretend you're a soldier again."

"Fuck you," I whispered.

"No, fuck you. Admit it."

"You're wrong."

"Admit you sold your soul to a mercenary organization—"

"No."

"With zero accountability."

"Wrong." My denial was barely a breath. It was a river in Egypt.

"Admit it."

Slapping my hands on the desk, I shouted, "I sold my soul to *you*, you fucking asshole!"

He fell back, slouching and staring past the camera into some middle distance inside himself.

What did he see there?

Guilt. He harbored it for things he hadn't done and fed it meals of things he'd never intended.

"Caden."

"Yeah, I... I don't know what to do."

"There's nothing to do. I'm coming. I sold my soul to you because I love you. I need you. I can't live without you."

He rubbed his forehead and looked toward the window. The light washed out his features. "It's not safe here."

"I know."

"The contractors. They're not protected. Not accountable and not protected."

"It's going to be fine."

"When they die, there's no official count. Blackthorne doesn't release numbers."

"Caden, it'll be all right. I'm not going out on security details. I'm just in some kind of office. They got me a house with a gate to live in."

He huffed a derisive laugh, as if his wire trumped my gate. "I shouldn't have done this," he said more to himself than me. "I should have just learned to live with it."

He was talking about the experimental *soo-hoo*s and the shots I was becoming more and more suspicious of.

"Are you living with it now?"

The question was rhetorical. I expected him to say no. Then I'd tell him it was worth it. He'd be mollified. I'd be soothed. We could continue normally. Maybe have a little fake sex.

But he didn't say no.

"Yeah," he said into the light from the window before looking back at the camera. "It's like it was. I can feel something's off, but I know what it is now. It's manageable."

Manageable?

Human beings were capable of selecting memories to suit their attitudes about present circumstances. We forgot the pain of childbirth to have more babies. We leaned over the toilet, swearing we'd never drink again, then said thank you when offered a fresh glass of wine.

"You almost killed me," I said, trying to state a fact rather than make an accusation. "You were in a constantly paranoid state that was pretty justified."

"I was managing. It's not worth this mess."

"We're going to be together. That's not a mess."

"It's a mess, Greysen. We're a mess."

I jolted, gulping breath, trying to think through the over-firing synapses. By defining our marriage as an unacceptable result instead of a difficult evolution, he'd broken through a limit I hadn't known I had. "Don't say that."

"I'm sorry. You don't have to like it, but it's the truth. We had something great, and we fucked it up."

"No," I growled through clenched teeth. "We still have something great. We're not past tense. We are a now. We are a future. We're happiness and hope, goddammit, and I won't let you talk like this."

The lips I'd been so happy to see pressed into a tight line. They lost their fullness, their generosity consumed in doubt. "I love you, Greysen."

"I know you do."

"This isn't about loving you."

"I know that too. But you're still wrong."

"I want you to stay home."

"This isn't about what you want either. I'll see you soon."

On the other side of the world, there was a knock at the door.

"I have to go," he said.

"Okay."

"Don't come. I mean it."

"I know you do."

The door behind him cracked open, and a bald white guy peered. He smiled at me, and when Caden turned to him, he jerked his head as if to tell my husband his presence was required.

We said our good-byes and cut the connection. The red camera with the line through it appeared again.

Nothing Caden had said had dissuaded me. I was more determined than ever to be with him.

Some forms of madness felt more lucid than sanity.

Chapter Fifty-Three

CADEN

The contractor we'd picked out of a giant comma of blood was in the ICU. Walter Benedict's chart put him at thirty-three, from Tucson. He'd needed two gallons of blood to replace what had been lost from his femoral artery. Agent Orange had managed to save his leg and his life. He was good, that guy.

"How are you doing?" I asked him.

"Feel like shit, sir." He didn't have to call me sir, but the fact that he did told me a lot.

"You lost a lot of blood." I sat by his bed. "Your body's busy making more."

"They're going to send me home, do you think?" His eyes were red-rimmed over dark circles. If he had been military, he'd have gone to Germany, then home, but he wasn't military.

"I have no idea how it works for you guys, but you made it. That's a good thing."

"Sure."

"What was your rank when you were enlisted?"

"Made it to staff sergeant. But the money... shit."

Contractors were well paid. He probably made twice as much running security details as he had when he was a soldier. Since Blackthorne was a private company, they could provide as much medical care to the wounded as they wanted. The VA was inadequate, but Blackthorne, again, could do what they wanted, be it too much or too little.

"You'll be on your feet in no time."

"Thanks, doc. For coming to get me. You didn't have to land under fire."

"Thank the pilot."

"Sure, sure." His eyes fluttered half-closed.

"Get some rest."

He obeyed almost instantly.

I didn't want my wife here. Not as a soldier. Especially not as a Blackthorne contractor. I did the rest of the rounds with my job on the perimeter of my mind and Greysen at the center.

She wouldn't be talked out of it. I hadn't married a pliable woman. The very things I loved about her were the things that made her difficult to keep.

She wouldn't come if she wasn't allowed, but I had no power over that.

She wouldn't come if I convinced her it would make the situation worse.

Or if she was needed at home.

Or if I wasn't here.

Bells rang in the back of my mind.

She won't come if I'm not here.

WHEN I KNOCKED GENTLY on Colonel DeLeon's door, the buzz of the Thing got lower and denser, as if it knew I was trying to get out of harm's way. Its presence had increased steadily since my last medevac, growing into an infuriating distraction. I needed to make it to my next Skype with Greysen. A long-distance pain play would put the Thing away, sleeping like a guest crashing on the couch after Thanksgiving dinner.

DeLeon's office was tiny with gray plaster walls, metal filing cabinets, and a window with white paint on the glass. She had her elbow on the desk and her fingers threaded in her hair as she hunched over paperwork.

"Yeah?" She didn't look up.

"I need to talk to you."

"Close the door." She sat back and indicated the black office chair in front of the desk. The upholstery was ripped on the right armrest and the edge of the seat.

I took off my hat and sat.

"What can I do for you, Dr. St. John?"

"No Asshole Eyes?"

"You look too serious for fucking around right now."

"I appreciate that."

"Good."

I didn't want to ask her—or anyone—for anything when I had no leverage.

When I'd taken too long to speak, she said, "I don't bite."

"I need leave." I didn't sound like I'd blurted it out, but I had.

Leaning forward on the desk, she folded her hands in front of her. "Why?"

"It's personal."

"Yeah. I know. But I get to ask. That's how it works."

She did, and I knew I'd have to answer.

"My wife signed on with Blackthorne."

DeLeon stayed stock-still except for two fingers she tapped together twice, then arched an eyebrow as she asked, "And?"

"And it's a bad idea. I need to go home."

"To talk her out of it?"

"Yes."

"I thought you were going to tell me she was pregnant."

"We don't get leave for that."

She smiled slyly. I was a grown man, and she was an open book. The first page read, *I'd like to fuck you.* "Why should I grant leave for that?"

Emphasis on why. Like, What's in it for me?

Would she sign leave papers if I agreed?

And if I could confirm that, would keeping Greysen safe be worth destroying my marriage?

No. Not even close.

We weren't there.

The choice between life and death wasn't clear-cut enough to make that deal.

"Because I'm asking."

"You obviously know the rules. You haven't accrued enough time for leave. You don't have a medical emergency. Nobody died."

"On my last deployment, I worked eight days on five hours' sleep. I was pumped so full of amphetamines I was having aural hallucinations. It was my job, and I did it. I've never asked for anything from the army. I did what I had to. Now I have to do this."

"How can you expect me to call your wife coming here an emergency when the army sent you here? Sent me here? Thousands of us are doing our jobs. You're concerned. I get it. But it doesn't hold up."

She was right. I'd have to think of something else.

"Thanks," I said, standing.

"Sorry I couldn't be more helpful." I had my hand on the doorknob when she called out, "Stop."

I turned, hand still on the knob.

"There's something," she said, hands flat on the desk as if this was hard for her. "I can call in a favor to get you leave."

"Okay."

There was more. There had to be more.

"But you have to do something for me."

There it was. A deal. She stood and came around the desk. She was going to try to seduce me, and I was going to refuse her.

"When you're a woman in this position," she said, "you have to deal with a lot of shit."

"Such as?" I took my hand off the doorknob.

"Such as my picture showing up in a Facebook group with the caption 'Who'd like to fuck this one in the ass?' Or getting assaulted in OTS. I'll spare you the rest of the list. But the worst? The body they're all so hot for is high-maintenance." She looked at my crotch and put her hands on her hips. "And what it needs is frowned on because not getting those needs taken care of isn't debilitating enough. No one says anything, but I know men and I know the fucking army."

She was going to touch me. I could sense it. I could use her body to stifle the humming madness. Satisfy the Thing. DeLeon was attractive in all the right ways. Except that she was wrong. I wouldn't have sex with her, not even to protect my wife.

"I'm not going to fuck you."

A smile spread across her face, and it turned into a laugh. "That's your loss. But I need something more practical. I need a procedure, and I can't miss a day of duty for it."

I was so relieved I almost laughed myself. "And you'll call in that favor? It'll get me leave?"

"One hundred percent chance of success."

She went behind her desk, and I sat in the chair across.

Chapter Fifty-Four

Four black-and-white monitors. Caden in a small room. Four angles. Frozen in a chair with the word PAUSED over him.

I thought, "I don't want to see this," but I didn't say it.

"Here was the problem," Ronin said with his arms braced against the countertop and his face lit by the four black-and-white monitors. He'd sat me down here after I'd checked in and filled out the forms. "He lied."

I exhaled the first N in *No, he didn't*, but bit the rest back.

Ronin glanced at me and twisted half his mouth into a wry grin. "He was the same about protecting you. It's cute." He hit the space bar on the keyboard.

The word PAUSED went away. Caden sat still, and again I had to stop myself from canceling the whole endeavor. I didn't want to see this, but I had to. I didn't know why. But I had to see it.

"What did he lie about?" I asked.

On the screens, Caden bowed his head, the muscles of his back stretching and contracting as he breathed rhythmically.

"He said he had no history of childhood abuse."

The man on the screen shook. I wanted to lay my hand between his shoulder blades.

"Maybe your question wasn't specific enough," I said.

"Sure."

Caden threw his body against the back of the chair, going rigid as he groaned in mental pain. The waveforms ran along the bottom of the screen with his lips as he said, "No, no, no." His pain was all over his posture. The light vibrated with it.

"It wasn't like this for me," I said.

"The treatment opens doors. Helps you face fears. You're not afraid of anything."

Caden shook his head vigorously.

"No. I am. I'm afraid of plenty."

"Different people, different results. But for victims of abuse, it's more than we can handle here."

Was Caden crying? Oh, Jesus on a ladder, we were separated by space and time. I was powerless in the face of his hurt.

"Is this hard for you to watch, or is it just me?" I asked.

"You get used to it."

"Why didn't you stop him?" My hand hurt. I looked down. I was twisting my fingers like a skein of yarn.

"We had no idea what this was. He gave one-word answers in his questionnaires. I thought he was reliving an experience in Iraq, but then he suddenly got very verbose in his surveys. Told us about some room in his basement."

"Was that six weeks ago?"

Six weeks ago, Damon had done the Blackthorne appointment. Damon would have been verbose and forthcoming where Caden would have finished his questionnaire with a scowl.

"Right about then." Ronin nodded.

On the monitors, Caden's face was buried in his hands, and he was weeping, but his back still expanded with the constant rhythm. He'd come to Blackthorne for me. I'd sold him on it. I'd done this. I'd forced him to dig up things he'd worked hard to forget. I owned every tear he'd shed in that room.

Dr. Frazier, the psychiatrist, knew he had to dig them up. Greysen Frazier, the daughter of a vet hounded by unexplored trauma, knew the same. But Mrs. Greysen Frazier-St. John had a burden of guilt.

"Why are you showing me this?"

"Because I can't show you the other subject who said they had no history of abuse."

I tapped the space bar, and Caden froze. "Who?"

"You're going to meet them in Baghdad."

"Now that I'm bound by your NDA, let's talk about the patients you sent me."

He leaned back on the counter and crossed his arms. "Let's do something even better. I'll send you the data."

Caden was covered by the word PAUSED, but I knew that under it, he was being crushed by memories he'd never shared with me. I must have been looking at it too long.

"You can get out of the contract, you know. You haven't been paid. You have an out clause."

Caden would be happy. My family would be relieved. I could go back to the hospital and manage the new program the way I'd pitched it.

I tapped the space bar. Caden changed. He stood straight, gripping the arms of the chair, legs spread, mouth open in an angry roar. His eyes were on fire, and he was ready to spring at something only he could see. My heart stopped, then pounded. He knocked over the chair and lamp. He was terrifying. I'd never seen him angry. Not that angry. Not like an animal.

Was this acceptable to me? And if not, how would going to Baghdad fix it?

I couldn't bear it. I hit the space bar to stop it. "Do you have a boss, Ronin? Or are you running the entire thing?"

"I have lots of bosses, but they prefer it if contractors have one point of contact. That's me. In the army, I'd never be more than a peon for someone. But this program's such a small part of this operation that I get to run it how I want. It's going to change everything."

"Everything?"

Gently, he started the video again. Caden lowered himself to the floor, bowed on his knees, hands in his hair. I wanted to touch the glass to comfort him, but that man was weeks ago and thousands of miles away.

"The way we go to war," Ronin said. "The way we use people. Imagine soldiers coming home with their trauma completely processed. They'd get off the plane mentally clear. Maybe healthier than when they left. All this from a few hours in a dark room? That changes everything." He turned to watch the video with me. "I know we give each other a hard time. But I consider you a friend. So, I'm going to give you some friendly advice."

I had a snappy retort about unsolicited advice rarely being friendly, but Caden's anguish slowed. Maybe with the *soo-hoo*s I couldn't hear but knew were there. Maybe on his own. He picked up his head, leaving his palms on his face, then lowered them as if he was being born out of his hands.

"I'm listening," I said.

Ronin could give me all the friendly advice he wanted. My mind was made up. Caden needed me.

"Call his CO directly. Tell him about the dissociation. Call it PTSD. You're perfectly qualified to assess him. They'll listen to you. They'll send him home. Then you bail on your contract."

On the screen, my husband stood up straight and righted the chair.

"He'll never forgive me. And I tried that."

"That's what I figured."

Caden buttoned his jacket, all posture and pride. He looked directly at one of the cameras and nodded.

WITHOUT A DOUBLE-BLIND CONTROL GROUP, Blackthorne's bioenergetics breathing data was inconclusive. All correlation. No cause. That would be their excuse when it all went to hell.

I recognized some of names and knew my patients by their rank and life's experience. Saw my husband and Leslie Yarrow. The ones with the mild dissociation I'd counseled had been going to Blackthorne for the treatment and had found it helpful. As hard as it was to measure mental health, the indicators pointed out that the patients I hadn't counseled who had done the breathing had also done well but not *as well.*

After hours poring over the file, I closed it.

Nice to know I'd helped. Really. But I'd been used. I called Ronin to chew him out, but he wasn't in the office. His cell went to voicemail.

Ronin had been in my life a long time. I enjoyed our constant exchange of witty insults and careless cruelties. His dream of a PTSD-free world was more noble than I'd expected from him, but he was clearly willing to lie to achieve it.

Words aside, his actions were louder and stronger.

He considered me a friend like I considered a roll of toilet paper a best buddy.

"YOU SHOULD HAVE SEEN HIM," I said, hugging my arms as I paced up the Central Park rock and down again.

Jenn had given up on our workout already and was sitting in the grass, touching her toes.

"He was distraught," I continued. "Really, really upset. Deeply. If you weren't me, you wouldn't even know how deeply, but I could see it."

"And now you're more dedicated to going than ever before."

"I can't leave him there."

"You didn't 'leave him there.' He went. He's an adult."

"I can't do this." I was walking back and forth so quickly I was almost at a canter. "Doing nothing is... no. Negative."

"Can you sit please? You're making me anxious."

I threw myself down next to her. "He says he's coming back." I flopped back and faced the canopy of tree branches. The leaves veiled the sky. "I should wait."

"So, you'll wait."

I put my hands over my face to block out the setting sun, but I couldn't block out the tourists, the traffic, or the laughter of children running through the grass. "I am so scared I can't even think."

"Okay, I would ask you what you're scared of, but I already know the answer, so I'm not going to waste your time or mine. You're welcome."

"Thank you." I took my arm off my face and looked at her. "For listening and everything else."

"Close your eyes. I'm working on a meditation for my guys."

"A meditation?" I made an *ick* face.

"Are you going to help me practice or not?"

"Oh, I'm *helping*? Okay." I closed my eyes, grateful to be given something to do. The light through my lids was broken by the shifting shadows of the leaves. I exhaled a small portion of my tension. "I'm ready."

"Focus on my voice."

I took a deep breath and listened, letting the noises of the park slip away, while my friend's voice rose and fell with the rhythm of the earth.

What is your fear?

Call it by its name.

Imagine the fear as an object.

Give it a shape and a color. Put it in a place and leave it there. Observe it. Note its dimensions and its depth. Describe its boundaries and its ability to move... or not.

Proportional to your own body, is it large? Is it heavy? Is the weight balanced? Could you carry it if you needed to? Or does it hold you in one place?

Now imagine it getting smaller.

And smaller.

Make it as small as the palm of your hand.

Note its new dimensions, color, texture. Note what's changed when its size is reduced.

If you haven't already, pick it up.

Hold it in your hand.

Feel the texture and weight of your fear.

Will you put it down and walk away?

Do you put it in your pocket?

Or do you crush it in your fist?

Now that you're holding your fear, the only thing you can't do is nothing.

Chapter Fifty-Five

CADEN

We sneaked down to an OR in the dead of night like lovers. Naked from the waist down, Colonel DeLeon had her legs spread. In stirrups. I wasn't surprised when she refused general anesthesia.

"Like what you see?" she asked.

"Looks healthy."

"God, this is going to be so good."

"Women usually say that before I scrape out their uterus."

She'd assured me she wasn't pregnant, and from what I could see, she had been telling the truth.

"You're being funny, but getting this bleeding to stop is going to change my life."

"This will pinch a little."

"He said."

She wrinkled her nose when it pinched.

"I would have done this for nothing, you know," I said as I worked.

"As your commanding officer, I don't like pushing for nontransactional favors. Hard limit. We're even. That works for me."

"Works for me too. You're going to feel some discomfort now."

"He said."

I didn't realize I'd forgotten about my Skype with Greysen until the procedure was done and I was snapping off my gloves.

WHEN IT WAS a decent hour in New York, I called our home phone from the base. Her mother picked up.

"Ma?"

"Caden! How are you?"

She was a truly nice person but strong. Stronger than my mother for sure.

"Good. I can't stay on long. Is Greysen there?"

There was clicking and shuffling before she could even answer me.

"Caden?" My wife turned my name into a question.

"I'm coming home, baby."

"When?"

"I don't know. I put in a leave request, and I have it on good authority it's going to be approved."

"But—"

"Just stay there. Can you just stay?"

A pause, bloated and heavy. I could practically hear her hardening her jaw.

"Don't come here," I continued. "Just wait."

"All right. I'll try. But temporary leave doesn't change anything."

"I love you. You know that?"

"Yeah. I do."

We hung up. I knew it changed nothing. I knew it left half the job done. But stalling would have to suffice for now.

WHEN I HEARD the whine overhead, I held on to the bathroom sink with my toothbrush sticking between my lips and foam dripping down my chin. I knew what it was before I spit. The siren wailed, and a voice over the loudspeaker said to take cover.

I rinsed and dressed quickly. I was an old hand at feeling nothing. As the new Thing got louder, I got better at stuffing my emotions, fears, and reactions away.

We were told the attack had come from a residential area over the Tigris, but that was later. It landed near the presidential palace inside the Green Zone, about two and a half miles from the hospital. The explosions were sharp, pounding, more resonant than when they fell in the Red Zone. The earth shook gently and quickly nine times. One for each mortar.

"That's some minty-fresh breath you have there, Asshole Eyes."

DeLeon and I were smashed against each other with our medical kits on our laps. Two paramedics had smashed us together in the back of the Humvee. A hit to the Green Zone felt personal. It felt like our neighborhood. We weren't staying inside the hospital.

"The better not to kiss you with."

"Your loss!" she shouted as we slammed over a pothole.

"How are you feeling?" I asked.

"Is this my follow-up visit?" The truck whipped around a turn, and we hung on.

"It's all your insurance covers."

She barked a laugh. "I feel great!"

We lost our smiles as we came upon one of the royal palaces. A corner had been knocked off. A block away, a crater opened in the road. People were running everywhere as the Humvee rolled into the blast perimeter. We were out before the truck fully stopped.

A paramedic with soot on his face ran up. "Nurse or doctor?"

"Surgeons," she said. "Both of us."

DeLeon was pulled toward an ambulance while I was taken to a patch of grass where the wounded were being triaged.

"We can't move him."

An Iraqui boy of about thirteen was sitting up against a tree. He looked fine until I got close enough to see the iron rod impaling his chest. I trotted up to him. There was no blood. His breathing was raspy. The medic called his vitals. She was obviously upset.

"We can't see if it's through the spine."

"You're making the lady sad," I said in terrible Arabic.

He turned to me. He was lucid. Good.

"Do you speak English?" It was my best Arabic phrase, but the boy shook his head. Great.

I tried to see the exit wound, but it was against and possibly through the tree. I ran my hand behind him as he whispered something I couldn't understand.

"Let's get his shirt open." We got the shirt open. Clean entry. Right of the sternum. "I can't determine the angle," I said to the paramedic. "But we have to get him to the OR. If he's pinned to the tree, we have to cut the pipe."

There had been another time an Iraqi had tried to talk to me. Another incident outside the confines of a hospital. It had been...

Dujon. Dujon.

... bad. I hadn't listened.

He whispered again.

I reached behind him again, then heard clearly what he was saying.

"Kunbulla. Is that your name, kid?" I stopped myself and asked, "Your name?" in Arabic as I felt behind him for the pipe's exit.

Around us, people ran, shifted, called out. They prepped a stretcher. Ambulances moved, and the earth turned, but I was focused solely on my probing fingers and the boy's bloody lips.

"Kunbulla." The boy made eye contact, trying to warn me. Apologizing at the same time as he was begging me to save him.

Dujon.

In complete emotional detachment, I remembered. I'd thought she'd been reading my name tape. I'd thought she'd been saying "Dr. John."

Right?

Kunbulla.

Dujon.

My fingers didn't find the place where the bar exited, but a solid mass, squared at the edges, thick as a pack of cigarettes, and as dense as a few metric tons of potential energy.

Qunbula.

Shit.

Chapter Fifty-Six

GREYSEN

The computer started making noise after five in the morning. I ignored it, then the night table phone rang.

"Mmh."

"Pick up Skype. I need to see you."

HE WAS FRESHLY SHOWERED. Hair wet. Face scrubbed and shaved.

It was noon there, but his hours had to be all over the place.

"Hi." When his smile turned back down, one cheek stayed red.

"Your face is scraped up."

He put his hand to it. Looked at his fingertips. No blood. The abrasions were too fine.

"What happened?"

"*Qunbula* apparently."

I gasped. "A bomb?"

"Yeah."

"Are you all right?"

"Yeah. I'm fine."

"What happened?"

"I told you."

His look through the screen, across thousands of miles, was as hard and cold as granite. He was quite possibly more beautiful when he was like this than when he was warm with love. But I couldn't compare what I couldn't see.

"You can tell me more without giving away locations. You don't have to say what time or who you were with. Come on. Stop treating me like I don't know the rules. And stop acting like talking to me isn't important."

"Why do you push like this? I just wanted to see your face."

I leaned into the camera. "You have what you want. Plus my unconditional love. Nothing you say is going to scare me."

"That's what I'm afraid of."

The only thing he feared was my fearlessness.

"Did you get the leave?" I asked. "Are you coming back?"

He bit his upper lip and let it pop out. If the resolution had been better, I was sure I'd have seen the dampness of that top lip and a pinkish blur where his teeth had scraped the skin.

"Do you know the Arabic word, sounds like *dujon*?"

"I don't, but my Arabic isn't that good." I wrote it down phonetically. I'd never learned the alphabet. "Is anyone fluent there?"

"Yeah. I'll try them."

"Where did you hear it?"

"It was a suicide bomber," he said.

Where? Medevacs got to the Red Zone after the bombs went off. Was it in the Green Zone? Why were you near him? How did they get in?

Tell me everything.

I couldn't ask any of those questions because he couldn't answer them. I put my hand over my mouth partly in shock, partly to shut myself up.

"A kid," Caden continued. "I was trying to move him. He was… I can't say without giving up the order of events."

"I understand."

"He warned us he was wrapped, and we got away."

"Are you doing all right?"

"I'm fine. I'm sure I'm fine." He was trying to convince himself.

"Tell me."

Those two words broke something in him. Was it the right time to ask? Had something changed?

"It's getting harder," he said. "The Thing. It's different. It's not fear and sympathy. It's anger."

Anger.

What would that split look like if it was allowed to happen?

"Sometimes," he continued, "I think it's all right and I can manage. Then days like today, it's a four-alarm fire."

He bent his body to run his fingers through his hair, turning his face from me for a moment. When he popped back up, I touched the screen where his lips moved.

"We have ways of keeping it down," I said. "But my parents are in the next room."

He looked at his watch. "Dad'll be up soon."

"Can you make it until tonight? I can send them to a movie."

"I'll spend the afternoon deciding where to bruise you."

"I miss you."

"About that...I have some bad news."

"Let me guess." I let my fingers fall from the screen. That needed to be the only expression of disappointment. I couldn't lay more on him. "After today's incident, all R&R passes and nonmedical leaves are withdrawn."

"Baby," he said softly, with a voice that never let me feel infantilized, only loved with the depth one loves their own blood. "I know I can't stop you from doing what you want."

"You didn't marry me for my obedience."

"No, I didn't."

The implication in his tone was that maybe he should have. I let it go. I heard my dad startle awake as if a bomb had just gone off.

"They're up," I said. "I love you, Major."

"I love you too."

We hung up, and I leaned back in my chair. If this Thing was like the old Thing and it was getting louder more frequently, we were back in the old pattern.

I could stay. I could be that obedient women he hadn't wanted. I could live in our house and patiently wait for something to happen. Be the bedrock of his chaotic life. It wasn't as if I had nothing to do in New York.

Trusting him came naturally. He'd never presented as a player or a cheat. Even when I'd broken into his locker, I had been ready to have completely misjudged him. But when I considered that if he needed rough sex to stay sane, he'd have to get it, and I'd have to deal with it. My blood curdled. Even the thought of him touching another woman made my palms sweat and my skin prickle with angry heat.

That wasn't on the table. If he'd wanted a milquetoast housewife, he'd had his pick. He'd married me because I pushed his boundaries and let him push mine. But not every limit needed to be tested.

Some lines had to be crossed so others wouldn't be.

Part Seven

Chapter Fifty-Seven

GREYSEN

The Phrog's dual rotors buzzed like a swarm of bees. My knuckles were striated in white and pink, and my palms already ached in the center. I kept my eyes on my boots and focused on the pain, feeling it in three dimensions as the shooting ache ran from my right wrist to my shoulder. That helped. Focusing on pain always did.

Nothing had changed. Not for me.

The Iraqi sky was still an infinite blue, but now I knew why that blue had always spoken to me, calling me into it. It borrowed the color from my husband's eyes.

On the way to the Blackthorne offices in Baghdad, I was flooded with fear that I'd drop out of that glassy vacuum and into the solid mass of the earth. Falling away from that blue was falling away from Caden.

"You all right, Frazier?"

I let go of the bench long enough to direct a thumbs-up at Dana Testarino, a PA and fellow contractor. She'd called me by my civilian name, reminding me that I was rankless and unprotected. I had no unit, no position, no military hierarchy. Ronin wasn't there to rib me. Jenn wasn't there to defend me. I was surrounded by a dozen other contractors. We were professional advisors. Experts in our fields. We'd bought our own kits and supplies mostly. I had a cold case strapped to the floor between my feet. It held prefilled syringes of the same compound they gave subjects before the *soo-hoo*s. It was called BiCam145.

"Some of the subjects are active military," Ronin had said. "They're in your files.

Major St. John and Specialist Leslie Yarrow have placebo instead of serum because we can't predict how they're going to react."

That was how I got confirmation on the other subject with childhood trauma. That was too bad. I liked her. I didn't want her to suffer, and I didn't want her to see me reenter Iraq as a contractor. I'd thought I didn't have a bone in my body that could feel shame, but I was wrong.

"What is it?" I'd asked.

"It triggers the bioenergetic breathing response. It opens doors. One dose for each subject, premeasured. When the hub touches skin"—through the plastic, he pointed at the rubbery white base of the needle—"it turns blue, and when it's removed, it's self-sealing."

I picked one out of the box. "Why?"

"To make sure the BiCam goes into a body, not another vial."

"To prevent corporate espionage, I presume?"

"Only the latest and best technology."

The latest and best was strapped down tight, and didn't budge when the Chinook swooped around, dropping in a stomach-twisting plunge that brought me closer to my husband and his grounded blue eyes.

BLACKTHORNE HQ OCCUPIED A U-SHAPED, three-story gray brutalist shithouse in the Green Zone. After they took our bags and we were split into military and personnel specialists, we were led to the plaza in the center of the U, next to a dry fountain. Birds chirped. Flowers and tree branches swayed in the breeze. People walked the verandas above, hustling from one place to the next.

Dana sat to my right. A rabbi in his twenties named David was on my left. To the left of him, two men who looked like really tough accountants stood in the shade. Dana and I were partnered. She could administer medications but not diagnose. David was a psychologist. We were the new mental health team.

"It's so nice," Dana said, indicating the trees, the birds, the infinite blue sky. "You'd never think there was a war going on."

"Yeah," I agreed, but I didn't.

A man in a dark suit approached with a file tucked in his elbow. He was six-four, under two hundred pounds, with a rubbery gait that made him look as though he'd fall down with each step. He was in his fifties, with black hair graying at the temples and a widow's peak.

"Good morning! I'm Ferhad Ghazi." He had a slight accent I couldn't place, and when he opened his arms, I saw a small notebook clipped on top of the papers. Like everyone there, he kept a handgun in a shoulder holster. "Welcome to Blackthorne HQ." He smiled like a salesman. My first instinct was to stand when approached, but I wasn't in the army anymore. "I am your ambassador for the Green Zone office."

HOW FAR AWAY WAS CADEN? What was he doing? Who was he with? He hadn't responded to my flight plans. Had he gotten the email? Did he know I was on the same continent, under the same flag, flying against the same sky?

We shed the accountants on the first floor. They went behind a set of double doors with a guy built like a toolshed. Ferhad brought David, Dana, and me to a large space with dozens of desks. Plants dotted the corners, and motivational posters hung on the white walls. Metal grates over the windows cut the sunlight in half.

"We take pride in our people," Ferhad said as we walked through the room. His voice was smooth and sonorous indoors. "So, we're fully staffed to take care of them. We utilize the military's medical facilities, but as you know"—he nodded to the three of us—"we supplement with our own professionals." He stopped on the other side of the room, at a door with a black box by the handle. "Your ID cards open this area."

He swiped his ID card over the black box. The red light turned green, and the door clacked. He opened it into a reception area. We were introduced to the receptionist and led to a clinic on the other side of the building. Examination rooms. Crash carts. Gurneys. Labeled plastic bins. The only thing that differentiated it from a military hospital was the quiet.

"Your office, Mister Rothstein." Ferhad opened the door to a relatively pleasant office with a desk and worn but cushioned chairs.

"Ladies..." Ferhad took us to the office next door.

Dana was shown her desk in the clinic. My office looked much like David's except for the cold case of syringes sitting ready on my desk.

"We need a refrigerator for this case," I said, pointing at the cooler of BiCam.

"Down the hall," he said.

I heard a loud *ho* from outside. Looking out the window, I saw a man fall off the roof of a four-story building. I gasped and pointed.

Ferhad laughed.

"Did you see that?"

"Yes, yes," he said, waving me to the window on the other side of the room. "Look from here."

He showed me the angle to look from. Another figure jumped, but now I could see them turn midair and rappel from the side of the building. "It's our training facility."

"That's so cool!" Dana exclaimed.

"That's so scary." I was still shaking.

"Yes, but look at the bottom. The blue and yellow?"

At ground level, around the corner of another building, I saw a sliver of blue and yellow stripes, like a pillow covered in a termite tent.

"I see it. Is it an inflatable bag?"

"Yes. So see? You don't have to worry." He pressed my shaking hands in his in a gesture that was not seductive but healing. "Have you seen your quarters yet?"

"Not yet!" Dana was chipper. You'd never have known she'd just been on a military transport.

"We got you a lovely place very close by. Let's get that put away, and I'll have a car bring you."

I HELPED Dana unpack her apartment first, then she helped me. It only took a few hours.

We were in furnished apartments in the Green Zone. The building wasn't new, but it was made from sturdy brick and cracking stucco.

Caden was inside the hospital compound, just under a quarter mile away. It was visible from the third-floor cafeteria at work, and if I could get to the roof of the apartment building, I'd bet good money I could see it.

My bones were made of iron filings, and he was a magnet, drawing my body's brittleness to the surface. Tonight, I'd go there. I'd fight exhaustion and jet lag. I'd see him. Touch him. Smell the coffee grounds and cut grass on his skin. I'd let him have me. I'd beg him to break me.

"You're smiling," Dana said as she wiped down my counter.

"Weird, right?" I put the last of my clothes in the old armoire and closed the door. It was next to the couch because there was no space in the bedroom.

"There's plenty to smile about," she said with the twang of an accent I'd noticed before. "We're making good money. Helping the country. Having an adventure. It's great."

"Where are you from?"

"New Jersey. You?"

"All over. But I landed in New York last."

"We're practically sisters!" Dana opened a can of Coke she'd picked up from the chow hall and leaned on the counter. "Have you seen the guy I'm next door to?"

"Nope."

"Name's Bob Trona, and he's totally hot in this Tom Hardy kind of way."

"Hm. Name rings a bell."

She picked up the novel I'd set aside and flipped to the inside flap. "He was in *Band of Brothers* and—"

"I mean Trona."

Putting a few cups and plates in the cabinet, I saw out of the corner of my eye a piece of paper slip out of the book. She picked it up and gasped so loudly I thought she'd hurt herself.

"What?"

She held up Grady's sonogram with a big shit-eating grin. "This! You're—"

"No, no. That's not me."

She turned it over to look. "The name's all rubbed off."

"It's been through a lot. It came from a soldier in Fallujah I never met. His wife. It's a long story. It's... I don't know. I feel obligated to take it around with me in case I meet a relative or something."

"You're so nice," she said, placing it on the table before turning back to the book.

I smiled. Of course she thought I was nice. That said more about her than it did about me.

I COULDN'T WALK to the hospital alone, especially after dark. Green Zone or not, security was locked down. I caught a ride with a guy armed to the teeth on his way to train the Iraqi Army in counterintelligence. We were stopped twice in the quarter mile and waved along once.

As the hospital came into view, my heart raced. *Soon, soon.*

Caden and I hadn't been separated that long, and I'd thought I was handling it okay, but I wasn't. Not until I stepped through the hospital doors and knew I could see him at any minute did I realize how nervous I was. Not until I was standing in the middle of the admitting room with no idea whom to ask what did I realize I was out of place. I approached the desk.

"Can I help you?" A uniformed woman looked up from a clipboard. She had a touch of lip gloss and had given her lashes a quick brush of mascara. Her long, straight hair was wrapped tight in the back of her head. It was lighter than mine and matched her eyes. She had a colonel's bird on her collar, and her name tape said DeLeon.

"I'm looking for Dr. St. John."

"Oh, yeah?" She put down the clipboard and looked me up and down.

No leaf cluster or name tape told her who I was. I could have been anyone or no one.

"I'm his wife."

Her gaze flicked over me again, making a different assessment. I held up the Blackthorne ID around my neck.

"Well, it's nice to meet you." She held out her hand. I shook it. "He's in surgery." She called to a black man who was passing, "Stoney. Asshole's wife."

Asshole?

"He's... wait..."

Not an asshole.

But Stoney was shaking my hand, as was a white guy with curly red hair and a short black woman in scrubs. They expressed surprise and shot questions about how long I was going to be around and why I'd come so far to see such an egotistical jerk. Good, solid army ribbing.

"All right," DeLeon said, putting her hand on my shoulder. "Come on. Let's go see what he's up to."

She brought me down a wide, well-lit hallway with a clean tile floor.

"This is much nicer than Balad," I said, letting her know I wasn't some civilian rube. I was jealous of her access to my husband and the place she had in his world.

"It'll do. Were you also there for Fallujah part two?"

"We met right about then."

"And now you're contracting?" The question was loaded, and the answer was worse.

"It's complicated."

"He's a complicated guy." The words left her lips with a touch of bitter syrup.

Something was going on with her. Any doubt I'd had about coming to Baghdad was swept away. I needed to be here.

DeLeon opened the door to a scrub room. "We got a medevac in about two hours ago." She went to the other side of the room to a set of double doors with windows. "He should be finishing up." She peered through. "Yep."

I looked through the other window. Caden's head was bowed over the patient, and his fingers nimbly threaded the wound closed. DeLeon tapped the window. He looked up, saw her first, and smiled warmly.

Too warmly.

When he saw me, the smile dropped into a frown.

Every drop of fluid in my body boiled.

DELEON WAS GONE, leaving me in the scrub room alone. When the surgery was done, the team came in, chattering about the operation. Caden entered last, snapping off a glove and yanking his mask down as if he wanted to say something. But nothing came from his beautiful, generous lips. He held them tight together as mine quivered, locking me in his gaze. The noise of the room was on the other side of a long tunnel.

He was here. No screen. No camera. No microphone. He was a foot away, living, breathing, sucking all the energy in the room. The sun was tucked under the horizon, but in his eyes, it was always daytime.

Wound tight as a man who's been disobeyed for the last time, he peeled off his other glove without looking away from me. "Welcome to Baghdad, baby."

HIS SPACE WAS the size of a dorm room. Still in scrubs, without saying any more than "Follow me," he'd led me across a narrow street to a heavy door, up a flight of stairs, and down a hall that echoed my footsteps.

He had a twin bed made so tightly I could have bounced a quarter on it. A sink with a mirror. A cheap pressed-wood wardrobe. His trunk. A desk with a plastic chair. He closed the door to his room and locked it but didn't turn to me. He just kept his hand on the lock.

"Greysen." The muscles of his back were defined against the fabric stretching across it.

"Caden." I held my hand out to put it between his shoulder blades and draw it down to his ass but pulled it back before touching him.

"You're here."

"I told you I was coming."

He put his forehead on the door. "I'm so disappointed I can barely think."

"I know."

"In myself."

"It's not your fault." Taking a deep breath, I put my hand on his back.

He curved away, turning around quickly, as if I'd stung him. "That's not what I meant. It's all locked up. I don't feel anything. I'm detached from myself. And when I see you, all I can think about is how you're the cure for everything that's wrong with me." His hands flexed open and closed as if they were ready to grab something and hold it tight enough to crush it.

"I am the cure," I whispered, unbuttoning my shirt. "Take your medicine."

Watching me unbutton, he considered, then put his hand on my bare skin. "I want to lay everything at your feet." He took me by the throat, digging his thumb and middle finger into each side of my jaw. "Leave it all on the table."

"Take it. Leave it." I undid the last button, exposing my simple white bra. He tightened his grip just enough to see if I was scared. I wasn't. I was a node of firing desire. A liquid conductor of sexual electricity. "I'm yours."

He murmured close to my face. I wanted a kiss so badly I was drunk with the need for it, but his lips didn't touch mine.

"Take off your clothes." He put upward pressure, making his hand the one thing to unbalance me and the one thing to keep me upright. I undid my pants on my tiptoes as he murmured to my face, "You're going to break without a sound. Not a word. Not a scream. If you want me to stop, you better say it quietly."

My pants fell around my ankles. I still had my boots on.

He let me go and leaned back, taking me in, then walked behind me. I felt his sky-colored eyes along the length of my body, from the hair coming out of its ponytail to the pants pooled around my ankles. He unhooked my bra and slid it off, then yanked my underwear down around my thighs.

"I can smell your cunt," he whispered into the back of my neck. "It's apples." He laid his lips on the muscle between my neck and shoulder. "It's delicious, just like your pain." He bit me slowly. His teeth were all pleasure with an increasing tension. I gasped, swallowing a cry. With the same slow control, he reduced the pressure of the bite.

"Caden," I whispered.

"Are you telling me to stop?" He wrapped his arm around me, grabbing a tit at the base and working up to the nipple.

"No."

With his other hand, he pressed four fingers between my legs, opening me. He ran his lips to my other shoulder and made a matching bite with excruciating slowness. Tears dropped down my cheeks.

"If you have something else to say," he said when he released my flesh, "do it now. Quietly." His hand stopped moving.

"Have you been faithful to me?"

I felt him shake his head, and taking that as a no, my tears increased.

"Oh, baby." He came around to face me. and his hand cupped my chin. "There's no one who can love me like you do."

"So, you didn't?"

"Never."

I tilted my face to kiss the palm of his hand. He stayed in the caress for a moment, then kicked off his shoes and twisted out of his shirt. I stepped out of my boots and pants, fully naked.

He cradled me in his arms, whispering, "I wish you hadn't come. I'm so glad you came."

Chapter Fifty-Eight

When I'd hurt her and she cried, the buzz had sighed, draping itself over me like a bedspread thrown wide over a mattress. I held it on a leash but let it get its satisfaction.

The raw potential of the Thing had rumbled behind a thin wall. Pure, uncontrolled rage. A hunger for destruction. Tearing her apart, destroying her, all those were figures of speech until I had to hold back what it wanted.

The leash was strong enough, but for how long?

WE BOTH NEEDED A SHOWER, and mine was down the hall. I was off duty, and leaving the hospital compound was generally overlooked if it didn't interfere with work and I showed up for emergencies.

So, I took Greysen back to her place on the Blackthorne compound.

"I've only been here once," she said in the dark, "so give me a minute." It wasn't dark for long. Motion-sensor lights flicked on when we passed entry doors. "This is me. Number three."

The door was a hundred years old, but the keypad next to it was brand new. She waved her card past the laser. It beeped and clicked open.

"Oh, hi!" A woman's voice came from behind, and I spun around to get between Greysen and whatever danger my brain had decided was creeping up behind us. It was a woman in her late twenties with a blond bob and bangs. "Sorry about the mess." She picked up the plastic cups, and I relaxed.

"It's fine," Greysen said. "Dana, this is my husband, Caden. He's over in the hospital."

"Nice to meet you."

We shook hands. Her nails were manicured. That wouldn't last long.

"Ferhad came by. He put an envelope under your door."

"Thanks," Greysen said. "See you tomorrow."

"Bye!" Dana said merrily and skipped off.

"She could stand to cheer up a little," I said.

"Don't give her any ideas." My wife leaned into the door, pushing it open.

As promised, a white envelope was on the floor.

OUR FIRST NIGHT IN BAGHDAD, I stayed in her apartment. It was on the upper floor and came furnished with linens and sheets, like a hotel. The cracked stucco building behind an eight-foot cinderblock wall had four doorbells and a keypad. Behind the iron gate was a small yard with swinging lanterns strung between the house and the perimeter poles over a beat-up table, with half-used candles and two plastic cups, surrounded by mismatched but functional chairs.

With the anger placated, I felt more in control. I didn't have to lock everything away to keep it quiet. Before I'd given her pain, my emotions had been locked away. Afterward, I faced the fact that I was upset that she'd come, and I was also relieved to see her.

With her, even insanity felt controllable. With her, I was strong enough, good enough, capable enough. She made a shitty world come up flowers and rainbows. She didn't erase the cruelty and ignorance, but when she was in the room, I couldn't deny that as ugly as shit got, beauty and perfection existed. The Universe with a capital U had something to aspire to.

She sat between my legs in the bathtub, her back to my chest. Her trapezius muscles were beat to shit where I'd bitten them.

"Dana's licensed to administer meds but not prescribe." Greysen told me about her job. "And she needs MD oversight. So, we've written up all the scripts in case of emergency."

I kissed her shoulder. "This might hurt when you lift your arm."

She leaned back against me. "It'll remind me of you."

"So what's the point of the shots?" I asked.

"It's for soldiers who've done the treatments you did."

"Really?"

"It reproduces the effect of the breathing exercises. Opens the doors of the mind so memories that cause mental trauma can be detached from negative emotions. If it works, it's years of treatment packed into a few days."

"And you believe this works?"

She sighed and leaned her head back against my shoulder, stretching her beautiful body against me. She pointed her toes against the far wall. "I don't know. I know how it affected you, and there's a sense to it."

"You know how it affected me, do you?"

She turned, kneeling between my legs. "You never told me the breathing was so hard on you." Her lashes were blacker when wet, stuck together like pen marks around her chocolate eyes.

I wiped a cluster of bubbles from her cheek. I shrugged. "I said I'd do the treatment. That means I do the treatment. If I complained, you'd either tell me to stop or feel guilty about it."

"You didn't tell them about your father."

"They didn't ask."

"They didn't ask about childhood abuse?"

She was working hard to be nonconfrontational, but some things were confrontations no matter how you phrased them.

"What do you want from me?"

"I want to know why you didn't tell them."

"I wasn't abused. My mother was."

She bit her lips back as if that would confine what she wanted to say. I knew what it was. Abuse of the mother is abuse of the child. But I didn't agree and I wasn't arguing about it.

She put her hand on my chest. "I'm on your side."

"I know. But it's my life. I'll characterize it the way I want. And not to change the subject"—I held up my finger—"you should have stayed home."

"It's my life." She repeated my words, then bit her lower lip against a smile that demilitarized the entire subject.

I put my hands on her hips and pulled her to me. "It's *our* life."

I sealed my answer with a deep kiss.

———

THE PRAYER CHANT woke me at dawn. Greysen was next to me, her hair spread over the pillow like a veil.

"I never thought I'd hate prayer," she said, eyes still closed.

"I have to go anyway." I kissed her cheek. "I'm on rotation."

She got up on one elbow. "I'm sore everywhere."

"Good." I got out of bed and put on my pants. My dick had its own sore spot after entering her so many times the night before. That was good too.

She sat with a groan and stretched as I got my shirt on. "You're doing the walk of shame."

"I've never been less ashamed of anything."

I kissed her. When I tried to pull away, she held me back.

"I love you, Caden."

"I know you do. No one would do such stupid shit unless they were in love."

Chapter Fifty-Nine

GREYSEN

There were a few cups and plates in the cupboards but no coffee. Without a commissary, I'd have to get it at a local Green Zone vendor.

The envelope was on the table by the front door. Flipping it over, I saw a sticker over the flap. CONFIDENTIAL. I tore it and slid out the stapled pages.

CLEAN MINDS PROJECT
List of subjects.

The cover letter gave instructions for use of BiCam145. Each was marked with the name and serial number of the recipient. No substitutions. No transfers. No changes in dose. To be administered by the psychiatrist or physician's assistant on staff after a traumatic event. Subject to be monitored closely afterward. Surveys given before and after. I knew all this already.

Under the letter was a list of names. I flipped to S.

Caden was there with an asterisk. So was Yarrow. The back-page footnote was clear.

*placebo recommended.

There was a quick, demanding knock at the door. Maybe Caden had forgotten something? I peeked out the window.

A dark-haired, fully-armed man in US Army-issued camouflage. His back was to me, but I'd have recognized that cocky posture anywhere.

I whipped the door open and leapt into his arms. "Jake!"

He held me up as if I was twelve all over again and he was my strapping big brother. "Punky!"

He spun me around.

"Oh my God," I said when he dropped me back to the floor. "So long. It's been—"

"Since your wedding." He smiled, drinking in the sight of me like a thirsty man. "I missed your crazy ass."

"Come in!"

"I only have a minute unless I want to go AWOL."

"I have to get to work. Come, come." I ushered him in and closed the door. "Sit. God, you look like such a *man*."

He had always been handsome, but he'd earned some toughness around the cheeks and a few lines around his eyes.

"You look skinny." He clearly didn't approve.

"Don't get me started. Tea? There are mint leaves growing in the front. I picked a few."

"Sure. They set you up nice."

"Perk of the job." I filled the teapot and plugged it in. "You should see the office."

"And you don't get bossed around as much."

I stuffed leaves into two glass cups. "Oh, there's plenty of bossing around. I heard you got your silver bar?"

"Again."

Jake had been demoted back to butterbar twice. He followed orders but had a habit of doing it in whichever way he found personally appropriate.

"Well, you'll keep it this time." I sat across from him while the teapot did its work. "How have you been? And get right to it."

"You never liked small talk."

"Not from you."

"Are you going to psychoanalyze me?"

"Yep. And we have about fifty minutes. No charge."

He leaned back in the chair, legs spread, hands linked over his chest. "I shouldn't have taken this deployment. It was stupid."

"Why?"

"I could ask you why you came back."

"You could. You first though." I was on the edge of my seat, not for the answer but for the comfort of his voice.

"Remember that time you called me from that punk club? The Spot or something?"

I did but barely. I'd been drunk, eighteen, and frightened our parents would be mad. He'd picked me up and taken me home.

"The Red Spot, and it wasn't punk. It was New Wave."

"The night before you enlisted."

A wave of panic went through me, as if talking about this was a toxic sea I was being asked to jump into.

"Let me check on the tea." I bounced up. The electric pot was already hissing. "Sugar?"

"No, thank you. Do you know, I've never felt as useful as that night? Every time I come here, I think I'm going to be doing something I can be proud of, and I'm wrong every fucking time."

I poured the tea. "You're useful. You just can't see the big picture. None of us can."

"Maybe the picture's too big for me."

I was supposed to listen without judgment or direction, but I could still feel the sulfuric sting of the toxic sea and changed the subject. "What about a woman in your life?" I poured hot water over mint leaves. "Anyone?"

He shrugged. "This and that. How's the moms and dads?"

"We did a little reminiscing when they came to visit. I found out about the talk you had with Scott Verehoven's father."

A smile spread across his face. "Yeah."

"That was gross, Jake." I handed him his glass.

"But I felt useful. See, that's the key. I wasn't looking for shit that wasn't there or securing a road we'd lose in a month. I could rescue a damsel in distress."

"Really, Jake?" I tucked myself into the chair across from him, cradling my glass. "That's sad. You could have let the lawyers take care of it."

"Fuck the lawyers." He blew on the tea. "We take care of business. It's the Frazier way."

That was how I'd found myself in Baghdad. Just taking care of business. That was why Jake had been bumped down to butterbar twice. We were a family of people completely unsuited to the military, yet there we were, three generations in.

I raised my glass cup. "To the Frazier way."

He clicked his cup to mine. "The Frazier way."

"I missed you," I said.

"I missed you too. Now tell me what the fuck you're doing with Blackthorne? You came for your husband."

I sighed. We had thirty more minutes, and I feared we'd spend it talking about me. "I did. I came for him. He didn't want me to, but I did it anyway."

He knocked his scalding tea back in a single gulp before clicking the glass on the table.

"That's how we roll," he said, and I knew that as much as he didn't approve of my decision, he'd never deny it was the right one.

DAYS WENT by without word from Caden. If I put my cheek to the window in my office, I could see the hospital. The soreness in my shoulders and between my legs faded. Whenever I saw a Blackhawk land on the pad by the hospital, I wondered if he was on it.

I counseled my fellow contractors in the mornings over marital and money issues. The afternoon's paperwork was ten percent less odious than the army's and geared more toward ass-covering than record-keeping.

The BiCam145 serum inside the "latest and best" syringes had been filed away in a refrigerator, but it weighed on me. I wanted to see if it worked. Through my work counseling Blackthorne's patients, I'd unknowingly had a small part in its development, and I felt responsible for it.

Ferhad's lunch tray was pushed to the side. He ignored Dana and me in favor of the little notepad he carried on his clipboard. He was a poet and could write it in the middle of a conversation.

"This is terrible," I said, dropping the rest of my chicken salad sandwich onto the plate.

"I hear it's harder to get food and stuff into the Green Zone since the bomb attack," Dana said before finishing the last of her sandwich. In addition to being a font of good cheer, she was a first-class news-gatherer.

"Everyone's on edge," Ferhad said, pencil still moving. "Zone isn't as green as it used to be."

"The Zone's always greener on the other side of the wire." Dana giggled at her own joke.

"They strapped bombs to a child." Ferhad put down his pencil. "If the doctor trying to help him didn't speak Arabic, another dozen would have been dead."

"He—"

—doesn't actually speak it.

No one needed to know what Caden spoke or didn't.

"What does *dujon* mean in Arabic?" I asked. "I speak a little, but I've never heard it."

"I don't know if it's Arabic," he said.

"Oh." I glanced at Ferhad's poetry. "I thought you were writing in Arabic."

"This is Sorani. It's Kurdish."

"Ah, I'm sorry to assume."

He waved it off. "It's a fine thing. *Dujon*"—he said it with a different inflection —"is Kurdish too. It means 'I'm pregnant.'"

THAT NIGHT, I reconstructed the conversation where Caden had mentioned the word. He had been talking about the suicide bomber, but I was sure he'd said it was a boy.

Who had been pregnant? And when?

Maybe Caden had gotten the word wrong and I'd made it worse. Maybe it was a different word altogether. There might have been no mystery there, but it nagged at me. Right next to the place where I doubted I should have come to Iraq at all.

I wasn't watching over my husband. Wasn't caring for him. I still missed him. I still didn't know if he was in danger, and even if he was, I had no way of preventing it.

In the middle of the night, I curled up inside myself, wondering if I knew what I was doing at all. I assumed I was wide awake until the phone rang.

"Dr. Frazier. This is Colonel DeLeon."

I shot up to a sitting position as if I'd been administered a day's worth of cortisol. "Caden?"

"No, no. Hold up."

"What?"

"It's not Caden. Old Asshole Eyes is just fine. I'm calling you as the psychiatrist on staff at Blackthorne."

I put my hand to my forehead and tried to think calm thoughts. "Okay. Sorry. Go ahead."

"I have two patients here. Just got pulled out of a fire this past morning. Both their files got a big note on them. I'm supposed to call you guys if they're showing signs of traumatic stress."

"Right. Yes." I swung my legs over the side of the bed. "Can I have their names?"

"What's this about?"

"They were part of a DoD-sponsored protocol. I'll bring releases."

"You better." She gave me the names.

I HANDED DeLeon the releases and a pamphlet describing how I didn't have to tell her shit either because of (or in spite of) the fact that Blackthorne was paid by the Pentagon.

She stuck her tongue in her cheek as she flipped through the pamphlet. "This is bullshit. You know that, right?"

"If I were in your shoes, I'd say the same thing."

"What's in the case?"

"It's confidential."

"Yeah, well, I'm not going to do chem tests on it. I want to look at it." She crossed her arms. "They're in my hospital. I could tell you to just fuck off."

She could, as a practical matter. If I wanted to challenge her, I'd have to make a series of phone calls I didn't want to waste time on. I put the box on the desk and opened it.

Without asking, she pulled out the plastic bag with the syringe numbered for Specialist Gregory Linderman. "What is it?"

"It's new. Experimental. And it partners with a lot of work he's already put in." Implying she owed it to the man to let him finish what he'd started.

"Why's there only one?"

I reached into the side pocket for the placebo marked with Leslie Yarrow's number. I didn't want to get them mixed up.

"Prefilled? They don't trust you to do your job?"

"Less transfer from container to container means less chance someone from Halliburton will get their hands on it."

She handed back Linderman's syringe. "If you weren't married to Asshole Eyes, this wouldn't fly, you know."

"If you weren't his CO, I'd throat punch you for calling him Asshole Eyes."

She whooped a laugh, pointing at me after she clapped. "Wifey for the win. Come with me."

Chapter Sixty

CADEN

Fighting through a barrage of fire and explosives for control over the blocks around some royal palace or another, they'd found a basement of children tied to hooks in the cement floor. All were malnourished. Three were dead.

Linderman was a mess. He'd come off the chopper with a broken leg an Eagle Scout could have fixed, but he was shaking so hard we couldn't set the bone. We gave him enough sedative to stop the shaking, but when it wore off, he stared in the middle distance with a notable lack of affect.

Yarrow seemed better at first. Burn wounds on her left side. They'd scar but heal. She started crying the next morning and couldn't stop.

"What the fuck?" On the computer, DeLeon had been scanning their files before calling in the psychiatrist. She picked up the phone. "I'll say hi to Wifey for you."

I looked over her shoulder. Blackthorne subjects.

I wondered if I had the same red box in my file.

I wondered about the children in the basement.

I wondered if there had been blood from the dead ones and if it smelled of copper in the darkness.

I COULDN'T GET the children in the cellar out of my mind. The cold floor. The weight of the dark. The smell of blood and the dying ones.

The anger Greysen had helped me satisfy two days ago faded into consciousness, and I was left with the buzz of emotions as a separate thing fought to push through the membrane of my defenses and swallow me in blackness.

It wanted her. It was drawn to her tears and her broken skin.

My better self needed her. She anchored me.

I hadn't seen her in days, which was nothing. But at the same time... too long. I kept half an eye on her as long as she was sitting in the ICU.

"How old are you?" DeLeon asked.

"Thirty-seven, why?"

"You're like a smitten teenager." She pointed at Greysen, whom I'd surreptitiously been watching through a window.

From afar, I'd watched her speak to Linderman for an hour with little response. She'd talked to their CO about what they'd experienced and taken notes. She waved when she saw me, and I nodded then pretended to ignore her. Now she was taking out the syringe, talking to Miss Cheerypants.

"For Chrissakes." DeLeon rolled her eyes. "Can you go over there and make sure she knows what she's doing?"

"She knows what she's doing."

"Go watch her anyway before I puke."

<hr>

"I'M SUPPOSED TO WATCH YOU," I said as Greysen unwrapped Linderman's shot.

He was still in his fugue in the ICU, one room over. Dana had scurried off to take notes on Yarrow.

"I'm capable of giving an injection. You should know that." She checked the prefilled amount with the amount on her sheet.

"How's he doing?"

"Bad. And she was one of mine, from New York." She shook her head slightly. She cared about her people, and this bothered her.

"They're both going home," I said.

"Good. What they saw. What happened." She put the needle on a tray. "I'd be traumatized."

"Yeah. Me too."

"Caden."

"Don't. I'm fine."

Still as a statue holding a metal tray with a single syringe, she clearly didn't believe me.

"Go," I said. "Before they send him home without your damn shot."

She went, and I walked behind her. She was the light in the infinite darkness. The fiery star in the blackness of space. With her, there were no cellars.

And yet, the cellar wanted to eat her alive.

I WATCHED from a safe distance as she administered Linderman's injection. The base of the needle turned blue, and she placed it on the tray.

Then she went to talk to Yarrow, and I still watched her—not because DeLeon had told me to, but because I couldn't take my attention off her. She sat at Yarrow's bedside for over two hours, leaning forward the entire time as if she didn't want to miss a single word.

That beautiful face, in a cry of pain. My pain. Pain I took from her. A part of me knew I was deep inside the darkest parts of the chasm I carried, but there was so much pleasure there for both of us.

DeLeon came up next to me and spoke softly. "Go look at Linderman."

"Why?"

"Shut up and do it."

I tore myself away from Greysen and went to the ICU, where Linderman was sitting up in bed, eating a cup of Jell-O, and joking with one of his buddies. He was animated, warm, seemingly unbroken.

It was as if the children in the cellar had never happened.

Could she erase the cellar for me? Could she make me normal?

Did I want to be?

I should have been happy for Linderman, but I didn't know whether to envy him or resent him, so I cut off all my feelings about it and added it to the buzz that tried to push its way through me.

Chapter Sixty-One

GREYSEN

The sadness worked its way through Yarrow's body, wracking it with sobs. For up to ten minutes at a time, she couldn't form words. I sat with her and waited every time. I liked her. Whether or not I should have come to Iraq for Caden was a moot point. This woman needed a familiar face. She made it all worth it.

"Oh, man," she said in an interstice between crying jags. "I'm so glad you're here."

"Do you want me to arrange a call to Molly?"

"Not yet. I don't want her to hear me like this, and I can't... I can't tell her about those kids." She folded a tissue into a square, absently creasing the edges. "She got upset when I told her about the bloody face. Couldn't sleep for a week."

The face was a man in her unit who'd died from a head wound. Blood covered his face, his teeth, the whites of his eyes as he screamed. She'd stayed with him as he died and brought him home with her.

"When you were working with me, you said there had been this feeling of being watched. Like someone else was always with you."

"Yeah." The crying had slowed now that she was distracted.

"You were doing treatments at Blackthorne for it."

"I wasn't supposed to tell anyone."

"I know. But..." I held up the contractor ID that hung around my neck.

"Right. So, you know about it."

Caden and Yarrow had experienced childhood abuse. If Caden's work in the black room was painful, Yarrow's might have been too. But outside that room, my husband's results had been remarkable. The psychic overload had slowed. Had he been able to keep up with it, he would have had enough respite to work through the issue normally.

I'd been taught the timing and tone of the breathing in New York. I could help her even with a placebo.

"Did the sessions help?" I asked.

"Yeah. They did actually."

"I know it's busy in here and the lights are bright, but can you do the breathing if I guide you?"

"I think so."

"If it gets too much, squeeze my hand, and I'll bring you out."

"Okay."

I put my hand under hers. "You're going to be all right."

"When I close my eyes, I see them."

"I'm going to give you other things to see."

"Okay. I trust you."

"Close your eyes and pretend you're in the Blackthorne offices. Walk through the halls. Your arm hurts where they gave you the shot. The tech lets you into the small room. See the yellow light of the lamp. The way it makes the black walls look dark gray. You sit and feel the chair under you. You see the cameras. They make you feel safe because you know you're not alone."

Her face relaxed, and her breathing got shallow and clear of sobs.

"The tech hooks up your monitors and leaves. The door clicks closed behind her. You're comfortable and safe." I waited, watching to make sure she believed she was safe. "Begin the circular breathing with me. *Soo-hoo. Soo-hoo.*"

YARROW WAS RESTING. She'd sobbed her way through the breathing, but it wasn't fear or powerlessness. It was cathartic. She came out of it renewed enough to call her wife and give her the good news. She was going home.

Dana came up to me as I was leaving the ICU.

"Hey, you signed off on all these." She handed me a clipboard with the signed releases. "We still have one in the bag."

"I didn't give her the shot yet."

"Why not?"

"It's a placebo." I flipped through the pages, signing. "I wasn't wasting time with it when she was in real pain. I'll give it to her before she leaves."

"Okay. Hey, have you seen Linderman?"

"I was about to go check on him." I handed back the clipboard.

"It's like a miracle."

DELEON HAD WOKEN me at dawn. It was now midmorning. I was hungry and tired.

I was also elated.

Ronin had used me. He was a complete shit. Always was and always would be. But after seeing Linderman, I knew this thing worked. Long-term effects remained to be seen, but in the short term, it fucking worked.

When Caden and I had been deployed together, a million years ago in 2004, we'd had inconsistent schedules. They'd been posted on a white board behind the nurses' station. If either of us noticed a crack of time where we could eat a meal together, we'd put a red dot by the other's name for the cafeteria or a T to meet in his trailer.

Baghdad had a similar setup. I didn't have my schedule posted, but there was a red R by Caden's. He was calling me.

HE OPENED the door and stood to the side so I could come in, then closed it behind me. I spun around and kissed him so hard and so fast it took him a second to catch up.

"It works," I said, peppering him with kisses. "All of it. It works."

"What—?"

"The breathing. The shot. Everything." I dropped my voice, remembering the thin walls. "God, I need you to fuck me now."

He threw me on the bed and stood over me. I hadn't taken a second to look at him before kissing him, but at that angle, I saw a shadow of Cold Caden's expression. The Not Damon. Always there, even with Damon gone.

I toed off my boots as he undid his belt.

"Caden," I said, "if Damon's gone, was he replaced with something else?"

He froze. I'd hit on something I hadn't known I was aiming for.

"Tell me," I said, opening my voice to accept an answer I wouldn't like hearing.

"There's something." He whipped his belt out of the loops. "It doesn't have a name."

"Damon didn't have one at first."

He undid his button and zipper. "This one's too angry to have a name. It wants to destroy everything. It's dumb and pissed off, and I have a handle on it."

"So, I shouldn't be scared?" I didn't feel scared.

He bent over and yanked down my waistband, whispering with a rumble, "I'll let you know. I can't welt your ass, or everyone will hear," he said. "But you'll cry anyway. You'll cry like you've never cried."

This was Cold Caden.

I could fix this man, but when he talked like that, I didn't want to.

"Always make me cry," I said as he tied off the tubing. He looked down at me, mouth firm. "Always find my edge."

"No talking." He held up the surgical clamp so I could see it. "Not unless you're telling me to stop. Understand?"

"Yes."

He calculated, blue eyes flicking side to side across my defenseless body.

"I saw Linderman. And I saw you with Yarrow. You want to do that to me. You want to make me your patient."

So businesslike he could have been closing off a bleeding artery, he peeled off his shirt and stepped out of his pants until he was wearing nothing more than his dog tags. Wedging himself between my legs, he kissed my cheek and murmured, "Your pain is beautiful. If you fix me, will I still think so?"

"I WANT the shot you gave Linderman," Caden said quickly, as if he didn't want to think too hard about it.

The afternoon sun shot through the window grates. We were dressed and satisfied. He was himself again, the two halves joined by my pain.

"I can't."

"Why not?"

I took a deep breath. He hated talking about his childhood. "It's for when you look like Linderman or Yarrow. Not for random Tuesdays."

"I'll have to get traumatized then."

"Hush, you." I poked him in the chest, and he held me tight.

"I want you to traumatize me." He tickled me, and I laughed.

"Stop or you'll traumatize me." I pushed him away, but he caught me and threw me on the bed, laughing, kissing my face and neck.

The knock at the door interrupted us.

He snapped his head around. "What?"

"Um, hey!" It was Dana. "Is Dr. Greysen in there?"

Caden opened the door. My PA hugged a clipboard.

"What's going on?" I asked her.

"It's Yarrow."

"FORTY-FIVE MINUTES AGO," Dana said as we strode through the hospital doors. "She seemed fine."

"Why did you give her the BiCam without me?"

"They had a space on the next chopper out. I knew you wanted to give it to her before she left. I came by your husband's door, but the bed was squeaking."

I'd been warned about the thin walls and was about to give her a talking-to about procedures when I heard the screams. We ran down the hall.

An ICU bed twisted at an angle next to a fallen IV tower. A signature of blood streaked the floor, and at the end of it, three MPs held a red-faced Yarrow on her stomach as she screamed. They weren't hurting her, but there was murder in her voice.

"Don't! Don't do it to me!"

"Wait!" I called to the MPs.

I ran, slipped on the blood, and fell, getting my wrist out of the way in time to land on my elbow. I scurried to her, getting on my knees. She'd been fine, just fine, a few hours ago. She'd been smiling and calm. Now she'd bitten her tongue and was bleeding out of her mouth.

"Ma'am," the MP said, "we have to move her out."

"Hang on. It's Doctor Frazier, Leslie. Can you see me?"

She looked at me. Or to be more accurate, her eyes landed in my direction.

I wanted to reach into her and pull out her pain. I wanted her to watch me wrestle it down and kill it for her. But it wasn't ever that easy. Ever.

"Don't," she pleaded. "Please."

"I won't hurt you."

"Don't let him do it to me again." She tried to get loose, but the MP held her more tightly.

I leveled my gaze at her. "You're sa—"

"Ma'am! Stand away."

"Don't let him hurt me!" Yarrow shouted. "Tell him tomorrow." Tears ran across the bridge of her nose and mixed with the blood.

"Not today. Not tomorrow."

"If you talk nice to Daddy, he listens sometimes."

"He's dead, Leslie. He died alone and miserable."

She broke down in tears. The doc on staff swabbed her arm and gave her a sedative.

I turned my attention to the MPs. The one who had told me to get away was firm but not without compassion in his expression.

"Be gentle with her," I said. "Please."

"We will be."

Caden stood in the doorway with his arms crossed. I couldn't look at him. He was my strength and stability. I was a buoy in a storm, and he anchored me to the sea floor. But he'd gone through the same treatments as Yarrow and gotten a placebo for the same reason. Knowing he could turn into a screaming face on the hospital floor was too much to bear.

"YOU ALREADY SIGNED off on the shot." Dana articulated every word as if speaking more slowly would help me understand. She had her hands folded between her knees, and she sat on the edge of the chair on the other side of my desk. "If she left without it, the paperwork would be wrong."

"I am aware of that. Thank you. From now on, BiCam is not to be administered without me."

"So, I should have *knocked*?" Confrontation with a side of sarcasm, because of course, who knocks on a bedroom door when they can hear the bed squeaking? People have *shame*.

"Yes, you should have knocked."

Her eyes went just a little wider.

"Dana." I folded my hands on my desk. "People fuck. They do it behind closed doors, in beds that sometimes squeak."

"Awkward."

"Would you rather feel awkward or have an episode like that?"

"You don't know it was the shot. You said it was a placebo."

"I know."

"Was it a placebo or not?"

I tapped my fingertips together. The pamphlet said it was a placebo. The staff at Blackthorne NY had said it was placebo. It shouldn't have affected her at all.

Was it the breathing? Had I done it?

The door clicked open behind Dana, and Ferhad poked his head in. "New York is on in Conference Room Three."

"WE NEED THE SYRINGE," Ronin said from the screen.

"We have it," I said. I'd already stowed the syringe with its blue-tinted hub to send back.

"I need a report with every detail. The circular breaths. The shot. Everything." He leaned on the end of a long, shiny table with chairs around it. Through the windows on his right, New York was overlaid with late morning clouds. "That's not supposed to happen."

I leaned against the conference table in Baghdad with the same sun under the same sky in the windows. "Was it a placebo?"

"Yes. I'm sure."

"Are you sure there wasn't a mix-up?"

"We'll test it and let you know."

"I don't care what you test. What about Leslie? What are you going to do for her now?"

He shook his head slowly. Nothing he could do. Out of his hands. A woman had bitten her tongue bloody, but if it happened again, it was just because shit happened.

"I want you to test Caden's," I said. "Before I administer it, I want you to make sure it's a placebo."

"I can't unseal it." Putting his hands behind him, he grabbed the edge of the table. "That would defeat the purpose."

"How about I just don't give it to him?"

"I'll see if we can send a new one. How is that?"

"Fine."

"Fine. Moving on."

"Moving on," I agreed.

"You can't tie your PA's hands. She has to do her job."

"She didn't waste any time going to you, did she?"

"We only hire the best, Greysen. If the job needs to get done, it needs to get done. She doesn't need a babysitter."

Maybe I was being ridiculous. I had signed for the placebo because I thought it was fine. I would have given it to Yarrow even if Dana had knocked on the door. Blaming her was useless and adding another layer of bureaucracy to our jobs wouldn't undo it. Prevention was in Dana seeing what had happened. She wouldn't want to be responsible for it happening again.

Chapter Sixty-Two

CADEN

Only the bottom ten feet of the Green Zone were actually green. High walls and barbed wire didn't keep out the rockets and mortars. I knew from personal experience that a suicide bomber could get past the gates and checkpoints.

The Green Zone was at least as dangerous as Balad Air Base had been three years before, yet it was different. Not more or less. Just different.

When I had been at Balad, Greysen was close to me. She was a major in the army. She was protected.

At Balad, I'd been sane.

Now, I wasn't.

I'd said a lot of things in New York when the whispers started, but I'd never let myself believe that I was truly insane. I'd admitted to a problem. A temporary illness. A set of symptoms curable with the right treatment.

But when I saw Yarrow crawling on the floor, overtaken by fears she thought she'd overcome, I called her insane in my mind. I had compassion for her plight, but at the same time, I categorized her neatly. She was crazy.

It was a dismissal, and I didn't realize I was doing it until I recognized the child's pleas that came out of her mouth. A woman's voice with a child's desperation. An identity twisted backward on itself.

What was the difference between her and me?

Nothing.

Nothing at all.

I came to this at my most lucid, right after tying my wife to the bed, but two days later, when the buzz started swarming, the reality of it had to be shut away. It had to be denied. I grabbed control, and the diligence it took to hold that control meant what it always did.

I had no feelings one way or the other about whether or not I was sane. I had a job to do. The Thing that buzzed and sometimes had a name sucked all the worry and fear into itself, leaving me in peace.

It was a great system even if it was crazy.

When the rockets fell after the midnight prayer, I got dressed. The casualties got to the hospital as the second round shook the earth.

"That was close," the paramedic said, wheeling in an Iraqi civilian who'd had a wall fall on his arm. He stopped where I told him, and the nurse cut the man's sleeve open while I got his vitals.

"Where were you?" I asked as I checked him over.

"At my daughter's house in Kardat Maryam," he said in accented but excellent English.

I didn't have a good sense of where the neighborhoods began and ended, but that was close to Greysen's apartment. It was late. She'd be home.

The nurse opened the sleeve.

"This hurt?" I pressed a spot on his swelling forearm.

He nodded vigorously.

"X-ray," I said to the nurse. "This is Boner's." I turned back to the patient. "We're going to x-ray your arm, and an orthopedist is going to take a look at you."

"Yes. All right."

"Was the neighborhood hit badly?"

"The house is half off."

"And the buildings around it?"

I was sorry about his daughter's house, but I needed to know if my wife was on her way into the ER or under a pile of rubble.

"Nothing. Like God was protecting them."

I DIDN'T BELIEVE in God without Greysen. Didn't buy his protection or his love. My faith only went as far as her well-being. It would snap back if anything happened to her.

I lay awake in the hours before dawn with the Green Zone quiet and my patients recovering. She was all right. She would have come through the doors if she'd been injured.

But the buzz didn't believe it. The buzz needed to check before it let me sleep. I was on medevac duty in three hours, where I'd sit in a room waiting for a nine-line that might never come. I'd stare down the black swarm. I'd keep it locked up while it pushed against its boundaries, forcing me to acknowledge its existence, while I tried to convince myself that I wasn't out of my fucking mind.

I was in my room, pacing. Pretending I had it under control. I wasn't panicked as much as I knew this wasn't right.

I tried to call her. The signal here was so bad calls dropped before they rang, and the one time I got through, my wife didn't pick up.

The shelling had stopped. I was off duty. If she was in danger, I'd know it by now. She would have been wheeled in.

And yet...

And yet...

You can't take care of her.

I froze.

The buzz didn't coalesce into Damon's voice. There wasn't a question in it. It wasn't immature and cowardly. The buzz growled its words. It was angry. I felt its rage like a knife in my thoughts, not a cloud over them.

What would it be to unleash this Thing?

I snapped up my jacket.

***

I RANG the bell outside her apartment. When she didn't answer, I took inventory of the wall. There were no streetlights, but the moon showed me no way to scale it. I pressed it again. If she didn't answer in sixty seconds, I'd check the perimeter. Maybe there would be a way to climb over in the back.

The light went from blue to yellow. Her light.

Voices. A woman and a man. The blade cut through my thoughts again.

"I don't know," she said.

Not Greysen. The blade retracted, but I was aware of its presence in the sheath.

The little window behind the gate opened, and a man's face looked through. "Who's there?"

"I'm looking for Greysen."

"That's Caden," the woman's voice said. "Her husband." It was Dana, chipper as always and, if I had to make a guess, a little tipsy.

The door snapped open. I recognized the man from a football game in Fallujah. With a hairline that had receded a few inches since the last time I saw him, he looked as if more than three years had passed.

"Pfc. Trona."

"Hey! Captain Fobbit." He held out his hand after Dana closed the gate behind me. "Oh, sorry. Major. Got your leaves, I see."

The front yard's hanging lights were on, and the little table had one plastic cup and a bottle of wine. Dana had the other cup in her hand.

"Yeah. I heard this neighborhood took some shelling."

"A little west of here."

"Everyone all right?"

He put his arm around Dana. "All good. I thought you went home."

"Didn't last."

"Greysen's upstairs," Dana said as my wife's door opened on the veranda above.

Greysen leaned over the railing in sweatpants and slippers, her back bathed in light from her apartment. The army T-shirt was worn to gauze, and she had to cross her hoodie over her hard nipples. "Caden?"

She hustled down, zipping her sweatshirt, and I went to the bottom of the stairs to meet her. "I wanted to make sure you were all right."

"I'm fine."

"Come sit," Trona said, "have some wine."

Dana reached under the table for the sleeve of cups. "Yeah! Hang out."

Neither Greysen nor I answered. I couldn't stop looking at her body. The brown eyes, warm in the chilly night, her feet in her slippers. The perfectly-shaped toes in front, a genetic gift, with the callouses from hard work in the back. Her hair was a nest from sleep, and her eyes were puffy. I didn't need to see the scar under her shirt or inside her right wrist to know they were there. This was what a woman looked like when she'd lived her life fully. The choices she made were all over her body and her manner.

"Sit, sit!" Dana said. "Was it busy at the hospital after the shelling? We didn't get a call that one of ours came in."

"Not too bad," I said with my eyes on my wife. I was so intent on her I didn't notice the buzz or concern myself with the angry voice.

Greysen sat on the bench and took a cup from Trona. She thanked him and, with a glance and a smirk, invited me to sit next to her. The night was quiet except for the wind and the crickets that dotted the white walls of the building. The buzz had been tamed for the moment. The woman I'd married was safe and beautiful.

"You knew these guys?" Dana asked Trona when we were all sitting. "Was it from Fallujah?"

"Yeah. Threw a football around with this guy."

"You have a good arm," I said. "Are you stationed here?"

"Contracting. Can't beat the money." He pointed his cup at the window next to Greysen's. "I live in the apartment right up there."

"Don't let him fool you," Greysen said with a smile. "He's been living in the apartment downstairs since he met this lady."

Trona put his arm around Dana, and they shared a kiss.

"At least when he's here," she said with a playful pout. "He's out doing security runs all the time."

"Fucking nuts out in the Red." He shook his head.

I let my hand creep over to Greysen's lap, sliding it over hers. We wove our fingers together.

"Tell me about it," I said.

"What are they calling you here?" Trona poured more wine. "Can't call you Fobbit anymore."

"Asshole Eyes," Greysen said with a scowl.

Trona cracked up. "I'm not even gonna ask."

"What's Fobbit?" Dana asked.

"It means he's an inexperienced rube who doesn't go over the wire," Greysen said, swirling her cup. "Which I preferred."

"Yeah," Trona said. "After that medevac you were on in Fallujah, I'm surprised you ever went out again. More power to you, man. I drink to your balls."

"What happened?" Dana asked.

"Nothing," I said. "Not that big a deal."

"We had sniper fire on a convoy out. He was good. Hit a full bird colonel."

"Colonel Brogue," Greysen said.

"Yeah, and civ haji were everywhere. Our guy hit a woman running away. I dragged her into the building we were holed up in, but she was bleeding bad out her leg."

"Femoral artery," I added. I didn't want him to recount this story. Not here. Not ever. But I couldn't react, or I'd overreact. It was easier to tamp it all down. "It was a mess, but we got there in time."

"For the colonel," Trona added. "But that lady with her screaming? Gave away our location."

I was about to change the subject, but Greysen leaned forward as if she was interested in his story. I put my eyes on my cup. It was half-filled with blood.

"Then what?" Greysen prodded.

"We held them off. But the medic's trying to put on the tourniquet, and she's screaming his name, this guy right here." He indicated me. "Or I thought that was what it was. St. John. *Dujon, dujon*. Like, okay we get it. You want the doctor. Can we not tell the world where we are?"

"Oh, my God." Dana was rapt, and Trona loved it.

I tried to take a sip of wine, but the liquid in my cup smelled like copper and discarded tissue.

"We dragged her and the doc into a fucking closet while we waited for a pickup and tried to get things under control. When we opened it…" He paused.

Maybe he was checking my reaction. I didn't know. The cup was full, and it reeked of death.

"She was dead. The tourniquet held, but there was blood everywhere. Man."

Greysen's hand was cold in mine.

"Our interpreter said *dujon* wasn't the name on Fobbit's uniform," Trona said. "He told us in the chopper, didn't you hear? It means 'I'm pregnant.'"

"She miscarried from blood loss." Greysen's voice was an electric blanket that warmed the air and fried the mind at the same time. "And it killed her."

"Dunno," Trona said.

"That's right," I said flatly. "That's exactly what happened."

Greysen let go of my hand, and my world narrowed into a long, endless hallway.

"Oh, my God, no more war stories!" Dana cried. "Let's polish off this bottle. Okay?"

My wife swigged the last gulp of wine and put down her cup. "You guys finish it. I have to be up early tomorrow."

She got up and went to the steps. I knew that if I didn't follow right behind, she'd slam the door in my face.

I was right. At the top, she got it halfway closed. I put my hand on it and passed through.

"Get out," she hissed.

I shut the door behind me. "What's the problem?"

"You lied. You said she lived. You said everyone lived. You *lied* to me."

"So what?"

She turned toward her bedroom, and I knew I wasn't invited there.

"How does what happened that night affect you?" I asked. "Or us? Or anything?"

"You. Lied." Her voice was as steady and thick as the air around us.

"I had my reasons."

"Good night, Caden. Be safe walking back."

My wife could yell. She could get spitting, kicking, screaming mad. But this? She was stating facts with utter clarity, as if she'd looked at the situation from down the block and decided to cross the street to keep her distance from it.

No.

She never walked away from a conflict.

Anger swelled, stretched, heavy as a water balloon filled to the breaking point.

In two steps, I had her arm clasped in my fingers.

"Don't touch me."

The man I'd always been released her, but the buzzing rage heard the hard flatness in her voice and wouldn't let go.

Hurt her.

"It's nothing." I heard myself growl as if I was an observer.

Hurt her until she listens.

"Let me go, or your balls are going to be removed from your body."

The threat didn't move me. I wasn't worried about my testicles. But I made a calculated decision that I had nothing to gain from holding her, and the angry man inside me, the one who was pushing to get out, agreed with the assessment and released her arm.

"You can do anything to me," she said. "You can hurt me. You can push every boundary I have. But lying? Lying's a line, and you crossed it."

"I had to."

She cocked her head and folded her arms.

"I didn't want to talk about it."

"Not acceptable."

"You have no right to be this way. Whether or not a casualty died has no effect on you or us. It's none of your damn business."

She was going to try to redefine her business, and I was prepared to answer her point for point, then I was going to fuck the—

"How many times?" She interrupted my train of thought.

"How many times what?"

"You lied about the woman. You lied about the word *dujon*..."

"I just forgot it."

"You lied about your father."

Now I wanted to choke her. My hands flexed into fists and unflexed. She looked at them, then back at my face. Her fearlessness was a clinical condition.

"You pushed too far, Caden. Multiple times. Over years. Lies of omission. Lies of minimization. Lies I don't even know about. And I let you get away with it. I pretended you hadn't gone over the line, but I knew. I knew."

"What's the fight for, *baby*?" Baby wasn't a coo; it was a gunshot, and I was too deep inside anger to mitigate the damage. "You want to sit here all night and grill me about every word I've ever said to you? What's your endgame? You want to split up? Walk away? If I crossed some kind of line with you, let's talk about how you react when I tell you things. Because you're pushy. You're stubborn. You don't do what you're fucking told, and you have no regard for me as a separate person. I only exist as I relate to you."

Anger is always a partner to righteousness, and I was fucking right. She was an impossible woman to deal with. A life-sucker. A divorce waiting to happen. Standing there looking at the floor between us, as still as a predator waiting for an opening. Not to kill me. No, an opening to love me to fucking death.

And yet... I wanted her, and I wanted her to want me. And I wanted her to move the damned line for the lies the way she moved it for everything else.

And yet... what I wanted was taking a back seat to something much more toxic.

"What?" I leaned toward her. "Nothing to say? Not spouting all the answers? For once?"

That lit a fire under her. "Go home."

Her anger opened a gate wide, releasing a swarm of hornets. I had to look away so she didn't see the full-throated rage, and when I did, I saw a paper rectangle on the table.

A sonogram. Early. Under twelve weeks.

It took a split second to analyze it.

I didn't know what I looked like when I turned back to her, but I was covered in darkness and the buzz, the leash broken, unable to pull back the need to break her.

It took her a single move to get past the threshold to her room. She slammed the door before I could reach her, and the bang of wood hitting wood made the earth shake and tilt.

Chapter Sixty-Three

At first, I thought he was banging on the door. I thought he was banging so hard the ground shook. I thought he hit the door forcefully enough to shake the plaster from the walls and ceiling with a deep, ear-splitting *pow*. He must have grown twenty feet tall, bursting through the upper story and the roof. His rage was an explosion of rock and a rain of dust.

I crouched, arms over my head to protect me from his falling debris. It didn't work. I was knocked over by it. It filled my lungs with fire and smothered me in darkness.

GREYSEN, Greysen, Greysen—baby, baby, baby—I want to tell you a story.

HIS VOICE CIRCLED the outer reaches of my consciousness. There was blood and black, air thick in my nose and hot in my lungs. A driving cramp in my gut and a sharp ache in my head. I couldn't move. I thought my eyes were closed, then I blinked. It was so dark I couldn't tell the difference. I coughed, and a warm flood soaked my pants.

What a time to get my period.

"Greysen?"

His voice. A bark. Close. Five feet? Three?

"Caden." I was alive. "Where are you?"

"Right here." His voice seemed deeper in the small space. A low roar. "Can you move?"

I took stock of my extremities. "My arms. There's something heavy on my legs."

Glass clinked as he moved toward me. "Can you feel them?"

I felt him near, but there was no light. I couldn't see, and my head hurt too much to move. "They hurt."

"That's good." He swallowed the last word into a rasp. A growl from deep in his chest. His hand fell on my hair splayed over the floor, gripping and pulling.

He released my hair, and our hands found each other in the darkness. He squeezed my fingers so hard he hurt me, and I became deeply aware of the small space and my inability to move inside it.

"Caden? Are you crying?"

No. This wasn't crying. He was hurtling air out of himself. This was something deeper. An inner battle I couldn't fathom.

He uttered a single word. It was rage and danger in a syllable, barked like an animal in a cage.

"No."

Chapter Sixty-Four

CADEN

The brain craves information. It starves in the absence of light. Pupils dilate like open mouths, crowding the irises until they're thin rings of color. That's all eyes are —collectors of information for a brain wired to make sense of the environment with very little data.

Modern people rarely experience complete darkness. Light pollution smothers out the darkness. Even without it, starlight can illuminate the path ahead. A sliver of moon behind clouds sends enough data to the brain to make out shapes.

When there's nothing, like in a cave or a windowless concrete cellar, the other senses collect more information, cracking open perceptions that are usually shut.

The smack of the mortar shell came at the same moment she slammed the door in my face, and the ensuing heat, fire, and rumble came as I cracked inside, letting the anger take shape, fully formed.

It had a name, but I wouldn't say it, and getting knocked over by half a wall took the wind out of its appearance. It was half in, half out, like a dog stuck in the cat door.

In the distance, more shells fell. I had to breathe. Take stock. The rubble had formed a pocket of complete darkness. A drop of warm liquid fell over my cheek. I was cut. My hands were free. I touched my face. Glass. I removed what I could. My foot was under something heavy. I shifted it, and a brick came off easily, but when I tried to turn, glass clinked under me, and a sharp pain seared the heel of my hand.

"Greysen?"

She didn't answer. The wall between us must have crumbled, because her breathing was close. I pulled my sleeves over my hands and crawled to her. My back scraped against something hard. Tight space. Dark. I felt for her body. She was so close. I could smell her. Hear her. I could sense the blood pulsing through her body, but I couldn't find her.

If she was dead, the Thing would eat me alive in fury.

"Baby. Please."

Rock. Just rock. Such a small space and such infinite darkness.

A woman I loved in such danger, in such a tight space, and me—helpless to save her.

This wasn't—

This didn't—

No. I was a grown man.

I wasn't—

I didn't—

"Greysen."

The smell of blood everywhere. She had to be all right. This couldn't happen. Not again. Not to me. The blood was copper and broken bodies. It flowed like a river, and it was my fault. The anger with the name I wouldn't articulate wedged its way out another inch, growling and hissing simultaneously.

No.

"Greysen!"

Her name was a shout in the dark, eaten by a small space without an echo. I didn't hear a response, but my hearing had been sharpened on the stone of darkness. I would have sworn I heard her heart beating. Maybe it was my own heart. Maybe they were beating with matching rhythms.

I wouldn't give up on her. Not now. Not ever. I wouldn't lose anything else in the dark. I'd lost too many women in the dark. Too many had hurt in my hands but out of my sight.

Not Greysen. Never Greysen.

I took a deep breath so I could call louder, harder. Bring her back from the dead if I had to. The air cracked into dust and shards, slicing my windpipe on the way down. I coughed before I could scream her name again.

"Caden." She was alive. "Where are you?"

Her voice. The sound of an angel choking on sand and broken seashells.

I reached for it and found a handful of her hair. I left myself. I was in a closet. I was in the bottle room. I was trapped in the smell of blood and hopelessness.

"Right here. Can you move?" My voice was swallowed by the air, pressed into impotence. Anger, unreasonable and explosive, pushed against judgment. It howled a single word with both insult and justification.

Dujon.

"I don't know," Greysen said. "Where are you?"

Her voice pulled me to reason.

I hadn't realized how dead still the air was until it moved from the swing of her arms. I found her hand, and the touch wasn't fortifying. It split the membrane, hitting me like a bomb on an apartment building.

Dujon.

"Can you move?" I asked, focusing on the moment, not the crowd of memories funneling into my consciousness.

She's pregnant.

She's pregnant.

"My arms. There's something heavy on my legs."

I'm trying to understand her, but nothing makes sense.

Her legs. My wife's beautiful legs.

Covered in so much blood, I thought she was wearing stockings.

"Can you feel them?" I was on my belly near her, squeezing her hand. I felt her pulse on my fingers, but the buzz was too loud. I couldn't count.

I blamed the darkness. I blamed my weakness.

"They hurt."

"That's good."

"Caden. Are you crying?"

"No."

I spit the word in a voice of pure instinct and raw fury. Maybe I was crying, but it wasn't sadness. Oh, no. It was something more powerful and far less manageable. It didn't have words. Just sounds meant to scare prey into shocked stillness. I was fighting a monster's release, pushing against two sets of events I wanted to forget while my most recent lucid memory was the love of my life slamming a door in my face.

I reached for her and was greeted with a hard, flat surface. Not stone. Wood.

"It's the door," she said. "I think it fell on me, and something's holding it down."

A door between us.

Not a wall.

Dujon, dujon

"I'm all right," she said as if she could feel my panic. "Someone will come."

Why is she saying my name over and over in the dark?

"If I change, Greysen baby, you have to leave me."

"What?!" Her alarm echoed in the space, bringing the realization of how small it was.

My heart rate picked up in panic, and my defenses weakened further. The swarm of hornets buzzed, pushing against the force of my will.

"Never see me again."

It's not your fault, sweetheart. It's just—

That slammed door. Her pushed in. The slap of the lock.

"What's happening?" she asked from far, far away.

"Promise me!" I demanded. "Promise *now*."

"No!"

Our hands found each other. I felt for the hard circle of her ring.

—you're going to have a little sister.

But I wasn't. Not after the lock of the door.

"Mmm," I said, barely audible to myself. I sounded like my own hallucination.

"Never."

It wasn't just the darkness; it was the thickness of it. The weight. The way it closed in while the sounds outside kept on and on like life moving without me.

And the smell. Cloying and coppery. Slurred words and panic swirling into a whirlwind.

"It was my fault."

"Caden?"

Caden?

Dr. John.

She squeezed my hand, and I was boy and man. Adult and child. I could make choices, and I was trapped in my impotence. Cut loose from her and twined with her forever.

"What's happening, Caden? Talk to me."

She needed me.

She needs me because…

"I knew she was pregnant."

"The Iraqi woman?" Greysen said in the darkness. "In Fallujah?"

"I had no idea she was pregnant."

Both were true. I lived two separate realities concurrently. The Iraqi woman spoke with my mother's voice in the darkness.

Dujon.

"She was bleeding," I said. "It was everywhere. She was dying. Because of me. Because I got a B on my history essay. It was the punctuation. The commas. He cut off her air to show me the difference between a *pause* and a *stop*, and when I ran downstairs…"

Boy, you're a coward.

"He put her in there with me. Bullet right through the thigh. The medic tied off the femoral artery, but her pressure dropped and her body got rid of the baby to save itself. I was scared he'd come down and see the mess and hurt her again."

I heard Greysen's response but didn't understand the words. I heard only strength and comfort, as if she was a guide through a frightening and alien land. She pulled me forward.

"She let him do it." I wasn't sure if I was speaking out loud or if the clay-thick air absorbed the sound before anyone heard. "Why did she let him? What the hell was wrong with her? Fuck her. Fuck her for letting him hurt her. God. There's so much blood. She's not moving. She's limp. Her arms and legs. She's—"

—dead. My mother is dead, and I killed her with a B in history because I wasn't careful.

—dead. This woman is dead because you didn't listen to her.

My wife was saying something. The syllables ran together to make one word said in my mother's voice, in a dark closet with gunfire on the other side of the wall and the smell of blood all over the cellar and my eleven-year-old hand being squeezed into pain.

Dujon.

Losing blood.

Duyon.

Blood pressure dropping.

Dayon.

Words slurring.

Danyon.

Heart stopping.

Damon.

The anger breached the crack, and its name became a hard buzz, drowning out the soft-bellied Damon. I was busting from the inside, swelling into a third person of unlimited, ever-expanding rage.

I articulated his name. It was no more or less than a roar without cadence or syllables. Unspellable, unspeakable, a sound that shook the earth and made the broken man inside me shrink into a pin dot.

The bag closed, only this time it wasn't a soft bag held with string, but a tiny room with a metal door. Black as night, I was alone again, listening to the sounds from the kitchen above as he tormented her for all the things I'd done wrong.

"Caden!"

I was so small. Four years old with fat little hands against the cold, concrete wall and the taste of stolen birthday cake on my tongue.

"Caden, listen to me." Greysen's voice from the kitchen. She was getting beaten up there, and she was calling me. "Fight it. Fight hard. I love you. I'm waiting for you. Push against it. You're bigger than this."

I couldn't feel my body. Every sense was muffled, but still she called me.

"I need you. Please. I need you. This is not your limit. You're bigger than this limit. Find it. Find who you are. Breathe. Breathe for me."

What was it about her voice that cut through the sound in my ears and the thick walls around me? She was so calm even as I was hurting her in the kitchen.

"Listen," she whispered, and I heard it. "*Soo-hoo. Soo-hoo.* Breathe with me."

The angry thing believed in destruction. The angry thing roared and growled. It didn't believe in bullshit meditative breathing. But my lungs did, and they obeyed, dragging the dense air in and out without a pause. Dizzying, confusing the angry thing taking me over, while the child in the basement felt the walls go soft.

Soo-hoo. Soo-hoo.

And Damon returned from a deep, deep sleep with his basket of needs and insecurities.

The buzz turned on him.

Soo-hoo. Soo-hoo.

You're weak.

You're worthless.

You're broken.

You are a blemish.

"Caden." Her voice was the pin of gravity, the edges of the Universe, and the anchor holding me to the center of it.

But I couldn't respond to her. It was too much. I was still breathing with a rhythm, even without her guidance, as Damon swirled into the same space as the anger.

I pitied him. I wanted to protect him. But he didn't need my protection. He was ready to die.

"Caden," she repeated without doubt or weakness. "Go into it. Don't run away. Embrace it. This is you. They're all you. I love you."

She was here, in the darkness—

Soo-hoo. Soo-hoo.

—with every mistake I ever made and—

Soo-hoo. Soo-hoo.

—she still loved me.

All the doors opened. A single space in my mind where blame and guilt and cowardice lived next to honesty and bravery and love.

I became aware of my body again, and in one gulped breath, I was whole.

Part Eight

Chapter Sixty-Five

I had a concussion from a falling wooden beam. Boner confirmed the door had saved my leg. It had cracked and fallen on me first, then distributed the impact force of the concrete piece that fell on it. I had a "dead leg," a quadricep contusion that looked as if I'd spilled black and red paint on my thigh just above the knee.

It hurt like hell, truth be told. The pain didn't bother me because my mind was completely occupied with Caden.

Under the rubble of my apartment building, I'd talked him through something neither of us had understood at the time. At one point, he'd just rested his head on my chest, and I'd stroked his hair. We'd waited in silence until we heard the trucks outside, then we shouted for all we were worth. As the voices of rescuers got closer, our shouts were mixed with relieved laughter. When the first shaft of light shot through the debris, I saw him for the first time since I'd slammed the door in his face.

"Wow," was all I could say. He was covered in a mask of gray dust, but the blue of his eyes reflected the morning light like windows to the sky, just like they always did, except for one thing.

The sky wasn't frightening. It was clear and calm, a protective shield not just over me, but over him as well.

"You look stunning yourself," he'd said from above me. "Not that you have a choice, but stay still."

Then he'd looked at the rescue team as they moved another slab, getting between me and the pebbles falling from the sky.

IF I'D STILL HAD my commission, they'd have sent me to Germany to recover, then decide if I had to go back to my unit or go home. But I was a contractor and part of the conversation about my own best interests. The military hospital kept me overnight to monitor the concussion.

In the dim light, surrounded by the soft hiss of machines, Caden leaned into my bed. "Dana and Trona are fine. Minor contusions. A few scrapes. They got sent home."

A rectangle of bandage clung to his forehead where he'd been cut by falling glass.

"For scrapes?"

"Home, Baghdad home."

"It's a pile of rock."

"Blackthorne owns a third of the Green Zone." He sat next to the bed and stroked my cheek. He wasn't the cold, detached man we'd fought to control, nor did he have the soft, insecure expression I'd come to know as Damon's. He was neither and both. He was impossibly complete.

"What's different about you?" I asked.

"Everything." Even his voice was somehow more whole, like a puzzle with all the pieces in place. "It's over."

"It can't be," I said. "Nothing's that easy."

"You call that easy?"

"I don't even know what it was."

"It was all the stuff I never told you." He slid his hand under mine and laid the other one on top. "I'm sorry, Greysen. I'm so sorry I lied to you. I thought if I relived it, I'd... I don't know. Die, maybe, if I want to overstate it." He brushed his thumb along the side of my hand with that perfect pressure I'd come to love. "Let me tell you what happened twice. No, two and a half times."

He was quiet for a long time.

"I wasn't afraid of the dark when I was a kid," he said. "I wasn't afraid of anything. I was like you."

"I'm afraid of plenty."

He shrugged as if I was splitting hairs. "If you say so."

"I'm sorry I interrupted. Go on."

After a short pause, he began again. "I went in the bottle room when I was scared. I could hear everything from the floor above, but I felt safe. I told you this, but I didn't tell you the last time I went down there. I was about eleven. I wasn't a careful kid. I didn't cross my Ts and or dot my Is generally, and composition wasn't my strong subject. I'd gotten back a history essay with too many corrections. Commas. Fucking commas."

I nodded. "Commas are sneaky."

He smiled in the dim light. "I was in a gifted school, and there was a lot of homework. I was tired when I wrote the essay, and I didn't check it over. He—my father—took it out on my mother. Sometimes I got mad at her for putting up with it, but I was always more mad at myself for not checking my work. Like she knew it, she always made sure to blame herself. The more I think about it, the more I think that was why I fell in love with you." He looked at me and squeezed my hand. "You'd never put up with that from me."

I held back a comment, but he read my mind.

"Except on your terms," he said with half a grin. "That's safe for me. Until it wasn't. Then... you know what happened."

"Damon."

"I protected myself from hurting you. I was already fucked in the head with him pushing on me because he was my protector."

"Did you feel split before then though?"

"No, I don't know what opened that up."

I had a feeling I knew what it was, but I wasn't ready to admit my hand in his breakdown. Not to him and not to myself. But I knew.

"Here's what I never told you." He cleared his throat and looked away. "That time, with the commas, he put her in the bottle room with me and locked the door from the outside. He did that sometimes with just me but not for long. This time, after the history essay, it was different. Jesus, this is hard."

I let it be hard. He hadn't dealt with any of it. Hadn't looked it in the face and taken control of it.

"I could hear her, but I couldn't see her. She was crying. She didn't cry in front of me. But she was across that little room, sobbing. And I was on the other side, feeling like it was all my fault but also resenting her for invading my safe place. Then she was groaning in pain. And I said, 'Mom, are you all right?' and she said, 'It's your sister.'"

He didn't have a sister.

"And that..." he said with a deep breath from the bottom of his lungs. "That was when I smelled the blood." His face scrunched into a knot, revealing every beautiful dimple. "It was sticky. So sticky and thick. The smell... and there was so much. Just on and on. A puddle. I thought she was dying. I thought..." Another deep breath he had trouble taking. "I thought I'd killed her."

"She was miscarrying," I whispered, and he nodded.

"I didn't know that. I couldn't see her, and she kept saying she was fine. I thought he'd stabbed her over commas. My commas."

"It wasn't your fault."

He pressed my hand to his lips and closed his eyes. "I didn't know what to do." His lips moved against my knuckles. "She just lay there and said it was okay. She said it wasn't my fault. She forgave me."

"Do you forgive her?"

"Not really. When she stopped groaning from the cramps, I crawled over to her. I got blood all over my hands and knees. She didn't move. I picked up her arm, and it was like a dead weight." He rested his head on my belly, the bandage disappearing in the folds of the sheets, looking at me with sideways eyes. "I swore to her that when we got out, I'd never miss another thing. I'd pay attention to every detail no matter how tired I was. She said, 'Okay.' That was how I knew she wasn't dead."

I ran my fingers through his hair. I was mad at Caden's father for being too dead to face justice, but I wasn't mad at Caden for lying. Not anymore. All the boundaries between us were false walls.

"And then," he continued. "The woman in the closet. The femoral artery. It was like I was eleven again. I asked her to forgive me, but she didn't understand my shitty Arabic."

"Because she was Kurdish."

"I think that was when I first felt Damon, but he was so small."

"And you were doing surgery all the time. The army too. So orderly it was safe to keep him in the background."

His eyes were transparent in the cold light of the moon. "In the rubble, it was different. No Damon. Just a monster. I swear, if you hadn't talked me through it, I don't know what I'd be now. I can do anything with you. I'm still fucked in the head, but it feels normal. I'm a fucked-up person but a *whole* fucked-up person. All the doors opened, and it's one room again."

"I think we stumbled on something," I said. "The breathing, plus the opportunity to face fear and get control. Maybe. I don't know. All I know is you look like the man I fell in love with before all this. You're the fucked-up, brave, honorable, strong asshole I love."

"I'm going to be everything you need from now on."

I believed him. I wasn't sure the world would let us be happy, but I was sure that if happiness was to be found, it was with him. All of him.

He sat up straight and got something from his pocket. He held it close before showing me.

Grady's sonogram.

"I understand why you didn't tell me," he said.

I laughed. He looked wounded.

"It's not mine."

"You lost it. I know." He took my hand as if I needed comfort, but he was the one who needed his hand held.

"No. No, no, no. It's from a soldier in Balad. He died, and I keep it for... I don't know why. Luck or respect."

He laughed once, softly, and the last of his tension fell off in a single breath. "Like a rabbit's foot." He plucked it off the bed.

"I would have told you," I said.

"I found it when we were fighting, so everything was upside down."

"Keep it for good luck or respect."

He slid it into his pocket and tilted his head right, then left to stretch his neck. "I have to get to work. I'll be in the next room if you need me."

"I need you. Trust me."

He bent to kiss my cheek, letting his lips linger on my skin. I turned, laying my mouth against his. Slowly, we entered into a kiss, savoring the taste and touch as if it were the first. His tongue gently met mine, and I melted into a pool of desire. With a leisurely pace, he opened his mouth, and I made my shape match his until we were bound by breaths and moans.

We jerked apart with a rustling of paper and the scrape of a chair behind him.

"I should go." He drew his thumb along my cheek. The corner of the bandage on his forehead had curled a little from laying his head on my chest, and I was struck again by the wholeness I'd taken for granted when we met and that I hadn't seen in a long time.

The Universe, assuming it even existed with a capital U, had a way of demanding Caden's attention. If there was any other explanation for his being repeatedly in dark rooms with bleeding women, I couldn't come up with it.

"We're very lucky," I said.

"There's someone up there watching out for us."

He was more prone to name divine causation than I ever thought possible. You never really know a person.

Chapter Sixty-Six

GREYSEN

They let me out of the hospital the next day. I bought a set of crutches and got a lift to my new apartment. The building was much bigger. Thirty units opening onto shared balconies around a barren courtyard. All Blackthorne personnel. Fortified with a thick wall and barbed wire that wouldn't keep out a bomb any better than the last place.

I was in a single-room studio on the second floor.

"I'm on three," Dana said, unpacking the stuff she'd managed to retrieve from the rubble. "It's a longer walk up the stairs, but it's so great."

I was sure it would be "so great" no matter where she was.

RONIN WAS at my desk like he owned the place. He had a stack of files at one elbow and a cup of coffee at the other.

"Make yourself at home," I said, putting my crutches by the door. I didn't need them to walk but to keep the pressure off a leg working to heal.

"Thanks. I got you coffee." He flipped his hand to a cup by the guest chair. "Black, right?"

I picked it up. "You didn't say you were coming."

"Last minute." He flipped a page.

"What are you looking at?"

"Leslie Yarrow."

"How's she doing?"

"No clue." He closed the file and tossed it across the desk in my direction. "Do you have something useful to add to this fucking shitshow?" He leaned back with his hands linked over his diaphragm. "Because it wasn't supposed to turn out that way. I mean, maybe she's fine now, but that's not an excuse."

I flipped through the file. My report was on top. "I think you need to hold off on this program until you know."

He got pensive on me instead of addressing my suggestion. "Every treatment addressing PTSD focuses on reducing the trauma's impact by serving the trauma back with a sense of control. Facing fears. Defusing memories."

Behind my report was her circular breathing treatment schedule, the BiCam145 dosages, and her questionnaires.

"It's got to be done with a teaspoon," I said. "Not a shovel."

"Is that why you didn't give St. John his syringe?"

Calling my husband by his last name was a way to detach himself and me from the decision. A cute way to remind me that I was a clinician.

"No signs of trauma. He looked better on the way out than the way in."

"Unlike Linderman," he said.

"Unlike Yarrow."

"I feel *bad*." He drew out the last word as if remorse was a foreign concept.

"Like I said, I think you should suspend the program." I got to her application to enter the treatment. Scanned it. "Unless you like feeling *bad*."

"The upside's bigger than my feelings. Speaking of, how do you feel? Heard you were trapped for hours."

"It sucked. However—" I was going to tell him about Caden and facing fears. Defusing memory. Giving control. I was deciding what was Ronin's business, what would be helpful to the program and thus everyone, and what was too private to share. But I got to the last part of Yarrow's file and stopped on a card paper-clipped to a report copied from *Stars and Stripes*. I'd seen her file before but missed this. Leslie Yarrow's unit had been on the front lines in the second battle of Fallujah.

"However, being stuck with Caden St. John was tedious?" he said, trying to get under my skin and failing.

I read while Ronin jabbed me about my husband.

Yarrow's unit had been under sniper fire for three days. Surrounded. Trapped in an abandoned orphanage. They were getting picked off one by one until they rallied and made a heroic escape.

"Are you okay?" Ronin asked.

A single orange card was clipped to the sheet. A form filled in with stubby pencil. A date in 2003, a dosage, and all her basic info scrawled as if in a hurry.

"When you were with Intelligence," I asked, "did they have people embedded on the front lines?"

He shrugged. "Defense? Sure. Are you supposed to be standing with that leg?"

"I have two legs." I handed him the sheet and leaned on my good leg. "This is before you came to Balad."

"Yeah." He scanned the pages and handed them back to me.

"When we were at Balad, I had two jobs, more or less—evaluate soldiers for PTSD and keep the surgeons on their feet. I came with caffeine shots, vitamins, and amphetamine."

He leaned back again, pushing away from the desk. "You saved lives with those shots."

"You came with a synthetic amphetamine."

"I'll repeat—those shots saved lives."

"And according to this"—I held up the orange card—"Leslie Yarrow got it, probably with the rest of her unit. Helped with knowing if you were being watched, right? It heightens sensory cues, which wakes up the mind for a surgeon. But if you're being watched by, say, a sniper? You'd know where they were and when they saw you. It was a cure for scopaesthesia. Unless your paranoid fantasies are real."

"And thanks to it, they found a way out of an impossible situation. The same way it kept Caden and two other surgeons working in Balad."

I sat. Leaned forward. Folded my hands together on the desk. "I don't believe you."

Mirroring me, he leaned forward and folded his hands together on the desk. "I don't care."

"How many others who got that shot are presenting with dissociative disorder?"

"None who told the truth."

Well. There you had it. He knew. Maybe too late, but he knew. I should have been surprised, but I wasn't. I was, in a way, relieved.

"Why didn't you tell me you were looking at the questionnaires?"

"You weren't supposed to know. You would have asked questions, and I didn't want to answer questions." He sighed and put his hands flat on the blotter, looking out the window. "My whole career is defined by what I can and can't say to whomever I'm talking to. There are a lot of things I've wanted to tell you. That was why I wanted to bring you into intelligence. One of the reasons. There were more. And don't look at me like that. This isn't about you or friendship. It's not about our past together. It's about keeping our eyes on the prize. Those dumbasses in Abu Ghraib threw a once-in-a-lifetime opportunity out the window. They went from making Iraqi prisoners uncomfortable, which was the idea—you know, just have a woman look them in the eye or tell them what to do—and they went right to torture. Right to forcing them to suck each other off. It was disgusting. We could have won this war in half the time with half the deaths, but no. They didn't stay in the lines, and now here we are with a private company picking up where the US government had to stop."

My face was covered by my hands. I pressed my eyelids down until I saw exploding stars.

"I'm sorry, Greysen," he said. "It's for the greater good."

I wouldn't be able to talk him out of his ideals, no matter how misguided.

I took my hands off my eyes. "Is there anything else I should know?"

"You should know you're doing good work. Worthy work. Don't just look at what's gone wrong. Linderman is doing fine still. You know, from what you've seen, there's no way a guy in that serious a mental state is restored like that." He snapped his fingers. "Until now. We have to understand what happened with Leslie Yarrow and make adjustments. She won't be the last one."

The way he lowered his chin and dropped his voice a touch? He meant Caden.

Chapter Sixty-Seven

CADEN

I felt great. For the first time since I'd first felt Damon's hiss or the nameless buzz, I felt truly whole. Six days went by with neither a relapse nor the threat of one. I went on a medevac, and though the heights still bothered me, I did my job and came back without a voice or a sound or an errant perception.

"You seem weirdly happy," Boner said over Thursday beers on the roof.

"It makes me uncomfortable, gotta be honest," Stoneface added.

"My wife." I shrugged. "What can I say?"

"Thanks for the mental images," Boner said, tipping his bottle to me in mock appreciation.

The evening prayer call arced over the city as soon as the sun dipped below the horizon.

"So," Stoneface asked, "what's she doing exactly?"

"That, my friend, is none of your business."

Agent Orange laughed. Boner shook his head. Heartland was on duty, but he would have changed the subject.

"Nah, I mean... here. What's that shot she's doling out?"

I sipped my beer. That wasn't any of his business either. Blackthorne had worked out a permissions system that didn't exactly override army medical, but since it was through the DoD, it didn't give them the authority to ask specific questions.

"I don't know," I lied, focusing on a grain of truth. I wanted out of the conversation.

"I'm asking because it's the fucked-up-in-the-head guys who get it."

As usual, I couldn't get a read on what he was thinking.

"And when they do, it's like…" Agent Orange spread out his hands. "Pow. They're cured."

"*If* they get it," Stoneface said. "Some don't. Some she doesn't do anything with."

"I noticed that," Agent Orange added. Him I could read. He wasn't accusatory. Not exactly. He was holding his judgment, but the judgment was getting loose.

"Guys, she works for Blackthorne. Who the fuck knows what they do? It's not like she tells me. She's got NDAs up the ass."

"That shot though." Stoneface shook his head.

"Fucking miracle," Boner added.

"Well," I said before finishing my beer, "I guess she's just magic."

"THEY'RE TALKING," I said to Greysen a few days after the rooftop beers.

We'd had a dozen casualties come in overnight, and one had been flagged for the Blackthorne psych. Everyone had watched as she spoke to the guy, and when she didn't give him the shot, they dispersed like a crowd after the firetrucks left. I caught her outside the hospital before she got back on the truck to the offices.

"Why?" she asked. "Because we haven't spent a night together in over a week?"

It had been busy, and our schedules hadn't overlapped. It sucked, but that wasn't what I was talking about.

"About your miracle shots."

In the desert wind, her hair crossed her face like a web. "It's not a miracle. It's research and preparation." She faced into the gust to clear the hair out of her eyes.

"They don't know why some people are getting it and not others. Or if it's going to contraindicate anything they're prescribing."

"I'll tell my boss. It may be something PR has to handle."

An errant strand crossed her face, sticking to her bottom lip. We didn't touch or show affection publicly, but I moved it without thinking.

"I miss you," she said.

The whoosh of the wind almost drowned her out. We stood in broad daylight, surrounded by people walking in and out of the hospital. But we were totally alone.

"What happens if I slip back?" I said.

"Back?"

"If I crack. If the split comes again."

Her brow knotted. "I don't think that's going to happen."

"How do you know?"

She shook her head slightly, slowly, thinking about her answer just a little too fucking hard.

"You don't know," I said.

"It's hard to explain."

"Try me."

She looked around, checking for ears and eyes. I led her to a window ledge wide enough to sit on.

She pulled the hair off her face and took a deep breath. "You're in a group that developed dissociative disorder because you had previous trauma. You're the only one who had a chance to relive the event while being talked through it. You faced your fear and got control. You're the only one who's been made whole."

I waited for more. Some proof. Some studies. Some evidence that it wasn't coming back. I got none of that. All I got was a look of devotion, which was nice but no cure for my concern.

"So, you don't know shit."

"No. Not really. But, Caden…" She reached for me, but I didn't return the affection.

"I don't know how I ever lived like that," I said. "If it comes back, I don't know what I'll be. Loving you isn't going to be enough to fix it, and I can't do it again. I won't."

What was I threatening exactly?

It didn't matter. I'd fought enemies I couldn't see because they were inside me. The memory of the splits, the constant battles, the lack of sleep, the torment of feeling that there was something hostile I couldn't escape was too much.

"I know you're scared."

"If I slip back, will you give it to me? The shot? Will I get it?"

"You're not going to slip back."

"I'm not playing this game with you. Yes or no?"

Through the veil of hair whipping over her face, I held her eyes with mine. The wind took on a rhythm that got louder and louder. I wouldn't move until she answered.

The rhythm turned into the *thup-thup-thup* of choppers. Paramedics ran out to meet new casualties. I'd be managing life and limb in minutes.

"Grey," I said urgently.

"There's a dose with your name on it."

Was that enough reassurance? I decided it was.

"Thank you," I said in an exhale of relief.

Chapter Sixty-Eight

Standing in front of the medical refrigerator, I held his syringe.

CADEN ST. JOHN

145-361-9274

To be given soon after an event as described in section 54a. Breathing methodology
B2.

A placebo, right?

Like Yarrow's.

Supposedly.

He had to medevac like everyone else. He was exposed to traumatic situations every few days. Which one would tip him? Which one would shut him down or split him apart? Was this a cure for a man who was whole? Or a detonator for an unprotected mind?

"Lunch?"

I jumped. Ronin peered in from the hall.

"You scared me." I put the syringe back.

"What are you looking at?"

"Just... dosages. Making sure we're consistent."

"We're not. They're different for everyone depending on height, weight, gender, how long we treated them stateside." "The medical staff is asking what the shots are about. How are they supposed to be sure it won't react negatively with something they're administering?"

"Legitimate concern, but we covered it in trials."

"Why everyone who needs it isn't getting it."

He shot out a derisive laugh. "Try giving it to someone who hasn't had the prep and see what happens."

"What happens?"

"Usually nothing. Usually."

NIGHT.

Caden and I on his narrow bed, bodies draped over each other. His chest rising and falling under my head. The beating of his heart. His fingers drifting over my shoulder as the doors of my mind clicked gently shut, one by one, in surrender to sleep.

I knew the sound of choppers overhead. I could hear them from miles away. I could tell if they were going to land on the north pad or by the hospital. I could tell a Blackhawk from an Osprey, speeding to save lives from a standard landing.

Caden's hand stopped moving just before I heard it. Blackhawk. If it came from the south, it was going to the airfield. If it came from the west, it was touching down on the hospital landing pad.

We remained twisted together, frozen as the *thup-thups* got louder, our full attention on the sky.

THE DAY HAD STARTED NORMALLY, but the insurgents had had a different plan. I overheard the soldiers and marines as they came in. US positions had been hit on four fronts. Massive casualties.

In Balad, I could have helped. If no one needed a psychiatrist, I could push paper, carry containers, take orders.

In Baghdad, I felt useless. Men were coming in torn apart, bloody, screaming for their buddies, and I couldn't help. Couldn't even talk to them until a doctor found a flagged file. Then Dana would come with the BiCam and I'd have a purpose.

I went to the chow hall to get out of the way and found Dana at a table with a cup of coffee and a gossip magazine.

"Hey," she said.

"What are you reading?" I sat down.

"Anna Nicole Smith died. So sad."

"Yeah, that's terrible. Aren't you supposed to be waiting at the office until they open a flagged file?"

"I brought everything," she said, tapping something between her legs. I looked under the table. It was a big medical cooler. "She was thirty-nine. Overdose."

"Yeah." I blew on my coffee. It looked like Dana didn't have the kind of gossip I was hoping for. "How's everything with Mr. Trona?"

She flipped a page, eyes still on the magazine. "Went on a security detail two days ago."

"I'm sure he's fine."

"He was on the run that was ambushed this morning."

"I'm so sorry," I said. "I didn't know he was part of that."

"Did you know Anna Nicole Smith dropped out of school at fourteen?"

"Yeah. I mean, no." I went from agreement to honesty in four words. A teardrop fell onto her magazine, leaving a dark-gray burst. "Do you want to go check the hospital? See if he came back?"

I handed her a tissue. She took it without looking up.

"There's still no word." She turned the page. "But I'm sure they're going to be fine once they get a medevac in."

"The medevacs have been back and forth. Maybe he's back."

"Nothing's gone out since the one that got shot down."

She did have the gossip I was looking for but not what I'd been hoping for.

There was no delicate way of asking if there had been a doctor on the medevac or if that doctor was my husband. Worry hardened over my confidence, crystalizing like ice on the window as Dana commented on every page of the magazine to distract herself.

Had Caden been on that Blackhawk?

I was cold and brittle, useless to Dana or anyone.

He wouldn't have gone up with casualties coming in. Even if they'd had an injury they needed a surgeon for, they couldn't possibly have spared him. Right?

He'd just been made whole again. God wouldn't take him away so soon after, would he?

The building trembled in answer to my question. The helicopter pad was above us, and something was coming or going. I leaned to look out the window. A Blackhawk with a big red cross on the tail sped across the sapphire sky.

My beeper went off.

"We're on," I said. "I'll help you with the cooler."

"FUCKING NIGHTMARE," DeLeon said to a nurse as she passed. Dana and I carried the cooler between us. "Wifey," she barked, peeling off the nurse and redirecting herself toward me.

I stopped short, jerking Dana to a stumble.

"You have three flagged on their way." DeLeon softened. "It was a rough ride. They're going to need you."

"Wait!" I called before she could turn her back on me.

"You're asking about him," she said.

"I am."

"I don't have time to give you a hug and a pat on the back."

"I know."

"Four hours ago." Her voice was flat and emotionless. Just the facts. "The medevac he was on was shot down over an active zone. We have reports of multiple fatalities and casualties, military and civilian, including chemical burns."

"Is he—"

"He's not dead, far as we know." A nurse pulled her away, but she called back, "Keep it together, Wifey. We need you."

TRONA WAS one of the first off the medevac. Third-degree burns from his right shoulder to his fingertips. Right behind him, children came without their mothers. Soldiers with uniforms burned off. Paramedics with blood drained from their faces and cheeks hollowed out as if joy had been sucked from their mouths.

A paramedic left the ER and promptly vomited on the floor.

"I'll get towels," Dana said.

I ran up to him. "Hey," I said, bent over so I could see the long drop of saliva from his profile. "Come sit."

He listened to me. I wasn't an officer without a commission. I wasn't an interloper. My status as a contractor didn't matter to either of us. I could listen to him, and he could distract me from worrying about Caden.

"It was so fast," he said. "One minute we're landing; the next, we're crashing. Me and the doc get out and we don't know what to do first."

The doc must have been Caden. I didn't react. At least I tried not to.

"I take the guys on the Phrog, and he goes into the street. Got shot at almost right away."

I clutched the fingers of my left hand in my right so tightly my ring pressed against my pinkie.

"But he tripped over this woman..." He took a deep breath in an attempt to keep it together. "Saved his life, but she was..." He shook his head.

"And you?" I said.

"She was melted."

I let him see it in his mind for a few seconds before steering him back. "You took care of the pilot and copilot?"

"Yeah. And two other medics. All fine. Not bad. Minor shit. But we were stuck. All of us. And it was..." He shook his head instead of using words.

"Greysen!" Dana called. She waved me toward the ICU. "Pfc. Karlson's in recovery."

"He was one of mine!" the paramedic exclaimed. "I pulled him out! Is he all right?"

"They don't put dead men in ICU," I said.

"Go find out!" He practically pushed me off my chair. "Then let me know."

He was suddenly like a kid, and I was suddenly carrying the weight of Caden's absence.

"The doctor," I said before walking away. "Is he all right?"

"He was when we left him."

They'd left him there, probably to make room on the Blackhawk.

I followed Dana into the ICU. She had the shot on a tray by Karlson's bed.

I put on my game face.

If Caden was dead, I'd know from the way the sky shattered.

Chapter Sixty-Nine

CADEN

I agreed to land under fire because I was there to get people off the ground, not run back to the Green Zone with my tail between my legs. And yeah, I was terrified. I'd imagined, more than most people, falling out of the sky. It was number one on the list of ways I didn't want to die.

But I'd medevaced dozens of times. Every time I went up, it got easier.

We were circling around a freeway with a hole in the center and debris at the edges. I couldn't say how close to the ground we were when we were hit, but my stomach had already flipped from the descent, then we started spinning.

It wasn't anything like I'd thought it would be. I'd always imagined the fall would be quiet and empty, with nothing but my thoughts and regrets. But it was loud. Centrifugal force pulled me against my seat, and I didn't have an inward-looking thought in my head. I heard and understood the pilot's mayday call. I saw the paramedics with utter clarity and noted that the instruments were all strapped down. I was as lucid as I'd always feared, but I was not afraid. My brain was too busy.

The Blackhawk screwed itself into the ground not far from the hole in the freeway, bending and creaking as a billion dollars in metal bowed around me. The prop smacked into the dirt, creating a ditch.

Then it stopped.

Arms. Legs. Fingers. Toes. Eyes. I took inventory of my body and senses. I was sideways. My ears buzzed, but it wasn't a discrete anger roaring to break free. It was just my ears.

"Doc?" A paramedic leaned over me. Frankie Beans. I knew him. Soft face. Brave heart.

"I'm good." I pressed the buckle of my belt and shrugged off the straps. Frankie helped. I moved slowly in case I had a break I couldn't feel. I'd ache in the morning for sure. "Who's hurt?"

"Unger took a hit to the head."

"No vital organs," I joked, crawling across the cracked space to what had been the front.

"Fuck you," Unger, the copilot, said. Blood covered his face, and his temporal vein was still gushing.

"Everybody out!" our pilot shouted. "Move!"

He shoved paramedic Mari Barron out his window, handing her box of supplies out behind her. Frankie was already putting pressure on Unger's head.

"Doc!" the pilot shouted. "You! Now!"

I grabbed my case and let him push me out.

———

I WAS JUST A GUY, not fearless, and I was no hero. But I was pretty good at my job under pressure. Everything narrowed down into tight focus. I made the decisions I was supposed to make and let the warriors do the rest. The wounded and the medical staff were put in a concrete bunker with stripped electrical circuits on one wall that used to route power to the highway's lights. I took care of men, children, and women—Iraqi, American, and one Australian.

"Trona," I said, leaning over the contractor. He'd taken a bullet in the arm. Clean exit. "Didn't expect to see you on the job."

"After a building fell on you, I didn't expect to see you ever."

The paramedics had cleaned him up. I started on the sutures. "We have a way of living through stuff, I guess. This is going to hurt."

"More than it already does?"

"Probably not. But you'll throw a football again."

"They were everywhere," he said as I worked. "I never saw anything like it. Benito got his head blown off right in front of me."

That would explain the blobs of green-gray on the front of his shirt.

"We're going to get you back," I said.

"It was quiet," he said. "We avoided Route Irish. I thought—" He cut himself off as I finished up.

"You thought you were safe."

He shook his head quickly. "Never safe, right?"

"Sometimes you're safe."

"I have to get Dana out of here."

"I know how you feel, man. I know how you feel." I took an extra second with my hand on his arm. I had nothing to offer him but that time.

As I got up, a sniper bullet grazed my back. It burned.

"Doc!" Trona yelled.

Mari scrambled over to me as I crouched.

"I'm fine."

"You've got to stay low." Mari checked me out, ripping open the back of my shirt. "This is going to hurt."

"She said."

"Jesus Christ," she mumbled as she checked the wound. "He missed your vertebra by a quarter inch."

"Easier to miss it than to hit it, right, Trona?"

"Right," he grunted. "When are they coming?"

The light from the tiny square window had gotten long and bright as day waned. A medevac wouldn't land under fire a second time.

"Soon," I lied. "They'll pick you up soon."

"I'm not worried about me," he said, gritting his teeth against pain. "I don't want them shooting you, bro. We need you."

THE FIRST MEDEVAC landed just before midnight. Mari and I stayed behind to fit in more wounded.

I didn't know what was going on outside the little cinderblock building, but it was quiet for long stretches leading up to a string of *pop-crack-pop*, then more silence. I had blood and dirt all over me. The room stank of bodily fluids, gunpowder, and flesh.

In the middle of the night, looking at the sky through the glassless window, I'd gotten lost in what some might have considered prayer.

I'd thanked the capital-U Universe for letting me be there to help, for letting me live, for the men who protected me so I could patch people up.

I'd thanked it for my clarity of mind. The end of the buzz of anger and the hum of cowardice. I was whole, and for that, I counted the stars in Orion's belt and thanked them for Greysen. I could die in an hour, but I'd die myself as one man, one unconflicted consciousness.

The moans of the wounded mixed with the high-pitched creak of crickets just as the *thup-thup* of a medevac came over the horizon. We mobilized everyone to move.

Trona got up on his own and flicked a piece of Benito's brain off a front button.

I had a young boy, about the same age as my *qunbula* kid, with an exploded foot. When they'd brought him to me, I'd frozen for a second with the memory but had shaken myself out of it.

Not the same kid. Obviously.

"Don't go," he said with panicked eyes as the helicopter landed. Decoding the Arabic took a second.

"I bring you." I was sure I'd gotten it wrong, maybe telling him he was bringing me, but he understood well enough to calm down.

"Doc," Mari called, helping a man with an open wound for a leg onto a stretcher, "we're out."

I picked up the kid with the shattered foot and carried him to the medevac. Shots were fired. I kept running, looking straight ahead, and fell.

Chapter Seventy

It was three in the morning. We were in a lull created by the fact that we couldn't get a medevac out to pick up the last of the wounded and two medical staff. One of whom was my husband.

The hardest thing I'd ever done was sit still in that hospital. Especially since I knew he wasn't that far away. Especially since I had working legs and feet. I couldn't do a damn thing, really. I'd never get there before they could send a medevac out, and leaving would make it all worse. Logically, I was exactly where I needed to be.

Yet I felt a physical pull toward him. When I went outside to get air, I saw the three bright stars of Orion's belt. Caden was under the same sky, and he was looking with me. He was my blue sky, my clear day, the protective shell over my world. At night, we were strung together by the stars.

"How's Karlson?" Ronin stood next to me, steamed and pressed, looking at the sky as if trying to figure out what I saw.

The beating of helicopter wings rose above us. It wasn't the first time I'd hoped it was a medevac going out for Caden. I'd given up on hope in favor of trust that he'd be back.

"Fine," I said. "And Humbert. Yarrow's the only one who fell apart."

"Good, good."

The helicopter took off, a black mass blotting out the dots of light and disappearing like hope.

"They're going to get the last of them," Ronin said.

"Thank you," I said to the stars.

"Past two days were like Balad Lite." He shook a cigarette out of a pack and offered me one.

I took my eyes off the sky to decline the smoke. "We didn't even know what we were looking at then when it came to mental trauma."

"Fuck, we didn't." He lit up. "We knew from Vietnam. Korea. But they weren't real soldiers, right? We kicked them out and didn't treat them. We pretended trauma was for pussies. Real men bucked up and went back onto the field. Played the game and won."

It was his turn to look pensively into the sky.

"What's your deal, Ronin? You're a callous asshole except when you're not."

He shrugged and blew out a cone of smoke. "I've seen things I never want to see again, and I didn't do shit. Didn't say shit." He tapped his ash. A single bright ember curled away in the wind and vanished. "You should have come to Abu Ghraib. You would have said something." He took a pull of his cigarette. "You would have saved me."

"And going up there would have destroyed me."

Smoke came from his lips when he laughed. "You? Nah." He stamped out his butt. "Nothing breaks you."

I looked at the night sky, waiting for the one man who made Ronin wrong. "Did you have PTSD from Abu Ghraib?"

"I'm just trying to balance the scales."

"How noble." I wrapped my sweater around my chest against the coldest part of the desert night.

"And futile."

"I'm going to wait inside."

He turned to walk with me, opening the door so I could pass.

"This was a shitstorm," he said. "It'll be a good time to give Caden his shot."

"No fucking way." I went through without looking back.

He caught up to me in front of the reception desk. "Don't you want to know?"

"If he's going to collapse in a heap like Leslie Yarrow? No, I don't want to know."

"It's a placebo."

"Is it?"

"Yes."

"Then let me set up a saline shot with my own hands."

"Do you not get how research works?"

I stood with my legs apart and my arms crossed. "No. At this point, I don't."

He lowered his voice. "This has been a traumatic trip for him. It's the perfect time. We need to show we had consistent treatments for both of them so we can isolate the cause of her breakdown. That's how we determine—"

"Blah blah blah. No. I'm not going to be responsible for breaking him."

I walked away before I had to hear more bullshit reasons.

He wasn't putting Caden in danger. Period. We'd worked too hard to throw it all away.

I WAS on the roof when the medevac landed. Caden had been over the wire many times since he'd treated a pregnant woman in a closet in Fallujah. Still, I half expected him to get off in a fugue and go to his room. But he was on his feet, shouting vitals and instructions.

Small things. I thanked the night sky and the rising sun for small things.

WE'D MET in a Balad Air Base scrub room. He'd been undressed and obnoxious. I'd been impressed with the least impressive things about him.

In Baghdad, I couldn't wait to see him. I went into the scrub room again. He was naked from the waist up as a nurse helped him change from a blood-spattered shirt into clean scrubs.

"Caden." I stood at the door. "I was so worried."

"For nothing," he said, getting his hands under the faucet. "You know I wouldn't die without asking permission first."

His next step was soap, but he kept his hands still under the faucet. I wove through the rushing surgical staff to stand by him.

His hands were shaking.

"Shit," he muttered. "Stoney!"

"Yo," Stoneface said through his mask. He was already scrubbed in. When he saw Caden's hands, he nodded. "I got this."

Caden shut the water and walked out. I ran after him, silently walking next to him until we were in a quiet hallway with a window at the end. He stopped and leaned against the wall.

"I thought I was dead," he said, looking at the hands that had betrayed him. His fingers still quaked as if they wanted to run away from his arm.

I slid my hands into his, squeezing as if I could keep them still.

"You're not."

"They were shooting at us and I tripped. I thought..." He took his eyes off his hands and met my gaze. "All the things we haven't done, it was all my fault for coming. I was leaving you alone. I wanted to have kids, and we never did. I could see them in my mind, and I was so sorry."

"It's okay."

"I can still see them."

"Are they cute?"

He laid his lips on my cheek for long seconds, breathing deeply. I felt connected to him by that breath. It was made of steel cables, connecting us near or far.

"They look like you," he said.

"I'm still with you. And if you're fine... I'll tell Ronin you're okay because he's going to ask you to get the BiCam shot."

"I saw Dana before I scrubbed in." He took his face from mine with a shrug. "I told her I'd take it."

The squiggle of the blood streak leading to Leslie Yarrow appeared in front of my eyes. It was the path her head had taken across the room as she was dragged while she fought with the chaos in her mind.

"What? Why?" I asked.

"It's the same shit they were giving me in New York. It's fine. It might even be *better.*"

The cables didn't fray. Didn't break. But my control was slipping away even as I tried to grasp our connection and pull it tight.

"Can you just not?" I took his hands and tried to reforge our link with a hard gaze. "Just don't take it."

"Do you know something I don't?"

I did. I knew the one thing that would make giving the shot futile, because the thing about placebos was that they were useless if the subject knew. "It's a placebo."

He laughed and kissed me on the lips with a deep sense of appreciation. "Then what's the problem?"

"The problem," I sulked, crossing my arms and lowering my voice, "is Yarrow got this placebo too, and she had a breakdown a few minutes later. So, either the thought of the shot created the reaction—"

"Which you just killed by telling the patient."

"—or it's not a placebo."

His eyes were so intense I nearly melted under their heat. Blue was a cold color associated with ice and distance, but when he directed it my way, it warmed me.

"I'm whole," he said. "Shaken, yes. But whole. Was she?"

I put my hands on his chest, wishing he hadn't put the shirt on before I had a chance to kiss his skin. "No, but—"

"Okay, take it easy." He took my wrists and kissed my palms. "I'm going to finish this treatment with them and be done with it."

He kissed me before I could protest, and there was so much love and trust in that kiss that I let it melt my objections away. I pulled him into me, and he wrapped his arms around my body as if he was afraid I'd run away.

When I felt his erection against me, I groaned into his mouth, lifting my leg over his waist. He pressed his hardness against my damp softness.

"My room," he said, cupping my breast.

"We're not finished talking about this," I said, grinding into him.

"We're going to talk about our life together. I'm going to give you the entire world. We're going to talk about which part you get first."

"You. You're the part I want first."

"Good, because—"

The doors at the end of the hall swung open. Dana appeared with a metal tray, stopping short when she saw us tangled together. "Oh! There you are. I, uh…"

I got both feet on the floor.

"It's fine," Caden said.

"I have to give you this," Dana replied, setting down the tray with a syringe that told stories.

"No—" I started.

"All right." Caden passed her on the way out, stopping long enough to say, "But give her a sedative."

The doors closed behind him.

"I'm not sure he needs it," I said.

"When he came in he looked a little—"

"He doesn't need it!" I shouted.

Ashamed of my tantrum, I went past her to follow my husband.

He was already sitting in the exam room, rolling up his sleeve.

"Caden, listen to me…"

"I'm fine."

Dana came in with her tray and, not wanting to yell again, I clammed up, crossing my arms and wondering how the hell I was going to get him out of this.

She sat next to him and pulled on latex gloves, smiling from ear to ear. "Thank you so much for taking care of Bobby."

"How's he doing?"

They chatted while she swabbed his skin.

I stood over them, remembering slipping on the squiggle of Yarrow's blood on the linoleum, her red face, the heat and depth of her confusion and pain. She screamed with the voice of an abused child. Would he sound like a little boy locked in a cellar when he got the shot?

"Baby?" Caden asked, his voice far away, drowned out by darkness and horror.

I couldn't risk stuffing him back in the bag. Not for his promises or mine.

Dana raised the needle.

"I'll do it." I held out my hand. Momentarily bewildered, Dana froze with the needle between herself and Caden's arm. "It's my responsibility."

"All right," she chirped.

She placed the syringe back on the tray and stood. I sat across from my husband and got gloves on, ready to deliver a death blow to his sanity or a round of nothing at all. Caden leaned forward with a smirk. He liked this. I knew he thought I was sexy with a needle in my hand. After this, he'd fuck me as if it would be the last time he used his dick.

Dana waited impatiently.

Ronin had told me she didn't need a babysitter. Well, neither did I.

"Can you get his paperwork for me?" I asked. "I want to make some notes after I'm done."

She nodded and left.

"You're really sexy when you boss people around," Caden said.

I pressed his arm down to hold it steady, feeling the way the skin gave but the muscle didn't. How complex the structure of his cells and nerves was. How touching him made me realize how fragile he was. How quickly I could lose him.

With my right hand, I held the needle to his arm, holding his elbow with the left hand. I felt him watching me. His impatience to do this thing so he could get me into bed.

The shot was nothing. Had to be. Ronin would lie, but about this? No. Not about the research.

But he had bosses.

Maybe they lied.

Maybe they'd made a mistake.

Maybe Leslie Yarrow and Caden St. John had become test cases.

"Come on, baby," Caden said. "I want to get moving here."

If I didn't give him the shot, Dana would. Ronin had authorized her to do her job with or without me. And since I'd asked them to send a second syringe? Squirting this one on the floor, if I even could, would just delay the inevitable. When the syringe didn't change color, they'd know I hadn't given it to him. They'd fire me. Send me home. When the new syringe came, Dana would give him the shot he was convinced he could handle.

I was trapped.

Caden was trapped.

The BiCam had to go into someone before Dana returned, and it wasn't going to be Caden.

Quickly, I turned the needle downward.

And away.

The diagonally cut tip turned toward me, the white rubbery hub hungry to turn blue when it touched my skin.

So fast, but carefully, with all my attention on what I was doing, I pushed it into my left bicep, lowering the plunger until the syringe was empty.

Caden leaned back.

"We're done here," I said. By the time I dropped the syringe on the metal tray, the hub was already blue.

HUBRIS IS EXCESSIVE, defiant pride or self-confidence.

That wasn't what this was. I'd given myself the shot out of certainty. Trust. I was sane and whole, so much so that even my fears and quirks confirmed my core mental soundness.

My body had been broken at the wrist, pierced at the sternum, snapped at the collarbone, but nothing could change what I was. Who I was. If you'd asked me if I believed humans had souls, I would have given you arguments about genetics and upbringing that added up to a denial. But I must have believed. When I gave myself that shot, it was because I trusted that I had a sane, unbreakable core. I was confirming the unconfirmable.

I believed in my soul. I believed it would never change. I believed that to protect Caden, I'd be able to shrug off whatever confusion this stuff created.

My attention was locked on Caden as he leaned back with his sleeve rolled up and the alcohol drying on his arm. His focus further established what I already knew. I was safe.

"Why?" was all he said.

"It's for the best." I stood, suddenly uncomfortable with inaction.

I had to move forward. Whatever that was, it was a direction. My heart pounded with anxiety. I felt trapped in an inert state that would corrode me. It wasn't an overwhelming feeling. It was more like an irritation. An itch on the sole of your foot in otherwise comfortable shoes. Definitely within the normal range.

I walked out. Forward into the lobby and outside, where dawn broke the blackness of the sky into blues. He was right behind me. I knew it without hearing him.

But I had to keep moving. I didn't even know where I was going except forward to an undefinable destination.

He grabbed my arm. "Slow down."

I stopped long enough for him to wrap his arms around me. I was locked in a stillness that was comfortable because it was him. "I'm sorry. I just got claustrophobic all of a sudden."

"Why did you do that?"

"I don't want you to have the serum or a placebo or anything. I don't care about the research, and I don't care what they say about what's in it. I don't want to risk it. Period. That's my professional assessment."

He ran his thumb over my cheek with that perfect casual pressure. His touch grounded me to the moment, soothing the itch to move.

"Okay," he said. "Are you going to be all right?"

"Yes." I ran my finger along the edge of his placket. "Now I am." The world was inside the spaces where we touched. Nothing could break us. Nothing.

"If the shot wasn't a placebo?"

"I'll be fine."

"Are you sure?" He lifted my chin so I could look at him. Behind him, the sky was lightening to the exact color of the eyes that saw right through me.

"Yes." I was five miles off the ground in his gaze.

"Greysen?"

"I'm fine."

"If you're not, I'll kill him." He meant Ronin, but I was fine. "I'll burn Blackthorne down. Do you understand me?"

"Yes." My voice was barely a whisper. I understood. He was forward motion and stillness. His eyes were the lock of gravity under a sky that melted, moved, shifted, cracked.

Behind his still points of blue, the sky was rent into two distinct halves, and the trust that my soul could bear anything shattered with it.

It was not a placebo.

Part Nine

Chapter Seventy-One

GREYSEN

Never take anything for granted.

Anything.

When a piece of metal had missed my heart by a fraction of the length of my fingernail, I'd stopped taking my safety for granted, adding that to my overall health and the health of my family. I never took Caden's love for granted, nor his well-being. Never money. Never my friends.

But I'd taken my sanity for granted. I'd leaned on it as the one thing I could always count on, no matter what. My mental stability was the rock I'd lashed the rest of myself onto as the earth shook and the winds tried to rip me away.

I was sane. My perceptions were keen and clear. My personality was steady, clearly defined as *me*, and with that collateral in my pocket, I could risk everything else. It couldn't be bartered, spent, or worn away. I could not be disengaged from it. My very existence had been poured into the vessel of my sanity.

Even after seeing Caden fall apart, I'd depended on that container to hold me together, assuming it was indestructible.

When I took the shot meant for my husband, the assumption remained. It was a placebo...or not. If it was, I'd be fine. If it wasn't, then I'd still be me, no matter what I'd injected into myself. No vial of experimental serum could take away the essentialness of *me* because that was where the unmovable object and the unstoppable force met. It was the only real thing in the world.

"Why did you do that?" Caden asked outside the hospital.

My arm throbbed at the injection site. I hadn't been careful with the needle, nor had I stuck it into thick-enough muscle.

"I don't trust him." I said, knowing Caden would understand I was talking about Ronin. "What happened to Yarrow, I don't want it to happen to you. And if I wouldn't give you the shot, Dana would."

He took me in his arms, and there the splitting sky was sewn shut. I thought I was just tired. A little stressed out. All I needed was a good night's sleep and Caden St. John.

"Why?" he asked. "Why not just dump it if you didn't want me to have it?"

"The syringe had a tell. If it didn't go into someone, they would have known."

"So what?"

"They'd just send more, and if I wouldn't give it to you, someone else would." There was more to it than that, of course. If I'd dumped it, another solution would have presented itself in time. But I took my sanity for granted, so I'd gone with the solution I had on hand because it would satisfy my need to save Caden.

"I had to know if it was a placebo or not," I said. "If I tossed it, we'd never know."

"Well?" He laid a kiss on my cheek. "Is it?"

His question wasn't urgent. He wasn't worried or uneasy, because he took my sanity for granted as well.

"Not sure," I said even though I was very sure something had shifted. I laid my lips on the bare bit of skin over his collar, breathing deeply of coffee grounds and lingering rubbing alcohol. The scent went from my nose, down my spine, between my legs, where it burst into a throb that beat with my heart. "Maybe it was an aphrodisiac."

"I'm off duty at oh four hundred," he said.

"Can you get to my apartment at that hour?"

"Probably. The army never sleeps."

Dropping my arms away from him, I stepped back. I felt the sky rip into two halves—two eyes watching me from deep in the past—and still thought I had it under control. I could watch the effects of the drug like a clinician and let them wear off like a person with a deep well of sanity.

"Be there," I said.

"Be naked," he replied with a smirk.

He took two steps backward to the hospital, turning when the doors *whooshed* open. I watched him walk away, yanking the tether between us tight, tighter, near breaking but not quite.

Not yet.

Maybe I took that for granted too.

I'D TAKEN the shot instead of wasting it because I didn't want Blackthorne to know it didn't go into Caden. Once I realized Caden's syringe hadn't been filled with a placebo, I got pissed off. That was not okay. Not for Caden. Not for anyone.

At 02:23:00, the Blackthorne offices were dark and empty. I sat at my desk and dashed off an email I was pretty sure I'd regret.

FROM: GFrazier@blackthorne.com
TO: RBlake@blackthorne.com
CC: DGionetto@blackthorne.com

Ronin:
Dana has logged subject Dr. Caden St. John's vial as administered because the syringe corroborates and because I told her it was.
This email is to correct the record. The dose was administered to me. The subject was the only witness. Dana is not at fault for the erroneous log. I will submit corrected paperwork first thing in the morning.
As an aside, the syringe did not contain a placebo. I am experiencing noticeable symptoms of scopaesthesia. As these syringes do not contain what I—the accountable physician— was told is in them, I will no longer be administering BiCam, nor will I sign off on the administration of BiCam by any physician's assistant under my purview.

Best regards,
Dr. Greysen Frazier

PS: Fuck you.

I deleted the postscript before I sent it. He needed to hear that to his face.

When I shut the computer down, my eyes needed a moment to adjust.

Medical books. Binders. A chair and a couch. An open door looking onto a large room with rows of desks facing north to minimize the sun's glare. My office had a window that looked out onto that wider room. Blinds shut.

The shut blinds bothered me. I kept them that way to protect the privacy of whomever was in the room with me. The door was open unless I was seeing someone or on a call. Normal.

But something was behind those blinds.

There was no noise. No visual. No sense other than a conviction I knew was wrong. I could see the large room through the door, and it was dead-of-night empty. If someone had come in, I would have heard the outer door.

Foolish, of course. I was just jumpy from the dark and years of fighting an enemy who could be anywhere. This wasn't the same thing Caden had experienced. It was manageable because I was in complete control of my mind.

I reached for cold common sense and felt the rip in the sky again. The bowl over all of us cracking in two and becoming sentient. Potential energy turned kinetic. Death turning to life.

I was tired, and it had been a stressful day. After gathering my things, I went to the doorway and paused before going through. Quietly, I leaned over and twisted the rod that opened the blinds and jumped at the sight of a shadow. I went back into the office and shut the door. Locked it. Jerking the cord at the side of the window, I raised the blinds.

The shadow was a coat hanging on a hook.

"For fuck's sake," I said to myself. My voice was a balm against the shifting reality, filling the crack like epoxy. "Just go home already."

BLACKTHORNE HAD a shuttle bus that ran between the office and the apartments all day and night. One was waiting outside for me. I chatted with the driver. The wheels moving under my feet felt right and good. I was moving. Going someplace. Forward momentum was exactly what I needed, and by the time I walked into my apartment at almost three in the morning, I felt normal again.

Caden might be hungry, and after he fucked me, I might feed him. I cut oranges and a stubby banana. Brewed mint tea and set out crackers. Then I stripped to bare skin and showered.

The injection site looked normal. The tiny pinprick would fade to nothing in a day.

For the first time, I considered that I might get fired for my impulse. I *should* get fired and sent home. Being separated from Caden would be the worst consequence, but maybe I'd done what I came here to do...save him from that shot. Maybe I could go home and just wait for his return, knowing I hadn't come to Iraq for nothing.

The idea of going home was like walking backward.

I paced naked to the opposite side of the studio apartment.

There couldn't be a backward. Stillness was death. There was only forward.

I couldn't go home.

A light rap at the door. I shut off the lights. I jumped onto the bed as he let himself in, a tall shadow against the outside lights. Like an animal, I could sense his scent and his energy. When he closed the door, I leapt off the bed, unable to sit still, and pushed him against the door.

We were open mouths and searching tongues. I was made of hands that opened, peeled, shucked his clothes away.

Forward. Forward. Forward.

I wouldn't be stopped or slowed. Moderation didn't find the limit. Safety didn't tease out the edges.

Caden flipped me to my stomach. I grunted in protest. I didn't want to be passive. I didn't want to be ridden. I wanted to ride.

He was inside me before I could explain, so deep I thought he'd crack me.

"Is this what you want?" he asked.

"Deeper."

He got on his knees, pulling me up until I was crouched over him. We were both facing the same direction, and that seemed more right than anything before.

Into. Forward. Through.

He found an untouched depth. An arcane secret in my belly that I'd been holding for him and only him. When he discovered it, he hurt me and broke through.

I shook. Or the earth quaked. Or reality trembled, threatening to break and spill its contents. It managed to hold together. For now.

HE'D EXHAUSTED me so much that even when I slept, I was awake, and when I woke, I was still asleep. I spun down a tunnel that was focused and clear in the center but more and more chaotic at the edges.

"No fever." Caden's voice, like the details of my world, was crisp and lucid as I heard it and fractured and shattered as it drew away, like a Doppler effect of cognizance. "Take this for the headache."

When I sat up to take the ibuprofen, the tunnel moved a little behind me, bending from inertia and snapping into place after a second.

"Did I tell you I had a headache?"

I was starting to doubt the words that came out of my mouth.

"I know when your head hurts, sweetheart."

I handed him back the glass. "Thank you."

"You don't look good," he said. "Are you going to be okay?"

I nodded, and the tunnel shook, waving lucidity before me like a red cape. When he kissed me, my consciousness shifted to where his lips touched my skin, and his voice was the focal point of my attention.

He laid my head on the pillow and covered me, promising he'd return as soon as he could. I barely heard him. My temperature was normal, but I was in a fevered half dream. The dashing thoughts repeated over and over like a mantra, falling into dissonance, only to echo as if I'd lost control of my inner voice.

At one point, between sleep and wakefulness, the bed seemed to drop from under me and the blankets hovered a few inches above.

Not really. I checked by laying my hand on the mattress and pressing down. But once I closed my eyes again, I hovered in space.

Not quite falling. Not quite flying. Stopped in time.

Cool air hit my face and my flailing limbs. It drove itself between my panties and my skin, making me aware of the angle of my body and the fact that no matter how much I flapped my arms, I couldn't will myself to fly.

I could still feel where he'd touched me. Where he'd violated me with his finger as if my body was his. The curdled nerves inside my vaginal wall were disgusted and greedy for more. One side of my bra was hitched over a nipple, hard from the damp and cold, and my lips were wet from inexpert kisses.

I'd escaped something but not what I'd always thought. Maybe rape but not rape. I'd escaped something I couldn't define.

Twisting, I could see the sky over the UCLA diving pool. The stars were cut out in the shape of Scott's perfect body perched on the edge of the platform, his knees bent to propel himself after me. The crescent of the moon looked as if it was balanced on my big toe, as if I'd cut half a glowing nail and hadn't ripped it away yet. The pool's filter churned like a diesel engine, and the mating song of the crickets that lived under the bushes on the other side of the fence was louder than an electric guitar.

Falls were survivable. Falls into a pool especially so. But doing it wrong hurt, and in my expanded airborne second and a half, I straightened as much as I could, watching the turquoise rectangle of the pool hurtle toward me. I closed my eyes. The wet touch of the surface hit my shoulder, and the cool air from it blew against my cheek for the shortest of split seconds in the elastic perception of time.

When I held my breath, time snapped back. My ears filled with the *whoosh* of bubbles. Pain shot through my shoulder when I tried to swim up. With a second *whoosh*, Scott broke the surface like a spear and scooped me up, pulling me to the surface.

I'd survived something.

I didn't know what, but I'd endured more than falling from the diving platform.

When Scott got me to the edge of the pool and I tried to grab the lip with my bad arm, I cried, "Ow."

"What were you trying to do?" he asked, getting out in one move like he did a hundred times a day.

His question was pure accusation, as if I'd done something crazy. He didn't know my collarbone was broken. He didn't know I was hurt, and I didn't either. I couldn't lift my arm, and I didn't care. I could hold on with the other one.

I was happy.

So happy I couldn't wipe the smile from my face.

Scott stood over me with his hand out, scowling, his body covered in dripping diamonds.

The happiness overtook me so hard I laughed in pure delight. Not because I was alive.

No.

I was overjoyed at the sight of the boy standing over me.

For reasons I couldn't explain in the halfway point between sleep and wakefulness, with my perceptions distorting at the edges, I was relieved that Scott was alive.

"Why did you jump?" he asked, truly concerned. He'd put his hands where they didn't go and scared me, but he wasn't a bad person. He was salvageable, and so was I.

My unreasonable joy grew like a water balloon stuck to a flowing hose. By jumping, I'd saved him.

I didn't know why I thought that, and I was afraid I was going to find out.

Chapter Seventy-Two

CADEN

Even asymmetrical war has a pattern. Days of nothing led into a barrage of casualties that lasted days about one third of the time. The other two-thirds were one-off IEDs or suicide bombers in crowded markets. Not fun. Every soldier who came in shaken to their core was proof that the system was broken, and every single hurt civilian convinced me it had to end.

But I had my detachment. I could still compartmentalize. Choosing it instead of having it thrust upon me brought a relieved kind of euphoria.

"She's going to kill me," the corporal said as the nurse, a petite brunette with freckles, used a ring cutter to get his wedding band off his broken hand.

"She's going to be happy you're alive. Look up." I shined a light in his eye. The cornea had been scratched by a flying pebble.

DeLeon poked her head in.

"*Dr.* Eyes." Recently, for reasons I couldn't get to the bottom of, she'd stripped the Asshole off my name. "Got a guy here to see you."

"I'm busy."

"Well, then." Her voice turned a little sultry. I looked around to see if she was directing it at me. "I'll have to wait with him then."

"Whatever."

"Take your time," she replied with a wink.

RONIN AND DELEON were chatting in one of the waiting areas when I came out.

There was a match made in hell for sure.

We shed my CO and went to a deserted corner of the chow hall patio.

"Sorry to pull you into a corner," he said.

"No problem. I love the cloak-and-dagger shit."

"We need to talk about what Greysen did last night."

"Do we?" I got immense pleasure from giving him a hard time.

"Did she tell you why she took the shot?"

"No." I blew on my coffee, considering the sanctity of marital privilege. "Why don't you ask her?"

"She's not in the office today, and she doesn't answer the phone, her email, or the fucking door."

"I'm sure she'll fill out a report or whatever you people do."

"I want to hear it from you."

"Really?" I sipped my coffee. I was taking it with less and less sugar these days. The sweetness seemed like a lie against the backdrop of ripped bone and flesh.

"Did you tell her to take it?"

The idea was so hilarious I nearly spit my coffee.

"What's so funny?"

"Have you met my wife?" Putting the cup down, I leaned back. "Can you imagine her doing anything I tell her just because I said so?"

He shook his head and looked into his coffee. "She didn't want to give it to you. She was afraid you'd react. She thought it might not be a placebo."

"Bad researcher," I scolded. "You're not supposed to tip your hand to the patient."

"Done is done. You're out of the study. Which is too bad. You were good."

"It didn't feel good."

"Trust me. You were great." He leaned his elbows on the table, circling his cup with his palms. "I never saw anything like you in Fallujah."

My cup froze halfway to my lips.

In Fallujah?

I observed Ronin only to find he was observing my reaction just as carefully.

I put down my coffee. "Is there something you want to tell me?"

"You should ask your wife."

He wasn't sitting that far away. If I stood, I could reach across the table and grab the collar of his Blackthorne polo before I punched him in the face. The coffee would spill. I might get arrested if he didn't beat the shit out of me first. A small price to pay for the implication that Greysen hid things from me.

"Here's the problem," he said, lowering his voice. Good strategy. In order to hear him, I had to pay more attention, which drained my anger of its explosiveness. "I don't know what was in the shot."

"How is that possible?" I growled.

He was fucking with my wife now. He could take his *soo-hoo*s and his benchmark tests and shove them. I didn't care what he did with me. I'd volunteered for that shit. But Greysen? Fucking with her wasn't okay. I must have looked like a wild animal because he went fake beta on me, averting his eyes and relaxing his shoulders as if he had no intention of attacking. Not physically.

"It's a big business," he said. "Blackthorne. If you count overseas income streams, it's bigger than AT&T."

"And?"

"And that means there are a lot of people. You just see me. That's by design. But my bosses have bosses, and there are parts of this program that are out of my control. We got those syringes sealed, with names and serial numbers already on them. We recommended a placebo as a control, but"—he shrugged—"I don't know."

One, two, three deep breaths. I said nothing.

"They're motivated to get this process to work," he continued. "As long as there's no childhood trauma, the shot plus the breathing has a two-pronged effect. It improves combat performance and releases the burden of battle distress. It's a win all around. But there's an actuarial component to this. Sometimes things are going to go to shit. The wrong people are going to get it, or a mistake in dosage will have side effects. The bean counters need to know what that's going to cost them."

"And the only way is to get it wrong and see what it costs."

"Right."

"What is that shit?"

"Does it matter?"

"Yes."

He pushed his coffee away and put a napkin in front of him. After slipping a pen from his pocket, he clicked it and drew on the napkin. Lines. Letters. A chemical compound.

"This is proprietary," he said, connecting lines and tucking abbreviations into the corners. "I could get sued into the poorhouse."

The chain of elements went on and on.

"I'm not a chemist," I said.

"I'm betting on that."

"I don't need you to prove a point."

He kept scribbling his molecule, opening the napkin to make more room. "The circular breathing's important. BiCam, the stuff we were working with in Fallujah? It was a breakthrough. But the army didn't want to hear anything from me. Not after Abu Ghraib." A short rip appeared where he pressed too hard. "I got busted down to Aberdeen piss boy after that."

He pushed the napkin toward me.

"Like I told you," I said, "I'm not a chemist. What does this have to do with Greysen?"

He took the napkin and crunched it into a ball.

"Dose and preparation." He took a Zippo and a pack of Marlboros from his pocket and poked out a smoke. "It's highly personalized." He bit the cigarette out of the pack and lit it, keeping the lighter open. "Your dose was raised over time."

He set the napkin on fire.

"The shots in New York weren't vitamins." I stated it as a fact because it was. I didn't need confirmation.

"Sure, they were. With more or less BiCam depending." He dropped the flaming ball on the table. "We were making you into a god. The split was going to be managed with bioenergetic breathing once you had the sessions under control. But the army brought you here and cut me out. So, I hired Greysen because she'd watch you until I could get transferred." A line of hot orange sped to the center of the napkin, and the black edges curled and flaked off. "Now she's taken your dose."

"Which is higher because I'm acclimated. And you have no idea what effect it's going to have on her."

"And here we are."

The last of the napkin turned to cold carbon. A ribbon of smoke curled between us and went dead.

"I know you're covered legally." I flicked away the black ash. "I know what I signed. I can only imagine what my wife had to sign to come here. So, when I say this, I want you to take it personally. This isn't about the law or military channels. This is about you and me. Nothing else. No one else. If she's damaged in any way, I'm coming after you. You're going to wish you were a piss boy."

He jammed his cigarette between his teeth and smiled around it as if relishing the challenge.

"Until then," he said around his smoke, "you need me."

THE APARTMENT WAS SO dark and still I thought she'd left. I turned on a lamp and shut the door. She was on the bed in the same position I'd left her, on her side, left foot poking from under the covers. When I took her hair off her face, her eyes were closed and she was smiling.

"Hey, baby."

Her lids fluttered, and she refocused. "Hey."

"How are you feeling?"

"All right."

"You haven't moved."

She got up on an elbow and looked around. The fruit from the night before had collected tiny flies, and her clothes were still on the floor. "I guess I haven't."

I ran my fingers over her forehead, the worst way to check for fever, but I didn't want to go full medical professional on her just yet. Her voice had a tenderness I didn't want to disrupt.

"Are you hungry?" I touched her lower lip. It was swollen from sleep, yielding and soft.

"I don't think so."

The sheet slid down her body, revealing the peaks of her breasts. I ran two fingers from her lip, down her chin, over the hardening nubs. She smiled again, looking down at my hand. Her dark lashes fanned out against her cheeks, fluttering as I moved the sheet below her waist.

"What do you want?" I asked, feeling the depth of the crease between her thighs. She gave no more than what the force of my touch demanded.

"Whatever you want."

"Open your legs."

She spread her knees apart. I ran my hand inside her thighs. She closed her eyes, releasing a gentle gasp. When I pushed her legs apart, she threw her head back, exposing the length of her throat.

"I talked to Ronin today." I slid my finger in her seam, teasing it open. "You told him you were having symptoms?"

"It's not that bad. I think it'll go away."

"What symptoms?"

"Feeling watched. But I know it's not true, so I think I'll get it under control."

She'd seen me break in two, yet she thought her symptoms would just go away because she knew the cause. Was it ego or confidence? I admired her stability and strength, but I wasn't imprudent enough to depend on them. I knew what this shit did to a person. I'd been like this before Damon peeled away and became his own man. Confident. Cocky. Foolish.

"I'm still pissed at Ronin," she said.

"He told me what they were trying to do."

She faced forward, looking at me but... not quite. Her gaze was slightly averted.

"Make warriors?" she said with a question at the end. "I didn't know. I still don't really know."

"I need to know how you're feeling. I need to know if it's hurting you."

"I feel fine," she said. "A little run-down. But fine."

I believed her. I trusted that she knew her own mind because I wanted to. I needed to tell myself she hadn't destroyed herself to save me.

I got three fingers deep inside her with no resistance, and she exposed her throat again.

I controlled her with one hand. I didn't need pain or bonds. She was hovering on the edge, and with every move, I halved the distance between her and her orgasm.

"When did you know it was the shots?"

"After you were stop-lossed. Then I saw the videos of you in the room. Saw your files. Ronin said… oh God. You should stop if you want me to talk."

"Breathe, baby. Just breathe. Tell me what he said."

Her chest heaved. "If they could cure PTSD, they could make better doctors and soldiers, but you had a childhood with… you didn't tell the whole story. And it was… so hard. The serum opened doors, and you split to… handle… the… detachment…"

"It was happening before I went to Blackthorne."

Her voice came back in soft groans. "Fallujah. It was the synthetic amphetamine in Fallu…"

I leaned over her as her mouth opened wide in a soundless cry and tears streamed down the side of her face.

I stretched my body parallel to hers. She was past words, breasts rising and falling quickly, eyes wide, expression drained. Exactly where I wanted her.

"What did you know?"

"I suspected something was off with the synthetic. But not this. I didn't suspect it would tear you apart."

Her expression pleaded with me to understand, but I already understood more than I wanted to.

"Why was it suspicious?"

"The indications sheet was keyed to the intake form. If you answered yes to certain questions, you couldn't get it, but I didn't think about *why* those questions. I trusted it."

"Trust is a mistake." I leaned into her until I could smell the regret on her skin. "Precision is the only thing that matters."

"It's my fault," she whispered with her eyes closed against my stare. "I know."

It wasn't her fault. I shouldn't have even let the thought cross my mind. She'd been as much of a pawn as I'd been.

"I told you that you loved me," I said. "Did I lie?"

She turned from the middle distance, steadily meeting my gaze for the first time since I'd come in. "No."

"I lied." I sat up straight with my hand flat between her breasts, feeling her heart beat against my palm. "Precision isn't the only thing that matters. Love matters too. You broke me, but you loved me whole again. What am I supposed to do?"

"Love me back."

It was the first demand she'd made of me since I walked in. Her voice had become steady and certain.

"I do," I said. "Before you, I was sure of everything. I had it all worked out. Now, because of you, I don't know anything. I'm lost in my own life, and I love you for it."

She reached up to my neck and pulled me over her. I kissed her. The taste of regret was gone.

"Be sure of me," she said, shifting her body under mine.

IT WAS STILL DARK when I turned on the shower. The showerhead was built into the wall above a drain in the floor, making the entire room into a shower stall. A makeshift curtain cut the room in half. I could have made it back to base and put my clean body into clean clothes, but her water was hotter and I didn't have to share the bathroom with two dozen other guys.

The door opened, and the curtain snapped aside.

"Hey," Greysen said. I only noticed her eyes stayed on mine when I stopped staring at her body.

"It's three in the morning," I said. "You have time to sleep."

She walked past the curtain and got under the water. "I have a lot to do." The streams fell over her hair, turning it from medium brown to sable. "And I can't just sit here and wait around for hours."

Magnificent. I ran my hands down the fall of her hair and to her lower back. She snatched the washcloth off the ring and soaped it.

"I want to see you tonight." I cupped her ass.

"Sure." She worked the cloth over her body with disappointing efficiency.

"Why are you in such a hurry?"

"Antsy. That's all."

Catching a line of lather making its way down her back, I stroked her, letting my erection press gently against her bottom.

"Ten minutes." I kissed her shoulder.

She stepped under the water and let the soap run off her, turning to face me with her head back. Her exposed throat made my balls ache.

I grabbed shampoo with my free hand. "Half an hour tops."

She straightened her neck, looking at me with my boner and shampoo in my hand, a cascade of water dripping down her chin. "Can't. I'm skipping hair."

She got on her tiptoes to kiss me, then went past the curtain to dry off quickly and economically, as if she had somewhere to go.

Chapter Seventy-Three

Caden was in the shower when I woke. I'd opened my eyes, compelled to do something, but I didn't know what. Everything. Up and out of bed. In the shower. Out the door before the sunrise. It was a work day in the Green Zone.

I blew through reports, writing up the final destination of Caden's vial without excuses or reasons. Just the facts, ma'am.

How had only two hours passed since I'd woken up? Only a few seconds to cross the cafeteria to the already-burned coffee the night staff had set up by the empty steam table? It seemed as if time used to be a flat sheet of paper that was now folded into an origami box.

I looped two mug handles in one finger and dropped them on the stainless countertop.

"We need to do a workup on you," Ronin said.

"I'm fine." I poured coffee into each cup. "The effects are less and less. I felt the jolt and crash from the B12."

And the splitting sky—

You were tired.

—as if the bowl over the earth had cracked—

You were stressed.

—into two blue eyes watching me—

You were worried about Caden.

—and I was going to slip into the dark fissure between them.

Quit it. You're sane. You have this.

"I believe you," he said casually, dropping creamer into his cup. "But we need data."

"Of course. Speaking of data, I need to go to the hospital and check on two subjects before they're shipped out."

"Then let's get started."

I WAS JUMPING out of my skin, but I'd answered the questions on the form fully, using complete, cogent sentences. Some repeated the same query with different words so that inconsistencies could be noted. I wasn't born yesterday.

The black-walled room was identical to the one in New York. It even smelled like the gilded grime of Manhattan.

"You ready?" Ronin's voice came over the speakers.

"Yes." What I meant was "Get on with it."

With a click, the *soo-hoo* recording started. The anonymous woman's soothing voice seemed drunk to me, like a 45 rpm record played on 33, but I closed my eyes and stayed with it. No reason not to do it right.

I started to feel light-headed. Floaty. The pressure of the chair under me lessened. The flyaway hair on the top of my head bent as if it were touching the ceiling, which I knew was impossible. I was just—

Upward

Crunching overhead

Eyes shut, I saw everything

And nothing

Above and below

Blue, so blue

The sky above crunching

Paper-thin layers of glass cracking

The pressure on my head was enormous

Flakes of sapphire falling on my cheeks

Pushing through the bowl over the earth

Scratching my face

Gravity in reverse

Falling up

Shattering the sky

Into infinite, starless space

And falling so far, so fast

The pool below, glowing turquoise in the underwater lights

A sky-blue rectangle in darkness

It raced toward me
Cool condensation on my face
I hovered an inch above it, flailing
A moment of conviction
I did the right thing
Before I dropped like a stone

THE END of the fall was the surface below. I expected pain. Consequences. Death.

Instead, there was relief. Release. Like bonds untied so aching shoulders could move and a sense that where submission ended, responsibility began.

But responsibility to what? To whom?

Thankfully, I got a call to the hospital. I couldn't be in that office another second. I had to *go*.

Once outside, I stood stock-still right outside the Blackthorne offices, in a sand-floored parking lot.

What had been Caden's cure? Trapped in complete darkness with a woman he loved. A pregnancy. The smell of blood and a feeling of responsibility.

I saw more differences than similarities between what had happened in the basement and what had happened under the rubble, but they had been enough. Not that it mattered in my case. I didn't have a childhood trauma. I'd been loved and nurtured by my parents, then my friends, then my husband.

I didn't have a moment to recreate.

What if I didn't have a cure?

What if the thing that had broken Caden was the only thing that could have cured him?

What if the fact that I wasn't broken meant I couldn't be fixed?

I backed up to the wall, trying to breathe slowly and deeply. After the bioenergetics session, the split was louder, more demanding. I couldn't ignore this. I couldn't pretend it would go away.

What is your fear?

Call it by its name.

Heights. Losing Caden. Cancer. Death.

Imagine the fear as an object.

Which one? They were normal. All standard. None stuck out as something that needed to be dealt with.

Give your fear a shape and a color.

Put it in a place and leave it there. Observe it. Note its dimensions and its depth. Describe its boundaries.

This wasn't working. My fears had no boundaries.

Fears with shape and weight were the demons of a sound mind.

God help me.

RESPITE WAS A WORD.

The word had a force, and it pushed against my consciousness like a bulldozer on a building. I heard it in the silence and in the whisper of the desert wind. The hum of the computer fan and the edge of Dana's words as she came to tell me to go out to the landing pad to see off two of our subjects. I was late, and I had to sign them off.

They looked great. They were great. Mentally, all great. But the whispers with counterarguments were everywhere.

Not great.

This was what Caden had gone through. I knew it. Belief that I could handle it was a habit. Running through lists of reasonable explanations was a professional routine. I still assumed I was tired or hungry but in control of my mind. If I could think about something else, it would go away.

But I couldn't run fast enough to the landing pad. Couldn't find distractions deep enough in the feel of the air on my face or the fingernail I dug into my palm.

Respite.

If I could just taste the thought, I'd know what it was. I could accept or reject. In the rattling of the earth as I went to the waiting chopper, I let it touch the tip of my tongue, accepting its push on my consciousness.

It tasted like poison.

"Thank you for holding them!" I shouted over the beating chopper blades, my hair whipping out of its ponytail strand by strand as the chopper took off with Blackthorne's two subjects.

Colonel DeLeon gave me a thumbs-up and jogged off the pad. I followed, glad to be moving.

"Did you get what you needed?" she asked when it was quiet enough to talk.

"Yes. Sorry it took so long. I got held up at the office."

The *soo-hoo*ing had seemed to go on forever, but not as long as it had taken me to write down what I'd felt and seen during the circular breathing exercise.

"They looked better," she said. "Whatever you're doing, it's good work."

"Thank you."

Her hand was on the door to the hospital. I wanted to go forward, but she was stopping me, and this created a nagging irritation.

"Your last name's Frazier?" Another nagging irritation. Easy rhetorical questions.

"Yes. Why?"

"California? Your family's from San Diego?"

I assumed Caden had told her, but the question was ill-timed, and I had to bite back a snotty retort for Caden's sake. "Officially."

"Follow me, please."

She strode through the halls as though she owned the joint, chin up, looking ahead in such a way as to say, "Don't stop me with anything less than a life-and-death emergency." Opening a nondescript door, she ushered me through and closed it behind us.

The desks were wide shelves mounted to the wall. Three computers and a line of binders. Two beat-up office chairs. She held her hand over one, and I sat in it, then she leaned over a keyboard.

"I hope I'm wrong," she said as she tapped. "But it's not a secret, and I don't know if your employer's looping you in."

She got out of the way of the screen. It was split into six boxes, each with a photo of a soldier. All men. Four white. Two African American. One I recognized.

Jacob Frazier.

"What—?"

"His squad was ambushed outside Al Taqa. These six were captured."

Captured.

Jake's been captured.

I said it to myself over and over, looking at his deadpan expression on the computer screen.

"Is he related?" she asked.

"He's my big brother."

And I owe him everything.

I didn't know where the debt came from. It was more of a feeling than a narrative.

"They're searching for them," she said. "I'd rather you found out from me than some rumor in the cafeteria."

What were they doing to him? How much pain was he in? How much panic?

Jake was tough, but torture broke the strongest of us. It bent the mind around the body. I'd seen it in my patients. Resilient men and women were broken by the force of it.

"Wifey," DeLeon said tenderly, "they're going to find them."

Behind her, my brother's face and five others looked flatly through a screen. Lies of time.

Chapter Seventy-Four

CADEN

Maybe I wasn't the most perceptive guy who ever walked the earth. Maybe I was a little detached and self-involved. When it came to other people, I could be slow. I processed vital data about patients and casualties quickly, but data about their moods and thoughts? I had no idea how to analyze that, and I didn't care to.

At the morning staff meeting, we were warned a dozen diplomats were landing at Baghdad International. They'd take Airport Road twelve kilometers to the Green Zone. We were all on call because that was the only stretch of road between the airport and the Green Zone, and it wasn't called IED Alley for nothing.

A couple of choppers dropped down like clockwork, and the meeting ended as we all ran to the landing pad.

"Wasn't bad," said the kid with a bullet bite in his calf. "We got 'em through."

"What's the trick?" I asked just to keep him talking while I examined the wound.

"Keep pushing. Just keep pushing."

I WAS CLEANING fragments out of someone's flexor carpi when I decided not to say, "He'll be home getting his wife off in no time." One, it was inappropriate, and I had functioning social filters.

But there was a second reason I didn't say that or anything, and I put it together during the busy work of cleaning shrapnel out of a wrist and arm.

I couldn't stop thinking about Greysen.

How she'd changed.

When I'd arrived the night before, she'd been lethargic, but more precisely? She'd been emotionally listless as well. She hadn't asked questions or answered sharply. She hadn't pushed back on my manipulation.

It wasn't the first time she'd been sick, but it was the first time she'd been mentally weak.

And in the morning?

Fully in motion but without the cutting sensitivity I took for granted.

She'd said she was feeling the effects but she was fine. Had she split?

My Damon self had battled for expression when the sun set, but she'd been changed during the night.

If she'd changed. Big *if*. But if she'd changed, it wasn't with the appearance of the sun. It was something else. I stitched up the hand, putting together every word she'd said and how she'd said it.

Be sure of me.

Last words I remembered her saying before good night and the soft breaths of sleep.

A command or a request?

I should have told Ronin about my suspicions about her split, but I wasn't in the mood for him. I didn't want to commiserate or brainstorm with him about the state of my wife's mind, especially with Jake in Iraqi hands.

Finding her was like hitting a moving target. Someone said she was in the supply room, then the chow hall, then the parking lot, then the landing pad. Once I got off work, I continued the chase to the Blackthorne office.

"I'm sure they're going to find him," I said when she closed the door, cutting off the sound of keyboards and ringing phones, leaving only the traffic and wind from the open window.

"You don't look sure. You look hopeful. Not sure."

"Fine." I threw myself onto the couch. "Hopeful. He welcomed me into the family on day one, and he was always good to you."

She didn't sit next to me. She leaned on her desk with her arms crossed. "You're talking about him in the past tense."

"Are you all right? Are you upset?"

"Of course I'm upset. What do you think? Who knows what they're doing to him? I don't know if he's even alive or if he wishes he was dead." She covered her face with her hands as if she wanted to mask her emotions with her hands. "And I can't do anything. I'm a few miles away, and I can't do anything."

"You're going to meet an intelligence guy tonight apparently?"

She dropped her hands. "I just want information. I have to know as much as they'll tell me."

"What are you going to do with that information besides make yourself crazy?"

Her lips tightened to the length of a matchstick. She bowed her head quickly, turning away so she could face the open window. She hooked her finger in the grate.

"If you're at the right angle, you can see the Tigris River from here." She pressed her cheek to the grate to find the angle. "Sometimes I watch the Humvees and trucks going out to the port and see the boats and I wonder what it's like to go someplace. To just run into the unknown. It's like I'm stuck in a matrix of limited possibilities. Going around in a circle, like that carnival ride where you stand against the walls of a round room and it spins and spins. Then the floor drops out, and you don't fall, but you're stuck to that wall by centrifugal force, just spinning and spinning." She turned to me fully, leaving her thumb and pinkie hooked in the grate. "What does it take to get out of it?"

"The walls drop, and you go flying."

She sat in the chair perpendicular to the couch, knees apart, leaning forward with a keen attention to what she said and what she meant. "My brother is outside that spinning room."

"You're not talking about *going*. You're talking about *being thrown*. You're talking about being powerless."

"I don't think I can find out how far I can go on my own. I don't think any of us can."

"Greysen." I sat up.

"Listen, think about it."

"What, exactly, are you talking about?"

"We can't push against our own limits because they're *our limits*. It's like a pot can't ever get any hotter than the flame under it."

"I mean, what are you trying to do? You want to get out of some loop, but you can't do it yourself, and hell knows I'm not on board for this. Who's pushing? *What*'s pushing?" My hands were clawed as if I wanted to strangle her. My muscles were coiled tight.

She saw my frustration, and it did not interest her. "Don't worry about it."

"Greysen..."

"I'm just thinking out loud." She dropped her hand and stood behind her desk, shuffling papers from one side to the other. She stopped at a small slip of paper I couldn't see from my angle. She slid it away from the stack and continued moving the papers around.

"Did you split?" I asked.

She froze with a page in each hand, six inches over the desk, hovering.

"After the shot, did you split like I did? Is there a part of you trapped in darkness?"

"No." She put both pages in a single pile. "I just want to know where my brother is."

Her intercom buzzed, and Dana's voice came over it. "Dr. Frazier? Your appointment is here."

"Please excuse me," she said. "I have work to do."

I THOUGHT my respect for my wife immense. I'd assumed I was maxed out on admiration. But when I realized what was happening, that respect unfolded again and again, taking up more space in my heart than I'd thought I had.

In New York, she'd faced an impossible situation. A new city with few friends. A husband acting in strange and dangerous ways. She'd stayed strong and competent where I would have fallen apart.

At least, I assumed I would have. Faced with her need, maybe I had the strength. I wouldn't abandon her.

Maybe I was the one unfolding.

SHE ANSWERED the door to her little studio with the phone wedged between her shoulder and ear.

"Okay, I understand," she said into the phone. "I love you too." She hung up.

"Who was that?"

"My mother."

"How is she?"

"We agreed on twenty-two hundred," she said, closing the door behind me. "You're late."

I looked her up and down. Her hair was brushed and clean. She wore sweatpants low on her waist and a tight, dull-green tee that ended just above her navel, casually exposing the soft curve of her hips and stomach. Her feet were bare on the cheap Persian rug.

"Nice to see you too."

Her hand was still on the knob, as if she wanted to open it and run out. I flipped the deadbolt.

"Were you the one to tell your parents?" I asked.

"They knew. Dad blew it off. Says Jake's going to be fine. Worrying won't help."

"And?"

"And he's right. I know he's right. But I still feel trapped in a spinning room."

There were a few ways to ground her. One came to mind quickly.

"Take your clothes off," I commanded.

She walked to the other side of the room. Not walked. She *stalked* there as if she was agitated and there was a purpose to the relocation.

This was new. All of it was new. I had no idea what she wanted, much less needed. Did she need to release her energies? Go for a run through Baghdad? Did she need to be soothed? Controlled?

I sensed the adrenaline running through her veins. I wanted to take her pulse, but I already knew her blood was pounding.

"I can't... I have to keep going."

"Where?"

"Anywhere. Something isn't finished, and it's not getting finished here."

When she finally met my eyes, I saw dark circles under confusion and aggression. She'd gotten up before three in the morning, and unlike me, she was a sleeper. Ten hours if she had her way.

I stood in front of her. She looked at me, then over my shoulder.

"You keep looking at the door like someone's going to walk through it."

She looked up at me. All the confusion and aggression were there, along with something else. A plea for help.

"You don't need to go out. You need to get some sleep."

And, with that, maybe the change. I needed to see if she'd wake a different woman.

Again, I was struck with my ignorance of how to help her and my trust that whatever I did was what she needed. I couldn't imagine one without the other. My ignorance without confidence would break me. Confidence without knowledge of my ignorance would break her.

"I can't sleep," she said. "I tried."

"Do you want to speak frankly?"

She tried to push past me, but I wrapped my arm around her, pulling her close so I could growl in her ear. "I'd rather you tell me what's going on."

I threw her on the bed. She landed on her back, and I expected her to leap up and punch me in the face. Instead, she got up on her elbows.

"Are you going to take your clothes off, or am I going to do it?"

"Is this how it's going to be?" The question was so pointed it had a vector all its own.

"You tell me." I leaned over her, knees on the bed, knuckles digging divots into the mattress. "Are you going to be honest with me?"

"Fuck you! I am being honest. I've never lied to you."

"Then are you going to be honest with yourself? Because I'm not as patient as you. I'm not half as nice. You're going to talk to me, or I'm going to take what's mine."

"What if I tell you to stop?"

"Then it's not mine, is it?"

A shade of her aggression wore away, and a few layers of confusion turned into attention.

"Are you talking?" I asked. "Or am I taking?"

She laid her hands on my chest. She was going to push me off her, which meant she either needed space for talking or she was telling me to stop.

"I'm not in the mood to talk," she said. "I'm not stripping for you just because you say so."

"Then I'll fuck you with your clothes on." I pulled her shirt over her bare breasts. "I really don't give a shit."

I kneeled over her as I undid my pants and pulled out my erection. When she looked at it the way she always did, like a lioness terrified of her prey but too hungry not to pounce, it throbbed harder.

I toyed with her until her body was slick with sweat and every touch made her shudder. Then slowly, so slowly, I slid my dick inside her.

"All the way," she whispered, hungry, begging.

"I'll take what's mine. Any. Way. I. Want."

With the last four words, I pulled out and in just enough to be felt. Just enough to drive her crazy. Then I buried myself so deep she howled.

Her legs over my shoulders, the pants against my chest, my own waistband restricting me, I took her hard.

I knew my wife. I knew how to fuck her. I knew what she liked and how she got off.

But no matter how hard I drove, she didn't come.

No matter how deep I went, she stayed on the edge.

I bit her breast, pinched her hips, gave her as much pain as I dared, and still, she cried and scratched but didn't come.

"Fuck," I said, coming inside her.

I kissed her neck and down her belly when her fingers tightened in my hair.

"Stop," she said. I looked up at her, and she stared down at me. "I need to drive this."

"Excuse me?"

She sat up and pulled off her pants. "I can't be a passenger right now." She peeled her shirt off as I got up and stood by the side of the bed with my dick out.

I helped Greysen up and led her to the cheap loveseat. I sat on the edge and pulled her close until her knees were on either side of me, and I leaned back as I let my hands roam her body, finding the crook between her legs.

She stayed my hand. "Don't."

She put my palms on her hips, lowered herself onto me. When I moved my hands to her breasts, she moved them to her hips again.

I let her set the pace. Let her push against me. Let her move any way she liked.

She took my right hand and laid it between her breasts. "I'm spinning." She put my hand on her throat, pressing my thumb and middle finger to opposite sides. "I need a straight line out. Give it to me."

Her veins pulsed under my hand, and the lump in her throat shifted when she swallowed. The control she offered was so precious that I took a moment before agreeing to it.I tightened my hand just a little. Her eyes on me, her jaw in the cradle of my hand, she moved again, and I drove a little, moving with her. All my focus was on her reaction, her pleasure, the release of tension from her face.

When her lips opened and her eyelids fluttered, she was back on the edge. I tightened my hand. "Say no while you still can."

"Yes."

She groaned under my hand. The orgasm was pushing at the boundaries, looking for a way in.

Tighter.

She went rigid mid-orgasm, shaking uncontrollably. I wrapped my other arm around her to bring her into me, pushing heragainst my body as the last of her air gave out. I couldn't come. I couldn't lose control while I had her life in my hands.

When I was sure she'd peaked, I let go, and she pulled in air like a drowning woman, then let out a long vowel sound that told me her body had elongated the orgasm while it dealt with the lack of air and exploded when she breathed again.

She collapsed on me.

"Hey," I said, pulling her hair away from her face. "Let me look at you."

She groaned, getting her arms under her with her head still bowed.

I reached past the curtain of hair for her chin. "Hey. Come on. Look at me. I need to see if you're all right."

I wanted to check her body, but when she looked at me, it wasn't her body that needed my attention.

"Greysen?"

She just looked at me, and I wondered what her name was.

Chapter Seventy-Five

GREYSEN

Distant in the darkness, a blue dot appeared, coming faster and faster, revealing its shape.

Speeding toward me, the blue rectangle glowed and shimmered. Under the water, black lines divided lanes.

Diving pools didn't have lanes, but the one hurtling toward me did.

Black hashes joined the lines, defining themselves into letters, numbers, instructions. The edges of the rectangle curled, and when I hit the surface at an impossible speed, the water was as dry as paper, and I was plunged into darkness so Respite could remember.

SAN DIEGO
JULY - 1992

I TRIED to keep my printing tight and clear, but I didn't feel well. My stomach felt like a dirty washcloth, wrung out and stuffed too high up my rib cage, regurgitating bitter yuck into my dry mouth that toothpaste couldn't cover. My head had a rock embedded on the left side where my brain should have been.

I saw through a layer of gunk as I tried to copy my driver's license number onto the blue form. I shook the pen. Copied the first three characters. Blinked gunk away.

Was that a 5 or an S?

"Do you have an idea when you'd like to start?" The recruiter folded her hands over the stack of papers I'd brought. She was white with a gash of red lipstick at the bottom of her face and flat platinum hair tied into a bun. It had the faintest line of brown at the roots.

My purple nail polish was chipped, and I had to tilt my head just so to see her through the fall of hair over my face. I'd dyed it Nuclear Black in the bathroom sink. I liked the idea of a black so black it could wipe out a city. "I get to pick?"

"You test now but... might want to go to college first?"

I went back to the forms. "I'm done." The pen made a colorless M-shaped furrow in the paper.

"Get married?"

"Not happening." I shook the pen and made circles in the corner of the page until the ink ran.

"Those are just examples."

"I can start right away."

She cleared her throat. "Do you have any idea what you want to do? As a job?"

"Whatever." I stopped writing. Tapped the pen. Put my nail between my teeth and removed it quickly. I wasn't supposed to bite my nails. I looked at her to see if she'd noticed, then I realized my answer wasn't going to fly. "I don't..." *Tap-tap.* "I don't want to hurt anyone. I want to serve. Not kill."

"There are plenty of ways to try to avoid that, but in the end, you'll have to serve in the capacity you're required."

"I can live with that."

"You're probably going to want to cut your hair before you test."

I flicked my head to get the fall of hair off my eye. "Sure."

"And if you come in without makeup, that's fine. Just get it all off."

She touched the outer corner of her eye, and I mirrored her. A streak of sludge was left on my fingertip.

"Yeah." I snapped a tissue from the box on her desk. "Okay."

"Greysen?" Her voice was kind but firm as she tapped my hand. "Don't worry. We're going to turn you into a soldier."

I believed her, and in that belief, I found comfort.

FEAR DIDN'T KEEP me still, nor did an inability to leave. I didn't want to move. I wanted to watch my story play over and over. The phones ringing at the recruitment office. The way the recruiter's lipstick ended in a crisp line across a bump that crested the boundary of her lip. The tang of alcohol seeping through my skin. I could remember every detail as if I was living it—except the reason I was there.

When I got up to go to the bathroom, it was with a certain resentment of my bodily functions. Caden was gone; I didn't know for how long. I was supposed to go to work but wouldn't.

A part of me was crying to get the fuck up, get the fuck out, move it like it mattered, but that part of me wasn't in charge.

The part of me on an infinite loop of past details was in complete control, and I had no choice but to watch as the story unspooled backward.

JAKE PULLED into the strip mall recruiting office and put the car into park. It was hot as hell, and it wasn't even noon.

"You go quicker if you have everything." His eyes were red-rimmed, and he smelled of sanitary wipes. "Passport. Driver's license."

"I have them." I pulled my knapsack out from between my knees.

"All your transcripts?"

"Back to third grade."

"Did you find the immunization records?"

"Jakey, I have everything."

He looked in the rearview. I didn't know what for. Maybe he was checking his own face to see if he'd aged in the past six hours. He had. "All right. I'll go talk to Mom and Dad."

"You don't have to."

"I know."

I pulled the latch on the car door. The dashboard beeped. This was it. The moment my life split into the dozens of things I could have done and the one thing I did.

"Thank you," I said without looking at him. I was looking into my lap, where I could see my raggedy nails half-covered in chipped purple polish. I'd wanted to clean them up but had run out of time.

No. It hadn't been time.

I'd run out of desire to do anything to make this easier on myself.

"I love you, sis." Jake laid his hand on the back of my neck and gave me a little shake.

"I love you too."

"You're going to be fine."

"Don't make me cry, fuckhead."

He put both hands on the wheel. "Then get out of here."

I flipped the fall of hair out of my eyes and got out, dragging my knapsack. I closed the door, took three steps to the double glass doors, and...

"GREY, BABY."

His voice overlaid the hundredth time I walked the strip mall pavement from the car to the recruiting office, skirting a beige wad of gum shaped like a rabbit.

Grey baby grey baby grey baby.

My face tickled when he pulled hair away from it. The screen telling the story flickered, and the details got muddy. They needed my attention. They needed to be memorized and cataloged. But with the flicker of that screen, desire came through. A desire to do things. To move. To lurch forward with big steps toward a goal.

The flicker straightened itself again, and I read every sign, decal, and flyer on the glass doors as if time had slowed down and I'd stopped myself from going in.

"How long has she been like this?"

That was Ronin.

"Twenty-three hundred."

"What was happening right before?"

Before.

His hands were on my throat. Would he tell Ronin that?

"She slept for a moment."

CADEN: "I'm taking her to the hospital."

Ronin: "Let us take her. We know what we're dealing with."

Caden: "No, you don't. I'm not interested in protecting you or the people you work for. I'm interested in protecting my wife. Get in the way of that. Just try."

Ronin: "I'll get the car."

Footsteps and a door closing. None of it was as clear as the changing smells and sounds as I walked into the army's office in a strip mall in San Diego.

"Grey," Caden said, "I'm going to take this sheet off you and get you dressed. It's just me here."

The sheet tickled my torso as it slid down. Cool air on damp skin. His hand on my shoulder to turn me. The touch wasn't sexual, but it was a flicker in my attention. A place where two universes melted together.

I felt the desire to desire again. It pushed through and grabbed his hand.

"Grey."

I was too muddled for words, but actions were feasible. I pushed his hand to the place my legs met.

"What's happening?" he asked.

I kept the pressure on his wrist as a world opened up in the places our bodies touched. Everything was there. The screen sped up, flicked, went slow. Where we were together was where the loop ended.

"I didn't know if it was the orgasm that changed you. I guess you're telling me."

He removed his hand. The recruiting office smelled of coffee and off-gassing. There was a tip-tapping of keyboards and the buzz of overhead lights. A deadbolt slid and clicked. The bed leaned, and Caden's voice was in my head.

"I want you to know," he said, running fingertips along my collarbone, breaking the loop, "I know what you're going through. I think I do. If it's similar. I'm trying to stay calm about it because I can't help you otherwise. But I have to tell you…I hate to see you like this. I hate it. I know this is as much a part of you as the woman I married, and I love every fucking piece of you. But I'm afraid we're being forced to live our lives in pieces."

With two hands, he opened my legs. I was on fire. Bloated with desire. The insides of my thighs were tender where he stroked, sensitive as new skin. My universe revolved around his touch. Everything else was bathed in a silvery gray that shimmered like a movie screen.

His hand stopped. There was a fly in the recruiting office. I heard it buzzing like a circular saw.

"I need you to say yes," he said. "I can't do this without that."

My will was tied up in my backward story, but another will needed to speak, and it would not be denied.

"Don't…"

He stopped. That wasn't what I wanted.

"—ess." I couldn't make the Y. I could only hope I was clear enough.

Caden didn't say anything. I wondered for a moment if he'd heard me, then the bed shifted with him. His hands ran the length of my body and back again, pausing to toy with my hard nipples. He opened my legs all the way, leaving me exposed, unable to resist or comply. A doll in his hands as he stroked and kissed inside my thighs before bending my knees over his shoulders.

Cool fingers slid inside me, and I screamed for more, harder, faster, but nothing came out. I was trapped into submission by my own fugue.

"Yes."

Fingers gone, I heard his belt. His button. A zipper. The rustle of clothing and the creak of the bed, and he bent over my folded body.

"I can't wait to hear your voice again," he whispered in my ear as he entered me.

Warmth spread like a stain into me. My knees were pressed against my chest as he fucked me.

As the pleasure grew, so did my will. It pushed through the screen in the shape of a woman trying to run through a latex wall.

"Come on, baby," he said. "Give it to me."

The rubbery wall broke at the sharpest points. Knuckles. Knee. Nose. Yielding to the force of the oncoming climax, giving way with tiny rips that grew around the contours of my body, breaking as I came through and living inside a pleasure whose gratifications were so satisfying, so all-consuming, so temporary.

The screen was in tatters.

I was out.

CADEN SAT on the edge of the bed, rumpled but clothed.

"What do you remember?" he asked as I got dressed.

I didn't care. Remembering was the past, and I was in the future, living my next second, not my last. But where was I going? What was my future? "Nothing."

"Noth—?"

"Like I said..." I pulled my button-front shirt over my head. Easier than fastening and unfastening a bunch of—

"If you'd stop moving for a second, you might."

"I'm hungry." I jammed my heel into a shoe. "I can't think."

"It's been three days since you—"

"Let me eat first." Second shoe.

"Ronin's bringing the car. I want—"

"There's an American place a few blocks away."

I opened the door. The world. The earth. Huge. Massive. Accessible through a doorway, sucking me into the curve of infinity. I could walk straight forever and wind up exactly where I'd started... but only if I got out.

He stood. "I'll walk with—"

"You can catch up."

"Can you let me finish a sentence?"

Sure. He could finish a sentence. Outside.

THE SUN WAS a diffuse disk behind a thin veil of flying sand and heat. A convoy rolled by at half a mile a fucking hour. Five tanks and a bunch of Humvees draped in armed men. They waved. Some nodded. Two jumped off and kept us from crossing the street.

"You need to get out of the way," I said. "You're going so slow I can make it between."

"Sorry, ma'am."

I wanted to slap the mirrored sunglasses off his fucking face, but Caden had my right arm in a vise, and he growled in my ear, "Calm the fuck down."

"I *can't*."

"Listen to me. Just pay attention to my voice. You've been in a fugue since last night. Ever since the last time I fucked you. Do you remember?"

The sex. I'd ridden him to orgasm. Could I walk down the block and go around this snail parade? No. They were standing at each intersection to prevent exactly that.

"Do you remember?" he asked again.

"I remember."

"What happened after that?"

If I wanted to think about it, I'd be thinking about it. I swung my gaze away from the troops at the corner to his eyes. The blue was not comforting. It was a reminder of everything that was broken.

"Please." I didn't know what I was pleading for.

"After that. What happened?"

I swallowed, paying attention to the way my throat opened and contracted. Sand bit my eyes. I narrowed them, bringing my husband into greater focus.

"I was enlisting. I remembered that day. It was with Jake, and I'm sure it's because he's on my mind. But it feels *bad*. I don't know how else to explain it." Bouncing, I looked up and down the block. Still trapped for the next few minutes. "It was the shot. The BiCam. Not a placebo, Caden. Not a placebo. I don't know what effect it would have had on you. Jesus, I want to strangle someone for trying to do this to you. It's awful. So awful. This isn't worth it. Nothing's worth it."

He cupped my jaw in his hands and held my eyes in place with his. "It's going to be okay."

"How?"

"I swear it, Greysen, I swear on my life I'm going to fix this. Can you believe me?"

Could I?

I believed he believed it, but the feeling of being on defense was so awkward that relief seemed impossible. The need to move-move-move to get away-away-away before I was overtaken was as mentally uncomfortable as I'd ever been.

"I feel it. It's another me. It's a me who knows things that she wants to show me. My God, Caden, she has a name. I split, and she has a fucking name. How did you cope with this?"

"I had months. This came on you quicker."

"Why?" I was suddenly desperate for some kind of answer.

"The dose maybe? Maybe years of repression made the doors open slower? I don't know." He moved his hands to my shoulders, squeezing where they met my arms. "All I know is we're going to fix it."

"When?"

"What's her name? The one you've locked away?"

"I don't want to say it."

"Say it so I know what to call her."

"Respite." I said it as if I couldn't believe it. It wasn't a name, but it was the word that came to me over and over. *Respite.* A reprieve. A suspended sentence. And the name of mental discomfort. The name of its opposite.

The convoy creaked by, and the soldier blocking us moved to the left to block two women wearing abayas that blew in the wind.

I ran across the street—toward-toward-toward.

Chapter Seventy-Six

There were so many things I'd wanted to do. Bring her to the hospital. To Blackthorne. Home. I wanted to try circular breathing. Anything and everything... but one thing at a time.

Then she was off like a shot, across the street through a break in the line of military vehicles. She was hard to catch under the best of circumstances. When she ran, she took off as if she was taunting me to catch up.

I was in heavy boots and a uniform built for protection against harsh elements. Not speed. Not comfort. My feet were heavier than hers, and her timing had been as catlike as her risk-taking.

Guns swung toward her. Clicks echoed off the sky.

I had a choice.

Use the air in my lungs to run after her and catch her bullet-ridden body before it hit the ground. Or use that air to stop the shots.

"Hold fire!" I shouted from the deepest, widest part of my lungs.

I had no authority over these men, but I was a major and I was in uniform. I held my hands out to both hold them and show I wasn't a threat.

The convoy shut down, and men piled off the Humvees.

The guy who'd stopped us from crossing the street jogged to me. "What the fuck—?"

"She's with me!"

"Who was that?" A dusty sergeant came to the sidewalk. I looked small and sad in the mirrors of his goggles. That was intentional. Self-reflection was intimidation.

"My wife," I said, straightening so I looked a little more authoritative in the mirrors. "She's with a contracting operation."

"Is she trying to get shot?"

In his mirrored glasses, I looked at myself expectantly. Small or not, I had leaves on my collar.

"Sir," the sergeant added. "Is she trying to get shot, sir?"

"Just in a hurry, Sergeant. If you give me room, I'll be following her."

He stepped aside and kept his opinions to himself. "Let's move out!"

They hustled back to the line of trucks, and in the moments before they moved again, I dashed across.

THE GREEN ZONE was both militarized and demilitarized, with one making the other possible. The *pop-pop* of live rounds went off sixteen hours a day at the Blackthorne training compounds, where the sight of a person rappelling or jumping off the roof of a building onto a yellow-and-blue stunt bag coexisted with a Subway franchise and a makeshift Burger King.

The restaurants didn't stop me in my tracks as much as the man falling in a controlled jump. My eyes widened and my heart stopped until I heard the *smack* and *whoosh* of him hitting the safety bag.

Get it together. It's just a stunt.

The American place Greysen had mentioned existed in the nether region between the white-tablecloth restaurants the diplomats and businesspeople frequented and the fast-food joints the low-rent contractors went to.

I jogged after her, avoiding the piles of rubble that dotted the streets as a reminder of how we'd gotten here. When I turned the last corner, she was half a block ahead and walking into the diner. I slowed down, relieved she hadn't changed course on a whim.

"I ordered you an egg sandwich with cheese," she said when I walked in. "They only have cheddar."

Too early for lunch and too late for breakfast, the place was nearly empty. She was standing by the front counter as if she was ready to make a getaway.

I leaned over to the woman at the register. "We're having it to stay."

"Caden," Greysen said behind me, annoyed.

"Sit anywhere," the hostess said.

I took my wife gently by the elbow and guided her to the back.

"I don't want to stay," she hissed.

"Neither do I, but the convoy could be another ten minutes at the rate they were going."

She slid into the back booth facing the rest of the room and folded her hands together on the table. I got in across from her. The window to my left was coated with a fine layer of dust.

I clasped her hands in the center of the table, squeezing briefly as if that could transmit my level of empathy. "I know what you're going through."

"Is it wrong that makes me feel less alone?"

"That's a question for a priest." I pulled our fists to my mouth, kissed her hand, and put them back on the table.

"I feel like my mind is a record that's skipping. I have this nagging pressure from 'her,' and the only thing that shuts her up is moving forward, and the space between them is just on and on."

"Where does it tell you to move forward to?"

"Just anywhere." The space between her brows knotted, and her hands tightened around mine. "And Jake. I'm so worried about him. It just says, 'Do something,' but there's nothing I can do."

"They'll find him."

"What if they don't?"

A waiter in a stained white polo shirt brought our breakfast on paper plates and left a fistful of metal silverware in the center of the table.

"Please eat."

"I'm not hungry. I mean, I'm starving actually. But this anxiety." She pressed her thumb to her sternum.

Being married to a psychiatrist had its downsides. She thought everything could be solved with talking. She had clinical terms for everyday discomforts. The upside was the fact that she could identify what she was feeling and verbalize it without a song and dance. Right to the point without a hedge or word of denial.

I picked up a fork and reached across the table to cut a section of her omelet before spearing the piece so I could hold it up to her mouth. She glanced at it, then at me with big, brown eyes that considered my offer to do half the work for her. With parted lips, she accepted, chewing slowly.

"What do you think her name means?" I cut another piece.

"It doesn't mean respite, that's for sure." She took the food.

"The core of my problem was in Damon's name."

"What about the other thing?" she asked. "You split again. That didn't even have a name."

"It might have come out if a bomb hadn't hit the building."

"Do you realize this means it can go on forever? You think you solve one split, and another pops up?"

"We didn't solve Damon with the deployment. Come on." I waved another forkful at her. "Eat. Don't make me do the plane and the hangar."

Ruefully, she opened her mouth and ate. After she swallowed, she said, "I'm glad I took it. Instead of you."

"I'm not." I pushed the half-eaten omelet around to get a better angle. "I didn't want this for you. And we could have handled it if it was me."

"I can handle it."

As I fed her the last of her breakfast, I had no doubt she could manage at least as well as I had. I was worried about my ability to handle being the sane one.

"I'm going to kill Ronin," she said.

"He thinks he's doing the world a favor." I put the fork down and put my plate in front of me. Dark spots had formed under the egg sandwich. "Fucking dangerous, that attitude."

I took a bite. It was salty and tasteless at the same time. I was starving. This thing was going down in two bites.

"I don't care if it works half the time," she said. "I want to destroy every one of those syringes."

"They'll just send more." I finished the sandwich with one last bite.

"I'm bringing it down." Her voice was determined, and a new fire lit up her face. "If it's the last thing I do, I'm ignoring the NDA and bringing it down."

The wind was picking up. Sand ticked against the windows like sleet. They could prosecute her for destroying property or revealing trade secrets. This Greysen was impulsive and action-oriented. This wasn't a side of her that thought through consequences. I had to do that for her.

"If you do," I said, "if you do anything to lose your access to Blackthorne's data, you won't have a case. They'll just hide."

"I don't care."

"And if they have a fix, you'll never get it."

"There's no fix. Nothing short of a completely accurate recreation of past trauma."

"You don't know that."

"I *do*."

"Damn it, Greysen." The force of my voice was raised, but the volume was as low as I could make it. "You need to bend a little."

"I'm bent near breaking." She took her napkin off her lap and tossed it on the table. "I'm going to work."

I stood with her, blocking her way. "Don't do anything reckless. Please."

"I won't."

"Promise me."

"I won't do anything reckless." She had mischief on her mind. Worse, it was mischief with a purpose. "Not today."

Chapter Seventy-Seven

The wind whipped. The sand pelted my skin. I covered my mouth with a scarf to get into the building. I wanted Caden. I wanted to stay with him. He soothed my need to be in motion. Without him, I was bigger than my skin. A balloon filled and filling faster, stretching thin as I tried to focus on getting into my office. I passed the storage room. Behind the coded door was a refrigerator stocked with prefilled syringes that, depending on the patient or the dose, delivered either madness or relief. All I had to do was go in there and smash them to pieces.

"Greysen!" Dana called.

Shocked out of my reverie, I waved and rushed to my office before closing the door behind me. Back to the window, I put the heels of my hands on the ledge and breathed as if it was my only job.

Wow. Okay. I could handle this. I was totally okay. A part of me could see how my desires and behaviors weren't consistent with rationality. I could see myself crumbling under them as if I was watching a movie.

Ronin opened the door.

"Get out."

He closed it. "You and Caden disappeared on me."

"Sorry." I shoved away from the ledge and pushed paper across my desk. "I have work to do. So, if that was all?"

He bent to see my downturned face. "I want to help you."

"I'm fine."

"Prove it."

PROVING it turned out to be harder than it seemed. My blood pressure and pulse gave me away.

"You really did a number on yourself," Ronin said as the Blackthorne nurse took the cuff off my arm.

"It's just stress."

The nurse showed herself out, and I put my jacket back on.

"I can't tell if you're consistent with other unprepped subjects taking a high dose unless you're honest with me."

"And how are those subjects doing now?"

He tightened his jaw for a moment. "Fine. We had some early testing in 2004, and they're fine."

He was minimizing or lying outright.

"So, there's no problem," I said.

"I didn't say that. We're working to develop a counter-treatment to undo the effects. Some of the subjects are at our complex in Texas."

"Some? Where are the rest?"

"We have a facility in Saudi."

I crossed my arms. "Long way from Abu Ghraib. That's where they're from, isn't it?"

"We're taking very good care of them."

"I'm sure that outside the destruction of their psyches, they're having a great time."

"You said you were fine."

He'd caught me in a fat lie.

"Touché."

He didn't rub it in. Had to give him that.

"I can't offer you a cure. But I can offer a little respite."

The name of my alternate rang like a bell. He didn't know. He couldn't know. It must have been the random use of the word that bent me enough to agree to a little of what he was offering.

Soo-hoo-soo-hoo-soo-hoo.

Sitting still in that little room was hard at first, but the breathing did calm me. I had to hand it to him.

Makeup in your eye.

Respite pushed against the barrier with a whisper. She showed me things I didn't want to see, and I had nothing to fight her with.

He said you looked like a raccoon.

She was showing me Jake in the front seat of his Chevy, smoking a clove cigarette. A sight and taste I hadn't remembered in years and didn't want to ever, ever think about again. He said something I couldn't hear over the wind. The picture flashed and disappeared, but Respite spoke clearly when she made me recall the scene.

Calm down, calm down. Jake told you to calm down.

A flicker of a Coke can. The hole at the top flashed with a flame inside it. Smoke.

Jake: It's done.

Jake's statement had cut through the fog. He was like Caden, deeply flawed and powerful beyond measure, as the flash from inside the Coke can lit his face.

Jake: He's got the cleanest fingers in the county.

This was before Scott had pushed me off the diving platform.

Respite whispered a correction. *You jumped.*

I'd jumped off that platform even though I was scared of heights. Why had I insisted he'd pushed me? Because it was easy to believe I'd had to save myself from his probing hands?

You jumped.

That was impossible, yet I knew it was true. He'd had his hands on me even when I'd said stop. They went between my legs, and I knew bad things were going to happen. I would resist it and like it and hate it, and bad things would happen.

You jumped to save him.

Respite was talking too damn much, and she could go fuck herself.

Chapter Seventy-Eight

CADEN

Casualties of the sandstorm, civilian and military, started coming in as soon as I reported for duty. They'd been hit by flying garbage, gotten knocked off their feet, been found wandering and disoriented. People came in coughing up orange grit.

I shouldn't have left her. She wasn't herself. If something happened to her, I'd be responsible. If she went off half-cocked and broke every syringe they had, the consequences were on me. I'd let her go. Worse, she was splitting in two, and I couldn't do a damn thing about it. Couldn't even stay with her when she needed me. I'd abandoned my duty to her. All the times I'd walked out the door of our house in New York while carrying the weight of Damon on my shoulders, had she felt like this? When I'd deployed, had she been crushed by this level of failure?

Surgery was done, and the wall between my personal life and the job on the table disintegrated. I was going to call Greysen repeatedly until she answered. From behind, I felt a vise grip on my arm pulling me in the opposite direction.

"I need you to stay calm." DeLeon said as she guided me down a hall with a sun-soaked window at the end.

"I'm calm."

"I didn't say *be* calm. I said *stay* calm."

The view through the window got clearer as we got closer. I could see the streaks and finger spots on the glass. By the time we stopped, the rest of the hall was dark and we were bathed in the light.

"Where's Wifey?"

"Why? Do you have one of her people again?"

"Answer the question."

"Is this what I'm staying calm about?"

"Major. You will answer the question."

Damn that bird on her collar. I had no interest in admitting the answer to her any more than I had in admitting it to myself.

"I don't know," I said.

"Okay. As long as she's not here."

"Why?"

"I don't want her hearing this from anyone else."

"If you wanted my attention—"

"That unit that just came in? The ones that were booby-trapped bloody?"

"Yeah?" She definitely had my attention.

"They were looking for the Al-Taqa Six."

"They found them?" I wasn't even finished before I knew I would have seen them if they'd been found or wired with C4. "Or... they were the bait?"

"Their dogtags were the bait, apparently. I couldn't get more than that. But this unit raided the house thinking they'd found them. They were moved. The scene was a mess, then once they tried to take the tags..."

"Boom."

"Blackthorne has ears everywhere." She put her hand on my arm. "She's going to find out. It should be from you."

"Thank you," I said, but it wasn't enough, so I repeated it. "Thank you."

"You have an early morning shift. Oh five hundred," she said. "I need you here. No excuses."

———

GREYSEN and I were safe in her apartment with the windows shuttered against the storm. I'd given her a sedative, but that seemed to only make her agitation worse. Telling her about her brother would send her through the ceiling.

"Have you tried the circular breathing?"

"At work." She crossed from one side of the room to the other. "We did a session."

"Can you do it now?"

"I don't think I can."

"Why not?" I sat on the sofa and invited her to join me.

She sat. "I can't sit still for it." She got up. "There's so much I want to tell you, but it's hard to keep my thoughts together to do it." She cleared her throat and cringed against pain. "It's hard to stay in this room."

"What's hard about it?"

"I need somewhere to go. Some purpose, you know? Or it's so uncomfortable I can't think."

I got up and held her arms at the elbow, keeping her still. My gaze met hers. She looked like a caged animal. Frantic, panicked by her surroundings.

"Your purpose is to talk to me. That's your goal. Do you hear me?"

She swallowed. Nodded. A little of the frenzy drained away.

"Say it." I knew talking would hurt, and demanding it was unfair and sadistic, but it was for her own good. "Tell me what you're here to do."

"I don't think that's going to work."

"Say it anyway. You know it's true."

Deep breath. "I have to tell you everything."

"That's your purpose."

"That's my purpose."

"Now believe it."

I held her stare for a while, trying to catch the frenetic energy as she released it and redirect it back with confidence.

"This," she said. "This is me. Running and driving forward. It's not mania so much, because I don't feel all-powerful. I don't have an unrealistic idea of my own abilities. But there's this push. Like I have to advance some agenda even if it changes once I finish."

"Stay with me. Right here." I led her to the couch so she could sit as long as she was able.

"When you had this thing," she said, "when Damon was around, did you feel incomplete? Like not a whole person?"

"Yes. I didn't think of it that way. But yes."

I ran my fingers over the top of her hand. She was in so much pain. I knew that pain, yet she seemed the worse for it.

"I feel like Respite took half of me and hid it behind a screen." She tried to get up, but I held her hands in her lap and she stayed. "She wants to show me things, and Caden, I don't know what they are, but I don't want to see them. And this half of me is running while she's just waiting. I feel it. It's like a dead weight on me. How did you deal with it? How?"

I didn't have an answer that would satisfy myself or her.

"Don't let her own you. Don't let her take over."

"She's not trying to be me. She's trying to help me. That scares me more than anything."

"Why? What's going to happen if she helps you?"

"Then I'm alone with it. With something. I need her to stay, and I need her to stop. It's both and neither. I can't make her stop, and I can't make myself stay still."

Her brown eyes went glassy with a layer of tears, and her words bypassed her torn throat so she could speak in a breathy whisper. "If you took my arms and legs away, I'd know who I was. Take my eyes, my ears, I'd still be me. But my sanity?" She blinked, and the tears fell. "Who am I?"

I tried to hold her, but she pushed me away and stood.

"Even if I get this fixed," she continued, "I know it can happen. I can be broken. There's something wrong inside me. How will I ever be the same?"

I could barely hear her through the tears and the shredded throat. When I reached for her, she tried to get away, but I grabbed her and pulled her back onto the couch.

"Your job is to sit here."

"That's not a purpose."

"Yes, it is."

"It's not forward."

"You're exhausted." I wiped her tears, but there were so many I couldn't dry her face completely.

"I can't sleep. Not when I'm..." She hitched a breath. "Not when I'm this way."

"The other one sleeps. Respite. And I think I know how to get her out."

"No." She shot up. "No, I don't want her. I'll be this until we figure it out." Pacing. Again. To the closed window. To the door.

I jumped up and put my hand on the door to keep it closed. Her lips twisted into a snarl.

"Get out of my way."

"I'll tie you down whether you like it or not." I pushed her against the door, hovering over her so closely I was a cage.

"You can't control me, so you threaten me?"

"Keep feeling sorry for yourself, and they won't be threats."

She pushed me away, and I pushed her back.

"You're crossing the line, Caden."

"Oh, fuck the line." I took her chin and made her look at me. "Fuck all the lines. Draw me a million fucking lines, and I'll cross all of them to get to you."

She swallowed against the pulse inside my wrist.

"Let me go," she whispered.

"Let me help you."

"Help what? I can't take this. I can't take another minute. I can't live in my own head anymore. I don't know who I am or what I think. I'm at my limit. I can't take it. I'll do anything to make it stop."

"Let me help you." My hand slid down to her chest. I held her in place gently, letting her know I was there without trapping her.

"Help me what? Tell me what, and I'll do it."

What did I want her to do? I was at as much of a loss as she was. I'd have done anything for her, but there was nothing to do. "You need to rest. We need to relieve the pressure from the other... Respite. Let her through. Let her help you."

"I don't want to."

"You're never going to get on the other side of this unless you do."

"How do you know that?"

"You just told me. You just said she'd disappear when she was done."

She pressed her mouth shut and averted her gaze from mine. She didn't have an answer.

"I know how to switch it," I said. "Damon was triggered by the sunset. The darkness. You have a different trigger."

When she looked at me, she was open and curious. "What is it?"

I couldn't help but smirk. "Orgasm."

"Only you would come up with that."

"Hardly. It was you." I unbuttoned her fly with a twist of my fingers. "You flip when you come."

She relaxed her shoulders, moving her head to the side as if she was considering the proposal. "I think you're wrong, but it won't hurt to try."

"That's my girl."

I backed up to give her space, moving aside so we could go deeper into the room, but I'd underestimated her again.

She spun around, opened the door, and walked out.

When my wife decided to self-destruct, she went at it the same way she went at everything—with grit and resolve. I'd expected that. I hadn't expected the speed.

She didn't go out. She went *up*, and even if she didn't know what she was doing, I did.

She didn't want a rest. She wanted this to end. She was going to recreate her fear and face it.

The stairs were outside the building. Drifts of sand had accumulated in the corners. She took the steps two at a time, using the bannister to hoist herself up faster, with me at her heels.

"Greysen!" My voice sounded like wind.

My view of her narrowed and folded as she stepped from the stairs onto the roof. The wind was more powerful up there, and it came from every direction. She had her knees bent and her elbow crooked over her face.

I grabbed her free arm. "What the fuck are you doing?"

She didn't answer. She stretched herself toward the edge of the building. I pulled her to me.

"I am not going to let you hurt yourself."

She twisted away but didn't run. She was out of her mind. Free of sound judgment. Listening to voices that wanted her to act without thinking. I knew those voices. They'd told me to punch a wall to break my wrist. They'd made me jerk my dick bloody. They weren't foreign intruders but the voices that we dismissed when we were in our right minds.

We were both compelled to do something, anything, but we were being pushed in opposite directions. The difference between us was that for the moment, I was sane.

That was the final realization. I put my love away. My compassion took a back seat to professional detachment. There were things that had to be done to save her. She had to be stabilized before she could be cured.

She got two steps toward the edge of the building, crouching against the push of the storm.

The wind slowed her down enough to catch. I grabbed her arm, then her waist, pulling her back against my chest. We fell to our knees with her writhing and me trying to get control of her.

"Caden," she said without reprimand. It was a call to her husband.

I put my hand into her waistband. "Let me, Greysen! Help me!"

She bent over, and I followed, jamming my hand all the way down until I felt where she was soft.

"I don't want Respite." Her voice was nearly lost in the wind, but I was close enough to hear.

"You need it." My hand deeper between her legs, I could barely move it against the weight of our bodies and the restriction of her clothes. "Let me in. You want it too."

I rubbed her, and she bucked under me. Her legs relaxed and opened a little.

The last time I'd made her come when she was a woman in motion, she'd been on top, commanding the situation. I let her have control again, moving my hand with hers as we grinded against each other. Sand skittered across her cheeks and lips. Her face was lost in pleasure. Magnificent and mine alone.

"God, baby," I growled.

She answered with parted lips and a stiffened spine.

We balled up on the roof, breathing against each other while the wind whipped around us. Who was under me? When she spoke, what would she say? Would it be active Greysen telling me how wrong I was about her trigger? Or would it be Respite, whose name was a lie?

I knew before she opened her eyes or spoke. I knew by the lack of tension in her joints and the easy rhythm in the rise and fall of her back. Getting up on my hands and knees, I observed her, and she opened her eyes, squinting against the flying sand.

"Respite?"

She smiled wanly. More awake than before. More aware and somehow more dangerous.

Part Ten

Chapter Seventy-Nine

RESPITE

Most people don't know when they're going to die, but I did.

I had an all-consuming drive—and it went backward.

When I was at the beginning, I was at the end. I'd have fulfilled my purpose, and past it, there was nothing but a void.

It didn't matter. My will to survive was nothing compared to the will to go back.

When Caden got off me, I got to my feet. I was wobbly because I couldn't pay attention to the act of standing. Every bit of energy went to remembering.

"Can you walk down?" He held me up by the waist.

I nodded, squeezing his hand. What a beautiful creature he was. With the orange sky behind him and his eyes squinting against the storm, he was deeply rooted in the world and all its troubles. He was a god causing the pain he cured.

"I can."

He led me to the steps, keeping his hands on me as if I had the will to run away.

I was grateful to him, but he wouldn't make me come again. Not until this was finished.

The screen flickered to life, and I was eighteen.

I COULD IDENTIFY two separate cricket sounds and tell the difference between a breeze from the west and a wind from the north. I was more sober than I had any business being. The happy, swoony feeling was gone, as was the sick swimmy feeling. My lucidity was painful.

Nighttime was a devil of clarity. All the doors open. Owls. Crickets. Birds. Scuttling in the bushes. Things breathing. Hearts beating. Somewhere. Anywhere. The cracking of nail polish being worried off sounded like a jackhammer in slow motion. The moon and stars were hidden behind a thick layer of clouds that caught the lights from the ground, diffused it, and sent it back as a shadowless mass.

The lights were off, and the engine clicked as it cooled. In the passenger seat of Jake's Chevy, I chipped my nails from solid purple to jagged gray.

Snick-snick-snick.

Waiting for my brother to get back, I congratulated myself when I got a big piece and brushed it off my skirt when it fell.

Snick-snick.

I got right back down to business. My full attention on cracking the polish meant I could move forward without looking back. This project in the cacophony of the night kept me from turning my mind back in time. Kept me from thinking about the weird brokenness between my legs. The soreness that reminded me of my deep corruption. The thing that caused all the other things that...

Snick-snick-snick.

If I'd known where I was going, I could have run there. If I'd been avoiding something my whole life, I would have hurtled myself into it full force. But I'd been adrift. I had nothing to run to any more than I had anything to run from. Until now. Now I had something to run from, but it was everywhere. You can't escape if you're running in circles.

Snick-sni—

"Ow." My voice sounded alien, and when I put my finger in my mouth, it tasted of enamel and blood.

I opened the glove compartment. The light went on. I wasn't supposed to shine a light or make a sound, so I hurried to grab a Burger King napkin from the compartment before the light cut too much of the night.

I closed it softly. Maybe the shock of light woke up a part of my brain that had gotten used to the darkness. Maybe my corneas had a temporary burn. Maybe some higher power had something to say. I don't know why the picture of what was under the napkin was imprinted in my mind, but even with the return of dark and the bleeding under control, it remained.

BE ALL YOU CAN BE.

Jake had enlisted six months before and had only been home a few days. He loved the military. The order. The routine. The challenges. Even the hierarchies.

ALL YOU CAN BE.

What was I?

Snick-snick-snick.

Was I who I had been yesterday? Or was I who I'd become in the past three hours?

YOU CAN BE.

I'd sneered at him when he came home, but he'd just smiled as if he knew something I didn't.

CAN BE.

I considered myself a pretty shrewd customer. A real cynic. I could sniff out falsehood. I knew PR when I saw it. "Be All You Can Be" was pure public relations magic, even to a girl who had made eyeliner into an art and wanted hair so dark it could take out a city block.

BE- snick-ALL- snick-YOU- snick-CAN- snick-BE.

But what could I be?

Could I live in a straight line?

Could I have forward motion?

Quickly, I opened the glove compartment, got out the pamphlet, and snapped it closed. I could barely see it, yet I had the pitch memorized. The front photo was deeply saturated in orange-and-yellow sunrise with the silhouette of cavalrymen marching, arms raised in command, every one a leader. In the rusty sky, a line of parachutes opened.

WE DO MORE BEFORE BREAKFAST THAN MOST PEOPLE DO ALL DAY.

Onward. I didn't have to look back if I was going toward something. I wouldn't be blindsided by the things I'd done if I could just keep momentum.

The back had a business card clipped to it. The recruitment office on Shiloh Street. Lieutenant Barry Driggs. US Army.

Lieutenant Barry Driggs knew who he was and where he stood. He knew where he was going because the army told him so. The army pointed him in a direction and didn't let him look back. He was one of them. So was Jake. That was what he had been smiling about when he got home.

Escape. The hope of a beautiful escape into purpose.

The dome light snapped on as the driver's side door opened. Jake got in and closed the door before the dashboard beeped twice. He smelled of alcohol wipes and twenty hours without a shower.

"Hey." I tucked the pamphlet under my leg. "How did it go?"

"Uneventful." He cracked a can of Coke. It hissed as he sucked the bubbles off the lip. The diffused light hit his sculpted cheekbones and the scrub of hair growing on his chin.

"You had time to get something to drink?"

He handed it to me. "Finish it."

"Why?" I didn't like the sticky brown crap with an indefinable flavor.

"Just do it. For once, just do what you're told."

I used the spotted Burger King napkin to wipe the bubbles off the side. Jake circled his finger as if to say, "Move it along." I drank as much as I could before the buildup of carbonation stopped me. My brother tapped the steering wheel and stared out into the darkness.

"Are you all right?" I asked.

"Yeah. I'm fine."

"You don't seem fine."

"Drink up, Punky."

I took a deep breath and drank as much as I could.

"I'm fine, but…" He paused for a shallow breath while I got the drink down to a third of a can. "I've been taking sniper courses. They make us think of them as targets. Not people. Like if we tell a part of ourselves that it's really a person, it poisons the part that does the shooting. But I don't know. I don't know if I can do it. After this, I don't know if I can lie to myself."

"Don't ruin your life because of me."

We looked at each other a long time. Condensation dripped onto my finger and slid along its length. Jake was my older brother. He'd given me noogies and made fun of my body when it started maturing, falling into silence on the subject when it was finished.

Now he was a man.

And me?

What did that make me?

I finished the remaining cola and handed him the can.

"What are you going to do?" he asked, reaching into his pocket and pulling out a used alcohol wipe. It had a faint streak of blood on it.

"Lie?" My headache started there, right when the alcohol wore off. At the moment I told the truth about lies.

He stuffed the wipe into the can until only a small triangle of white stuck out. "Smart."

"Do you think so?"

"Yeah. If anyone asks, tell them I picked you up at one thirty and took you home. Do you have a lighter?"

"Sure." I got out a pack of clove cigarettes and offered him one.

He took it and the black Bic. He lit us both, then touched the flame to the white triangle. When it caught, he shook the wipe down. Yellow light flickered from the little hole, replaced with acrid smoke.

"I'm sorry," I said. "I did ruin your life."

He cracked the window and blew the smoke out, coughing. "This shit's going to ruin me way before you do." He dragged again and choked. I laughed. "It's like smoking broken fucking glass."

I took a long pull before licking the clove flavor off my lips. "Yeah." I smiled, flicking my ash into the empty can. "Ruins the shit out of you."

***

BACK IN GREYSEN'S SPACE, Caden sat me in a chair. He pressed his fingers to my wrist as if the answers were in my pulse. I smelled the smoke from the can mixing with the clove cigarette. Tasted the Christmas on my lips. He was with me, staring at me as if he was trying to understand me, but he never would. I was the memory of what I'd forgotten. I was the events during a drunken blackout. I was Greysen's darkness and the light that banished it.

"You're thready," he said. "You need to rest."

"All right." I wasn't tired. I was drained.

"And eat."

"Sure."

I closed my eyes, letting the room slip away, going backward to my brother's car as he parked it on a back road and told me to stay there. I was to sit in darkness and silence. I was to duck if someone came. I agreed to everything, submitting to culpability for something that I'd done but couldn't remember.

The pressure of the chair under me disappeared. Caden had taken me in his arms and was carrying me to the bed, where he laid me down and stroked my hair from my face.

"I'm going to fix this," he said.

I opened my eyes. Above me, he was a protective force that had no idea of the harm he could do. I wished I was worthy of him. I wished my sins were as unintentional as his.

"No," I said, "She and I are going to fix it."

Chapter Eighty

CADEN

Hours had passed with her narrating the sound of the leaves in the wind. I'd sat still for it when I could, but mostly I took her pulse and her temperature, looking for something to latch onto.

Solutions. I needed solutions, and all I had were problems.

I didn't know what Respite meant by fixing it, but if she was anything like Damon, she wasn't going to fix shit. She was going to fuck it up.

Phone lines were down. Neither of our cells had signal. I didn't have a car, and I couldn't carry her to the hospital. I still hadn't told her about Jake because I couldn't decide which one of her would take it worse. Respite, whose world seemed to circle around him? Or Greysen the Unpredictable?

If she were injured, I'd carry her back to New York if I had to. But I hadn't yet taken her to the hospital because I didn't want to put a dozen doctors between us. I didn't want to answer questions, and I didn't want her whisked away from me to some mental facility. Because they would. The army. Blackthorne. Someone would take her away.

Greysen had a few granola bars in the cabinets and a bruised apple on the counter. A half-eaten container of hummus and a round of pita that still had a day or two in it. I unwrapped a bar and sat on the edge of the bed.

"You have to eat."

Her eyes opened halfway, as if she wasn't committed to looking outside herself but for the first time in hours, she'd try.

"Respite," I said. It felt wrong to look at my wife and call her a different name, but she wasn't Greysen either.

"Hello, Caden." She glanced at the bar that poked out of its wrapping like a bloom, then back at me. As Respite, she exhibited an emotional flatness I associated with distraction. She was never fully present in the room with me, and it made me impatient to see my wife again.

"What kind of name is that?" I asked. "A little on the nose, don't you think?"

"She turned my name into her wish." She sat up, sliding her bottom back and leveraging against her right arm. The sheet fell down her body. I'd stripped her to her underwear, and I was glad I hadn't finished the job. I didn't want to look at those beautiful tits on another woman.

"So that's not your name?"

"No."

I pushed the granola bar at her. She took it reluctantly.

"What's your name then?"

"Something like that."

"Like Respite?"

She nodded and bit off the tiniest corner.

"But not?" I continued.

She shook her head. This new personality took years off Greysen's demeanor. There was something very knowing about her but something petulant and naïve as well.

"I don't know it yet, but I will." She bit off another corner and chewed with more attention than chewing deserved. "I'll know once I play the entire thing back."

I waited. Did she think I knew what she was talking about?

"Do you have water?" she asked.

"Sure."

As I filled a cup, I watched her in the reflection of a tiny mirror tile. Greysen in a black bra and rumpled sheets but not her. Not her at all. I'd married a woman, and there was a girl in the bed.

"Thank you," she said, taking the glass.

I pulled up a chair. "What's this about playing something back?"

She handed over the glass, then the half-eaten granola bar. "A thing that happened. The memory is deep, but I had eight kamikazes. So, it's there? I can get it out, but only one thing at a time, from the end. Like I have to unpack the box from the top?"

I heard what she said. The words were fine, but the tone wasn't Grey. It had question marks all over it. I couldn't blame her for not knowing which way was up. I didn't either. Couldn't tell how long this would take either. Was she unpacking a two-year-long event or a bad few minutes?

"When is the memory from? How old were you?"

"Eighteen."

"Where were you?" I kept my tone casual. I didn't want to freak her out. She seemed fragile.

"Um, Jake just pulled up to a... like a side back alley-ish thing? It's a lot of cinderblock and gray. Light industrial, maybe. It's really dark, and I'm glad about that."

I'd thought I knew what my wife was going through because I'd lived it with Damon. But Respite was different. She spoke about her alternate as if she was the same person. Past the emotional flatness, there was a soft compassion for the girl whose story she was telling. A forgiveness. Respite's tone confirmed she existed to help, not conquer.

"Also," Respite continued, "there's kind of a gross swimmy feeling, and my tongue tastes like burn."

"The eight kamikazes."

She may have heard me, but judging from how her gaze went blank, it didn't matter. "The crickets are really loud. I feel like they're going to give me away. It's cloudy, but the light pollution from town makes the clouds bright enough to see by. And Jake is mad. He gets out of the car. He's got big muscles on his arms. When he left for the army, he was skinny. Now he's like a man. He scares me?"

Again, the question at the end illustrated how different she was. I wanted to shake her loose. It had been hours, and I wanted my wife back.

She put up with Damon for weeks.

"Why is he mad?" I asked.

"It's three thirty in the morning," she replied without looking at me. "He wants to know why the hell I haven't gone home. What's on my freak mind? He always called me a little punky freak. And then I cry so hard he stops being mad."

She went silent.

"Respite?"

"When Jake gets out of the car, the gravel crunches under his feet. He's not wearing the boots he came home in. He's wearing his old Adidas while he's on leave, but he keeps his dog tags on. He leaves the car door open. The dashboard's beeping, and his lights are on."

She'd started from the beginning, adding new details but going no further back.

"Why is he there?" I asked.

"He's saying, 'Oh, fuck, Grey. Fucking fuck. Where?' and I point at a dark place behind the building. Jake goes, but I sit sideways in the car with the door open. I take the keys out and turn off the lights so the beeping stops. I wait a long time."

"What's happening, Greysen?" I called her by her real name because she wasn't respite any more than I was a back rub.

"There's a break in the clouds, and I can see some stars through it."

"Greysen." I try not to growl and fail.

"When I rub my thumbnail, I feel a place where the polish is flaking."

She was rubbing her thumbnail as if she was there, wherever *there* was. She was infuriating, making no effort whatsoever to dig out of this. She was just sliding into the details of a memory that could go nowhere and not answering the relevant questions.

She was about to talk again. She opened her mouth to reminisce about the light reflecting off the sky or some bullshit. I didn't want to hear it. Not another word.

I took her by the shoulders and shook her. "Listen to me!"

She focused on me for the length of fingers snapping. For that moment, she was herself. It was like taking a rib spreader out and putting the thorax back in its place. It all fit.

"Where are you?"

Before I even finished my sentence, she was gone. Heart, lungs, ribs—taken apart. Insides outside.

I was bereft. My body was inside out. I was the one with parts out of place.

"He's gone a long time," she said. "The crickets pause enough to let the sound of the rustling leaves through."

"No, no, look at me."

"I'm hungry."

"Okay, I'll—"

"I can hear my stomach rumbling in the pause."

"Stop!"

She did. I thought I'd be relieved, but her silence wasn't a refocus of her attention. She was deep inside herself and not bothering to tell me what was happening. This was worse.

My watch beeped, cutting my thoughts like a scalpel.

I had to report for duty in half an hour.

"Grey, listen, if you're in there. Listen."

I lifted her chin until she faced me. With my other hand, I moved my finger across her field of vision, left to right and back again. Her eyes did not follow.

"Jesus, baby, what's happening?"

My watch beeped. So close to her ear, yet she didn't move a muscle.

"I have to report for duty in half an hour. Talk to me. Tell me what to do."

The watch stopped. Like the silence of the crickets, it opened the door to heartbeats and breaths.

"Greysen."

Twenty-eight minutes to report, and if you're not ten minutes early, you're late.

"Greysen."

No answer, but her lips were puckered in my fingers. I smashed my mouth on hers. The woman in my hands felt like her. My tongue fit between her teeth just the same. She tasted like my wife. But she didn't respond. I pulled my lips away but held her head still. I was torn between staying with her and reporting for duty. The hospital needed me. The army needed me, and I'd made commitments.

"Talk to me," I said.

"I beg him not to leave me."

"I won't leave you."

"He says he never will."

"I won't. Ever."

"He's my brother, and we're all we have."

"We're all we have."

Did she hear me? Did she understand? Was I even talking to her? Or was I reminding myself of what was important?

Her eyes focused and found mine. I let her jaw go. She was my wife again. Partly, at least. She was still soft and docile, but she didn't seem as young or fragile. "Caden."

"Yes?"

"That part? It's over. I remembered everything I had to."

"Everything?"

"Everything that was there. I feel the things before bubbling up."

"Are you all right?"

"I didn't know you back then. It's weird to think there was a time in my life without you."

"I was there."

Her brow knotted, and she sat perfectly still, as if breathing and remembering couldn't coexist. Finally, her eyes met mine and she spoke. "I don't remember that."

She took memories and facts very seriously.

"Always. We were a promise the Universe made before we were born."

She looked away but not back inside herself. "I don't know if I felt it."

"You don't need to feel it to make it true." I gathered her hands in mine and laid them in her lap. "I knew it the first time I saw your face. You were a promise kept. I knew that if I let you go, I'd be breaking something bigger than me."

She slid her hands out of mine and around them until my palms were on her bare thighs.

I saw my watch against her leg. Twenty-seven minutes. I was going to have to walk a quarter mile in a storm to get to the hospital. I had to leave... or not. There was another issue: an orgasm would bring back the other Greysen.

"I have to report."

"Okay." She lay back, legs still open, the fabric of her underpants creased in the center where moisture made them stick.

She was going to get herself off. If I reported, I'd come back to an empty apartment. She'd be somewhere in Baghdad, walking toward some purpose she made up just to give herself forward motion. We'd be separated again, and I'd have no control of the situation.

That was not acceptable. The US Army was going to have to deal with my absence.

Leaning over her, I hooked my fingers in her underwear. "Pick up your butt." I slid them off her and balled them in my fist. "Bra off."

She unhooked the front and wiggled out of the bra. I took it. She closed her legs.

Grabbing her ankles, I pivoted her until she was lined up with the direction of the bed.

Stroking her legs, I said, "What do you remember about us?"

"That I love you."

"About sex."

"Nothing."

"Nothing? Do you remember the spankings?"

Eyes wide with shock, lips parted. The idea shocked her.

"So, you don't?"

"No!"

"What about pain?"

"It hurts?"

She was my wife, but she was different. What had Greysen gone through with Damon? Had it been anything like this? Had it felt just short of infidelity, or had it gone over the line?

I put a knee on the bed and pressed her inner wrists together. I wrapped her black bra straps around her pretty elbows.

"I'm going to tie you to the bed."

"Why?"

"So you don't run away."

I tied her elbows to the bed, letting her hands clutch the bars. Her big, brown eyes watched me.

"I won't," she said. "I promise."

You can still make it to the hospital.

I could. But I couldn't leave her tied up for ten hours, and I couldn't leave her untied alone to switch back to a woman on a mission, any mission as long as it took her forward. No. This was the right thing. Shirking duty went against every fiber of my being—except the ones that prioritized Greysen. Those fibers far outnumbered the dutiful ones.

"Do you remember the last time I fucked you?" I asked, standing over her.

"No."

"Right before, you were soft and detached like this. Were you remembering things?"

"I think so. Scott. At the pool."

"Let me tell you how it's going to go then." Gently, I ran my finger between her legs. "I'm going to taste you. You're going to come in my mouth, and if I'm right, you're going to flip. I have to talk to Greysen."

"But I have to *remember*." She tried to sit up, stretching the bra straps against the cheap piping. "She can't remember."

"Remembering can wait."

"No. It can't."

I slid two fingers inside her, and she gasped. "It will wait. I need to talk to my wife."

"I won't come," she said. "I just won't, and you can't make me."

My wife was my wife no matter which side of her personality was on display, and when she decided what she wanted—or didn't—that was the last of it.

"Challenge accepted."

I got up and undressed. She watched as piece by piece, I stripped my uniform. Each article of clothing I took off made it less likely I'd report for duty. Each badge and buckle laid itself down in service to my wife until I crawled between her legs, fully naked.

"I'm not going to come," she said. "I can feel the next memory coming."

I pressed her legs apart as far as they'd go and sucked gently on her nub before running my tongue down to her entrance. "You're going to come now." "We're calling Jake on a payphone. The quarters won't go in. There's gum in the slot."

"Oh, no, you don't."

Three fingers inside her.

"Pick up, Jake." Her voice was lower, less demanding. I was losing her. "Pick up. We don't know what to do. He answered! Jake! Jake. We need you!"

"Come, Respite."

"He sounds sleepy and pissed off. He's asking where we are. We don't want to tell him because we said we were at Anna's."

"You're almost there."

"Don't tell Mom and Dad...We're at the Red Spot."

She elongated the O and came as if it was the last vowel she'd ever utter.

With Respite.

We're at the Red Spot.

Respite.

Red Spot.

Her name was a slurring of Red Spot.

I knew why Respite didn't keep the promise of her name. She was the reminder of a night eight kamikazes had hidden.

"Get off me," my wife growled.

"Welcome back."

"YOU'RE GOING AWOL?"

She'd gotten up like a shot the moment I untied her.

"I'm not leaving you."

She was already getting into her pants as if she was late for an appointment with the president. "I don't need a babysitter."

This woman was impossible. Both personalities tested what little patience I had.

"You need to stop long enough to listen."

"I can talk and move at the same time. First we have to talk about what's going on with you."

"With *me*?"

"Caden doesn't go AWOL." She pulled a clean shirt over her head. No bra. "Caden shows up." She stepped into a shoe. No sock. "You'd better get in before they court-martial you."

"I am showing up. I'm showing up for you. Listen. We can beat this if we make a plan. I can't keep going without your agreement."

"To what? Let you spend five years in Leavenworth? I won't be party to that."

"We need to hole up here and let Respite finish. Go backward far enough until she finds out what you're running away from."

"I'm not running away. I'm living my life."

I'd assumed I'd have a minute to talk to her, but I didn't. She went for the door. I leapt off the bed and stood between her and the exit.

"I'm tired of trying to talk sense into you," I said.

"Then this is the perfect opportunity to stop talking."

"This? The way you're acting? This is not you."

"Who is it then? Because this is the real me. The other one is a shadow of me. Maybe a subset of things I haven't done. Or have done. Or the bits I don't like... or traits I don't use... the waste all bundled up and shoved into the light. But she's not me."

"When I had this, I felt like one of me was real and one was an intruder too. But that wasn't it, and you know it."

"You're you, and I'm me."

"Meaning?"

I knew what she'd meant, but I thought she'd backpedal. Soft-shoe it. Say she was sorry or pretend she was talking hypothetically.

No such luck.

"Let me spell it out," she said. "You were always unstable. You were a psychopathology study waiting to happen. The moral rigidity with the personal impulsivity? The trauma denial? The detachment? The way you joyfully cut people open?"

"That's enough!"

"Did you start fires when you were a kid and forget to tell me?"

"I see what you're trying to do."

"Did you dissect your dog?"

"Yeah. I jerked off into the open carcass of my dead fucking dog. But I never, ever fucking said shit to you like you just said to me."

She folded her arms over her chest, inspecting the floor with her mouth pushed to one side of her face. She was cowed for a few seconds before she set her jaw and stared right at me. "Deal with it."

She put her jacket on, which she should have done before the first time she tried to leave, but she literally didn't know whether she was coming or going.

"I'm not going to turn my back on you because you insulted me," I said.

"Everything just got really clear." She zipped her jacket, and I realized just how naked I was. "You're in my way. You've always been in my way. You're an obstruction I don't need."

"I need you. I need the woman who could listen and think. What I have now is two people, and neither of them has a fucking brain in their head."

"You didn't hear me."

"I heard you."

"You didn't. So, let me say it again. I. Don't. Need. You."

I knew better than to take her words personally. She wasn't herself. Anyone with an ounce of detachment could see that. But I'd used my last ounce listening to an old story about a nightclub. I had no armor left, and she was on the attack.

"You just proved you do," I snapped. "You just proved Respite is your filter. You're a real bitch without her."

"Sorry to step on your toes. Get your clothes on and get out."

She threw my pants at me. They unspooled in midair. Their full length landed against my naked body and collapsed onto the floor when I didn't catch them.

Was I just an obstacle? Did she feel nothing at all? Or did she feel plenty, none of it affection?

"What's the Red Spot?" I asked.

"The what?"

"The Red Spot. It's where Respite got her name."

She stopped long enough to register the way Red Spot fell right into Respite, then she snapped right to the issue at hand: getting away from me. "If I tell you, will you leave?"

"Yes."

She leaned on the arm of a chair and laid her hands flat on her thighs. "It was a club in Logan Heights. They took our fake IDs. They played the music I liked, and it was just a completely unexceptional cinderblock box."

"Did Jake go there?"

She answered with a derisive laugh. "Jakey wouldn't be caught dead at that freak show."

"What if I told you he did?"

"You'd be lying."

"Respite remembered."

"Then she's lying. Damon was unreliable. She's unreliable. She's manipulating you."

In a single unguarded moment, the creature in my wife's body looked at my dick. She shifted, as if feeling the sore dripping I'd left between her legs from a fuck she couldn't remember.

She felt something. Even if it was jealousy, It was something.

"If you won't go, that's fine." She slapped her thighs and stood. "I'm hungry."

I was sure she was telling the truth, but I also knew this side of her as well as I'd ever known anyone. Greysen never changed a subject without a greater goal in mind.

"Me too." I snapped up my pants.

"If we go to base chow, you can check in at the hospital."

Check in. As if I could just say hello and walk out. That wasn't going to work, but getting thrown out of her apartment wasn't sustainable either.

"Good idea. You can save me a seat."

"Deal. I'm going to the bathroom, then we can leave."

She went into the bathroom and closed the door behind her, trusting that I was a complete fucking idiot.

Chapter Eighty-One

GREYSEN

The sand crackled against the narrow bathroom window, then stopped. It opened onto an air shaft that sometimes caught a burst of wind that spun into the funnel of the space, then petered out. I considered climbing out, but even if I could swallow my fear of heights, the door had no lock and the window squeaked when raised. He'd be in here like a shot.

Peeing was a chore because I had to sit still for it when I could have been on the way to base. I'd catch DeLeon, and she'd tell me what she knew about Jake, or she'd send me to someone she knew or whatever. But when I sat still, I had to think about what I was going to do with the information, and that just slowed me down even more.

I had the nagging feeling I was missing something. Convincing Caden to go to base to eat had been too easy. But I couldn't look back and take it apart. All I could do was get to the base and slip away while he got chewed out for being an hour late.

Maybe everything was just easy and I should have been thankful.

I washed up, checking myself in the mirror.

Stopping was mentally painful, but I had to figure out what I was looking at.

I didn't recognize myself. I looked the same but different. Like my own twin sister. How interesting. Was I different because of my expression? Was it the peeling off of weakness that left behind a cold mask? Or was my way of seeing different?

Thump-thump-thump.

Three hard, quick knocks turned me away. Not the bathroom door, but the apartment door. A voice from outside.

"Greysen? Are you in there?"

And then Caden joined me in the mirror. Still naked from the waist up, he burst in and put his hand over my mouth.

"Quiet." His breath was wet in my ear. I struggled, but he held me in a vise of bone and muscle.

Thump-thump.

"Greysen!"

It was Ronin. I didn't necessarily want to see Ronin any more than I wanted to see Caden in the mirror, trying to burn silence into me.

I didn't like being told what to do. I especially didn't like being held down and hushed.

"I want you to understand something," he murmured. "This is what they wanted. They want to create people without emotions. Better doctors and soldiers. We fell right into it. What you're going through seems right to you because you've had all your bad feelings moved over to some separate part of you. You're a surprise success story, and they want to bring you back to Blackthorne. They want to poke you and prod you, but they aren't interested in helping you."

I spit sharp syllables that added up to "Get off me!" into his hand while the pounding on the door continued.

Thump-thump.

"Stay still."

He had a fucking boner pushed against my ass. My pussy was still dripping from fucking *her,* and he was erect all over again.

I hated that I wanted it. I hated how the painful constriction of his bare arms turned me on. I hated that the only thing that soothed my need to run out the door was his body. Stopping to go to the bathroom had been mentally painful, but stopping to fuck him? Not painful.

The thumping stopped, but he still held me. The sand ticked against the window. Silence reigned. We watched each other in the mirror, and the blue eyes I could always spin up into were just a color to me. No sky. No canopy. No bowl of protection. Just blue.

Since I'd taken the BiCam, I'd known something was wrong with me. I was sick with a mental flu. But a flu came with the assumption of recovery. It wasn't until I felt nothing in Caden's gaze that I knew I was broken.

And even in that knowledge, nothing changed. Caden could slow me down with sex, but he couldn't protect me or heal me. I was crowded with the need to push forward even though I knew my drive toward purpose was fake. It was a result of this brokenness. I still had to move.

It was as if my self-knowledge had been split from myself.

"I'm going to move my hand," Caden said. "If you scream and he's still there, you'll go with him and I won't be able to get you."

His palm lowered, leaving behind a chin wet with spit. He leveraged his arms on the counter. The pressure of his hips still pinned me to the sink.

"He's gone," I said.

"He's coming back," he whispered, "and he won't be alone next time."

"You don't know that or anything." I looked away. Opposing him was a knee-jerk reaction. I had to fight him. I didn't even know why.

"They're going to take you away, and they're going to lock you in a room. Maybe for a day. Maybe a week. Maybe I'll never see you again."

I'd already told him he didn't know that or anything, and he still didn't. But I knew plenty, and he was right. I'd be taken away.

What would I fight then? What would I push against?

"What's your plan?" I asked the man in the mirror.

"You need to remember, and we need to use the memory to fix this."

He must have said it at the exact right time because in the crack between how messed up my head was and what Ronin wanted out of me, I heard him.

"I don't want to."

"I know."

"I want to run."

"I know, baby. I know." He turned to kiss my cheek

When he looked back at the mirror, the protection of the sky was back in his clear blue eyes. For a second, I was home inside him again.

And then it was gone, and blue was just meaningless mutation in eye color.

My skin was too tight. My boundaries too close, and I expanded into a burst of tears.

No.

I was not crying. This was not the time. I took a tight breath through my nose, expanding against his chest.

"Tell me what to do," I said.

"Agree to remember."

"What if it doesn't work?"

"You'll get carted away, and I'll be court-martialed for desertion."

With Damon gone, it was easy to forget Caden had a deeply manipulative side. He was going to use his own decisions to direct me. He'd destroy his life to make sure I didn't destroy mine, which was noble, crazy, and calculating.

"Don't worry about me," he said, taking his hands off the counter so I could turn and face him. He must have been reading my mind. "I'll be fine. Remember for yourself. Do it for your own sanity. Not for me."

He leaned away, giving me more space. I could get to the door. I had shoes on already. All I had to do was *go*. The impulse formed and grew the longer I denied it.

"Invite her back," he said, eyes on mine as his hand drifted down my shirt to the ridge of my waistband. "I'll stay here. She won't take over."

"It feels like she will."

He increased the downward pressure on my pants. "I know."

He did. He knew how painful it was to let the other take over, yet he wanted me to go there.

This was Caden. If I trusted anyone with my soul, it had to be him. I trusted him more than myself with my well-being. I'd forgotten that, but even in the mess of urges I was fighting, that one truth was clear.

I pushed his hand away. "I'll do it."

His lips tightened slightly, and one eyebrow twitched. "Go ahead then."

"You're staying to watch?"

"Hell yes."

Getting down to business, I put my hand down my pants.

"How's that feel?" he asked.

"Freshly fucked." I started to yank my hand out, but he held it down.

"Remember how it was with Damon?"

"Fuck you."

He smirked and pulled my shirt up to kiss my breasts. I was wet and firm under my fingers but felt nothing. I stopped moving.

"Too pissed to come?"

"I think I'm scared."

He reached behind me to the medicine cabinet. "I bet you are." He searched over my shoulder and took something off the shelf. "Let's see if we can distract you." Holding up a pair of eyebrow tweezers, he said, "Go on. Touch yourself."

The tweezers were angled at the ends, creating a sharp tip. He pinched them together in front of me.

He pressed the two points against the skin over my left breast.

"I've wondered," he said, drawing the tweezers across, "which one of you likes the pain?"

The sting crackled along my body, humming down my spine and awakening the nerves under my fingers.

"I've been hoping it's this side of you. I'd hate to lose it."

Across my sternum, lightly perpendicular to the scar, and circling the nipple of my right breast. I gasped when he increased the pressure.

"Watch me."

I did, but he didn't look back. He was working the tweezers over me like an artist on a masterwork.

"Touch yourself just a little harder," he said.

Harder than before, he pressed the two points over the tender flesh of my left breast, lifting his eyes to mine. "Finger yourself while I mark you, and don't come until I finish."

"Okay."

"What do you say if you want me to stop?"

"Stop?"

"Very good. Begin."

I circled my clit as he drew a hard, hurtful line down to the nipple. The pleasure followed the double line of sharp pain as my skin broke just enough to scrape but not enough to bleed. I watched his face as he worked, the sweat gathering on his brow, the short breaths that told me he was as aroused as I was. When he went too hard, I yipped.

He looked up and pushed the points hard against me. The pain was a shot of pleasure, but I was held back by the distracting noise in my brain. I didn't want to flip. I didn't want to go into the darkness. Into the nothingness. If he was almost done, I was going to fail.

"I'm going to bend her over this sink and pull her hair back so she has to look at the mark."

He put the tweezers below my scar and pressed hard down my body.

"Fuck her in the ass before you bring me back. Make it hurt."

"Come now."

I hurled myself into the orgasm and darkness.

Chapter Eighty-Two

RESPITE

I couldn't remember in the darkness. Not clearly. Not with detail. Not without forgetting it immediately. I was in a deep, dark hole. Hopelessly ungrounded even as I was so deep I couldn't think about anything but getting out.

Then a tingle of consciousness. The sound of soft chatter and crickets. Night birds and his voice. His hand on my thigh and the desire that came with the unexpected touch.

I crawled out of the hole with the pleasure as my glue, sticking to it to pull myself out, and after a burst, the light came, and with it, the memories.

I COULDN'T MOVE my legs. My scalp was a thousand points of pain.

"Wake up," a voice said close to my ear. Caden. "Open your eyes."

Light budded in gray bursts, then got warmer. Lines formed.

Day fought with night. Caden's voice echoed another man's. The mental and the physical swirled together until I couldn't tell one from the other, until a real physical discomfort defined itself. I was being defiled. Hurt. My ass was being probed.

He jerked my hair. "I told you to open your eyes."

A slick finger violated my anus, and I made a noise that was half grunt, half squeak.

"I told her I'd fuck you in the ass, and I will if you don't come out and talk to me."

I opened my eyes. A bathroom. Caden behind me. A mirror.

"Good."

"Ow."

"You want another finger?"

"No. Please no."

"But I promised."

"Please."

"Look in the mirror. Look at your body."

I focused. The mirror over the sink reflected me from head to navel. Behind me, Caden was shirtless, pulling my hair to make me look up, his expression a cruel, dangerous fire.

My body was marked in hot, pink double lines. Spots of blood had broken out.

"What does it say?" he growled.

I didn't answer right away. I was too shocked. He placed a second finger at my entrance, and I clamped down.

"Keep clenching. Just makes it tighter. What do the marks say?"

I blinked, clearing out the last of the distractions. "They say *HIS*."

"Who is he?"

"You."

He let my hair go. "That arrow points at your cunt. It's mine. When I say it's time to come again, you come. Do you understand?"

"Yes."

He slid his finger out of my ass and pulled up my pants. "I want to hear everything you remember."

We shifted position so he could wash his hands. His dick was hanging out of his pants, touching the edge of the counter as if it was looking for stimulation.

"She made you promise you'd have anal sex with me?"

He shook the water off his hands. "I promised I'd fuck you in the ass until you cried. That's a different thing."

"And you're not going to?"

"No."

Even after the invasion of his finger, I was grateful. "What else did she make you promise?"

"You don't want to find out." He wiped his hands on the towel. "But you have to cooperate." He pressed the white towel to my chest. It came back with a tiny spot of red. "And you have to let me take care of you."

He let me have the towel and washed his hands, watching me in the mirror.

"I can take care of you too." I brushed my hand along the hard rod of his dick. I wasn't surprised at how it felt as much as I had a very clear memory of being surprised. It ran through me like a gunshot, coming out the other side through a bigger hole.

"Not necessary." He snapped open the medicine cabinet and took out Neosporin and gauze.

"Someone told me it's painful if you don't get it."

"Someone was trying to get in your pants." He closed the cabinet door and let his hand stay there while he looked down as if deep in thought. "I forgot how young you seem."

"At least I'm not telling you to hurt anyone." I started to pull down my shirt, but he stopped me.

"Let me look at your abrasions, then you eat. Do you understand?"

"I can." I must have sounded confused because I wasn't answering his question.

***

SAN DIEGO

JULY - 1992

"I DON'T KNOW if I can do this." I clutched the sides of the metal ladder so hard that even through my fingerless gloves, my hands hurt from the unbuffed steel edges. The thick treads of my heavy boots were good for staying on a ladder, not jumping from one.

I can.

The side of the building was so close my breath bounced off it. The fire ladder that led to the roof had a latch at the top that lowered it the final six feet. I hadn't unhooked it because I didn't think I'd be able to rehook it from the ground. I didn't want to leave a trail of actions and intentions.

Up or down, Grey.

I looked down. It wasn't that far. Worst case, if I landed wrong, my femur would get shoved into my pelvis.

Imagining the smashing bones and ripped muscle delayed me another thirty seconds. Then a bird chirped. I didn't know one bird from another, but what if it was a morning bird chirping to welcome the sun? I had once chance out, and it was down.

I can.

And I did.

The air whooshed in my ears, the fall of hair in front of my eyes stuck upward, and my skirt flew up, cooling the damp tear in the crotch of my tights.

I landed on my feet like a cat, legs bent, arms forward with my palms down, pausing to assess if the shot of pain in my hip was anything more than a momentary shock.

I did.

I can.

I ran to the phone, patting my pockets for a quarter. I was still wobbly but sobered by the jump and all that had preceded it. A headache was growing, my stomach tightened and flipped, and my mouth tasted like topsoil.

MY CHEST WAS EXPOSED and cooled with the astringent sting of antiseptic.

"What happened then?" Caden asked, patting a section of the S with wet gauze.

"We called Jake." I was lying on the bed with my back to the headboard and my shirt gathered over my breasts.

"I wish you'd remember forward." He put the gauze on the side table and dunked a half-stale pita in a container of hummus that had been in the back of my fridge. "Open."

I opened my mouth, and he placed the food into it.

"I'm getting full," I said as I chewed. He must have been feeding me for a while.

He pulled down my shirt. "Good."

When the phone rang on the other side of the room, Caden went from relaxed to rigid. It wasn't until then that I noticed the storm had subsided to a strong wind.

"They got the lines back up quickly," he said.

It rang again.

"Are you going to get that?" I asked. "Or should I?"

"I have it."

He was at the phone in two steps. Clear of the last memory, I could pay attention to the details of him. I watched the efficient grace of his body and its perfect proportion, heard the deep sonorous layers of his voice as he said, "How did you find me?"

He was near, but without his attention, I fell down the hole into a black-on-black square with his voice booming from the sky.

"I'm coming back."

He promised someone he was returning as the roof got closer.

"I'm not deserting."

Caden got farther away. The new memory loaded and flicked on like showtime in a movie theater; his last words were a whisper before the lights went down.

"I have to finish something."

OVERWHELMED WITH FEELINGS.

Fear.

Regret.

Anger.

Confusion.

Anxiety.

I paced the edges of the roof, corner to corner, the hole in my magenta tights growing with every step. The Red Spot closed at two. The music below was dead. No more Visage or Thompson Twins. No more dancing to The Cure by swaying my body and moving my hands in complex, geisha-like movements. The patrons gone. The employee section of the lot was all parallel white strokes. The line of cabs out front had drawn down to the final rider half an hour before.

Must have been three in the morning. I had to get out of there. I couldn't stay up on the roof like a princess in a tower. I was a sitting duck. A lame duck. A girl whose options were limited by fear.

I stood at the edge of the ladder and looked down. I could lower it from where I was but not from the ground.

How did I get up here?

He'd hitched me up so I could reach the bottom rung, which was six feet over the ground. Then at the top, he'd gone around me so he was up first and he could help me over.

I'd been impressed by that.

Stupid, stupid girl.

Now the bottom rungs were still six feet off the ground, and if I unhooked it from the top so the entire ladder slid down, I wouldn't be able to get it back up once I was on the ground.

I paced the roof counterclockwise so I wouldn't have to go past the back of the building, but I had to check. What if...

No!

"NO!"

I sat straight up in bed with a full bladder and a heart pounding as if I'd run a four-minute mile. The moon was full in the window of the darkened room. The digital clock's red numbers read 0200, and Caden was rushing to the bedside.

"Help!" I shouted.

He took me in his arms and held me. My impulse was to push him away, but something stronger surrendered, and I fell into him.

"Tighter," I said.

He wrapped himself snugly around me until I could barely breathe. I was anchored inside him. Not moving forward or back, he held me in the moment. I needed that. It was uncomfortable, but I needed it.

"What happened?" he asked.

I didn't answer because I didn't know yet. I let the protection of his embrace surround me and took in the details of the room. The chair with the little light had a book on it. The clock flipped to 0201. Our moonlight shadows made the shape of a face against the wall.

"You stopped talking," he said. "I thought you went to sleep."

"What was I saying?"

"You kept describing a roof. I assume it was the Red Spot."

I pushed him away. "I don't want this anymore."

"Want what?"

I threw off the sheets, ready to get out of bed, but I saw what I was wearing. Underwear and a T-shirt. I leaned back. Reaching behind me, I grabbed the bars of the headboard and spread my knees apart.

"What are you doing?" he asked, eyes on the damp fabric between my legs.

"You didn't come before," I said. "In the bathroom. How about now?"

"It's tempting," he said. "But no. Not yet."

His words were pretty definite, but his face wasn't. Neither was his body. His hand twitched as if he wanted to touch me so badly. Fingertips circling thumb. I imagined one inside me to the knuckle, then the web.

I took a hand off the headboard and laid it between my legs, groaning as soon as I touched myself.

He took my wrist and moved my hand away. "No, baby. You're not flipping back until you're done."

"I am done."

"On a rooftop? I don't think so."

The way he was leaning, I could see his erection.

"It's true."

He leaned over to speak softly in my ear. "If it was true, you'd be gone." I could practically feel the throb of his dick against the air in the room. "Why do you want to flip back so badly? Are you afraid of not existing?"

"No."

"What are you afraid of?"

My purpose was to not exist. To push back until I knew all there was to know. My voice would be silenced, and only then would I find peace. I was pregnant with the unknown, heavy and clumsy, waiting for the pain that was promised before the inevitable.

But somehow, in the anchor of his arms, I didn't want the pain. I didn't think I could stand it. If I could hide away in the darkness, maybe I could avoid it.

I didn't want to tell him. I wanted to convince him it didn't matter.

"Once I'm finished, something else will come."

His face was buried in my neck, but the weight of his body gave him away, getting heavier at the shoulders as if they drooped in despair. "I'll be with you if that happens."

He wasn't lying, but there was a touch of doubt in his voice.

Two quick knocks at the door interrupted.

"Don't get it," I said, afraid of losing the protection of his body over mine.

"I have to." He freed my wrist and got off me, exposing me to the curse of freedom. I could move. I could get up and move forward even as my mind craved backward.

Neither. I wanted nothing to do with it.

Caden leaned down to the floor to get something.

I put my hand between my legs, pressing against the damp fabric. Caden grabbed my wrist again. His belt was in his other hand.

I must have projected fear, because he said, "I'm not going to hurt you. Turn over."

Another knock.

"Wait downstairs!" he called, then pushed me a little.

I followed, getting on my stomach. He straddled me and put my hands over my head, through the bars of the headboard. I really thought he was going to fuck me away from all this.

Instead he put my inner wrists together.

"Who is it?"

"Time," he said, looping the belt around my wrists. "I'm buying you some time."

"It's tight."

"I know." He got up. "I won't be long."

I had to twist painfully to look at him as he put on his shirt.

"How long?"

"Before you can work your way out and get yourself off." He flung the sheet over me so I was covered. "Which you will not do." His voice was a little lower. A little clearer. Stating a fact, not a request. "Or I'm going to fuck your ass raw."

He stood over me for a second before walking to the door, then he turned with his hand on the knob, checking his work.

He opened the door partway, slipped through, and left me alone in my darkness.

Chapter Eighty-Three

CADEN

The storm had died a quiet death sometime in the night. The air was clear and still, as if it wanted to make up for the wrongs of the previous two days.

Ronin waved from the courtyard below.

If I never saw that asshole again, it would be too soon, but this wasn't about what I wanted. Nothing was anymore. I needed him and his sorry, unaccountable ass.

I took the stairs down to him. The only thing keeping Respite from turning back into Greysen too soon was a belt that wouldn't hold for long, but I couldn't invite Ronin in. I didn't want him to see her. Not in her underwear or fully clothed. I didn't want him saying a word or making a promise. Respite might fall for anything he said, and I couldn't physically restrain her in front of him.

"Doctor." Ronin offered his hand. I took it. "I hear you're AWOL?"

"You heard right."

"May I ask why?"

"No."

Ronin huffed a laugh and took a pack of Turkish cigarettes out of his breast pocket. He offered me one, and I declined.

"So," he said after lighting up. "You're going to make me beg you for the reason you called me at three in the morning? Or can I assume you finally decided to really help her?"

"Can you reverse it? Or is this just a pitch to take her to Saudi?"

He took a long drag of his cigarette and let out a shit-stinking ribbon of smoke.

"There was never a need to reverse it. The breathing controls it for most people. For cases like you, who never should have gotten it? You showed us the cure."

"A recreation of trauma."

"You were the most successful subject we had until a building fell on you."

"What about Greysen? People who took too much, too fast, and broke."

"We're working on it. We're this close." He didn't bother holding up two fingers close together. He flicked an ash instead.

I thought I knew what was best for her. I assumed her cure started with us, together. But for a single moment, I couldn't tell if I was being irresponsible.

Was my first plan of action correct, or did I need to change it?

I couldn't decide, and that alone was uncomfortable.

"You have two people watching us across the balcony." I changed the subject, pointing up at the veranda across the yard. While Respite was in her reverie, I'd noticed the café table outside the apartment door was occupied by two people playing cards at all times of day.

"Just making sure everything's all right," he said.

"And I thought you were in love with me."

"Only a little. You showed us the outer limits of what we could do."

"And Greysen?"

"She's showing us the limits of what we *should* do. Listen. I didn't want this for her or anyone. I want to fix it. Bring her in—"

"No." The decision came from my heart, unfiltered by doubt.

"—you report for duty—"

"Not happening."

"What do you want then?"

"I want food. Light food. Fruit. Yogurt."

"You're holing up?"

"And empty that apartment. I don't want to see another one of your goons up there."

"You're worried about *us*? There are going to be MPs with a battering ram at your door if you don't report for duty. DeLeon isn't covering for you much longer."

He was right. The clock was ticking. I was going from AWOL to desertion.

"Get me the food while you get me a car and a helicopter out of here."

He plucked the cigarette from his mouth mid-drag. "You are out of your fucking mind."

His gaze shifted suddenly, moving over my shoulder. I followed it.

Greysen was coming down the stairs.

Ronin and I exchanged a look.

"Grey?" I said.

"Hey." She had on sweatpants and a hoodie, and she was the sexiest woman alive. "Hi, Ronin."

"Hi." His voice cracked with youthful insecurity. He dropped his cigarette on the ground and stamped it out. "Hi, Grey."

What the fuck? He seemed totally disarmed.

I put my arm around my wife. She jammed her hands in her pockets.

"What did you need?" I asked her.

"Just got lonely upstairs."

The silence was so heavy and uncomfortable even the birds and crickets couldn't make a sound.

"So," Ronin finally said. "I'll work on that thing we talked about?"

That thing?

He'd never looked so guileless. Something had happened to him in the flash of a second, because the Ronin I knew had guile. Plenty of it.

"The food," I reminded him. "Light food."

His eyes on my wife. I wanted to gouge them out and cut the optic nerves. I wanted to do violence I'd never wanted to do before. I'd known Ronin for four years and hadn't seen him look at Greysen like that for three and a half. I snapped my fingers in front of his eyes, and he looked back at me.

"Was there something else?" he asked.

"You'll figure it out." I tightened my grip on Grey. I wasn't leaving her for a second. Not for a court-martial or anything.

Ronin smiled ruefully. "Bye, Grey."

"Bye, Ronin."

He walked to the other side of the courtyard, hunched over like a kid.

"Go on upstairs," I said. "I'll be right up."

"You all right?"

"Yeah." I pecked her lips quickly. "Don't touch anything you're not supposed to, you hear?"

She didn't answer. She just headed for the stairs. I ran to Ronin. He turned when he heard my footsteps behind him.

"What the fuck was that?" I asked.

"What are you talking about?"

We were the same height, so meeting his stare wasn't a show of force. Not initially. Not until he looked away like a submissive puppy giving way to the pack alpha.

"I know you can fight," I said. "I'm just a doctor. But I promise you... if you separate us, I will find a way to destroy you."

"Yeah. Okay." He tried to leave, but I grabbed his arm.

"Ronin."

"What?"

I looked at his face critically. The light wasn't great, but I could see everything I needed to. "You took the BiCam."

He shrugged as if he didn't want to admit guilt.

Ronin didn't have *guilt.*

"Why?"

He jerked his arm out of my grip. "Just back off."

"Seeing what it did to me wasn't enough? What it's doing to my wife?"

"He did it to prove it was safe."

Talking about himself in the third person was jarring enough. The tone of petulant resentment overshadowed even that.

"That if all the prep hadn't been done," he continued, "the breathing, the graduated dosages... everything... it could still be effective. He thought Greysen must be hiding something or she had PTSD she wasn't admitting. Or her dose was too big. So, he took it. He did a whole bunch of math, came up with just enough to crack him open, and took it because he was the only subject he trusted."

I respected his ability to do to himself what he did to other people. I respected his thoroughness. At least, I respected the guy who gave himself the BiCam. This man standing in front of me could have been anyone.

"What's your name?"

He smiled with that same rue. "My name is Abe Grey."

For the sin of taking part of her name and making her a piece of his sickness, I almost punched him in the face right there, but he kept talking.

"She has a man's name," he said, looking at the top of the steps. "Isn't that funny? Did you ever wonder why?"

"Her parents thought they were having a boy and kept the name."

"She tried to tell him not to go to Abu Ghraib. Everything revolves around that moment, you know? When she said no to him and yes to you."

"On the landing pad?" I asked. "In Balad?"

Years before, Greysen had been caught between my marriage proposal and Ronin's offer to assist in Abu Ghraib. She'd chosen me, and after news of the torture in the prison had come out, she'd been horrified and relieved. I'd just been horrified. I knew she wouldn't have had anything to do with it.

He nodded. "If she'd come... if she'd been there, she would have saved him. She would have raised alarms. It all hinged on her. But she wasn't there, and he stayed in ABG. He tried to sort it out. Take the torture down a notch."

I was torn between feeling sorry for the guy and wanting to surgically remove his nuts for shouldering my wife with his sanity.

I was the only one allowed to do that.

He looked up at her apartment on the other side of the courtyard, eyes wide with adolescent adoration. "She looks the same as when he met her in basic."

They were about the same emotional age, these two, and that bothered me like a hot poker in the ass.

She was mine. At every stage of her life. Before she even knew she had a soul mate. Before she even desired one. Every facet of her personality and every spark of every neuron in her brain belonged to me. Birth to death.

Mine.

"Listen to me." I snapped my fingers in front of his face. He looked away from the light in her window and back at me. "You get me what I asked for."

"What did you ask for?"

What caused his flip? Not orgasms. Not the dark and the light. Was Ronin's split triggered by the sight of my wife? I hoped not, because he wasn't seeing her again. Not as Ronin or Abe Grey.

"Helicopter out. A Blackthorne bird. Don't make a deal with the army. Call me on my cell when you have it. I'll get you further instructions when I have them."

He bit his lower lip.

"Do it," I said. "Do it, or you're never going to know how to get back to normal."

Chapter Eighty-Four

RESPITE

I'd gotten out of the belt by twisting my hands. It had seemed impossible at first, but I stopped feeling the pain when the pressure to roll a memory got to be too much. The screen in my head was firing up. House lights down. Projector threaded. Curtain open.

The next part was going to hurt, and I didn't want to hurt.

So I went outside to talk to Caden and Ronin.

I was Caden's. I knew that. I knew we were married. I knew he was mine. But Ronin confused me. I'd met him in basic, and my memories started there before going backward. He was familiar in a way Caden wasn't.

Dismissed from the courtyard, I paced the apartment, twisting one hand in the other, singing songs in my head and giving words to details so I didn't have to think the things I didn't want to think.

Ronin had taken my virginity, her virginity—our virginity—but not really.

That had happened before. But not really.

It had happened in the depth of drunkenness, when my brain had been too scrambled to make sense of anything. It had wired the memory all wrong, then blocked it off because it was fucked up. It was all so fucked up. It took the scramble and just said, "Forget it."

And there, the crack appeared. Light shone through, blasting the screen white for a moment before it all started at the first moments of a very long memory.

SAN DIEGO
JULY · 1992

"I LIKE THE PLIMSOULS TOO," he said, talking about the band, trying to be cool in front of the punk girl who was actually new wave.

I knew he had to have a name, but no matter how many times I replayed the scene, he never said it. Maybe our introduction had been the only utterance of it and it was before the roof. Maybe the music had been too loud to hear. In my mind, he was Bryan Adams. The furry blond hair he'd wrestled into some kind of conservative shape and the chambray shirt left my head playing "Summer of '69" on repeat.

"I meant the shoes," I said, jerking my chin at his blaringly white leather high-tops. "Plimsolls go good with jeans. Even stonewashed."

We were sitting on the edge of the Red Spot roof, legs dangling twenty feet in the air. The building had been a warehouse. Pretty tall for one story. He had little cuffs turned at the ends of his jeans. I hadn't noticed that inside the club.

"I'll try that." He smiled. He had a nice smile for a regular sort of guy.

I knew the type. They came around because the Red Spot was the closest club, or the only one open, but they belonged at McSweeny's or Bar None, where they played Huey Lewis and the News and served Heineken by the gallon.

"So, where'd you get that name?" he asked.

He'd asked my name, and I made something up because I didn't want to be boring or explain mundane things.

"Trouble?" I said. At the bar when I'd made up that name, I'd picked a maraschino cherry out of the bartender's tray, feeling quite satisfied with myself.

"Yeah. Where's a girl get a name like that?"

"I was born trouble."

"GREY," a voice cut through the memories. A deep voice from another time. A voice that came after I did things. A voice from after that night. "What's happening?"

"The cherry bursts on my tongue."

"You were on the roof a minute ago."

"It's sweet, and the skin gives way under my teeth. I like how he watches me eat it. I feel sexy. Like a woman."

His fingertips brushed my cheek to remove hair I hadn't felt. "Where are you now?"

"The roof of the Red Spot. He's there."

"Who?"
The projector stopped, and I snapped to attention.

Chapter Eighty-Five

CADEN

The morning after Ronin walked out of the courtyard as Abe Grey, a plan came together, but everything had to be right. A certain precision was required to get rid of this completely. When Damon retreated, I'd thought I was finished, but another Thing had come. A more dangerous, more destructive split. Only the perfect parallel situation had healed me, and I had to create that for her, or she might split again once Respite was done with her.

She was slouched in her chair, one foot braced on the table in front of her, stroking her lower lip even as she spoke, then suddenly, she snapped to attention, looking at me in a panic. "I can't."

I kneeled at her feet and cupped her face. She looked like a woman in unbearable pain.

"You can."

"Make me her again."

I couldn't. The answers were close. Whatever they were, it felt as if the moments she was reliving were coming toward clarity. We didn't have time to flip back to Greysen, who would resist everything about this process.

Four thirty in the morning. I was calculating my next move when there was a knock at the door. I was so wrapped up in our little world I thought it was Ronin with the food or news of a helicopter.

"Hang on!" I called, then stood before my wife. "Give me your hands."

She gave them, trusting me like a foolish young girl. Like a prick, I took advantage of her trust and led her to the bed.

"Lie down."

She did, but when she saw what I had in my hands, she started to get up. I lowered myself onto her, letting my weight hold her.

"No!"

"It's for a minute."

I'd cut the pull strings off the blinds and fashioned them into a knot I could fasten quickly. I got her arms around the leg of the bed and had her tied in one move.

"Let me go!"

I leaned close to her face. "I'll untie you when I close the door. Then you're going to eat and you're going to finish this so I can have my wife back. Do you understand?"

"You're going to bring her back?" Her face was lit up with hope.

"Yes." I stood. Her body was relaxed, and her face had the beginnings of a smile. "But I want to be the one to do it."

"Thank you." She blinked, and tears fell on each side of her face.

I put my finger to my lips, and she nodded.

That was as good as it was going to get.

I answered the door, assuming it was Ronin. Who else would it be at this hour?

"Asshole Eyes," DeLeon hissed. "What the—"

I stepped out and shut the door behind me. "I'm sorry."

"I don't want your fucking apologies. You're fucking AWOL, and I can't cover for you."

"I know. Don't cover for me. It's not worth it."

She crossed her arms and leaned on the railing, looking me up and down as if taking inventory. There must have been a lot to see. I could only guess what I looked like to her. No sleep meant bloodshot eyes, periorbital swelling, and hyperpigmentation, skin that looked as if it was coming detached. I hadn't shaved. Had showered so quickly I hadn't washed my hair.

"You look like shit." She confirmed my thoughts. "Are you sick? If you're sick, they won't court-martial you."

"I'm not sick."

"So, what's the problem?"

"The problem."

I didn't say more because the problem was too deep, too wide, too complex to explain on a doorstep.

The problem was I couldn't leave Respite alone for too long or I'd walk in on Greysen, or more accurately, Greysen would burst out the door running.

The problem was, if I told her the problem, she'd order me to bring my wife into the hospital and I'd lose control of the situation entirely.

The problem was I needed to get back inside before Respite got to the beginning of the story. I needed to hear it in fine detail so we could recreate it, have her face it, conquer it, and walk away. It was the only known cure, and I wasn't getting talked out of it or distracted away from it.

"Is it her brother?" she asked. "She's upset?"

"She's upset." I hadn't even told Greysen about Jake, but I was telling DeLeon the truth. Like an upturned apple cart, Greysen was upset. "Have they found him? Dead or alive?"

"No."

"Shit. No clues? No leads?"

"Not that I've heard. And every day that goes by? Gets less likely they will." She put her arms down. "I didn't take her for someone who'd collapse about this."

"You never know a person until they're in crisis."

She sighed and rubbed her eyes. "Okay." She dropped her hands, letting them slap against her thighs. "I owe you, Asshole, and I like Wifey. But my debt's paid once we go from AWOL to desertion."

"I'm not deserting."

"After a certain point, you don't get to decide that. And I'm sorry, I know you want to be with her and you have control issues, but you're going to have to give it up. You're getting court-martialed either way. You can either turn yourself in by oh eight hundred, or I have to call the MPs on you."

With a dull, flat cadence and a volume barely enough to be heard through the door, my wife's voice came from inside the apartment. She was remembering again.

"Thanks for the warning," I said, putting my hand on the knob. DeLeon was supposed to dismiss me, but we were past formality.

She raised an eyebrow as if I'd made a threat. Or maybe she'd heard Respite's voice from inside as she started reciting her memory again.

"If you run, they'll find you. They'll lock you away and shove the key up your ass."

"I understand."

She jerked her chin at the door, indicating Wifey, who needed me and whom I needed. "There are no conjugal visits in Leavenworth. Leave her alone now for a little while, or be separated for fifteen to twenty. Your call."

"Thank you," I said. "I mean it. I owe you one."

"See you in the morning?"

The evening prayers began, echoing over the walls of the city, an underlayer to Respite's recital. Because of language or physics, I couldn't understand either.

"Yes."

"Okay. Good." DeLeon started down the steps.

I watched her go, unwilling to open the door while she could hear my wife's voice relay a story about a boy on a club rooftop. She waved to me at the bottom. I waved back, turning my hand into a thumbs-up, promising I'd be there in the morning and almost believing it. She strode out of the courtyard, leaving the morning birds, the Arabic prayer chant, and the muffled tale of a young girl in trouble behind.

Chapter Eighty-Six

RESPITE

This part was too long. It started too early, on the roof with Plimsouls and plimsolls. The tension of going forward was stretching me thin. I felt as if I'd break in the middle. At the chest. The way a rubber band got translucent before a tiny heart-shaped hole appeared at the center of the thinnest point. It would snap sometime after I started anticipating it and before I expected it, stinging skin where the kinetic energy clapped against nerve endings.

But still, I pulled the rubber band because I had to. Forward was backward. If I stopped, I didn't know if I'd go back further to begin again. So, I had to tell the story even after sunlight blasted my face and the sounds of a prayer chant on the mosque's loudspeaker stopped being muffled by the door. I told the story through the folded darkness of the door closing and the *click-clack* of locks.

"I'm back," he said, sitting on the short table in front of me.

"Is everything okay?"

"Everything's fine. He was kissing you."

"There's a lot."

"Take your time."

SAN DIEGO

JULY - 1992

THEN HE KISSED ME. He was sloppy, mouth too wide, tongue a whirligig around mine.

The music had stopped.

His hands were up my shirt.

All the people were gone.

I couldn't actually taste his tongue, and I was pretty sure he couldn't taste anything either.

How was I getting back to Lia's? Or was it Anna's? Dina, maybe? I'd lost track of the lies I'd had to tell my parents to stay out past midnight.

His hands were under my bra before I could say no. It was fine. It felt okay. I put my hands on his body. Under the chambray shirt, he was tight and muscular. This was okay.

I didn't go for a guy like this. He wasn't the right type, but the heaviness that settled between my legs was more demanding than my taste in men.

We rolled onto the surface of the roof. Drunk. Not caring about the dead leaves and dirt. The grit of tarpaper and the jutting roofing nails. Just doing the thing. His penis was rock hard under his jeans. That wasn't new to me. There had already been copped feels through pants and grinding in cars. But no one had ever done what he did next.

He unzipped his pants and pulled it out, then taking me by the wrist, he put my hand on it. I was too shocked to pull back and too drunk to consider the consequences.

"Stroke it nice."

His mouth was a sloppy whirligig again. The skin of his dick was soft and paper-thin, stretched over a hard core. He rolled on top, pinning my thighs under hard knees.

"Wait."

When I took my hand away, he put it back, pressing it against the head. "Wait for what? You feel so good."

"Just wait." It was all too fast. The world was spinning.

"Don't be like that."

Twisting. Trying to get up past the sickening, drunken spin of the earth. He pushed me back down, immobilizing my struggling body under him.

"Stop! Let me *go*!"

He reached under my skirt and, with a hard grab, ripped a hole in my hot pink tights. He was bigger and stronger. His dick was already out, and with two fingers that didn't tease or cajole, he wove past my underwear, and with two fingers—

Knock-knock.

Chapter Eighty-Seven

CADEN

She sat on the edge of a worn chair, looking into the space between the imaginary horizon and the deepest part of her soul, filtering details through a wider and wider net. Her timeline jostled, putting the wrong dialogue in the wrong scene, moving events around like puzzle pieces that wouldn't fit right until everything landed in its place. She took hours to describe minutes with a young man who scared the shit out of me, but I listened carefully as the moon ran her course over the sky.

When my attention wavered, it went to remembering Ronin's schoolboy glances. I knew when a man wanted my wife, and though I'd been jealous and possessive when Ronin was around in the army, once we were civilians, he'd never made a sign that he had any interest in her.

Until she was this sweet, vulnerable version of herself that I didn't recognize. Now his interest burned so hot I could feel it on me. He hadn't been interested in Greysen until she'd become this woman describing a boy's chambray shirt, the white buttons, the upturned collar.

Respite, to me, never seemed like Greysen. She seemed defenseless. She was talking about this guy on the roof with questions in her voice, and I knew he was going to take advantage of her. I knew he was going to do something she didn't want and my wife would come at him like a lion. This girl would describe it as if it was happening to someone else, which it was.

He ripped a hole in the crotch of her tights a dozen times before she put all the details in their slots. I was girded for a violation I wouldn't be able to avenge. I wouldn't even be able to get angry because it would scare her, and she needed me to keep my emotions in check.

I could do it only when I reminded myself that this girl was getting sent back where she'd come from. Respite was going to be reabsorbed, and Greysen was going to come back.

Again, her tights were ripped. Again, he pinned her and reached under her underwear with two fingers. She'd gotten this far so many times before finding a new detail to backtrack. My anger over his fingers was just as heavy, but it had been dulled smooth.

Knock-knock.

Her mouth went tight, and though her attention stayed inside herself, she was aware enough to stop talking.

"Wait here," I said.

"Yes."

"I'm not going to tie you up."

Her eyes met mine. I couldn't tell if she was surprised or if she wanted to be bound, but after the implication that she deserved pain, I was reluctant to do anything she might see as punishment.

"Just..." I stood. "Just don't bring Greysen back yet. We don't have time."

"Yes. I agree."

Why did she agree? When she was remembering, she didn't seem aware of time. I doubted she'd heard DeLeon's warnings.

"Good," I said, putting my finger to my lips.

I opened the door as far as the chain would let me, letting in the sound of crickets and the whoosh of pre-curfew traffic. The knocker was backlit by the building's floodlights.

It was Ronin with a box under his arm. He had a puppy dog look on his face, and even though I had never been a fan of the sneaky bastard, at least I'd always known exactly what kind of sneaky bastard I was dealing with.

I closed the door behind me and reached for the box.

He stepped back. "No."

"No? What the fuck did you come here for then?"

"We should talk. All of us."

"All five of us?" I went for the box, but he twisted away.

"I want to see her."

"Why?"

"I want to make sure she's all right." He swallowed hard, glancing at the door, then back at me. "This stuff, it fucks with you."

"Tell me about it."

"Just one second," he said expectantly. "Then I'll go."

"Jesus," I said, "I bet you were a nice kid before the army fucked you up."

Her shriek came from the other side of the door. "Let me *go!*"

I should have gagged her. That was my first thought as Ronin's eyes met mine. Behind him, the two Blackthorne contractors at the café table shot up and ran around the linked verandas to get to us.

"Ro—" I started to explain, but he shoved the box into me, sending me off balance enough to push me out of the way so he could open the door.

We spilled in. Me. Ronin. The two Blackthorne agents.

My wife was twisting on the floor. "Caden! Help."

Ronin was ahead of me. He leaned down to her, and there was a moment of them truly seeing each other before she spoke.

"Only Caden."

I pushed him out of the way to kneel by her. "What happened?"

"I got out," she said to me in a quivering voice. "It was terrible. So bad."

"It's okay. I'm here now."

Arms free, she wrapped them around me as we crouched on the floor. Ronin and the agents cast a shadow over us as I rocked her. His posture was wider, and his face was harder. He'd flipped like a coin. The sincere boy had left, leaving behind the sneaky bastard I'd always known. Except... not. Without that sincerity or that deep well of caring for his friends, he was just plain untrustworthy.

Ronin turned to the two contractors. "Close the door on your way out."

They left, and Ronin put his attention back on us.

"Leave," I said. My wife was shaking in my arms, and he didn't need to see it. Her weakness wasn't his business.

"I'm going to our facility in Saudi," he said. "We're close—really close—to making this reversible. I want her to come."

"You're not separating us."

"Either I will, or the army will. You're AWOL. At least if she comes with me, she's in the hands of people who know what this is."

As soon as he left, I was getting her out of here. We were sitting ducks here, waiting to get picked off and pulled apart.

"She's in *my* hands," I said. "Just go."

"They're getting a warrant."

So this was how it was ending. With military police and a forced separation. And when they found her, what would they do? Nothing? Or would they deliver her to a black site run by her employer? We'd be at square one with the memory unfinished.

Greysen was in full Respite mode, staring in the half distance between herself and the floor, brushing her thumb against her lip, watching her life flash before her eyes. I didn't want to leave her, but I wasn't sure I had a choice. Surrendering meant separating. Going with Ronin meant we could both be trapped.

I could make a decision one way or the other. Six of one or half a dozen of the other. But I wouldn't decide alone. I wouldn't decide this for her or without her. She wasn't a child, and she wasn't my charge.

"Do I have until morning?" I asked.

"Maybe. We're arranging transport, but I don't know how long the army's going to take getting it together."

"Give us until then."

I'd let him think we were going with him, but that hadn't been decided. He'd leave his people at the door no matter what I said. Crouching in front of my wife, I tried to break her stare, but I didn't. She kept on seeing what she was seeing.

"Oh seven hundred," Ronin said. When he opened the door, blue floodlights blasted half of Greysen's face, narrowing the pupil. "You're doing the right thing. For her."

I ignored him. We had a few hours and no more. Maybe our last hours together.

"What you have," he said. "Between you two? I admire it. It's what we all wish for… that one perfect partner." He stood, unmoving in the doorway until I looked at him. He spoke before I had a chance to chase him out. "She made the right choice. You were the right choice."

"I know."

He nodded and left, cutting the light with a click. Her pupils dilated again, but she didn't move.

I needed Greysen back. She was hard to deal with, but she was the side I could make a decision with.

Watching Respite think, I couldn't flip her yet. She was close to her moment.

"Respite," I whispered, "what's happening?"

Her head jerked once, slightly and sharply to say no.

Kneeling in front of her, I took her hands. "Tell me."

Her brows knit.

"Please." I had nothing else. No demands. No strategies. No manipulations. I could only submit to the will of my wife's frailer half.

"He says…" She stopped, and I waited. And waited. "He says, 'You're wet.'"

The last thing I'd heard was her shout, "Let me go." It had progressed with whoever this guy was. Bryan Adams. Plimsolls. Chambray Shirt. I had to catch up without speaking or making assumptions, but God damn, it was hard when my heart was pounding with rage and the only person around to hurt was the one who had already suffered.

"He puts his fingers in deeper. All the way. I'm not prepared. It hurts."

I am not angry. Do not get angry.

"He does it hard. It hurts and…" Swallow. "Something breaks. I'm bleeding."

"Grey..." I wanted her to stop. She was going too fast. I wasn't ready.

"He says I'm wet. He... he says I want it. I say no." She was hopping between pieces of dialogue, one after the other, speeding up. "He hears me. I'm sure he hears me. But he pushes inside me and..."

Her face exploded into messy, open-mouthed, saliva-string sobs. I took her hand. She could stop now. She could leave it for tomorrow. The next day. Never.

"I come," she says around the sobs. "He makes me come. It happens so fast, and he calls me a... a slut."

I'd told myself I was ready, but I wasn't ready for shit.

I knew those orgasms.

I loved them.

I cherished every single one.

When she cried over the one he took, she was my wife again, and that orgasm was mine.

It was hers to give, but it was mine.

What was stolen from me had been ripped from her first.

I pulled her into my arms. My wife. She was vulnerable and weak. She was sensitive and broken. She had always been those things, but I hadn't loved all of them. I hadn't loved the vulnerability. I had only loved what was easy to love. Strength and tenacity. Bravery and power.

Now she was sobbing against my chest. Not a young girl. Not a separate person I wanted to banish, but an indispensable part of the woman I loved.

All of her.

I loved all of her.

"Respite..."

"Call me Greysen. That's my name."

"Are we at the end?"

Chapter Eighty-Eight

RESPITE

SAN DIEGO

JULY - 1992

The orgasm was still hot between my legs.

The guy in the chambray shirt leaned heavy on my body with a look of surprised satisfaction. "You hot little slut."

Without thinking, I landed a hard clap on his face. "Get off me!"

"That's how you want it?" He slapped me.

I touched my face in horror. That wasn't how I wanted it. Not at all. But he thought so, and he pushed me down with one hand and reached for his dick with the other. In a moment of imbalance, I rolled and got out from under him, crawling away while he got on his feet.

"No!" Swaying, blood dripping down my leg, I got my feet under me, feeling everything as if I'd been abandoned by the numbing of the eighth kamikaze.

"Fuck you," he growled. "You came. The least you can do is suck me off."

"If I suck your dick, I'm going to throw up."

That wasn't an idle threat. My stomach was eager to expel what felt like half a gallon of vodka and triple sec. He must have known it. His tone changed back to the guy I'd kind of liked for a couple of hours.

"Come on." He came a step closer. I took half a step back. "Hand job. You already touched it. Don't leave me hanging. It's going to hurt like hell if you do."

"I'm sorry. I just... I'm not ready."

He held out a hand for me and saw the blood on his fingers. "Man, I busted your cherry?"

"It's okay," I said. "Not a big deal."

"Fuck." He was staring at his fingers.

I walked toward him a little, thinking he felt guilt. I was foolish.

"I bet you're so tight."

Was that supposed to be a compliment? I couldn't tell.

"Listen," he said as if he was the most reasonable guy on the planet, "it's busted. You might as well. You came already."

His cajoling tone made me very, very angry. Rage filled me like a foul, sulfuric burn.

"You mean like a hot little slut?"

"That wasn't an insult."

"Like fuck it wasn't." I stepped forward, and he took half a step back. "You put your fingers where I didn't want them."

"You seemed to like it." Defensive. Irritated.

I should have been worried he'd come at me again, but his moment had passed. This was a guy who didn't think of himself as a rapist even when he raped.

"I. Said. No."

"But you *came*." He put his dick back in his pants and zipped up. "If you don't appreciate what I just did for you, then fuck you."

I hated my orgasm because it made me into a liar. It made me into a prude who —deep down—wanted it. It made me into a cocktease. It made him *right*.

"I'm sorry."

What was I apologizing for?

I'd said no, but I'd come right onto his hand.

He offered a slice, and I'd taken the whole pie.

I was too drunk, too young, too fragile to know I didn't owe him an apology. But he was shrewd. If I was drunk, young, and fragile enough to apologize, maybe the night wasn't over.

"It's all right," he said, using his forgiveness to take a step closer. "Did it feel good?"

He asked as if he was curious, not as if he wanted to weaponize the answer.

"Yeah." I shrugged. "Thank you."

He reached for me, and I let him move the fall of hair away from my eye. "You're really pretty when you're mad."

"Thanks. We should—"

—*go.*

I never got to finish the sentence. He was on me. Trying to push me down. He was going to take what he wanted no matter what I did.

Once I was down, I was done. I knew that much.

There wasn't a middle ground. I had to resist all the way or not at all.

My anger coalesced into a fine laser of energy, a force directed squarely at his chest, propelling me forward with all my weight. I pushed him not just away, but back so hard he stumbled with one leg crossing over the other, losing his balance until his calf hit the ledge and he disappeared over the edge.

IN THE MIDDLE space between the mind and the world outside it, I watched the shape of his body change as he fell over, the expression on his face. The second before I heard the *hssp* of a one-hundred-seventy-pound sack of bone and tissue hit the ground lasted a lifetime.

In the hours/minutes/seconds between that sound and the sight of his body on the ground, bent like a swastika with his head in a pillow of black blood, I went cold. Everything emptied out of me. Every emotion, thought, personality trait spilled out as if a bucket had been shot full of holes.

And while it all emptied out, another orgasm filled me. This one was real, given not taken, meant to heal instead of break.

It would be my last.

My last as me.

The memory had been found. The dark place touched. I had no more secrets from myself.

As the pleasure opened, I collapsed into the same shape I'd been in when I was released. I'd snap back into Greysen the way I had before but aware of how I was folded and how I fit.

When I came, she came, and when I went back into my place, something else cracked inside her.

Us.

Me.

The thing on the other side of the crack was cold, calculating, deadly.

It took my place in the darkness. It was only a matter of time before it got out.

And then, with nowhere else to go, I went home.

Chapter Eighty-Nine

GREYSEN

Pleasure held hands with pain as a soul-emptying orgasm ripped through me. I felt as if I didn't have a body at all except for the place where his tongue met my clit and his hand twisted the soft skin of my thigh.

When I opened my eyes to the ceiling of my studio in the Green Zone, I felt reborn. My husband's gentle mouth left my body, and I loosened my grip on his hair.

"Grey?" he said from below. "Baby?"

"I remember."

"Are you all right?"

"Caden." When I said his name, I felt that part of me that had cracked off and shaken loose. It rattled like a car part that would need replacing. It would drop out of the chassis in the driveway or going eighty on the freeway.

He crawled up until his body was a bridge over mine, eyes flicking over my face as if gathering data. "Are you whole? That's what I'm really asking. Is it over?"

His eyes were the blue of the Iraqi sky, with all its promise of comfort and spectacle of power. I ran my fingers over his jaw and neck as if for the first time. I didn't want to disappoint him, but I didn't want to lie either. "No."

He bowed his head, cutting me off from him and his protection.

"I'm so sorry for what I did," I said.

"I know."

"I killed him."

"It was self-defense." He kissed my cheek as if that made it any better.

"And then I sent my brother to clean off his fingers. That wasn't self-defense. That was a crime."

"That was his choice."

"Caden, I wanted to turn myself in but…"

"But Jake. You did the right thing. Your brother protected you, and you protected him."

He was right, but he was wrong. Where law met order, he was dead wrong, but where the burden was shared, he was right. God damn him, and God damn me. I didn't know how to live with this.

"It was wrong," I said. "He was somebody's son, and it was *wrong*."

"We can dissect this later," he said, sitting up. "They're coming for you soon."

"Who?" I got up on my elbows.

"Blackthorne. They're working on a treatment for this in Saudi." He got up. When the mattress went flat, I felt the abandonment of his weight. "They want you to go."

"What treatment? What is it? Behavioral? Occupational? Clinical? What are we dealing with here?"

"I don't know. I don't know a damned thing. I didn't know which questions to ask, and I still don't. I don't trust him or the company he works for, but there's no one else and nothing else unless we're going to recreate you killing someone and making a different decision. Or gaining control of it. Or whatever it's going to take. I'm not willing to do that."

He looked lost. I didn't often see him in the space between knowing who he was and making a decision, where the variables weren't organized and the choices led to unknown ends. It was from this crack that Damon had gathered his traits.

"What if I don't want to go?"

"Then you don't go."

I got off the bed. "Then I'm not going. There. Done." I stepped into my clothes. "We stay together and figure it out together."

"There's a problem."

"We'll figure it out." I buttoned my pants as if I was punctuating a sentence.

"I'm AWOL. We're not going to be together much longer."

My loose, cracked-off part rattled. It spoke to me by freezing and hardening my decision into a solid mass, breaking it off until it wasn't a decision anymore. It was an old thing that didn't work. I was left with a cold calculation from a dangerous piece of myself…

Let him go.

… and a hot need directed outward, at him…

He cannot go.

"How long?" I asked, hoping to settle the tug-of-war inside me.

"Too long. Way too long."

"Jesus Christ on a ladder, Caden. What were you thinking? Have you talked to anyone? Have they issued a warrant? Are the MPs coming?"

He didn't have to answer. All he had to do was look away, and I knew.

Let him go.

He cannot go.

I cracked again. His forgiveness and unconditional love were the only things gluing me together. I cracked harder than he had after Damon slipped away.

"Grey." He was near me, on me, holding me up as my legs lost the ability to keep me standing. "Grey. It's going to be all right."

Let him go.

He cannot go.

The decision wasn't rhetorical. Coldly, I didn't care if we separated, but if we separated, I was sure I'd die. If I chose, I'd be rent in two again. It took all my concentration to exist between the two choices, leaning in both directions and neither.

Let him go.

He cannot go.

Once I chose, I'd split, and one side would show herself while the other got locked in a bag. I knew this like I knew I had two feet and ten fingers, because I was sane and that sane part of myself could see it all happening but was helpless to do anything about it.

Let him go.

He cannot go.

"Baby, listen." He was on his knees with me, crouched between the erect and the supine, keeping me from complete surrender. "I'll go with you. Both of us to Saudi. They won't separate us. Come back. Come back to me."

He turned my face to his. He was so strong. He'd decide. All I had to do was follow, and I'd hold together.

"I can't take this anymore," I said. "I can't live like this."

Far, far away, there was a knock on the door.

"You can, and you will. Do you hear me?"

The way he ignored the knocking and focused on me and me alone gave me the strength to hold the pieces of myself together. "I hear you."

He helped me up after another, more urgent, knock. "Are you ready?"

"Stay with me."

"I'm with you, baby. I'm always with you."

He reached out to answer the door. I grabbed his arm.

"What if it's the MPs?"

He paused, arm around me, close enough to feel his heart beat.

"I love you," he said, and while still holding me, he opened the door and sunlight flooded in.

Chapter Ninety

CADEN

The Suburban's windows were tinted so black they were nearly opaque, dimming the Middle Eastern morning into a dull twilight. Thank God, because a Humvee with MP spray-painted on the side passed in the opposite direction, engine roaring.

Ronin wasn't in the car. He was meeting us at the landing pad. The driver was a bald white guy built like a bookcase. In the passenger seat sat a Latina with her hair twisted into a biscuit at the base of her neck. They wore charcoal-colored Kevlar and had spiral wires looped from their back collars to buds tucked in their ears.

"You all right back there?" the white guy asked, making eye contact in the rearview.

"Yeah." I had my arm around Greysen.

She was looking straight ahead. The look wasn't like Respite's middle-distance stare, which was a passive gaze inward. This was a look of deep, scalpel-sharp concentration.

"Should be eight minutes to the chopper," the Latina said. "Hopefully you'll be in the air before they catch up."

And if not?

If we got held up at a checkpoint? Blackthorne might intervene for Greysen, but I'd be hauled off for a well-earned court-martial. Our separation would break my wife's heart, and like a virus of despair, mine would follow.

"It's okay," I whispered to her. "It's all okay. I have this. I have your back."

We hit a pothole, and her head bounced a little. It could have been a nod, or I could have been losing her second by second.

IN FRONT of a six-story Blackthorne building not far from my wife's old office, I held my hand out, wondering if I'd have to carry her, but she took it and slid down to the pavement.

"Can you walk?" I asked quietly.

"Hold my hand."

She didn't have to ask. I had no intention of letting her go.

A phalanx of Kevlar vests and curly earpieces surrounded us. Six of them, armed to the teeth, led us into the building, through the marble-and-brass lobby built to show the opulence of an oil-rich country. We were hustled into a plexiglass elevator. Even though they surrounded us so we couldn't be seen from the street, Greysen squeezed my hand hard enough to hurt. Heights. Her least favorite thing. Maybe because of her fall from a diving platform, but maybe because of the boy at the Red Spot. Falling and dying had been a buried reality for her for a long time, manifesting as the most rational of irrational terrors.

The walls of the top floor rattled, and when one of the guards slapped open the door to the roof, I heard the reason for the shakiness in the *thup-thup-thup* of a chopper.

Greysen and I climbed together, side by side, my arm tightly around her to let her know I was there. I wasn't leaving. I would hold her up until the world forced us apart. Until there were no more options. Until they took me away kicking and screaming. Until death did us part.

Ronin stood by the open door of the helicopter with his head turned away from us. His profile was somehow so deliberate I had to question it for a moment, then when he waved without turning, I knew. He was trying to not look at Greysen. He knew she made him change.

The noise of whooping air beat my ears, but as we crossed the roof, the sound of sirens cut through. The ledge around the roof was low enough to let me recognize the Humvees by their speed and the MPs spray-painted on the roofs. They raced away from Greysen's part of the Green Zone right toward us.

We were going to make it, yet I was frozen in place.

I knew how long it took a chopper to get off the ground. I recognized the building I was on. I knew its placement in the Zone. We were going to make it before the cars got to us. She and I would go to a Blackthorne site where a cure might wait. We'd be together.

It was all going to work out.

Ronin stood by the open door, hands in his pockets, gaze averted, wind whipping his hair into a nest.

I'd be a fugitive, and my wife would be in an institution in Saudi Arabia.

But we'd be together.

Right?

She started for the chopper, slipping from under my arm. I grabbed her hand, and she snapped out of the controlled mental effort she'd been making. She looked at me without asking the questions I saw all over her face.

We'd pushed this as far as it was going to go. We'd arrived at a destination. The end of the line. We were at the boundary of our ability to control our fate.

And yet, looking over the edge of the roof to the street below, I had a chance to push harder. I didn't want to, but I had to.

Greysen would have, and she deserved someone at least as resolute as she was.

"Come on!" Ronin called, looking directly at us for the first time.

My wife never accepted a boundary. She'd have pushed a mountain across the desert for me. She wouldn't give up when she saw a wall. She'd break it down, dig under it, climb over it, and conquer whatever was on the other side.

"I love you," I said, the roar of the Humvees getting closer. "I'd marry you again."

"Okay?"

The question at the end of a statement. Respite. The part of her personality that looked to the past for answers wanted to know why I had to tell her I'd marry her again.

"You're everything, Greysen. My life with you is all I have. But the only way to protect you is to let you go."

"Wait." She shook her head quickly, as if getting the bees out of her ears. "No."

"They'll chase me, and if they find me, they'll find you. It'll be ten times worse."

"Let's *go*!" someone shouted.

I took a big step backward, until my heel was on the two-foot-high ledge of the roof. She put her arms around me, clamping me in the cage of her body.

"No!" She looked up at me, pleading.

I wasn't sure I could go through with this, yet I had to do it. I had to detach myself, cut her open, and watch her heart beat before it broke.

"I'm sorry!" I reached behind and pulled her hands away.

She did exactly what I'd expected, clinging harder, pushing into me, trying to wrap her legs around me. "Don't you do it! Don't you leave me!"

Our bodies twisted together in a push and pull. A locking of limbs and muscle. I took her by the wrists, fingers pressed to the scars inside them.

Over her shoulder, Ronin was jogging toward us.

Shit. Time to push.

I let her arms go.

"I have to," I said coldly, calling on the surgeon and the sadist to do the speaking for me. "You have to go alone."

"You promised."

"I had to get you here." I shrugged.

Her face darkened from desperation to rage. Betrayed. Abandoned. Lied to. With eyes afire and hair whipping around her, she was beautiful and terrifying. Pure power and splendor.

"Grey!" Ronin said, three steps from us.

She grabbed my arms, and I tried to pull her off, but she didn't budge. The Humvees stopped at the street below, six stories down and one step backward.

"Good-bye, baby."

I yanked my arms away, and she pushed me, trying to stay connected but also showing me her anger. She pushed too hard. I lost my balance, knees cut to bending by the ledge, and let her go so I wouldn't pull her over the edge with me.

What I let go of, she grabbed for, catching my shirt, clamping onto it hard as if she had the strength to pull me back.

Which she didn't.

My weight pulled her over.

We were in the air, the beating of the chopper blades snuffed out by the wind in my ears, grounded by neither earth nor the safety of a cable.

Free floating.

Subject to the single-minded will of gravity.

We spilled down.

A second lasted forever in frightening lucidity. The blue of the sky. The smell of sand and gas in the air.

She was next to me and a little above, hair flying back, one shoe lost to wind shear, fingers shaped into hooks as she reached for me.

What gravity pulled down, the wind pushed up. My hand reached for hers, and we touched, sliding our palms together in the split moment before impact.

Chapter Ninety-One

GREYSEN

Lucidity isn't always sanity. Illusions can seem clear and reasonable.

That may be the very definition of insanity. Not that a mind is muddled or confused, but that it's too clear and concise when facing its own misrepresentations, without the ability to turn to reality. Not without help.

Which is to say, everything got clear on the way down. My life was a deck of cards being bent from the bottom and shuffled. I could see the face cards flipping by, each one an event in my life.

A person who touched me. Events, meaningless and otherwise. A thing I saw once.

Lia, who shows me how to make the Egyptian points on the corners of my eyes.

Jake, who yells when I break his Walkman.

July Fourth barbecue. The smell of chlorine and ketchup. Colin drinks a beer. He has Dad's chin.

My sixth birthday. I'm at the head of the table. I pretend I am queen.

The *thup-thup* of hundreds of helicopter rotors.

In the backseat, the way the sun bursts over the line of the mountains while my brothers argue.

A clown on stilts hands out bananas.

My mother at the kitchen table, doing a crossword.

And Caden.

Half-seen in slow motion as we parted on the way down—I wouldn't let him fall alone. Not this time.

Caden.

Whose love woke me so slowly I didn't realize I'd been sleeping.

Whose body was the source of my deepest aching need.

Whose arms shook as he carried me to the CSH in Balad. The sun peeking from behind him, bursting as if he was my horizon line.

Whose body was life.

Who opened the mail with a rip and a blow.

Who never let me fall until I pushed him.

Whose eyes held the promise and protection of the sky above.

Caden.

Who was suspended in the air next to me, his posture a scribble of unlikely angles, released from the constraint of gravity even as he was imprisoned by it.

He was reaching for me, and I didn't have to abandon him.

I couldn't save us, but I'd tried. I'd grabbed his shirt and tried to pull him back. Physics and inertia sent me over with him, but I wasn't an observer to my foolishness.

I'd tried.

Time stretched. All was still. The pressure of the air under me was leverage enough to reach for him. Touch him. Hand to hand. Skin on skin. I had him.

I was so sorry. Wrecked with a regret I'd never have time to process.

But I'd tried.

Everything was clear.

And real.

Clicking into place—Forgiveness matched with responsibility. Sorrow with hope. Contentment with worry. Death with love. Acceptance with elation.

Caden with Greysen.

The complete puzzle came together, and clarity matched with reality.

Which is to say, I knew I was going to die sane.

Chapter Ninety-Two

CADEN

SAN DIEGO
OCTOBER, 2005

I hadn't thought I'd ever get married. I didn't love bachelorhood or despise the institution of marriage. It wasn't a position I'd staked out and defended. It was simpler than that. I'd long ago accepted the fact that I was emotionally unqualified for the job of husband.

Then she'd come, and it didn't matter.

Nothing else mattered. Not my rented tux or the wedding gown she'd plucked off the rack like a pair of jeans. Not Doug, the photographer who worked for the local paper. Not the brown sludge seeping into the hem of her dress or the grit between my toes.

What mattered was the sun setting behind her, the way her laughter rose above the bang and gurgle of the crashing waves, the wind pulling her veil behind her toward the infinite ocean.

She was connected to the sun, the sea, the wind, and the sand, and I was connected to her.

I'd never thought I'd get married, but how could I have known a woman like her existed?

"Stop kissing for one minute, guys!" the photographer cried. "I can't see your faces."

I opened my eyes. She had sand in her lashes.

"We should let the man do his job," I said.

"If we wanted posed pictures, we would have hired that other lady."

I turned to Doug and smiled, keeping her close. Behind him, her parents watched. Dad held Mom's shoes. Jake and Colin were to the right, still arguing about politics as a cover for deep personality differences. Cousins, uncles, aunts, none mine before this day, played in the sand or wrinkled their noses at their sullied finery.

I heard the hiss of the foaming wave before I felt the cold rush on my feet, and as Greysen squealed, I sank an inch into wet sand and laughed. Doug *click-clicked*, and we ignored him.

"I just lost the deposit on this tux."

She picked up the skirt of her dress. "It's ruined," she laughed. "I guess I can't wear it again."

I swept her in my arms and spun her. "I'll shred it later just to make sure."

"Oh no!" she cried when I put her down. "Look!"

Five feet away, a sand castle was getting waterlogged.

"Let's move out," Dad called. "The caterer's going to start in half an hour."

"We have thirty minutes to save it!" Veil dragging, she ran to the castle. "Mom!" She tossed her mother her shoes.

"Twenty minutes," I said. "Ten minutes to drive back."

She got on her knees and patted the base of the castle. "Help me!"

"You can't be serious?"

Looking up at me with a streak of sand on her left cheek and the last bits of the sun catching the hairs flying out of her up-do, she caught me in the web of her higher expectations.

I got on my knees across from her, the castle between us.

"Just this one thing." She pointed at a tower that had survived the wave. It had been made by a careful child, with evenly cut turrets and a window with sticks for bars.

"Hurry." I got my hands under it, and she did the same.

A wave smashed and foamed, ripping toward us as we carefully lifted the tower without a second to spare.

"Slowly," I said. "Careful."

"Okay. We got it."

Doug took his pictures. Jake and Colin stopped arguing. The kids watched with wide eyes. Everyone held their breath, rooting for us to move the tower to safety.

We stepped over the newly wet sand, balancing the piece of the castle. With every step, the tower cracked and split, and as we stepped out of the tidal zone, it collapsed in our hands.

A collective *aww* went up.

"We tried," I said, slapping the sand off my hands.

She looped her arm through mine. "We did."

When I kissed her, she tasted like sea foam, so I kissed her again and again on the way back to the house.

We tried.

We did.

Epilogue

CADEN

Death changes you even when you don't die.

I'd recognized the Blackthorne building as soon as we got to the roof, and I saw the yellow-and-blue striped airbag below. I had a second to decide if the opportunity to have Greysen push me off a building would occur. I didn't have time to ask if the bag was inflated or if it was safe. I didn't have time to train in the proper way to fall.

If I'd had a second more to think about it, I wouldn't have put her at risk.

Maybe I just did impulsive things when she was about to get on a helicopter with Ronin. Maybe I'd never know, and maybe it would never matter.

The bag had been inflated, and we fell side by side. Not quite safely, but not quite dead either.

"Baby!" I wrestled the inflated bag to turn to her.

"Caden!"

Anything could be wrong. I hadn't seen the angle of her fall, and it took very little to paralyze a person from that height.

"Can you feel your hands and feet?"

"Yes." The sound of her voice was a song, and her expression was sharp and aware. "Are you—?"

"I'm fine."

I rolled on top of her, pushed by the movement of the air in the bag. Four hands clasped between our chests.

"We're fine," I said.

"We're fine."

I was promptly arrested.

I WAS COURT-MARTIALED, demoted, and had my bonus taken. It wasn't fun. I stated my case, expressed regret, took responsibility, but also made it clear that I would always do what I had to do to save my wife. Greysen was a character witness, as were her father and Jake, whose survival after capture was a miracle. Ronin testified with eyes averted from my wife's face.

What kept me going through the shame of it all was Greysen. She was whole. We'd recreated her pivotal moment, and she'd taken control of it the way I'd taken control of my own.

That was the only cure so far.

By the time I was a free man, Blackthorne had quietly ended the BiCam study. They'd shuttered the medical study division, wiping it from their website as if it had never existed. Ronin went into the Saudi facility. I hoped they found a simpler cure, but knew they'd never tell me.

In the end, I was treated fairly. I negotiated staying in the army even after I could have been discharged. Greysen didn't admit to wanting to keep her connection to the military, but I knew she did. Once she told me she was pregnant, I knew I had to stay.

I SURFED. A few months to forty-two years old, army captain, New York City born and raised, I'd taken up surfing at five in the morning before I had to report at the Presidio.

Monterey was on the wrong side of dawn. The sky over the water didn't change from dark to light as much as it went from navy to cadet, and when the ocean swelled, it looked like a black plastic bag being shaken out.

The surfer rides between the shore and a force that threatens to throw him against it. The push is stronger than any one man, and riding it means using it, respecting it, knowing it can pick you up and slam you against the earth if you're not careful.

Which it did. A lot.

I spun in the brine, tucking my body into itself as I was rolled against the sand and spit up onto the beach with grit between the edges of my suit and my skin.

Shaking out my hair, I located my board and tucked it under my arm. My watch said I had time for another shot at it and—

"Caden!"

Sun rising behind her, Greysen was pulled forward by our son. He was named Hank, but we called him Yank because he pulled us in all directions as hard as his eighteen-month-old body could. I stuck the board in the sand and held my arms out for the baby. The fat, brown curls he got from my side of the family had been bleached blond by the sun, and the dark eyes he got from my wife were big with delight when I picked him up.

"You're up," I said facetiously.

Of course she was up. Hank didn't actually sleep. It was unusual for her to drive to the beach before seven in the morning. I kissed her, but her lips were tight.

I turned to Hank. "What's Mommy mad about?"

He reached over my shoulder to the bright-yellow board. I put him down.

"I'm not mad," she said.

"Boo!" Hank peered around the board and popped back behind it.

Distracted, I chased him around the yellow barrier. "I'm going to get you!"

Crouching, chasing him in circles as he squealed, I was low enough to see what Greysen had in her hand. A white letter-sized envelope.

Snatching up Hank, I laid him over my shoulder and blew noisy air onto his belly, then I turned him upside down while he laughed and brushed the sand with his fingertips.

"What do you have there, baby?"

She held up the envelope. The front had the US Army seal. "Are you deploying?"

Since I was normal active duty, I would have known weeks ago if I was being sent overseas. Greysen knew that, but once burned, she assumed everything was fire.

Gently, I lowered Hank onto the beach. "No. It's not that."

"What is it then? Why didn't you open it?"

"Because." I snapped away the envelope. "I know what it is, so there's no point." I jammed my finger under the flap's corner and yanked, making a mess of the tear. "And you've been with patients, or I've been on shift. We're busy." I blew into the split to open it. "I was waiting for the right time."

Hank was pulling at my legs to get up.

I held the envelope out to him. "Pull that out."

I had to get it removed halfway before he could get the paper loose. I handed it to Greysen still folded. She took it suspiciously, as if I'd lie about being deployed.

No. She trusted me. She still thought the army could lie, and I didn't blame her.

"Open it," I chided, picking up Hank again.

She swung her head to let the wind keep the hair out of her face and unfolded the page, glancing at me as if to ask if I had anything else to say before I was proven wrong.

"Mommy is a suspicious lady."

Hank made a farting noise with his lips.

Greysen read the letter, every word of it, a satisfied smile growing across her face. "Major St. John. Congratulations."

"I'm off square one."

Her hands dropped, wrinkling the letter. "God, when can I stop worrying about this?"

I reached for her and pulled her close. Hank transferred his weight from me to her. "This is our life, baby. Is it that bad?"

"No. It's perfect."

I kissed Hank's cheek, then her lips. They yielded this time, and I tasted her mouth until Hank jammed his fingers between us, laughing.

"Hanky," I said, "are you ready for your little sister?"

"Yes!" He pointed at his mother's belly, which was just starting to show.

"All right." I gave him to Greysen and picked up my board. "So am I."

"So am I," Greysen said when I took her hand.

Hank wiggled to the ground and pulled us away from the ocean to the car, our home, our life together with its ups, its downs, its surprises and routines.

I helped Greysen onto the curb even though she didn't need it and kissed her until our son pulled her away. I watched her stuttering walk to her car as she tried to keep up with a child who wanted to see everything every minute and wanted to take us along for the ride.

She glanced back at me, smiling, and waved me forward. "Keep up, Major!"

I hitched my board under my arm and chased my family home.

Was our life perfect?

Yes.

Yes, it was.

GREYSEN

HOW MANY POSSIBLE futures did I have?

When we walked away from that air bag, I knew I was starting a possible future so unlikely that I needed to appreciate every minute of it.

When I found that envelope, I thought I was coming to another pivot point. A fork in the road where choices had to be made, because I promised myself that if he deployed, we were going with him, logistics and common sense be damned.

"You really dodged a bullet there," I said from the passenger seat. The front of the yellow surfboard stuck out from the roof like a giant duck's bill in the windshield.

"How's that?"

With the windows open, the cool morning air whipped his hair every which way. I'd married a man who was rigid and yoked by darkness, but my husband had a burden-free spirit.

"I was going to take Hank wherever they sent you."

He laughed and put his hand in my lap, twining it with mine.

"Don't ever change, Grey. Never."

"Don't ever leave me. *Ever.*"

Hank made little boy sounds in the back, holding a toy helicopter against the window so the sky would be a backdrop.

"I got an email from Ronin," I said.

"Which Ronin?"

"That's the news. There's only one. They used the visualization procedure."

"Yours?" He stopped at a light and turned to me, brows raised. Big smile. God, this man was beautiful when he was happy. "The one you developed?"

"Yup."

He slammed the car into park and put his arms around me. His kiss was insistent and jubilant, made through a smile. He pulled away.

"I'm proud of you."

"I'm pretty proud of myself."

His eyes left mine for a second and he pushed the neckline of my shirt aside, exposing the mark he'd left on me the night before. It was sore to the touch. He was still good at hurting me just enough.

"You better have a doctor look at that," he said.

"Good idea."

"G'een, g'een!" Hank shouted from behind me, kicking my seat. A horn honked behind us.

"Let's go!" Caden said, looking at Hank in the rearview as he crossed the intersection.

"Let go!" his son repeated.

"Onward!" I joined in.

"O'wad!"

"Onward," Caden said, taking my hand as he turned onto our block.

Forward we went.

Always forward, with nothing but the earth beneath us, the blue sky above us, and the horizon line before us.

If you want me to let you know when new books are planned or live, I have a mailing list on my website - cdreiss.com

You can follow me on Facebook, Twitter, or Goodreads.

Or you can text cdreiss to 77948 and I'll send a text when the next book is live.

Acknowledgments

Thank you, thank you, thank you for joining me on this journey. This series was for you but also for my own soul. It's not often that the id of a writer and the needs of readers are the same, so I cherish this series for that. My goal was to deconstruct a marriage, piece by piece, examine it, and put it back together. It's because of you, my faithful readers, that I was allowed this conceit.

Throughout the writing of this series, Sarah Ferguson and her husband answered stupid questions about the military in sixty seconds or less. Rebecca Yarros was great help for the Fallujah flashbacks . I learned so much I can barely fit it all in my head. These women make their husbands' sacrifices possible. They serve our country as bravely as the men they love, and they are not to be underestimated.

Sarah is also on my PR team, and it's because of her and Jenn Watson that I was allowed time to write. Yes, this thing was a month late, but they held down the fort while I struggled to make this series what I needed it to be.

Fort-holding-down credit also goes to Jean, Serena, and Michelle for their help with my Facebook group. Cameron makes the gorgeous graphics on Instagram and profile pictures. Ashley makes my emails so effing pretty. Anthony keeps the money where it belongs and is amazingly good at being the soothing voice that cuts through the panic. Thank God for all of them.

Chanpreet Singh used her medical training to help figure out what happened in that closet in Fallujah. A lady from my fan group helped me find the right Kurdish phrase for "I'm pregnant." I've searched my Facebook inbox and cannot find her name. If you're there, wonderful lady, message me again so I can place your name here.

Cassie was a goddess and editor of grace, as always. Her staff, especially superbrain Devon B, proofed the series, and can I tell you something? Devon puts the CMoS numbers in the comments. Super sexy.

Lauren Blakely and Laurelin Paige mentor the hell out of me. I can't even begin to list how many times and ways they extract my head from my ass.

I tried to calculate how long Caden's parents were in the air as they fell. With the help of the internet, it should have been a snap. It wasn't. I finally broke down and asked Penny Reid if she knew anyone who could help me calculate it, and she came back with a number in less time than it took to fall from the 101st floor of the World Trade Center circa 2001.

I took liberties with history, military procedure, and medicine. I've listed them below in the order they occurred to me. There are probably more I'm not aware of. I apologize if any of these took you out of the story.

1. There was no major *shamal* (sandstorm) in Baghdad in 2007. There was one in 2005 and 2008. The May storms are called Al-Haffir or "the driller," which is a fact irrelevant to this list but delightful nonetheless.
2. Surgeons didn't go with medevacs regularly until 2011. Their presence saved lives, but not in 2007.
3. Medical teams at Balad Air Base worked for eight days straight at the outset of Phantom Fury (the second battle of Fallujah) with minimal rest. I have no evidence they were being given amphetamine or any other performance-enhancing drug.
4. Abu Ghraib was the site of horrible acts of torture I never want to see again. As far as I am able to ascertain, the Department of Defense did not order these specific acts as a way to "use their culture against them." Ronin's quote is an expression of my belief that people do not act in a vacuum, not point of fact.
5. Military Service Obligations are eight years. After 9/11, AMEDD recruiters could negotiate the obligation down for medical personnel who didn't have an educational debt to work off.
6. This one isn't really a fudged fact, but it's worth mentioning. I have done bioenergetic/circular breathing many times. The effects are exactly what's in the book. You should give it a try.
7. The characters' personality problems were the result of an experimental

drug that I made up, so the presentation of very real, very serious dissociative disorder wasn't even close to textbook. Mental illnesses, in general, are not as easy to cure as some made up drug side effect in a book. I hope I was clear in that.

8. The word "crazy" is only used in context of character. If the character would think or say it, they do. Greysen wouldn't. Caden would (though by book three, he was less dismissive). Mental illness is serious, debilitating, and worthy of compassion and resources. I hope I dealt with it in a way that expresses reality as well as respect. If you don't think I lived up to my ideals, let me know.

9. On capitalization: I know the military has their own style guide, but I don't like it. I follow the Chicago Manual of Style. I don't capitalize army or rank unless I'm specifically talking about the US Army in a formal way or using rank with a person's name. This can get pretty fuzzy in casual prose. When there was even the slightest bit of doubt, I opted to not cap army or rank. The word "soldier" should never be capitalized unless it's the first word in a sentence. It's my book. I do what I want. End.

10. Same for internet, web (as in world-wide), and wi-fi.

11. You can pry the Oxford comma out of my cold, dead hands.

12. Jake's abduction is loosely based on the capture of US military personnel in May 2007. It is not meant to match the historical record or erase the stories of the lives that were lost.

13. Getting these two to jump from a plane/helicopter/building without her knowing she'd live was a puzzle I was putting together, taking apart, and rearranging until the last minute. Seriously. Do those bags just stay inflated all the time? Doesn't someone have to be there to deflate at the point of impact? Six stories? Really? I hope I didn't push credulity too far in this or anything.

As always, thank you to all my readers: The new ones for taking a chance on a genre-straddling series and the old for sticking with me. I hope I can continue to entertain you for years to come.

Also by CD Reiss

The Games Duet

Adam Steinbeck will give his wife a divorce on one condition. She join him in a remote cabin for 30 days, submitting to his sexual dominance.

Marriage Games | Separation Games

The Submission Series

Jonathan brings out Monica's natural submissive.

Submission | Domination | Connection

Corruption Series

Their passion will set the Los Angeles mafia on fire.

SPIN | RUIN | RULE

Forbidden Series

Fiona has 72 hours to prove she isn't insane. Her therapist has to get through three days without falling for her.

KICK | USE | BREAK

Contemporary Romances

Hollywood and sports romances for the sweet and sexy romantic.

Shuttergirl | Hardball | Bombshell | Bodyguard